CROSS
& CROWN

CUT & RUN SERIES BOOK 9

ABIGAIL ROUX

RIPTIDE
PUBLISHING

Riptide Publishing
PO Box 6652
Hillsborough, NJ 08844
www.riptidepublishing.com

Crash & Burn (Cut & Run, #9)

Cover art: L.C. Chase, lcchase.com/design.htm
Editors: Rachel Haimowitz, Chris Muldoon
Layout: L.C. Chase, lcchase.com/design.htm

ISBN: 978-1-62649-203-5

First edition
March, 2015

Also available in ebook:
ISBN: 978-1-62649-202-8

CRASH & BURN

CUT & RUN SERIES BOOK 9

ABIGAIL ROUX

RIPTIDE
PUBLISHING

To every reader who walked through fire with Ty and Zane.

To every life that's been changed.

To every word between us, from beginning to end.

Thank you for making this possible.

TABLE OF
CONTENTS

CHAPTER 1

Zane Garrett sat in his cushy chair in the Baltimore field office, staring at the frosted glass on his door. It read Special Agent in Charge, and it was the title he'd been working toward since he'd entered the academy. Aside from a post in Washington, it was the pinnacle of any agent's ambitions. In charge of one of the fifty-six FBI field offices.

Five years ago, Zane would have been doing a Snoopy dance behind his closed door the moment he'd taken possession.

Now, though, Zane hated—no—Zane *despised* sitting behind this desk all day.

He tossed his feet up and clunked his heels on the corner, leaning back in his chair. Fuck this desk.

Zane glanced at his watch. It was a gift from Ty, a surprise from last Christmas. Underneath, the engraving read simply "Yours." Classic Grady: succinct, romantic, and not at all incriminating. It made Zane smile whenever he checked the time.

He still had ten minutes to his nebulous lunch hour, so he pulled out his phone and dialed Ty.

"Grady," Ty said after just two rings. Even though he'd resigned from the Bureau a year ago, he still answered his phone as if he expected someone to be calling him to go kill something.

"Hey, doll," Zane drawled. "How's your day going?"

"Pretty good, actually. What's up?"

"I had a thought."

"God help us," Ty said under his breath.

"Do you think Burns was the endgame?"

On his first day in the new office, Zane had swept it for bugs. He'd only found one, which rather surprised him. He'd already known it was there, hidden beneath the desk; Richard Burns himself had shown it to Zane and Ty before he'd died. Zane had destroyed it: an opening gambit in a game of chess where pawns were people and kings lived or died on how soon they realized they were playing.

Ty was silent for a few heartbeats. "What?"

"I sweep this office every fucking day, waiting for another bug. Nada." Zane rocked in his chair and rolled his head from side to side. "Nothing on our phones, either. Do you think it's possible we were being watched because of our connection to Burns? That *he* was the target, and I'm just spinning my wheels here when I could be in bed with you all day?"

"Well. Are we still going with your chess metaphor?"

"I like my chess metaphor."

Ty laughed, and the sound warmed Zane to an unhealthy degree. "Okay. Isn't chess all about patience and strategy?"

Zane groaned and rubbed at his temple.

"You're going insane, aren't you?" Ty asked fondly.

"I feel like this must be what *your* brain does all the time. Squirrels juggling knives in there."

Ty snorted. "I think, on the larger scale, it's our move. You know? We've been quiet since Scotland. You're stuck behind a desk, I'm playing Mister Fix-It. What's there to spy on?"

"But how would they know that if they're not spying on us?"

Ty made a clucking sound. "Maybe they are."

When Zane hung up a few minutes later, having secured a dinner date with his fiancé, he was still frowning. *Maybe they are.*

Ty's words haunted him for the rest of the day. *Maybe they are.* But how? He scanned the office one last time with his device, but registered nothing. He waited until most of his agents were gone for the day, until the floor was clear, and he walked through every cubicle, methodically checking every nook and cranny. He even checked the bathrooms.

Well, at least he knew the entire fucking building was clear of listening devices now.

Finding their mole was Zane's final mission, and it was eating him alive. The mole who'd been spying on them for God knew how long.

The mole whose connections and motivations were still mysteries to them. The mole who'd damn near gotten them killed in New Orleans.

The mole who'd caused Richard Burns to be murdered.

He stood waiting for the elevators, muttering to himself as he checked the batteries in the damn detector. "You're obsessing, Garrett. You've been spending too much time with Ty."

He shoved the batteries back into the thing and tucked it into his leather satchel as the elevator dinged. He glanced up, eyes wide as he realized what he'd just said.

Why the hell would anyone bug Zane at work if half of his or her interest was in Ty? It had been effective when they were partnered; they'd been together all the time. But now? Ty wasn't here. Ty was at home.

Home. The row house.

"Fuck!"

Ty paced through the living room of the row house, listening to Zane's voice mail greeting for the fourth time in the last hour. Zane was hours late now. He was never this late.

"Oh, I'll leave you a message, you son of a . . ." He left a one-word message at the beep this time: "Asshole!"

He tossed his phone at the couch as he prowled by. He hated being stuck like this. And Zane knew he hated it! Zane never did anything even remotely dangerous without calling Ty first, because he knew Ty would rain down hellfire on Baltimore looking for him if he went radio silent. The cartel was still out there, lurking. And Ty didn't have Zane's back now.

He stomped out to the back stoop and threw himself down on the top step. This step had seen him through many of his dark moods over the years, and now he sat out here a lot, staring at his Mustang, while Zane was at work. She was Nightmist Blue, a hauntingly beautiful and historically accurate deep hue, with two thick white racing stripes going up her center and a white interior to match. She was finally done, inside and out, and Ty had stuck with vintage parts right up until he got to the electronics, when he'd found pieces online made to *look* vintage but that were entirely modern. She could sync with an MP3 player, keep your ass warm in the winter, and start up with the press of a button from the comfort of your home.

She was so beautiful that Ty hadn't had the heart to cover her up since he'd finished her, even though the weather this winter had been especially harsh and dark.

Ty was fairly certain that was more about his state of mind than the weather, though. And now it seemed that Zane was going to start disregarding their dinner plans and not bother to tell Ty when he'd be late coming home.

Ty shook his head. One pass, that was all that bastard would get before Ty threw a fit of epic proportions.

He could only sit here for a few minutes before concern and restlessness got to him again and he headed back inside, going for the cabinet under the kitchen sink where he kept his new stash of Cubans.

His sharp ears caught the scratch of keys at the door before he could reach his stash. He stomped to the front door, prepared to give Zane an earful. The door didn't open, though. Ty heard the keys jangle and a soft curse from the other side. He threw the dead bolt and yanked the door open, and Zane stumbled inside as he tried to get his keys out of the lock.

"Where the fuck have you been?" Ty shouted.

Zane waved a hand at him, and the smell of alcohol wafted off him with the cold wind.

Ty gaped. "Are you . . . are you drunk?" he asked, voice going higher.

"If I am?" Zane challenged as he leaned against the open door.

Ty opened his mouth to respond but nothing came. He stood blinking at the man in his doorway like it wasn't the man he'd been living with for almost three years.

"God, Ty, don't be so fucking uptight," Zane said with an exaggerated roll of his eyes. He discarded his wool overcoat and his suit jacket and kicked the door closed. Snowflakes wafted in with him, drifting to the wood floors as Zane tossed his satchel aside.

Ty couldn't even decide if he was awake right now, much less what to say if this wasn't some sort of hallucination. The last time Zane had fallen off the wagon, he'd tossed Ty through a table. The time before, he'd ignored Ty's bid for assistance and left him alone to be hung over the side of a cruise ship by two Italian goons. Zane wasn't exactly a good person when he drank, which was why he'd been working so fucking hard at sobriety.

Zane was digging in his pocket for something, and as he scrounged around for it, he took hold of Ty's arm and pushed. Ty moved with him more out of shock than anything else, gritting his teeth as Zane shoved him against the wall.

"God, did you swim in it? What is that, tequila?" The smell was so strong he could have licked Zane and gotten buzzed. Anger began to boil deep in Ty's gut. After everything that'd happened, after everything that could still happen, and Zane had just . . . decided to go out for a drink? The rage came out in a shout that echoed off the brick wall of the row house. "You don't even like tequila! What the hell is wrong with you?"

Zane pulled a piece of paper from his pocket, then brought his finger to his lips in a shushing motion. Ty growled at him, but Zane raised the paper before Ty could rev up for a retort. Ty read the note with barely concealed contempt.

House is bugged. Play along.

Ty blinked at the paper, and then Zane kissed him. There wasn't a hint of alcohol on his lips or tongue; the scent was coming off his shirt. Ty had taught him that trick. Zane shoved the note into Ty's pocket, then grabbed his hip and pressed him hard against the wall to deepen the kiss.

The row house was bugged? Ty wasn't quite sure how Zane pretending to be drunk would help with that, but he was willing to play along until he could get a better explanation. Mostly because Zane had him shoved against the wall and was kissing him like he had when they'd first met: sharp and messy, mean and desperate.

Ty returned the ferocity of the kiss, pushing back. It was rare that he could convince Zane to really manhandle him, but it was fun. Zane doing it without provocation was downright legendary.

Zane ground against him, rough gasps escaping as they kissed. It was as if he were trying to eat Ty alive, a sort of passion they'd kind of forgotten about over the years.

Zane started pawing at Ty's shirt. "Fucking buttons." The volume of his grumbling was exaggerated, but it worked to make him sound inebriated. He shoved his hand into Ty's pants as he rubbed himself against Ty's thigh.

"Hey," Ty barked, and he swatted at Zane's hands. He lowered his voice to a bare whisper, speaking against Zane's cheek to further muffle his words. "Careful with the goods there, Hoss, you break it, you bought it."

"I already bought it," Zane whispered, smiling against Ty's lips. "You got to fight back a little if this is going to work."

Ty scowled. Zane went to work on his neck, licking and sucking, and Ty's eyes drifted closed as a thrill ran through him. Zane wanted a fight that sounded bad enough for Ty to kick him out of the house without alerting anyone that they knew about the listening devices. And he apparently thought a nice violent round of sex would do.

Fair enough. If there was one thing Ty and Zane knew how to do, it was abuse each other for fun.

Ty gave Zane's shoulder a shove and sneered at him. "Go sober up! I'm not dealing with you when you're drunk."

Zane nodded encouragingly, looking relieved that Ty had caught on. He mouthed the words, "I love you." Then he shoved Ty's shoulders back against the wall. "Hold still," he ordered in a tone he so rarely used that for a moment Ty did exactly as he'd been told rather than putting up the fight he was supposed to.

This was some next-level role-play. Ty bit his lip against a grin. Fuck, this might turn out to be too fun. They could have accomplished the same thing by throwing shit at each other and shouting, but this at least gave them a chance to whisper to each other, to get a little bit of a plan together. And hell, when had they ever passed up a chance to maul each other?

Zane pushed at Ty's pants, then grunted in frustration when he couldn't get the fly undone. Ty had spent most of the day at the bookstore, tearing out its insides, and he was wearing a pair of work pants stiff enough to protect him from sharp edges and hot surfaces. They weren't exactly made for being groped in. Hell, they were more suited to being burned alive in, as tough as they were.

Ty gave Zane a taunting grin. "What's wrong, Garrett, got butterfingers? What else is limp tonight?"

Zane retaliated by grabbing Ty's work shirt and ripping it open. A button flew up and pegged Ty in the chin. He closed his eyes and snorted, then let out a muffled grunt when Zane's lips met his. Zane bit him hard enough to sting.

"Ow! Jesus, Zane!"

"Get these off." Zane tugged at the pants.

"Get them off yourself! You can't handle a fucking zipper, you sure as hell can't handle me."

Zane gave him a pointed look and tugged at the zipper again. He leaned closer and whispered, "No seriously, I can't get these off."

Ty rolled his eyes. So much for a spontaneous mauling. He tugged at the zipper to his work pants, but they were stuck. He glanced up at Zane, his cheeks heating as he bit the inside of his lip, trying not to laugh. "Uhh."

Zane didn't waste more time on buttons. He pulled his dress shirt over his head, tossed it away, and slid one of his knives from its sheath at his wrist.

"Garrett." Ty held up a hand, trying to press himself further into the wall. He didn't have to fake the fear in his voice. "Don't you fucking dare! Not the knife!"

"Hold still," Zane ordered again with a hint of sadistic glee.

Ty squeezed his eyes closed and turned his head away. If he was going to lose a chunk of himself in a sex-related accident, he definitely didn't want to watch. Zane sliced his waistband cleanly, though, the cold edge of the knife against Ty's hip sending a shiver up his spine.

Zane shoved Ty's pants down his hips, his fingertips gliding reverently against Ty's skin. The knife blade was still down there somewhere, but Ty forgot all about it when he met Zane's eyes. They were nearly black, not their usual warm shade of brown, and filled with real heat. It made Ty's breath hitch.

His eyes flicked to the knife still in Zane's hand. "You think you need that?"

Zane hummed and pressed his bare chest to Ty's. He rubbed his nose against Ty's jaw, then ran it up to Ty's cheekbone, his lips grazing skin. Ty's eyes drifted closed when Zane kissed his cheek.

He was peripherally aware of Zane putting his knife back into its sheath, then removing both of them from his wrists and setting them on the table next to the door where they kept their keys, badges, guns, and miscellaneous weaponry. Ty held Zane's gaze, though, and Zane smiled warmly. How many times had they fucked and forgotten to disarm first? It had caused some odd injuries over the years.

Zane's hand slid down the taut muscles of Ty's stomach, fingers grazing the juncture of his hip and the base of his cock. Ty was only half-hard, but Zane would soon remedy that if he continued in this manner. He nosed his way along Ty's jaw again and nuzzled against Ty's neck to kiss and nip at his favorite spot right above Ty's collarbone.

"Zane," Ty begged. Then he remembered they were supposed to be fighting and he was supposed to be angry, not begging Zane to touch him. He grunted in frustration. This wasn't going to work.

Zane winked at him, his eyes sparkling with mischief and lust. God, how Ty loved the man. He had to dig deep for harsh words that would sell their little act.

"It's going to take more than a couple licks and a sloppy handjob to get me off, jackass."

Zane raised an eyebrow, a smirk flitting across his lips. Ty mirrored the expression, offering a silent challenge. What, Zane thought they were going to *fake* angry sex and not get down and dirty for this one? Please.

Zane jerked open his fly and shoved the fabric out of the way. He jutted his chin out to kiss Ty, then with one last squeeze, let go and spun him around to thump his chest against the wall. Then Zane kicked his ankles apart, gasping as he curled one hand over Ty's shoulder and shoved his hard cock against Ty's ass, nudging between his cheeks.

"Fuck," Zane whispered, and they both groaned. Zane rested his forehead against the back of Ty's shoulder, their bodies pressed tight from thigh to chest, warm and hard and familiar. When he spoke, he muffled his words by pressing his lips into Ty's skin. "We've got to figure out how to move this upstairs."

Ty nodded. If they weren't careful, they'd enjoy this too much and forget to sell the conflict. "You think you're fucking me without lube, you've lost your damn mind."

Zane laughed almost cruelly. "Can't have you bitching because you're sore."

Ty shoved away from the wall, and Zane stumbled back. He barely caught himself before he tripped over his satchel on the floor. Ty kicked out of his ruined work pants and his briefs, and then yanked his shirt off his shoulders. They were never going to find all the damn buttons to it anyway.

"Go to Hell, Garrett, go sober up somewhere," he snarled, and he stomped off toward the stairs. When he reached the foot of the steps, he glanced over his shoulder to find Zane following him, head cocked, blatantly leering at Ty's bare ass. Zane met his eyes and winked. Ty gestured for him to come at him. They'd make another scene here to sell the charade . . . and Ty was pretty sure there was some lube stashed in one of the kitchen drawers, within reach if they wound up getting carried away.

Zane moved in front of Ty, and then trailed the backs of his fingers down Ty's cheek, giving him a chaste little kiss before he stepped back and shoved Ty into the wall. The rough brick bit at Ty's skin, and Zane's body hit him a moment later, knocking the breath out of him.

"Easy!"

Zane kissed him, silencing him, and Ty's fingers found their way into Zane's mess of dark, curly hair. He hitched one leg up Zane's hip, and Zane grabbed the back of his thigh, thrusting their cocks together. They both groaned, loud enough that even a discount listening device from Walmart could have picked up the sound.

"Right here," Zane growled, and he raised a bottle of lube he'd grabbed from somewhere.

"Where the fuck did that come from?"

"My bag."

"You take lube with you to work?" Ty shouted, genuinely outraged.

Zane bit his ear and whispered, "It's from the trip to Seattle, baby."

Ty's body responded to the memory of that particular business trip. Zane had taken Ty with him, knowing he'd have more downtime than work to do. They hadn't exactly spent their free time sightseeing.

Ty set one foot on the stair railing and pushed, helping Zane to hoist him up the wall. Zane was jacking himself with one slick hand, coating himself in preparation. He bit down on Ty's collarbone hard enough to make Ty cry out, then he did it again as if the sound had spurred him on.

Zane was either actually losing control, or he was pretending so well even Ty believed him. And Ty liked it. A lot. "Come on," he whispered, and he rose up onto his toes, pushing harder against the stair rail with his other foot.

He tried at the same time not to tense, but it was near impossible when he was holding himself against the wall. Zane shoved one slick finger into him, and Ty gasped. Yeah, this was going to hurt a little. He scrabbled against the rough brick for something to grab, then settled on grabbing Zane.

"Okay?" Zane whispered against his ear.

Ty nodded.

"Tell me to stop if you need to," Zane bit out before jerking his finger free and lining himself up.

Ty nodded again, and Zane started to push in. He was going to leave his mark on Ty tonight, fake or not.

Then Zane stopped, his body stiffening and the head of his cock just barely breaching Ty. He shuddered in Ty's arms, and his cock pulsed, pushing at tense muscles. He dug his fingers into Ty's thigh and set his forehead against Ty's neck. "Fuck, Ty."

"Zane," Ty gasped. Then he grinned, nipping at Zane's ear. "Sell it, baby, come on. Fuck me."

Zane raised his head, his dark eyes flashing.

Ty shivered with anticipation and nodded. "Hard."

Zane huffed and snapped his hips, once, twice, forcing himself in with a low growl. Ty banged his head against the brick wall, eyes squeezed shut, gritting his teeth through the burn of the entry. "Come on, Garrett," he taunted even as his voice trembled. "That the best you got?"

Zane thrust in again, his cock spreading Ty open further. The brick dragged against Ty's skin, and his muscles were screaming as he tried to hold himself up with the banister. Zane's grasping fingers found their way into Ty's hair and yanked his head to the side as he shoved deeper into him.

"Fuck!" Zane finally shouted, sounding frustrated when he couldn't get Ty's body at the right angle to sink all the way in.

Ty grunted and tried to push against him, but he had no leverage. Zane was gasping with each thump. He growled and bit down on Ty's shoulder, his teeth dragging over bone. His thrusts grew even more frenzied as he used all his strength, taking more of Ty's weight.

Ty threw his head back and groaned wantonly. It was as close to getting mauled as he could come. Zane gripped him tight, aiming to bruise, to maim and claim, and bit down harder as his breathing went ragged.

It seemed like Zane was close to coming, and they'd forgotten to keep up their little charade. Ty'd forgotten to make even a peep of complaint over the fake abuse, and Zane had forgotten to abuse.

"God damn it," he ground out. He kissed Ty again, the heat banking to a low simmer, his thrusts slowing until the swollen head of his cock once again pushed at Ty's muscles until he wanted to scream for Zane to move. Zane pulled out, loosening his hold. Without the solidity of his body or his hands holding him up, Ty had to thump his foot back to the top step. His entire body throbbed with need and pain and frustration.

He swallowed hard. "What's wrong," he managed to ask. "Can't even finish?"

"Get your ass upstairs," Zane snarled.

"Or what?"

Zane grabbed his jaw, holding his head still as their eyes met. "Or nothing," he said, voice pitched just loud enough to be picked up.

Ty gazed into his eyes, a smile growing. "So hot," he whispered.

Zane's lips twitched, and he nodded his head toward the stairs.

Ty had to slide against Zane to take the first step up. The way Zane was looking at him, all fire and desire, sweat dripping down his temples, Ty sort of felt like a squirrel slipping past a big dog. He only made it two steps before Zane's resolve apparently went up in smoke, and he tackled Ty to the stairs.

Ty grunted when he hit. Zane was on top of him before he could even try to right himself, biting at Ty's shoulder, dragging his teeth against the skin until he could place a kiss on Ty's neck.

Ty cursed loudly, struggling to hold back a groan. Zane had a hand on Ty's hip, pulling Ty's ass toward him, and his damp belly and chest were pressed against Ty's back.

The head of his cock pushed against Ty again, his hands digging into Ty's ribs as he held him still, and he only waited long enough for Ty to push his ass against him before he shoved inside again.

Ty cried out, turning it into an outraged scream for the sake of the bug. Zane's hand smacked against the step beside Ty's head, and Ty grabbed for it, holding on as Zane moved inside him, his thighs slapping against Ty's, his free fingers grasping Ty's flank and leaving stinging trails behind as he tried to hold Ty's body still for those brutal thrusts.

Ty raised his head long enough to look up to the doorway where a nice cushy bed was waiting for them. Instead, he was on his fucking knees on the stairs, gripping the iron railing as Zane fucked him into the sharp corners of the steps. Then Zane's cock hit his prostate, and he screamed.

Zane grabbed his hair and yanked his head back, forcing Ty up onto all fours. Zane kissed his neck, then his ear. "Why haven't we fucking done this before?" he panted.

"Broken bones," Ty whispered back, huffing a laugh as Zane buried his face against Ty's shoulder and groaned.

"You know you fucking love it," Zane said, voice louder.

Ty gritted his teeth, fighting off the very real pleasure to try to find the right words. "Just get off and get out, for Christ's sake," he finally growled.

Zane shook his head. "Not that easy."

His hand snaked around Ty's body, groping, lingering in the sweat forming on Ty's tense muscles. He pulled Ty close, then shoved his weight sideways. He wound up sitting on a step, lounging with his long legs reaching the floor, and Ty straddling him.

His hand closed around Ty's cock, and he leaned back, taking Ty with him. Ty's USMC ring clanged when he grabbed for the railing. Zane's cock boring deeper into him as his weight pushed him down had him close to coming.

"Move," Zane ordered.

Ty banged his head against Zane's shoulder. "Go to Hell. You want to get off, you do the work."

Zane laughed, and though it wasn't genuine, he did a good job of selling the evil chuckle. He wrapped his slick fingers around Ty's cock, sliding them around the head and down the shaft.

Ty groaned, not even sure what sound he'd intended to come out. He jutted his hips toward Zane's hand, moving Zane inside him. "Fuck you, Zane. Fuck you so much," he murmured, earning a very real, gentle chuckle that he felt against his back.

Zane jacked him harder, forcing his hips to move and his body to contort. He grabbed a handful of Zane's hair and yanked at him, begging for a kiss. When Zane curled down to deliver, he shifted inside Ty, hitting his prostate again. Ty broke the kiss by shouting Zane's name against his lips.

"That's it, Grady, come on!" Zane yelled against Ty's cheek.

Ty growled for the benefit of the listening devices, and Zane's grip tightened on his chest, nails digging in.

"Move, Ty, for God's sake," Zane pleaded with short, gasping breaths.

Ty shimmied his hips, then dropped down, crying out as he reseated himself. Zane lost his hold on any remaining composure, bucking his hips and pulling Ty back to lie flat with him as he came inside him. Zane's hand never stopped moving on Ty's cock, though, and Ty struggled against the coming orgasm. It wouldn't really sell their fight if he got off in the end. He turned his head toward Zane, desperately seeking anything to muffle the sounds.

Zane clapped a hand over his mouth, and that was all it took. Ty bucked his hips, squeezing his eyes shut and grasping at Zane's hips and ribs as Zane jacked him through it. He spurted over his stomach and thighs, and his toes curled as he moaned against Zane's hand.

They were both panting and sweaty when it was over, and Zane was straining beneath him as he tried to keep them both from sliding down the stairs. Ty's breathing was ragged against Zane's hand, and Zane let him loose cautiously, as if releasing a wild animal.

Ty arched his back, forcing Zane out of him. They both bit back their groans, and Ty rolled to his belly again.

"Fuck, Garrett," he said softly.

Zane put his hand to his ear as if he hadn't heard.

Ty growled, then pushed to his hands and knees. "Fuck!" he shouted. He slammed his hand against a step, and Zane jumped. "Fuck you, Garrett!"

Zane whirled his finger in the air, telling Ty to continue, then pushed himself to his feet and darted to the front door, not making a sound. Ty watched him for a moment before taking a deep breath and starting in on a loud, rambling rant that would cover any sounds Zane made as he moved around the lower floor. He had his bug detector in hand now, moving past all the usual places.

As Ty was bitching loudly about how Zane never did the dishes anyway and fuck him, Zane signaled to an electrical outlet near the kitchen.

"Get your shit, and get out until you can fucking handle yourself, Jesus Christ!" Ty shouted.

"Whatever, Ty," Zane said as he headed for Ty and the stairs. "Work's hard enough. I don't need your whiny bullshit on top of it." He stopped long enough to grab Ty and kiss him, whispering something unintelligible against Ty's lips. Then he stomped up the steps.

Ty followed, silent on the balls of his feet. When he reached the landing, Zane indicated the table on Ty's side of the bed. Ty nodded, then headed back downstairs.

A few minutes later, Zane thumped down the steps, wearing sweatpants and one of Ty's T-shirts, a gray one with stylized pink writing that read "The 3rd rule of fight club is have fun and try your best." He had a garment bag and Ty's go bag full of emergency supplies slung over his shoulder.

Ty pointed at it, frowning. "Mine," he mouthed.

"Mine now," Zane said back, smirking as he gave Ty one last kiss and then headed for the kitchen. Their little scene ended with the slamming of the back door and the revving of Zane's Valkyrie.

CHAPTER 2

Nick O'Flaherty didn't hear the intruder until he felt someone sit on the end of his bed. He opened his eyes, trying to shake off sleep that felt unnaturally heavy. Something was wrong.

The only two people who visited him regularly and had access to the security on the harbor and keys to his yacht were his partner and his boyfriend. Kelly was sure as hell the only one who'd risk sneaking down here and crawling onto Nick's bed to wake him. But Kelly was in Colorado, leading a group of at-risk kids from the camp where he worked through the winter wilderness.

"Good morning, darling," a voice said in the darkness, and that British accent most certainly was not Kelly's.

Nick reached for the gun beneath his pillow even as Liam Bell laughed and tapped the butt of his gun against his own knee. He was sitting on the corner of the bed with his legs crossed primly, the gun pointed at Nick.

"Hands where I can see them."

Nick withdrew his hand from under his pillow and raised both palms out toward Liam.

Liam put a finger to his lips and gestured for Nick to sit up. He kept the gun on Nick until Nick was standing in the corner, far enough away that Liam apparently felt comfortable moving.

He reached beneath Nick's pillow, pulling the gun out first, then Nick's phone. Nick mentally cursed as Liam held it up, one eyebrow raised. Nick had managed to hit Send on his emergency contact, and the phone was ringing, Kelly's name and photo on the display.

Liam ended the call just as Nick heard Kelly's distant voice mail message.

"You still tell him the vibration under your head wakes you easier than the noise?" Liam asked. "To explain hiding your phone beneath your pillow? I suppose that's better than telling him you keep it under there to call for help when I show up, hmm?"

Nick felt the blood draining from his face. "You've been listening to us?"

"Only key words. And not even those after the first week or two."

Nick cleared his throat, torn between embarrassment and rage. "How the *fuck*?"

"You're not as paranoid as you used to be. Slipped you a little token of my love in your water filter to make sure you'd sleep nice and hard." Liam frowned as he jammed Nick's gun into the back of his jeans. "One thing I didn't hear while I was listening was the two of you talking about your engagement."

Nick remained silent, forcing himself not to swallow against the nerves building.

"Do you remember the time after your surgery?" Liam asked, and Nick would have sworn there was concern in his voice.

"Some of it," Nick admitted.

"But you do remember our deal, don't you?"

"Yes."

"You let the Doc believe you don't remember proposing?"

Nick's heart stuttered. That was exactly what he'd done. Kelly had never brought up their conversation, the one where Nick had said, "Marry me," and meant it with all his heart and soul. Kelly was waiting for Nick to say it again—to say it again sober. And Nick had remained silent.

He'd remained silent because he knew this day was coming.

"Smart," Liam said with a nod. "My intention here is for both of us to live through this, so don't go thinking I take pleasure in you breaking his heart or anything."

"No?"

"You can propose again when we're done. I promise."

Nick took a deep, calming breath. "Can we just get to the point of why you're here and what you want?"

"Of course. Accompany me upstairs, would you? And put some more clothes on."

Nick rolled his eyes and moved toward the closet. Liam stood back, gun on him. He grabbed a T-shirt, moving slowly, knowing despite Liam's casual attitude that the man was on a hair trigger. He had the look of someone who'd been on the run for a while. His beard was scraggly, his blond hair a little long. His clothes were dirty, too, and his jeans had holes in the knees. He looked nothing like the man Nick knew.

Nick glanced back at him as he pulled his T-shirt on. "Do you . . . want some new clothes and a razor? Maybe a shower?"

Liam raised an eyebrow. "Is that concern for my well-being? Or for your sensibilities?"

"Let's call it both."

Liam grinned. "Later. Shall we talk business first?"

Nick led him up to the main deck, looking around the salon and galley, trying to figure out how Liam had gotten into the marina and onto the boat without tripping any alarms. To his horror, he saw nothing but open ocean out the windows. He forgot the gun at his back and rushed forward, searching for the docks, the marina, for land.

"Holy shit!"

"Yes," Liam said with a pleased grin. "Now. You're wondering why I'm here."

"Where are we?" Nick shouted.

"I don't know, you're the nautical one. I just piloted the boat out of the harbor."

"Pirated! You pirated it out of the harbor!"

"Semantics."

"Did you anchor us, or are we drifting? Do you even fucking know how to handle a vessel this size?"

"Don't be flirty. I anchored us. I think." Liam scowled. "Actually, you may want to go make sure."

"You could have killed us, you fucking shitstick! How long have we been drifting?"

"Calm yourself, mate, you're turning red."

"There are shipping lanes that . . . shoals . . . oh my God." Nick growled when every curse word he knew failed him, and hustled to check the yacht's radar and make sure they weren't drifting into dangerous waters. He also wanted to know how far away from Boston Liam had managed to get them while he'd slept.

Liam followed, obviously knowing from past association that Nick would have weapons hidden all over the boat. He wasn't going to give Nick a chance to get the drop on him. He also didn't give Nick a chance to do anything more than make sure they were safely anchored. Nick got a quick glance at the charts, but he still had no idea where they were, not close enough to send an SOS.

"Now sit," Liam ordered.

Nick cleared his throat. "Okay." He stepped back from the controls and let Liam get a good look at him, then led Liam into the salon. He gave the open ocean one last frown before he settled on a couch. Liam sat across from him, gun resting on his knee and aimed at Nick.

"What's this about?" Nick demanded.

"What else? The only thing we have in common anymore."

"Ty."

Liam smiled almost sadly. "Indeed."

"What about him?"

"Well. I'm here to save his life. And I need your help."

Nick blinked at him.

"Really? I was expecting something more witty."

"Get used to disappointment," Nick advised. "I don't play games anymore."

"But you used to be so good at them, darling."

Nick took another deep breath, nodding in acknowledgment. "This is about the cartel?"

"And Richard Burns. But then, you knew that, didn't you Nicholas?"

Panic ripped through Nick, but he schooled his expression. "I don't know what you're talking about."

"Of course you do."

Nick met Liam's icy blue eyes for a long moment, until Liam smirked and Nick had to look away.

"We need to get Tyler to take action. We need him on the offensive. That's his wheelhouse, and you and I both know it."

"Valid," Nick said. "But the Feds and Interpol are bringing heat on the cartels all over the world. The Vega cartel has been quiet for a year; they've even pulled their operations in the northern cities. They cleared out of Boston two years ago. You really think they're still after Ty and Zane when they have bigger problems now?"

"Yes. In fact, I know it."

"You know it," Nick said, deadpan. Liam nodded. "Through your super secret government contacts, I'm guessing. Isn't that beard a little against NIA dress code?"

"Call me a master of disguise." Liam quirked an eyebrow as he waited for Nick's reply. After a few seconds, he waved his gun through the air and set it on the table with a metallic thud. "Oh, come on! You used to be so good at witty banter!"

"I also used to like you. Made the witty banter easier."

Liam's mask broke, and he looked genuinely surprised. He covered it quickly, though, retrieving the weapon. "Well. I suppose I don't blame you."

"Why are you here, and what do you want me to do?"

"As I was saying, Tyler and his fiancé have all but forgotten the threat to them."

Nick scoffed and looked away. "That's not true."

"Is it not? Have they made any progress on which of their allies is spying on them? Have they made any headway in building a case against the cartel? Have they done anything but restore that old building they'll never live in and plan a wedding they're not likely to live long enough to see?"

Nick lowered his head. He couldn't answer any of those questions, mostly because he didn't know the answers, but also because Liam was probably right. "So. You want to push Ty into action instead of letting him get complacent."

"Precisely."

"Why?"

"Well, for one, I want the Vega cartel to go down in flames. That's my assignment."

Nick snorted. "No."

"Pardon?"

"You're lying," Nick spat. "That's not the reason. You're not on assignment. Look at you, you're so off the grid there's only one explanation: You've been burned for something. You're being hunted, and you're so desperate that I'm the only ally you could drum up."

Liam cleared his throat and shifted.

"You want me to help you? Tell me the truth."

Liam sighed like a petulant five-year-old and lounged on the couch, his foot on the table and the gun resting on his thigh, still pointed at Nick. His finger was on the trigger guard, though. Nick could have launched himself at Liam and possibly gotten to him before he could transfer that finger to the trigger, but something stopped Nick from taking action. Liam noticed him looking and smiled crookedly as he moved his finger to rest on the trigger.

Their eyes met, both men acknowledging what *hadn't* just happened.

"Fine," Liam said. "This is about revenge, pure and simple. And proving my innocence to the NIA to get me off the kill list."

"Now that I believe."

"I'm glad we're on the same page."

Nick ran both hands over his face. "You're using Ty as a chess piece. Just like they used us in Afghanistan. Just like you used us in New Orleans."

Liam was quiet for a long moment, letting Nick's bitter words melt into tense silence. "You and I both know it weren't me who set your team up in New Orleans," he finally said.

"Oh yeah? How do you figure?"

Liam looked puzzled for a moment, his brow furrowed, his frown obvious even through his beard. "*You're* the one who called them to New Orleans."

"Yeah? So?"

"*You're* the one who alerted the cartel. *You're* the one who sent the NIA warning to be there."

The words hit Nick with the force of a linebacker. Was Liam actually accusing him of orchestrating the shitshow in New Orleans? If Liam thought it was Nick's doing, then they'd been wrong about him being behind it. Or was he just playing games again? Nick tried his best not to react; the more Liam talked, the more information he'd get out of him. But the shock obviously bled through to his eyes, to his expression, because Liam tutted.

"Don't try to act your way out of this one, Irish. You called all of us there. And you were the one who switched that bullet on me. Why would you want Tyler to think I wanted him dead, by the way? I never could figure that one out."

Now Liam was implying Nick had actually tried to kill Ty. If Nick could have thrown a table at him with his mind, he would have. But he sat silent and subdued, letting Liam talk.

Liam sat up and placed the gun on the table between them, mirroring Nick's stance with his elbows on his knees, hands clasped together. "No matter. The reason we always got on so well, you and I, was because we both knew when to be a player, and when to be a piece. Tyler, he never even knew he *was* a piece. He still doesn't. You played us in New Orleans. You lost. It's my turn to play the board, Nicholas, and your turn to be the piece."

It took Nick several seconds to shake off the shock of Liam's accusations, but he nodded as if accepting the role, and the responsibility. "So what piece do I play in your game?"

"You? You're the opening gambit."

"We're not exactly on the best of terms right now. Ty's not going to listen to me if I try to convince him to take action. Especially since I know taking action is going to get him and everyone around him killed. You think I want him dead, you've miscalculated. You can hold a gun to my head, to Kelly's, but I can't convince him for you."

"Yes. You can. Just not with words."

Nick inhaled sharply and nodded. "With my death?"

Liam's smile grew. "Maybe not yours, necessarily."

Nick could feel the blood draining from his face. "Garrett?"

Liam's smile broadened. "With a finger pointing at the cartel to blame? Tyler will be unstoppable, inconsolable, a Tasmanian devil filled with rage and guilt and mourning. He will gather every force in his artillery, call in every favor from every mercenary and killer he's ever met, build an army to march on Miami. All for revenge."

"You're going to kill Zane to turn Ty into some sort of atomic bomb?"

Nick tensed as Liam reached into his pocket, but he brought out a small box instead of a weapon. "Firstly, I don't kill my friends, it's rude. Second, he'll be quite useful once the game is afoot, so no, I don't intend to kill Garrett. Or you." He placed the box on the table and opened it. Inside was a frozen finger, bloodied where it had been severed.

"Whose finger is that?" Nick demanded.

"I didn't catch his name." Nick glared at him, and Liam rolled his eyes. "Does it help if I tell you he was a very bad man?"

"No!"

"Well. He was. Do you have a computer aboard? Access to the internet?"

"Yes, why?"

"Is it secure?"

"Secure? What are you talking about?"

"Well, after we kidnap Garrett, we'll have to send Tyler this finger in the post. When he receives it, with Garrett's ring on it of course for easy identification, he will instantly believe it to be Garrett's. Others, however, will be more levelheaded. They'll print it. I need to alter the records to make Garrett's print match this one."

"You want to hack the FBI with my laptop?" Nick asked, growing more flustered the more he learned of Liam's plans. "No, my laptop is not secure enough *to hack the FBI*! You fucking half-wit!"

"Well. I'll make do." Liam stood, stuffing his gun in his holster. He closed the lid on the finger box.

"No!" Nick stood with him. "I'm not going to let you do this! I'm not putting my friends and family through that for some revenge kick! You amass your own damn army to march on Miami; leave us out of this bullshit war you're trying to start!"

"This war has started already, and believe it or not, I was a casualty, not an instigator."

"I have a hard time believing that," Nick sneered.

"It's true whether you believe it or not. My partner and I were planted in the cartel. Someone blew our cover, and she was murdered before I even made it clear of New Orleans. The NIA believes it was me who killed her. They called me a traitor, said I'd been turned by the cartel."

Nick was silent, trying to parse the truth from Liam's words. Everything the man said had to be taken with a grain or two of salt, but Nick was distressed to find that he believed this story.

"Now I'm being hunted. And Grady and Garrett are well embroiled in this and have been from the start. Zane Garrett? He was stealing information from the cartel. Do you know why the Vega cartel pulled stakes from Boston?"

Nick shook his head.

"Money. They were losing it faster than they could make it."

"You're trying to say Zane was siphoning cartel money when he was undercover?"

"Indeed. Stealing account details, to be precise. And Tyler? He killed Antonio de la Vega under orders from our dear friend Richard Burns, not to mention how many others while trying to cover Zane's tracks. So put your conscience aside and follow the plan, and *maybe* all your friends will come out of it alive. If not free from jail." He stopped suddenly, looking over Nick's shoulder with a new light in his eyes. "Wait, you're brilliant."

"What?" Nick asked with dread.

"If they think Garrett's dead, they'll pause to mourn, have a funeral, all that. If that finger comes with a ransom, they'll think he's still alive! It will kick them into instant action!" Liam grabbed Nick's face with both hands and kissed him. "Brilliant!"

Nick sputtered, trying desperately to stay calm as he wiped at his mouth. He took a step after Liam as the man turned to go find the laptop, and he grabbed Liam's elbow to halt him. Liam turned, gun appearing in his hand so fast that Nick didn't even realize it was sticking into his belly until Liam shoved him back a step with it.

Nick put both hands up. "I'll help you," he said, trying to keep his voice even. "But not if you intend to go through with your plan."

Liam raised an eyebrow, easing the gun out of Nick's abs just enough to let him breathe without pain. "I'm listening."

"You want to prove your innocence. You want to cripple the cartel. We can do those things without making Ty and Zane want to kill us."

Liam narrowed his eyes and cocked his head. "How?"

"Let me do the thinking. And you keep your fingers to yourself."

Liam jutted his chin out, icy blue eyes boring into Nick. He finally nodded.

Nick swallowed past the tightness in his throat. "You're playing with lives, you know."

"Yes." Liam grinned, his eyes sparkling. "What was it you used to tell me before missions?"

"You're bringing a chess set to a gunfight."

"Indeed." Liam reached out carefully and dragged a finger down Nick's cheek, then held it up as if he'd wiped something off his face. "And the white knight never left the board without blood all over him. Did he, love?"

Ty sat in the midst of a room full of chaos and disaster. The plywood floors were covered with scraps of wood and plaster dust, which he had been horrified to discover actually had horse hair in it. The walls were nothing but two-by-fours and exposed brick. The ceiling was letting light in through the second- and even third-story windows, and dust motes floated peacefully though the sunbeams.

Ty was cross-legged, forearms resting on his knees, lips pursed in a mixture of disgust and amusement. He'd worked on projects like this all his life, but he'd never had this many things go wrong on him. He'd spent the warm months of the summer and fall working on his Mustang, leaving the interior of the building for the cold of winter. Now, sitting in the freezing cold without heat or insulation on the first day of February, he was regretting a lot of his decisions.

At least he could be positive this building wasn't bugged.

The front door, made of old, dirty glass covered with peeling and faded stickers, grocery bags, and duct tape, opened with a terrible creak.

"Hey, Bulldog," Zane said as he stepped over the threshold, a box under one arm. "How's it going?"

Ty cleared his throat and pointed up at the ceiling. "I put a hole in the house."

Zane tipped his head back to peer up as he walked toward Ty. "What were you doing?" He sounded like he was trying not to laugh.

"I was . . ." Ty cleared his throat, blushing. "I was poking it with a stick."

Zane propped the box on his hip and raised an eyebrow at Ty.

"It made sense in my head," Ty insisted. "Did you bail from work early? What's in the box?"

"I left work early, brought you lunch. Why were you poking the house with a stick?"

"I was looking for wiring," Ty answered, blushing harder.

Zane set the box down, then carefully went to one knee before thumping to the dusty floor to sit next to Ty. "Wiring? Did you find any bugs?"

"No, so I guess it was a win."

Zane took Ty's hand in his and laced their fingers together, and Ty smiled even though he'd had a backbreaking, frustrating day. He squeezed Zane's hand as he stared at the jagged hole in the second floor.

"We could have built a building from scratch, you know," Zane said, waving at the inside of the old, three-story brick building on the edge of the harbor in Fell's Point.

Ty gazed at the room too, seeing the architectural details beneath the years of paint, dust, and misuse. He shook his head and smiled as he cut his gaze to Zane. "Old and broken-down is more my style."

Zane cast a glance around them, then settled on Ty again, smirking. "Whatever makes you happy, doll."

Ty narrowed his eyes. "You're being agreeable. What have you done?"

Zane gave him an innocent shrug. "I didn't do anything. I'm just agreeing." He slid his fingers along Ty's palm to caress the inside of Ty's wrist.

Ty turned his hand over in Zane's. Then he sighed. "Your office is bugged, isn't it?"

Zane laughed. "No. But it's kind of sad that you think that'd put me in a good mood."

"Wouldn't it?" Ty asked with a smirk.

"Probably." Zane sat back, seeming entirely too pleased with himself as he looked around the building again. He finally pointed to the back wall. "I think the section on horses should go right there, what do you think? Maybe a picture of you in the saddle?"

Ty shook his head, rubbing at a spot of tension between his eyes.

"Oh, I picked up the mail when I went by the house." Zane rummaged in his box for a small package that he handed to Ty. "Did you order something? What is it?"

"I don't know." Ty used his pocketknife to get into it, gazing at Zane fondly as he did so. The silver feathering at the sides of his hair was getting more pronounced, and every time Ty took notice of it, he wanted to tackle Zane to the ground.

He pulled a small jewelry box out of the package and turned it over, then narrowed his eyes at Zane. "Was this you?"

Zane shook his head and reached to pluck a card off the inside of the packaging, flipping it open to read. "Says it's from Owen." He handed the card to Ty.

"Weird." Ty muttered, and popped the jewelry box open.

Inside was a nickel.

Zane chuckled. "Your friends are so strange."

"Hold on," Ty said, a grin spreading across his face. He picked the nickel up out of the box and examined it, finding a slit near the edge just big enough for a thumbnail. When he pulled on it, a tiny curved blade popped out of the nickel. Ty laughed delightedly. "It's a knife!"

"Oh my God," Zane groaned.

"Looks like he found a new supplier. Secret Santa next year is going to be awesome." Ty put the nickel in his pocket, still grinning.

"You realize most of the things you get from your friends should be illegal, right?"

"Hey, that go bag you appropriated is full of illegal things I got from my friends, so either stop judging or give it back."

"No, I like it. And you're not getting those boots back, either."

Ty grunted.

Zane's smile turned into a leer. "You coming to the hotel tonight?"

Ty laughed and nodded. The night Zane had left the row house, Ty had waited a few hours, then tracked Zane's ass down and crawled into bed with him in the luxury suite he'd booked.

"You going to tell me how you found me?" Zane asked for perhaps the twentieth time.

Ty stole a languid kiss, then whispered, "I'll always find you, Zane."

Zane rewarded him with a fond smile. He kissed Ty again, humming happily. "Give me a hint."

"Please. The Admiral Fell Inn? It's the only hotel nearby that's a pun; of course you headed there."

Zane chuckled, closing his eyes as Ty nuzzled at him. He finally ducked his head, reaching over to tug the box closer. "I stopped by that deli you like so much near the office."

Ty's smile turned melancholy at best. He was glad he'd made his decision to quit the Bureau, but it had been a trade between having Zane at home and having him at work. And he kind of missed work. "Are you going to be happy here when you retire? Selling old books and keeping me occupied?"

Zane met Ty's eyes. "I can't imagine being anywhere else. Although I suppose if it becomes worrisome, we can take a trip out to Austin for a couple of weeks now and then. You know. Vacation."

Ty frowned. "No need to be mean." He ran his hand up Zane's back, letting his fingers trail up the soft material of his dress shirt. He was about to zone out when he remembered what he'd wanted to show Zane. "Oh! Want to see what I found in the back room?"

Zane laughed and held out a cold bottle of water. "Sure."

Ty took the bottle as he pushed himself to his feet. He grabbed Zane's forearm and tugged him up. "You're going to love this."

Zane smoothed one hand over Ty's ass. "Uh huh. Go on." He was humoring Ty, but Ty didn't care.

He led the way into the back room, which had been a kitchen in the original building but had since been turned into a storeroom with a sink and a refrigerator hookup. Ty had removed everything but a hammer, leaving the room just as bare and pitiful as the rest of the structure.

He was grinning from ear to ear when he waved his hand at one of the walls. It was covered with cheap paneling and painted a garish green, and there were several holes where Ty had taken the hammer to it.

Zane looked from Ty, to the wall, back to Ty, and back to the wall before shaking his head. "What am I missing?"

"What, you don't see it?" Ty's smile grew bigger. "Your finely tuned spider sense hasn't realized that this room isn't as wide as the front room?"

Zane frowned and twisted halfway around to check the room's dimensions. "Someone closed in a bolt-hole?"

"Better." Ty picked up the hammer and stepped over to the panel that had first caught his attention. He used the claw to pull the panel back, then took the flashlight from his back pocket and clicked it on. He gestured for Zane to lean closer, and he let the light shine on the wooden treads of a stairwell, hidden for at least half a century.

"Oh hell," Zane said under his breath. "No wonder you're giddy. The survey didn't show a basement on this lot."

"I know!" He'd been excited when he found it, almost excited enough to grab the flashlight and investigate. But he would never do such a thing without Zane, and he was sort of scared shitless of dark basements. "Want to check it out?"

"How long did you have to wait for me to get here so you could have me go down there?" Zane asked, a wry smile twisting his lips as he crossed his arms. "You could have called."

"Wasn't long before I poked the hole through the ceiling," Ty admitted. "As soon as I found this, I left this room. Please take this and go down there so I can see what it is!" He shoved the flashlight at Zane.

Zane chuckled and took the Maglite. "Open it up," he said, gesturing to the rest of the paneling blocking the stairway.

Ty slid the hammer back into the paneling and tugged it off the wall with ease. He set the first strip carefully aside, then tugged at the next one to open it up. The cobwebs in the old stairwell alone would have kept him on ground level if he'd done this earlier.

Zane was pulling on the pair of work gloves Ty had worn most of the day. Ty wanted to go with him and see what was down there, but he knew his limits, especially after his ordeal in Scotland. His limit was right here at the first step.

Zane moved to the landing, and Ty peered over his shoulder. "If it's big enough down there, I might be able to handle it."

Zane settled a hand at the base of Ty's neck, squeezing as he pressed a kiss to the corner of Ty's lips. "My brave bulldog."

Ty huffed. "Just go see what's down there!"

Zane took the first couple of stairs cautiously, testing each before settling his full weight on it, and then moving on. The stone wall along the stairway was bare, no railing, no evidence of one ever being there. Ty watched until the flashlight's beam found the ground floor of the cellar.

Ty shivered. There were obviously no windows or doors, since no one knew the damn room was down there.

Finally, Zane called up the stairs, "I'm at the bottom."

"Uh huh. And?"

"Stairs are pretty sturdy. The floor is paved with stone; looks like there was a wood floor over it at one point. It's so dusty it's hard to tell. There's shelving along the walls, not in very good shape." Zane raised his voice to carry up the stairs as he moved further away from them. "Broken glass. It looks like it was cleared out in a hurry."

"What else?" Ty asked as he fought the urge to go down there and investigate.

"Wait a sec." Zane went quiet for a long moment, and then Ty heard a crack, a whump, and a crunch that sounded like wood falling. "I'm okay!"

"Don't make me come down there, dude."

"So brave," Zane called from the dark. "There's a grate here."

"What kind?"

"Big-ass grate in the floor," Zane answered, his voice a little more distant and muffled.

Ty grunted, frowning. "Might have been Prohibition era," he called back. "Made it easy to dispose of evidence during a raid. You know, that makes sense with some of the other architecture in this place. It might have been a speakeasy at some point."

"Would explain the shelves and boxes, anyway," Zane said as he started back up the stairs.

"Is it usable space? Worth renovating? Or should we board it back up and pretend it's not scary?"

"It's usable. Pretty solid, really, stone floor and walls, doesn't look like it's leaked, even being this close to the harbor." Zane emerged from the dark and joined Ty back on the main level. "Definitely good for long-term or secure storage."

"You could make it your art studio when you go through your dungeon period."

Zane snorted and shook his head.

"Although . . . I might be wrong, but if it was used as a storage cellar for illegal alcohol, they would have had a chute to get in there in secret. Load it from the street, right into the cellar. Maybe we can get some more lights down there and check it out better later."

"It's totally open down there," Zane said, patting Ty's arm reassuringly. "Not closed in at all. Just one big room with foundation pillars."

"One big, dark, underground room," Ty said with a nod. "With three stories towering over it."

Zane set his hands on Ty's hips. "You don't ever have to go down there if you don't want to. We could just board it up and forget about it."

"That would take all the fun out of it," Ty said, and placed his hands on Zane's waist. "We'll paint it white, it'll be fine."

"Sure it will."

Ty kissed him quickly. "Let's go back to the hotel, huh? I'll tell you some ideas I've got for your bookshelves."

Zane's hands were slow to let him go. "You need a shower," he said, brushing some dust and dirt out of Ty's hair.

Ty's smile grew more predatory. "That something you'd like to help me with?"

Zane's hum of approval was nearly a purr.

Ty kissed him again, this one much more heated than the last, and then stepped away. "Let's go. I've got dust caked in places it was never meant to get."

Zane sprawled on the king-sized bed in the suite at the Admiral Fell Inn where he'd been living for the last week. And yes, he'd come here because the Inn's name was a pun.

Every night, he would wait impatiently for Ty to come prowling in. And according to Ty, every night at the row house Ty would make a fuss about going to bed, make a commotion and grumble to himself as he got into bed, then turn out the lights and sneak out like the trained professional he was so he could spend the night with his fiancé. It made Zane laugh to think about a man like Ty, with all his training and experience, using those highly developed skills for the adult version of breaking curfew. How had it come to this?

Zane was trying to decide how they could use the bugs to their advantage. Julian Cross had once told them that if they were facing an opponent larger than themselves, the best way to beat them was to use their own strengths against them. He hadn't phrased it that way; he'd used an inane chess analogy instead. Zane had since become pretty adept at the game, so he finally understood what the man had been trying to tell them.

The only problem was that Zane couldn't decide how best to use bugs against their mole. They could feed them wrong information, try to get them to overplay their hand. But they didn't even know enough about the mole's game to do that. They were playing blind. Until one of them came up with a solution, the only way they could converse freely was at the bookstore, which they'd ultimately chosen to list in public records under the name of the Carter Garrett Ranch for the express purpose of keeping it out of the spotlight, or here in this hotel suite.

At least it was a nice suite.

The water cut off in the bathroom, and a few seconds later Ty stepped out in nothing but a towel, steam roiling behind him. Zane propped his head in his hands and stared.

The first marks of age were finally starting to hit Ty. A little gray in his scruff when he grew it out, which he did more often than not these days. Arthritis in the hand he'd broken so many times. But he was still cut and lithe, he still reminded Zane of a large jungle cat when he moved, and his mind and tongue were still as sharp as ever. Zane had never imagined himself loving a person like Ty, but now? Now he couldn't imagine his life without him.

Ty gave him a cheeky grin when he caught Zane staring. "Want a show?" he teased, his voice a low purr.

"What, like late-night cable?" Zane asked, trying to sound innocent. "Skinemax presents?"

Ty tossed his wet towel at him, then crawled into bed and laid himself out over Zane as Zane fought to disentangle himself from the towel. Ty's body was still hot and damp from the shower, but Zane didn't care. He ran his fingers through Ty's hair, grinning as he waited for some further form of punishment. But Ty remained silent, merely peering down at Zane with a slight frown marring his features.

"What?" Zane asked when he realized Ty didn't plan on sharing what was on his mind.

"Let's elope."

Zane laughed, but he realized almost immediately that Ty wasn't laughing with him. His grin fell into a frown. "Wait, what?"

"I'm tired of not being married, Zane. And God knows neither of us can make a decision to save our lives. Where do we have it? Do we do the whole nine yards or shorten the ceremony? Do we try to make it religious or keep it nondenominational? Do you have a best man or do you ask Annie to stand with you? Do we involve our families, make one of them travel? Does Chester get to put a corsage on his shovel? If we have to go to Texas, can I put Barnum in a bow tie and have him be the bouncer for the reception?"

Zane had to bite his lip to keep from laughing. He wished Ty were exaggerating, but those were all conversations they'd had in the last year, including Ty insisting that if he was ever made to go to Texas again he'd string Barnum the Bengal tiger along behind him on a leash until Zane let him go home.

"Screw the big ceremony," Ty said with a snarl of his lip. "Screw what our families and friends want or think. For once let's just . . . do it for us. They just legalized it in Maryland, we could go down in the morning and apply for a license. It's only a forty-eight-hour wait; that'd give us time to wrangle up two witnesses to get here, and by Monday morning we'd be hitched. And it's not like we don't have some federal connections we can abuse. There's a way you can get the wait waived by a judge, and I talked to Hank Freeman, you remember him?"

"The judge who always rushed your warrants for you?"

"Yeah."

Zane laughed and he wrapped his arms around Ty to kiss him.

"He said he'd do the ceremony if . . . when you agreed."

This wasn't just some whim Ty had come up with in the shower. He'd researched it, made inquiries, probably even greased the wheels with Judge Freeman so he'd rush the application and perform the ceremony on short notice. Zane nodded, a little in awe as he met Ty's shining eyes. "Let's do it."

"Yeah?"

"Right now. If we take the Valkyrie we can make it to the courthouse before they close and get the license. We could be married by Monday," Zane said. If Ty wanted spontaneous, Zane could give it to him this time.

Ty kissed him messily, then rolled out of bed and scrambled for his clothes.

"Are you . . . you heard me say Valkyrie, right?" Zane asked. Ty *always* complained about the motorcycle.

Ty straightened, pulling his jeans on and buttoning them. He was beaming. "You've always wanted me on the back of that death trap, right? Here's your chance."

"This might be the best day of my life," Zane said disbelievingly.

Ty crawled over him again, pressing him to the mattress and kissing him until they were both breathless. "I'll make sure of it tonight. Now get your ass in gear, let's go get legalized."

Come Monday morning they were in Zane's hotel room yet again, except this time Zane was tying his shoelaces over and over, trying to get them right as Ty paced in front of him, his phone held to his ear. They'd called Deuce as soon as they'd received their marriage license and told him to come to Baltimore and bring Livi, Amelia, and a suit. They needed two witnesses, after all, and Amelia would jump at any chance she could get to dress up and peg people with something pretty like flower petals or rice.

They'd decided not to call anyone else. Their families could wait, and this way each family could be given their own time, their own celebration, something that suited them. Understated and elegant in Texas for Zane's mother, moonshine and shovels in the mountains for the Gradys. And they'd be able to hold off the meeting of the families for a little longer, something Zane wasn't keen on seeing happen anytime soon.

Zane didn't really have any friends or family he desperately needed to be with him today, but Ty . . .

Zane glanced up at him with a sympathetic frown. His brother was coming, and Zane knew that was paramount to Ty today. But Ty had more than one man he considered a brother, and blood had little to do with it.

Ty cleared his throat and stopped his pacing, squaring his shoulders as if fighting nerves when his call went through. "Hey, babe, it's Ty again."

His voice sounded shaky, but everything sounded shaky right now. They were just a few hours away from getting to say "I do." He didn't remember much from his first wedding, but these moments of nerves building up to it were familiar.

Ty coughed, closing his eyes. "Nick, I don't know where the fuck you are, man, but I kind of need you here. Please call me back."

Zane stood slowly, watching Ty with a frown. "Still not answering?"

Ty shook his head, not looking away from his phone.

"You worried?"

Ty raised his head. "Little bit."

"I thought Nick disappeared like this without telling anyone pretty often. Isn't that why he lives on a boat, so he can go off the reservation?"

"He does, it's just . . . he usually still checks in with *someone* even if he's AWOL. He still checks his phone, calls back for emergencies. I . . . I thought he'd call me back by now, even if he's too far away to get here. You know? I told him we were getting married. I mean . . ."

"We can do this later," Zane offered, but Ty was already shaking his head. Zane took a step and rubbed his hands up Ty's arms, squeezing gently. "You want him here, Ty. We can do this later."

"No," Ty said, and his voice wasn't shaking any longer. "You're the only person I care about being here."

Zane pulled Ty in for a kiss. He was wearing the blue suit Zane loved so much, at Zane's insistence, and Ty had demanded Zane wear his charcoal pinstriped suit tonight. Zane was happy to oblige. By the time they went to bed, Zane would be able to call Ty his husband, and both of their suits would be wrinkling on a floor somewhere.

A knock at the door saved the blue suit from Zane's wandering hands, and Ty pulled away with a wink. He opened the door to his brother's smiling face. Deuce was dressed sharply, and was holding a plastic container in his hand.

"I'm so going to be the favorite after this," Deuce crooned as he stepped into the room.

"Deuce, the maid of honor *died* at your wedding," Ty said.

"Well, I didn't kill her," Deuce argued. "Ma's going to disown both of you."

Ty nodded and gave Deuce a hug. "We'd have to do this in Maryland regardless of what kind of ceremony we had elsewhere. Might as well do it now."

"Can't wait to watch you explain that to Ma." Deuce turned to Zane and offered him a hearty handshake. "Y'all ready?"

Ty met Zane's eyes. The hazel was glinting in the light, and his lips curved in a smirk.

"Oh yeah," Zane said, unable to fight his grin. "Yeah, let's do this."

"You nervous?" Deuce asked them.

Ty snorted and shook his head.

"That's a yes," Deuce said wryly.

"Shut up, I'm not nervous."

"Yes, he is." Zane softened the words with a fond smile in Ty's direction.

Deuce handed Zane the container he'd brought in, then patted him on the shoulder. "Take your time. We'll be in the lobby, ready when you are." He squeezed Ty's shoulder in passing and then left them alone once more.

Zane lifted the container. The plastic was clear, but fogged over from whatever Deuce had in there, so it was impossible to see the contents.

"What is that?" Ty asked.

Zane shrugged, then shoved the container at Ty. "He's your brother . . . you open it."

"I don't want to."

"Why not?"

Ty huffed. "Well, why don't you?"

"Because . . ."

"He handed it to you, it's obviously yours to open."

"But he's *your* brother. You should open it."

"I can't," Ty insisted.

"Why?"

"Because it might be alive."

"Why would it be alive?" Zane cried, and he shoved the container into Ty's arms.

"I don't know!"

Zane snorted and popped the lid. They both winced away from it, but nothing fuzzy or breathing jumped out. Ty lifted the lid and stared for a second, then broke into a wide grin.

"Deacon, you sly son of a bitch." He held up a small boutonniere and twirled it between his thumb and forefinger. It was made of a single orchid.

"Orchids?" Zane asked.

"I told him about the black market orchid thing when I first realized . . . well, that I was in love with you," Ty admitted. Then he smiled and turned the boutonniere over. "He made fun of me because he said black market anything was not romantic. God, I can't believe he remembered."

Zane took the container from Ty and set it on the desk nearby. There were three more boutonnieres in there. Deuce had obviously planned for Zane to have someone at his side, but Zane didn't need anyone else. He had everything he could have wanted today.

He took the orchid out of Ty's hand, their fingers lingering as their eyes met.

"Come here," Zane whispered, and dragged Ty closer, kissing him gently as his palm slid against Ty's cheek. "I love you. So much."

Ty had his eyes closed, his nose pressed to Zane's. He was trembling, and it made Zane smile. He never thought he'd see the day that Ty Grady was nervous.

Ty must have felt Zane grinning, because he took a deep, shaky breath and said, "Go ahead and laugh. I feel a little like I'm going to yark all over you, though, so you'll get what you deserve."

Zane took Ty's face in both hands and backed up just enough to look into his eyes. The boutonniere was still between his fingers, and he set it on top of Ty's head so he wouldn't squish it. He chuckled when Ty didn't even complain.

"Tell me why you're nervous," he said, low and gentle. "And then I'll tell you why *I'm* nervous."

Ty took another deep breath and let it out slowly. "I don't know. I desperately don't want to fuck this up."

"It's just an, 'I do,' Ty. Even if you fuck it up, who cares? We'll still be married. We'll still be us."

"I know. But I think . . . I think I never thought we'd make it here."

"You thought I wouldn't say yes?"

"No. I mean, no, I . . . I didn't think we'd live long enough to be here. And something about today feels like borrowed time."

Zane's brow furrowed, and he took a tiny step closer. "Then let's take that time and ride it hard and put it up wet, baby."

Ty laughed, closed his eyes, and nodded. "I love you."

Zane kissed him as warmth spread through him. "You want to know why I'm nervous?"

"You're not nervous. You're pretending to be so I won't feel stupid."

Zane was silent, a smile pulling at his lips. He kissed Ty again, lingering over the familiar taste, the scent, the beautiful fact that being able to take Ty in his arms and kiss him whenever he wanted wasn't unique anymore.

But it was sure as hell special.

"You're right," Zane whispered. "You want to know why I'm *not* nervous?"

Ty nodded against Zane's cheek. His eyes were still closed.

"Because there's not a thing in the world that could fuck this up. Including you."

Ty barked a laugh and finally opened his eyes. "Promise?"

Zane grinned. "I do."

Ty had convinced the Honorable Henry Freeman to meet them at the harbor that evening. It was a Monday night, and the harbor front was empty. The aquarium was lit up, though, and so was the USS *Constellation* out on the water. Ty hadn't intended for the nineteenth-century sloop of war and the neon waves on the side of the aquarium to act as their backdrop when they said their vows, but he certainly wasn't going to admit that when the others started talking about how perfect it was.

Zane took his hand as they strolled toward the water and slowed him to a stop, letting Deuce, Livi, and Amelia move ahead of them.

Ty turned to meet his eyes, taking a deep breath to try to steady himself.

Zane smiled warmly and squeezed his fingers. He took Ty's lapel in one hand and held up one of the orchids Deuce had brought them. He was already wearing one on his lapel, and he moved to pin the other one to Ty's suit, his brow furrowing in concentration.

Ty gazed at him, loving the way Zane looked when he was focused on something. Zane glanced up briefly, meeting his eyes. There was a lot of pain in their tumultuous past. There were a lot of things they'd said and done to each other that could have broken them. They'd been able to move beyond them, though, bracing themselves with love and loyalty and trust.

Ty opened his mouth to tell Zane that he loved him one more time, but he gasped instead when Zane stuck him with the pin on the orchid.

"Shit, sorry," Zane said, laughing breathily before he was able to curtail it.

Ty grabbed his face and kissed him.

"Not yet, you yahoos!" Deuce called from further down the water.

Zane was grinning when Ty let him go. He took Ty's hand in his and they moved to join the others. Judge Freeman had just arrived, carrying a small leather book and a traveling mug that may or may not have contained alcohol. He shook both Ty and Zane's hands, then handed Deuce his mug and waved his book.

"Where are we doing this?"

Ty glanced around them. They were near the edge of the sidewalk, with the water lapping at the concrete pilings and a rope that was supposed to keep adventurous sightseers from toppling into the harbor. The USS *Constellation* was so close they could hear her creaking. Music played from the restaurants and shops near the aquarium. Snow threatened with a few stray flakes, and the wind off the Atlantic was bracing. It was a little chaotic, to be honest, and the dichotomy of the busy harbor and the calm water were striking. Then Ty saw the massive chain on the *Constellation* disappearing into the depths where she was anchored, and he grinned.

"This is perfect," Zane answered before Ty could do it.

Ty turned to him, and suddenly all his nerves dissipated like they'd been taken by the breeze.

Freeman cleared his throat, opening his book as Ty and Zane faced each other. Deuce and Livi hurried to their sides, and Amelia reached into a little box she'd been carrying and chucked a handful of dissolvable heart-shaped confetti at Ty and Zane's feet.

"Not yet," Livi whispered, and she managed to grab Amelia before the little girl could dump the rest of the box on Zane's shoes.

Ty and Zane both had to bite their tongues to keep from laughing.

Freeman gave them a moment to make sure they were ready, then reached into a front pocket and extracted a pair of reading glasses. He slid them on and smiled at them, then put a finger on the page. "Here we are."

Ty couldn't take his eyes off Zane, who was watching him ardently in the glow of the lights off the harbor. He was certain that whatever Freeman said next, he would never remember anything beside the look in Zane's eyes.

"We are gathered here tonight to join these two lives, these two hearts, these two souls, in marriage. If there is anyone present here today who objects to this union, please take it up with the two armed federal agents who are getting hitched."

Zane winked at Ty, reaching for him. Ty gripped his hand, holding on to him like they were in danger of blowing away with the heart-shaped confetti swirling at their feet.

"Do you have vows?" Freeman asked.

Zane nodded, but he didn't move to take out a piece of paper or any notes. He licked his lips instead and took a deep breath. "Ty," he said, and the sound was almost lost in the night. "Some roads to love aren't easy, and I've never been more thankful for being forced to fight for something. I started this journey with a partner I hated, and a man in the mirror I hated even more. The road took me from the streets of New York to the mountaintops of West Virginia, from the place I born to the place I found a home. It forced me to let go of my past and face my future. And I had to be made blind before I could see."

Zane swallowed hard and looked down, obviously fighting to finish without choking on the words or tearing up. Ty realized his own eyes were burning, and it wasn't because of the cold wind. Zane squeezed Ty's fingers with one hand, and he met Ty's eyes as he reached into his lapel with his other.

"I promise to love you until I die," he said, his voice strong again. He held up a Sharpie he'd had in his suit, and pulled Ty's hand closer to draw on his ring finger. With several sweeping motions, he created an infinity sign that looped all the way around the finger.

When he was satisfied with the ring he'd drawn, he kissed Ty's knuckles and let him go, handing him the Sharpie.

Ty grasped the pen, but he couldn't take his eyes off Zane. He ran his thumb over Zane's palm. He had a set of vows he'd jotted down on a note card, folded up in his pocket, but he left them where they were and gazed into Zane's eyes, their past flashing in front of him, their future opening up in his mind.

He took a deep breath. "I promise to never leave you alone in the dark," he whispered.

He pulled Zane's hand closer and pressed the tip of the Sharpie against Zane's skin, curving the symbol for forever around it. When he was satisfied, he kissed the tip of Zane's finger and slid the pen back into his lapel pocket.

Freeman coughed and turned a page in his book. "Do you, Zane Zachary Garrett, take this man to be your lawful wedded husband?"

Zane's lips curved into a warm smile. "I do."

Freeman turned toward Ty. "Do you, Beaumont Tyler Grady, take this man to be your lawful wedded husband?"

"I do," Ty said, almost before the question was finished.

"Then by the power vested in me by the state of Maryland, I pronounce you legally wed." Freeman slapped his little book closed. "You may now share the first kiss of the rest of your lives."

Ty had fully expected to have the urge to grab Zane and plant one on him out of sheer impatience and joy, but as he stood staring at his brand-new husband, it was as if they were moving underwater. He touched the tips of his fingers to Zane's cheek, then stepped closer and used both hands to cup his face with the utmost care. Zane was still smiling when they kissed, and it was slow and gentle, Zane's hands at Ty's ribs pulling them flush.

"Okay, now," Livi whispered somewhere to their side, and a moment later they were both pelted with handfuls of heart-shaped confetti.

Zane laughed and finally wrapped his arms around Ty, squeezing him tight. The others continued to toss the confetti at them, even handing out bits to people passing by so they'd be sure to get covered from all sides. They laughed into the kiss, not caring. They were still locked in their happy embrace when Deuce turned the box over above them and rained little, bitty hearts down on their heads.

CHAPTER 3

Ty got the key into the door just before Zane hit him from behind and pressed him against it. He grinned and shook his head. "I have a surprise for you," he said as Zane kissed his neck.

"Oh, really?" Zane splayed his fingers against the door beside Ty's head. The brand-new tattoo on his ring finger was still red around the edges. Ty couldn't take his eyes off it. Zane had worn a gold one in the past, and they'd both had silver even if it had been fake. Ty had also lost or utterly destroyed two engagement rings, so Zane had refused to buy him a wedding ring, knowing it would just get crushed, cut off, or cost Ty his finger. The only solution, Zane had decided, was to tattoo it on.

Right after the ceremony, they'd headed for a local place owned by an artist friend of Zane's, and they'd made the rings permanent. The proprietor, Tudor, had even insisted they throw an impromptu wedding reception right there in the tattoo parlor. When Ty and Zane had escaped the revelry, Tudor had been waltzing with Amelia, and Deuce and Livi had been considering getting inked.

The tattoo Ty now had on his ring finger was the simple wrapped infinity symbol Zane had drawn, but when he moved his middle finger, it revealed an anchor woven in. A hidden reminder of what Zane was to him. Zane's was the exact same thing, only with a simplified compass incorporated in.

Zane had rambled about the symbolism as he'd added the compass and anchor with his Sharpie, about how they were both different things to each other and different people but part of the same thing. Ty had been too distracted by the utter ridiculousness of how much that tiny needle hurt on the webbing of his finger to engage in philosophy at the time.

"Ty," Zane whispered against Ty's ear. "Have you gotten distracted by something?"

"Yeah," Ty murmured, then grinned. "My husband."

Zane grabbed Ty's arm and turned him around, pushing him against the door and kissing him possessively. "That sounds so good when you say it."

Ty raised an eyebrow and nodded. "I'll be sure to scream it later. After I show you your surprise."

Zane took a deep breath. Ty got the door unlocked and shoved it open, pulling Zane into the row house. It was the first time he'd set foot in there for over a week. Their plan had been to come here to gather some clothes for Ty, but Ty hadn't quite divulged all the information he had.

Zane was silent as he followed Ty into the living room, looking around as if he thought Ty's surprise might be alive and need a litter box.

Ty spread his arms wide, beaming at Zane in the half-light. "It's clear."

"What?"

"I killed the bugs," Ty said with pride in his voice that probably wasn't deserved, considering he'd gotten rid of the listening devices by pretending to be the clumsiest ex–special forces person ever.

"The house is clear?" Zane asked, a smile growing as he looked around the row house again.

Ty nodded. "I know we wanted to use them to seed information, but it's been almost two weeks, and . . ."

"It wasn't working, I know," Zane finished for him. "That means I can come home?"

Ty sighed in relief. A part of him had been afraid Zane would be irritated that he'd acted without consulting him. "For now it does. You want to see what I've done?"

"What have you done?" Zane asked, dread filtering into his tone.

"Well, I needed a good excuse for destroying the furniture upstairs and throwing it out. And then . . . well, it ended up destroyed. So I got us a new bed."

Zane perked up as he moved closer. They hadn't even bothered turning the lights on, and his shadowed features in the dim living room sent a thrill up Ty's spine. "New bed?"

"It's a king-sized bed," Ty said with a slow, crooked grin.

"I hope it's sturdy."

Ty shrugged. "I haven't been in it."

"Oh, we'll have to fix that," Zane said, drawing the words out as he approached.

Ty snickered. He took the few steps to close the distance between them and brushed his lips against Zane's. "Welcome home, Zane."

Zane smiled and kissed him gently. "Husband."

"That's right. Now, come on, I want to show you your new bed." Ty took Zane's hand and tugged him toward the stairs.

"*Our* new bed."

"I thought we were going to need a forklift for the mattress. It's one of those memory foam ones."

"How'd you get it up there?"

"I utilized some surprise resources. John English stopped by."

"The Snake Eater? From Scotland?"

"Yeah, he had a few hours' layover, stopped by. I'll tell you about it later. He helped me move the bed in. I think we got it up there on beer fumes alone."

Zane chuckled but stopped at the base of the stairs. He took their joined hands and kissed the tip of Ty's ring finger. "I'll never feel the same about these steps again."

Ty laughed and closed his eyes. Zane's lips brushed against the nape of his neck, and he turned his head to meet the kiss before Zane could pull away. Zane cupped his cheek to keep him in place for the fervent kiss he delivered next. It was hot and wet, and Zane eventually broke it to pant for air.

"You mentioned a bed," he said breathlessly.

"It's a really nice bed, Zane."

Zane nodded and kissed him again. "Maybe we should test it to see how nice it is."

"Come on." Ty grabbed Zane's hand and yanked him up the first step, but Zane pulled Ty back and then took the first couple steps alone. He turned around, mischief written all over his face, then went up another step backward and started unbuttoning his shirt, trailing his fingers over the material of Ty's favorite suit.

Ty glared up at him as he put one foot on the bottom step. "I will catch you," he warned.

Zane smiled and licked his bottom lip while moving up and back again, undoing another button.

"Fine then, be naked by the time you get up there, less work for me," Ty told him, and took the next steps two at a time.

Zane laughed and hurried up a few more steps before turning toward Ty again and finishing with the buttons, leaving the shirt to hang open as he started on his belt. "C'mon, baby," he drawled. "I've got some motivation for you."

"Garrett," Ty warned as he put both hands on the railings and pushed himself up two more steps with a grin. He swiped out for Zane's feet.

"Grady," Zane singsonged as he moved up out of reach, the ends of his belt dangling. His fingers moved to the button of his suit pants.

"I thought we were trying to test out the bed, not the stairs," Ty whined as he watched Zane undress halfway up to the second floor. If he caught him before the bedroom, they'd be fucking where they landed. It was too big a day for them to mess around with such niceties as mattresses.

"We'll get there," Zane promised. He shrugged out of his shirt and tossed it over the railing.

Ty shook his head and peeled out of his blue suit jacket as Zane watched, tongue between his teeth. Then Zane turned and was gone, leaving Ty to hustle after him. By the time Ty caught him he was standing in their bedroom, pants discarded, the black fabric of his briefs stark against his skin.

Ty grabbed his hips as he sank to his knees and kissed Zane's belly, starting at the ridge of his lowest rib and working down toward his hip. His fingers curled under Zane's briefs as he nuzzled against his warm skin.

Zane moaned, sliding his fingers into Ty's hair. "Aw damn. There goes my motivation to try out that brand-new mattress," he muttered, angling his hips toward Ty's mouth.

Ty tugged Zane's briefs down, leaving the elastic to hug at Zane's thighs as he bit the tender skin of Zane's hip.

"Baby . . ." Zane exhaled shakily. Ty grinned up at him. He took an obscene amount of pleasure in doing this for Zane. His husband.

Zane could have anything he wanted as far as Ty was concerned. He climbed to his feet when Zane urged him to, and Zane's hands wrapped around him, holding him close as they kissed and Zane turned them until Ty's knees were against the edge of the new bed.

Ty sat hard, dragging Zane to him before he could get away. He kissed Zane's belly and chest as he tugged him to stand between his legs. Zane settled his hands on Ty's shoulders, then slid a finger under Ty's chin and tipped his head back. As Ty looked up, Zane traced the lines of his face so gently his fingertips barely touched the skin.

Ty gazed up at him adoringly, the heat banking under the intimate caress. Zane's fingers trailed down to his throat and the compass rose he wore around his neck before pausing.

"God, I love you."

Ty pulled him down and kissed him. He let his lips just slide over Zane's as he guided Zane back into the bed with him. Ty rolled them into the middle of the mattress, getting Zane under him. Zane stretched out, spreading his arms over his head and pulling one knee up.

Ty stared for a moment, entranced, and Zane closed his eyes and let his hand travel down his own body, palm sliding over his inner thigh as he arched his back.

"Memory foam," Zane purred. He moved his hand from his thigh onto the mattress. "Interesting."

"I'll show you interesting," Ty promised, and grabbed the bottle of lube from the bedside drawer.

His breaths were harsh and he was hard despite the fact Zane had barely touched him. He ran his fingers up the inside of Zane's thigh, urging him to spread his legs wider, and then he kissed the inside of Zane's knee. Zane whispered his name.

Ty hummed as he dragged his tongue up the inside of Zane's thigh to his straining cock. "First time as a married couple. How do we want it?" he asked as he opened the bottle.

Zane breathed hard through his nose, laid his head back, and closed his eyes, so Ty pushed one of Zane's legs to the side, stroking himself as Zane opened up for him. And then he gave Zane what he wanted, thrusting into him, past the clenching muscles and in deep despite the resistance from Zane's body. Zane cried out in agonized pleasure, body bowing and writhing. Heat coursed through Ty, and he grabbed at the sheets above Zane's head as Zane pulled both knees up and squeezed at Ty's waist, laying himself open and letting Ty take complete control.

Ty worked his hips until he was buried inside his newly minted husband, and then he stretched out over Zane to cover his hands. They laced their fingers together. "I love you," Ty breathed against Zane's lips.

"If you knew half the things I want you to do to me tonight," Zane managed through an overwrought groan.

"So tell me. But this won't last long if you do. Good God, Zane."

"It has to." Zane pulled his knee higher and hooked his ankles at the small of Ty's back.

With a grunt of effort, Ty flipped them over, and Zane wound up astride him, Ty's hands grasping his thighs.

"Now, I want to see you jack off." Ty emphasized his point by pulling up his knees behind Zane and using the angle to thrust into him.

Zane's back arched as he rode Ty's cock, rolling his hips and groaning. He slid his hand up his thigh to grip himself, eyes closing and head falling back as he stroked himself with Ty rocking deep inside him.

"Open your eyes, Zane," Ty insisted as he gripped Zane's hips.

Zane forced his eyes open and met Ty's gaze, rolling his hips and whimpering. Zane's hand continued to move as he lifted up and sat down again, knowing just how to get what he wanted. He slowed his hand, either trying to stave off the orgasm or torture Ty. Possibly both.

It was what Ty wanted to see and feel and hear, that inevitable snap of intense pleasure when Zane lost all control. Zane's body trembled over Ty's, muscles straining, his breathing coming in gasps and pants.

Ty had to fight with every ounce of control he had not to come inside Zane as he watched.

Zane maintained their gaze as long as he could, but he closed his eyes and cried out Ty's name when the orgasm hit him, curling over as he jacked himself. Ty held on to him as the climax ripped through him, keeping Zane in place while he thrust his hips up over and over, fucking Zane through it, jutting into those pulsing muscles until he couldn't stand it any longer and rolled Zane onto his back again. He fucked him hard and fast, forcing him into the mattress, hiding his face in Zane's neck, until he was yelling as well, his body jerking in Zane's tight embrace as he came in a series of loud and entirely gratuitous moans.

Ty collapsed against him once he'd spent himself. He was careful as he pulled out, kissing Zane so he could taste Zane's gasp when he pulled free, then rolling sideways with a plaintive huff. Zane rolled with him, still panting as he kissed him desperately. Their lips mashed and tongues got caught between teeth, but they kept at each other like they'd been starving for it. Ty finally stopped it by catching Zane's chin in one hand.

"It's okay," Ty said, still gasping for breath himself. "I'm not going anywhere, I promise."

Zane gave him a crooked smile, recovering still from the exertion.

Ty rubbed his nose and cheek against Zane, eager to just feel and smell him there so close. His husband. "I love you," he said.

Zane kissed him again. "I will never get tired of hearing that. I love you too." He drew Ty to him, not paying any mind to the mess of cum splattered between them.

They lay quietly for a while as their breathing calmed, and Ty felt Zane smile against his cheek. He sighed as he looked up at the ceiling, and then he rolled onto his side and pushed himself back against Zane to request he be cuddled. "Nice bed, huh?"

Zane shrugged and made an uncertain, almost negative sound as he wrapped Ty up in his arms. "I don't know."

"What do you mean, you don't know? You know how much this thing weighs?"

"I'm just saying. I think we should check it out again," Zane said innocently. "Just for some empirical data."

"You fuckshits! How you gonna go get married without all your friends?" Digger shouted. At least, Ty was pretty sure that was what he'd said, because his accent was definitely getting worse as he ranted. "Couldn't wait a day for us to get here? What are you, knocked up? I hope your mama whoops your ass."

"That's uncalled for," Ty muttered. He glanced at Owen, who'd been sitting on the couch in the living room of the row house, drinking a beer and watching Digger for the last five minutes.

Owen met Ty's eyes and shrugged. "Seems legit to me. We could have been here."

"What, you were looking forward to more glitter at the bachelor party?" Ty asked.

Owen pointed a finger at him. "That . . . we agreed never to speak of that again."

Zane chuckled as he settled onto the arm of the chair beside Ty and handed him a bottle of water. "Someday I'm going to hear all the Sidewinder stories and be traumatized for life."

"Word," Owen and Ty said simultaneously.

"Hey, when do O'Flaherty and the Doc get here?" Owen asked.

Ty cleared his throat, his smile fading. "Doc is flying in late tonight. I never got in touch with Nick."

"Seriously?" Owen's voice cracked with the word. Ty shrugged, and Owen arched his back and started digging in his pocket for his phone. "Come to think of it, he hasn't returned any of my messages either. Not for like a week or two."

"Yeah," Zane added. "We've been playing chess with this iPhone app. He hasn't made a move in so long our last game got forfeited. Ten days, or something like that."

"You two play chess on your phones?" Ty asked.

"Yeah." Zane shrugged, as if it wasn't at all odd that he'd had more contact with Ty's best friend than Ty had lately. "It's fun playing someone who actually knows the rules."

Ty harrumphed and settled back into his chair. "I know the rules. I just choose to think they're stupid."

"Where have I heard *that* before," Owen said under his breath.

"Shut up. So that's close to two weeks for both of you? No activity anywhere?"

Owen and Zane both nodded, glancing at each other with growing unease. They all looked to Digger, who was still muttering about Ty's mother beating him for eloping on them.

Digger shrugged and pulled his phone out. "Sent me a text a while back," he said with one last evil glare at Ty. "Said he was going fishing with a friend, and I'm supposed to feed his hamster if he doesn't come back. It was . . . phone says twelve days ago, now."

"Feed his hamster?" Zane asked, a tinge of dread in his voice like he wasn't sure he wanted clarification.

Ty was frowning, but he tore his eyes away from Digger and glanced up at Zane. "Means he was going off grid, and if he doesn't come back, Digger's supposed to wipe his life clean for his family. His mom, you know . . ."

"Monty Python?" Zane asked with a fond smile.

"'Your mother was a hamster,'" Owen said, not even cracking a smile. "Why would Nick go dark? I thought he resigned from the department."

"He did," Digger said with a careless shrug. "Well, he kind of did. He had a couple cases to clean up before he could go."

"They wouldn't let him leave?" Ty asked, preparing to be outraged.

"No, you know Nick. No unfinished business. But this ain't work; it's the same text he sends me whenever he leaves Boston. I didn't think nothing of it. He's convinced he's going to die away from home."

"Sounds like O'Flaherty," Zane grumbled.

"So he's not in Boston at all?" Owen asked. "Why would he go off grid *and* go out of town? Hold on, should we be worried?" He glanced between Ty and Digger. "Six, did you tell him on the phone that you were getting married?"

"Yeah." Ty's stomach turned with that same sense of unease he'd felt when he'd tried to reach Nick before the wedding. He'd attributed it to prenuptial nerves at the time, but now he wondered if it wasn't more. "I left a message. Several, over the course of two days. I just . . . I kind of figured he was still pissed at me."

"Nick would have called you back, man, I don't care what he's doing or how pissy he is. You call him and say you're getting married, he'd call back," Owen said. "We all would have. Jackass."

"Yeah, if we'd been invited," Digger huffed. "Has Doc heard from him?"

Ty shrugged, unable to shake that sense of dread. It even overpowered the minuscule amount of guilt he was starting to feel for eloping and not inviting Sidewinder. "I don't know. We'll ask him when he gets here."

"Doc's been on an adventure trek for three weeks," Owen told them.

Zane cocked his head. "What's that?"

"The camp he worked at," Owen said. "They took in underprivileged kids, foster kids, and first-time delinquent offenders and taught them the ins and outs of survival, basically. Doc was a counselor there. His favorite thing was running these adventure treks, where he'd take the older kids out into the mountains and fake a disaster they had to solve. Lose their equipment, pretend to break his leg, that kind of stuff. I went with him once, it was fun as hell. We faked our food supply getting carried off by a bear."

"Giving kids PTSD, that's what it is," Digger mumbled.

"Yeah, it's great," Owen said with a grin.

"Why the hell's he doing it in winter?" Zane asked, aghast.

"He has some Ranger buddies who were planning a controlled avalanche. He took the kids to a safe distance, and he's going to see how they handle the fake emergency."

"That's . . ." Zane shook his head, gaping.

"Awesome, right?" Owen said, his brown eyes sparkling. "So Doc's still doing these treks while Irish is finishing his shit in Boston. But where he went, there was no service."

"So he probably don't know Lucky's missing, just think he's undercover or something. So . . . when Doc gets here, we might have to tell him," Digger realized. "Not it."

"Not it," Owen added a split second later.

"Motherfucker," Ty grunted. He glanced at Zane, and Zane put both hands up to ward him off.

"No way in hell."

Ty rolled his eyes, but his stomach was turning over and over. How long had Nick been off the grid? Twelve days? And more importantly, why had he gone dark and not called any of them for help? What the hell was going on?

Owen and Digger stayed for a few more minutes to make a game plan for the next week, but then they geared up to go out for dinner.

"We'll pick Doc up when his plane lands. Y'all stay in, fuck like bunnies," Digger told Ty as he gave him a farewell fist bump.

"You sure you don't want to stay and eat here?" Zane asked as he walked them to the door. "I'll cook."

"Nah, man, I've been craving those damn crab cakes since the last time we were here," Owen said with an easy grin. He offered Zane his hand. "Congratulations, Garrett. Welcome to the family."

Zane seemed surprised when he took Owen's hand. "Thank you."

Owen's smile was still in place when his eyes hardened and his grip on Zane's hand visibly tightened. "You hurt our friend, we hurt you."

Digger clucked his tongue from behind Owen's shoulder. "Oohrah, bitch."

Zane laughed, albeit uncomfortably. He probably knew the threat wasn't an empty one. "Understood."

Owen threw Ty a wink, and then he and Digger stepped out into a cold drizzle, bundling up as they argued about who got to drive to the restaurant.

Zane turned on his heel and glared at Ty.

"Hey, I don't control who or how they threaten."

"Sure you don't." Zane threw himself on the couch, stretching his long body out with a sigh. He'd gotten up early for work, and though the evening had been a relaxing one with just Digger and Owen there, he was probably ready for bed.

But Ty sidled up to the couch instead and climbed on top of him, grinning. "Hey there, beautiful," he said with a kiss to the tip of Zane's nose.

Zane's hands landed on his hips, a smile pulling at his lips. "Hey, yourself. Are you starting something down here?"

"Maybe."

"Not on your fantastic new mattress?"

Ty grinned and raised an eyebrow. "Variety is the spice of life, right?" He kissed Zane gently, teasing at his lips and tongue, settling his body over Zane's. There was nothing heated or hurried about it—just the two of them, enjoying an evening alone as a married couple. The thought made Ty smile into the kiss.

A knock on the door drew his attention, but only briefly. Zane grabbed at his chin, shaking his head and smirking. "Let it go," he whispered.

Ty delved back into another kiss. But then the knock came again, weaker and slower, as if their visitor was using the palm of a hand rather than knuckles. Ty raised his head again and squinted at the front door.

"Ty," Zane groaned. "It's probably Johns and Digger wanting me to cook for them after all. Or some drunk at the wrong door again."

"That fucking bar down the street, dude, I'm ready to file a complaint with the city." Ty settled between Zane's legs, pressing him further into the couch cushions. Their lips had barely brushed before the knock came again. This time, though, it was merely a scratch and a thump at the door as if something had fallen against it.

Ty straightened with a frown, and Zane sat up to crane his head toward the door. They both stared, bodies tensing. They'd each spent too much time in the business to ignore a sound like that.

Zane patted Ty's thigh. "Go check," he whispered.

Ty rolled off him, and as he edged toward the front door, Zane retrieved a hidden handgun from beneath the couch where Ty had duct-taped it at some point. Ty waited until Zane had pressed himself against the wall, at the ready, before he cracked the door open and peeked out.

The man on the stoop had slumped against the doorframe, head lowered, shoulders hunched against the biting cold. He looked every bit like he had given up on the door being answered and intended to just sleep there tonight. He had a hood over his head, and his bulky shoulders were covered by a thin, green anorak.

"Hey buddy," Ty said carefully. "You okay out here?"

The man looked up at the sound of Ty's voice, and Ty gasped as he found himself staring into the faded-green eyes of Nick O'Flaherty.

"Six." Nick pushed away from the door with one hand, leaving behind a smear of blood as he stumbled toward Ty.

Ty caught him as Nick collapsed, but his knees buckled under the unexpected weight. "Zane!" he cried. "Help me!"

Zane moved to support Nick's weight, and together they dragged him inside. Zane kicked the door closed behind them, and they laid

Nick out on the hardwood floor. Zane lurched sideways and threw the dead bolt on the door.

Nick gasped and curled as he tried to protect his bloodied side. His anorak was soaked. It wasn't raining that hard, so he'd been in the elements for a while.

"I got you," Ty said as he leaned over him and patted Nick's cheek. "Irish? Look at me. Look at me!"

Nick focused on him, and he seemed to calm a little when Ty's tone became more of an order than a request. He was still breathing hard, but he closed his eyes and held still as Zane patted him down, looking for the source of the blood.

"What happened?" Ty asked, his hands still cupping Nick's face.

"Bell." Nick's voice was thin. He closed his eyes and took a shallow, shaky breath. "He turned on me. Knifed me."

"Liam Bell?" Zane shouted. "What the fuck?"

Ty couldn't tell what was blood and what was rain, but there was a lot of discoloration on Nick's shirt right now. He turned his attention back to Nick, forcing himself to keep calm. "What do you mean, he turned on you? What were you doing with him?"

Pain creased Nick's brow and seeped into his eyes. "I'm sorry. I'm sorry."

"Okay," Ty whispered.

Nick almost came off the floor when Zane found the wound in his side. Ty had to hold him down as Zane inspected it.

"He might be lucky," Zane finally whispered. "Looks like a knife went through his surgical incision. The scar tissue is thick there, acted as armor. It doesn't look like it was deep enough to nick anything."

"You sure?"

Zane nodded curtly and pressed his hand over the wound to stem the bleeding. "He's losing lots of blood, but he's okay."

"Thank Christ," Ty said under his breath, grabbing a couch cushion to elevate Nick's feet and a throw to cover him with, tucking the blanket as best he could around Zane's hand.

"Why was he with Liam Bell?"

"Zane, later," Ty warned.

Nick grabbed Ty's wrist, squeezing it hard, shaking his head.

"No, Ty, why the hell was he with Liam Bell?" Zane asked again. "What were they doing?"

"That can wait, Garrett, just call an ambulance!"

"No, no cops," Nick gasped. "No cops. I killed him." He closed his eyes and repeated the words, whispering them over and over as if they gave him comfort.

Zane ran a bloody hand through his hair and stood, pacing away a few steps. "Good riddance," he grunted. "Let's get him patched up, then we'll stuff him somewhere safe."

Ty stared at his husband with a hint of awe. Zane had come a long way from the agent Ty had met in Richard Burns's office, the one who'd done everything by the book.

Ty tore his eyes away from Zane and went to the kitchen to retrieve the old, tin first aid kit he kept under the sink. He also grabbed a few bowls, rags, and bottles of water. They had to plug that wound before Nick lost more blood.

He thumped to his knees next to Nick with his armload of supplies.

"No," Nick grunted when he saw Ty's first aid kit. "Hell no."

"What?" Ty asked.

"Don't let him near me with a knife or a needle," Nick told Zane, his voice breaking on the last word.

Ty popped open the first aid kit.

"Or that Rawleigh's stuff!" Nick shouted, voice reaching an almost panicked pitch as he grabbed for Zane's arm. "Oh my God, not the Rawleigh's stuff! Garrett!"

"Okay!" Zane said, patting Nick's hand. "Nothing but water and gauze until Abbott gets here, I promise."

"Kelly's coming here?" Nick asked, but he didn't sound relieved, not like Ty would have expected, anyway. Zane nodded, and Nick closed his eyes, still gripping Zane's forearm.

"What is wrong with my salve?" Ty asked, clutching the tin to his chest. "This stuff works miracles."

Zane snorted.

"Fuck you, Grady." Nick grunted. His grip on Zane's arm visibly tightened and he peered up pleadingly at Zane. "Last time he put that on me it peeled my skin off!"

Ty stroked the tin. "That was a bad batch."

"*You're* a bad batch!"

"Ty." Zane pointed his finger. "Put the salve away."

Ty did as he was asked, but grumbled the entire time. Then he tucked the throw blanket around Nick's legs and waist, cut Nick's shirt from the wound, and arranged the rags under Nick's body. He cleaned the area around the wound as Nick held on to Zane's hand and tried not to cry out.

It was a tidy stab, if Ty could call it that. Whatever weapon Liam had used when he'd attacked Nick hadn't been serrated, and he hadn't been able to twist it. Nick must have taken care of him before he could, and the blade had merely slipped in and then right back out with all the precision of a scalpel. It wasn't deep. It probably hurt a great deal, but the biggest danger to Nick was loss of blood.

"I'm surprised you pulled the knife out," Ty said as he dabbed at the wound.

"I didn't," Nick said tightly. His eyes were closed, and he seemed to have lost what little fight he'd had in him over the salve, but he was regaining some color in his face just from being warm and immobile. By morning, he might be rested enough to tell them what the fuck had happened without losing the narrative to exhaustion and confusion.

Zane used two Steri-Strips to close the incision, because Ty wasn't willing to call it anything else, and then pressed a square of gauze to it, letting the seeping blood hold it in place as Ty made a larger bandage to cover it.

When they finished, Nick was staring at the ceiling, gasping, his fingers clutching at the rug. As Ty watched him, he closed his eyes as if relief was washing through him. Ty fought the urge to hug him.

"Is there anyone after you?" Ty whispered.

Nick grunted and opened his eyes again.

"If there is, we need to get you upstairs, out of sight. Can you manage it?"

Nick nodded, wincing. Ty and Zane worked together to get him off the ground again, Nick cursing them both the entire way to his feet.

"One of you puts me in a fireman's carry, I'm kicking your ass," Nick threatened as he slung an arm over each of their shoulders. Just doing that seemed to hurt him, though, because he cried out and tried to pull away the arm he had over Ty's shoulders.

"You couldn't kick a puppy right now," Zane told him, and once they got to the bottom of the narrow stairwell, Ty was forced to let Zane take over. He followed up the steps, watching as Zane took on Nick's weight and Nick grew weaker with each step.

How long had he been out there, injured and trying to get to help? He'd been AWOL for nearing two weeks as far as they had determined. Had he been with Liam Bell all that time? Had he been a prisoner? Who the *hell* could keep Nick a prisoner by himself for almost two weeks? Even Liam wasn't that good. And how had he wound up in Baltimore? Ty was beyond confused, but he wasn't willing to ask Nick questions when he was in this shape. They just needed to get some fluids into him and keep him warm and safe until Kelly could get here.

Ty took up Nick's other arm when they reached the first landing. The guest bed was another flight up, and Nick sure as hell wasn't going to be making it up there. They carried him to their bedroom instead, helping him out of what remained of his bloody shirt before laying him on their bed. Ty rounded the end and sat next to Nick, taking his hand. Nick grasped his fingers like a lifeline, like he'd done so many times in the past, and Ty fought the tightness in his throat as he patted Nick's hand.

He could feel Zane's eyes on him, and then Zane placed a hand on his shoulder, squeezing. "I'm going to go call the others, okay? See if I can catch them. They should be here for this, don't you think?"

"Yeah, good." Ty glanced up at Zane. His eyes were soft with concern, and his brow was furrowed. He seemed to understand what this meant for Ty, to have Nick here and safe, to know where he'd been and to be able to physically comfort him. Ty gave him a weak smile. "Thanks, Zane."

Zane nodded, then left the room with his phone in hand, closing the door behind him.

Ty stared after him for long seconds, until Nick rolled his head to the side and drew Ty's attention back. He was looking at the closed door as well, green eyes still full of sorrow, sunburned face creased with worry lines.

"You two got married," he said.

The word brought a smile to Ty's lips, but it faded fast. He nodded. "You got my messages?"

"No." Nick jerked his chin toward Ty's finger. "I saw the rings. I like them. Like the ink."

"Thanks," Ty said, but he barely got the word out.

"I'm sorry I wasn't there." Nick eyes locked with Ty's, and they were glistening, but not quite tearing up. "I should have been there. I would have been there, Tyler."

"Hey." Ty tapped Nick's cheek with two fingers. He left bloody fingerprints behind and wiped them off with a corner of the sheets. "I understand there may have been some extenuating circumstances going on here, so . . ."

Nick grabbed Ty's hand with surprising speed, his eyes going hard. "The cartel's coming, Ty," he hissed.

"We know. Irish, just wait 'til you're better, okay? It can wait."

"No," Nick insisted, squeezing Ty's hand tighter. "They're coming after the two of you."

"Is that what you were doing with Liam?" Ty asked, despite telling himself not to interrogate his friend. "A cartel thing? How'd you end up with him? And how'd you manage to kill him wounded? I mean, I know you're good and all, but—"

"I didn't. Didn't kill him."

"But you said you did."

"No." Nick's eyes went distant for a moment. "He got burned by the NIA, came to me for help. *Forced* me to help. He needed evidence . . . couldn't get it alone."

"Why'd he come to you?"

"Leverage. And you have to know why I did it, okay?"

"Doesn't matter, Irish, it's okay." Ty's heart sped up at the mere thought of Nick being forced into working with a man like Liam. What the hell had Liam held over him? It couldn't have been just brute force; Nick wouldn't have taken that for two weeks.

"No, I need you to know before . . . why I did it." Nick's eyes fell closed, and his body was beginning to relax. It seemed he was coming to the end of his energy, but was refusing to give in to it until he got out whatever he was trying to say.

Ty put a hand on his shoulder and squeezed. "Why you did what?"

Nick opened his eyes and stared at Ty, brow furrowing. "Why I killed him."

"But you just said you didn't kill him."

"I'm sorry."

"I don't understand, Irish. You need to sleep."

"No."

"Okay. Then you need to slow your mind and try to make some sense for me."

Nick closed his eyes again and took a shallow, shaky breath. "You have to know why they're coming for you. For Zane. You have to know."

"Are you saying *you* know? You can tell me?"

"Burns," Nick said, his voice lowering even more. Ty couldn't tell if his mind was wandering or if he was just confused by the conversation now. Ty was sure as hell confused, anyway. There was no telling how much blood Nick had lost, and that made your mind do odd things. Nick continued, though, undaunted by Ty's quiet attempts to calm him. "They're coming because of Burns. Burns did this."

"Irish, we had this fight."

"No," Nick barked, and he winced as he moved to sit up. Ty pressed him back to the bed, holding him by one shoulder. That was all the force it took to keep him down. "Burns was using you. You and Garrett. He started this war. He's not who you thought he was."

Ty shook his head and lurched off the bed, pacing away before his hands could start to shake. "The cartel killed him, Nick. How can you possibly believe he was working with them?"

"He wasn't." Nick swallowed hard, closing his eyes like he was gearing up the last of his energy. "He was stealing from them."

"What?"

"Using Garrett to do it."

"That doesn't make any sense. Did Liam tell you this bullshit?"

"Using you to clean up his messes," Nick continued mercilessly.

"No."

"And Ty . . . you and Garrett were his last mess. He was coming for you next. For you both."

Ty whirled, trying to reconcile what his oldest and most trusted friend was telling him about a man he'd known since birth. "You're saying Dick Burns was going to kill me and Zane?"

"Yes."

"Bullshit."

"Other agencies were onto him, he was preparing for a clean break. You were the last pieces on the board who could take him out legally; he needed you both to take the fall."

"Bullshit!"

"Ty."

"No!"

Nick swallowed hard.

"He was like family to me!" Ty shouted, jabbing a finger at Nick. "He wouldn't do what you're accusing him of. Whatever evidence you've got has been ... doctored, or ..."

"No."

"Yes! Burns wasn't dirty! This is someone trying to cover shit up, that's all it is. Maybe the cartel is trying to loosen up the choke hold in Miami, maybe this is all the NIA and they need a fall guy." Ty ran both hands through his hair. "You know what? It might even just be Liam Bell playing with you! I don't care what it is; all I know is they killed Dick and it won't end until I put my fucking knife through de la Vega's eye."

"Ty," Nick whispered, and he looked sort of sick when Ty met his eyes. "The cartel didn't put the hit on Burns."

"What?"

"It wasn't de la Vega. It was the NIA."

Ty pulled up short, his chest twisting at the mere thought. "The NIA ordered Burns killed? How do you know that?"

"Because I was the one they pulled to do it."

"You ..." Ty narrowed his eyes. "What?"

"When you sent me home, to Suitland with that message. The NIA intercepted me. That was the whole reason they ordered you to tap someone for that delivery."

"What the hell ... that ... doesn't ..." Ty covered his eyes with his hands. "No, that doesn't make any sense."

"I killed him, Ty."

Ty lowered his hands to stare at the man in his bed. Nick was watching him warily, visibly struggling for breaths. Ty stared for so long he eventually registered the ticking of the clock on the bedside table as time creaked by. "What?" he finally asked, low and dangerous.

"I killed him. I broke his neck." Nick raised his right hand and turned it over. It was trembling so violently that Ty could see it from where he stood. "Did it right-handed, so no one would recognize it as my work."

Ty's mind and pulse were both racing, and there was an odd buzzing in his ear he couldn't quite place. "What are you telling me?" he asked carefully. "You killed Richard Burns?"

Nick still held Ty's gaze, but he was shifting his shoulders like he might be preparing to defend himself. "It was either him or you."

The continued calm of Nick's exhausted voice was beginning to make Ty's blood boil. He rounded the end of the bed, his fists clenching.

Nick deflated as if it took too much energy to be on guard and talk at the same time. "They showed me everything they had on him. He was dirty, Six, and you were next on his hit list. I accepted the orders to save you. You and Zane."

"You killed Burns?" Ty shouted. He lunged toward the bed just as the door burst open and Zane grabbed him around the waist. Ty fought as Zane lifted him off his feet and started dragging him toward the hallway. "He killed him, Zane!" Ty shouted as he struggled. "He killed Burns!"

Zane shoved him out of the room and slammed the door behind them. The last thing Ty saw was Nick turning his head away as Ty railed.

Nick woke slowly, like he was dragging his consciousness behind him through the shifting sands of a desert. He'd lost a lot more blood than he'd imagined he would on the trek to Ty's row house. He almost hadn't made it there.

A cold dread settled into his chest when he realized he was lying awake with his eyes still closed. He forced them open, shocked by how bright everything was. Weak moonlight streamed through the curtains. His limbs were heavy, almost numb. He didn't even try to move them. He did roll his head to the side, though, to check the door.

A man was hunched over the side of the bed, sitting in a chair with his head pillowed on his arms on the mattress. Nick squeezed one eye closed to try to focus on him.

"Ozone," he said, his voice hoarse.

Owen jerked up, blinking away the sleep and focusing on Nick, hand on the gun at his belt. "Hey," he said, relaxing and sounding a little surprised to be awake. Owen had always woken like that, though, moving before his brain registered awareness. "You feel okay? You lost a lot of blood, man."

Nick nodded. "I've had worse."

"Yeah," Owen whispered, almost as if he hadn't intended to say it. "Ty says you murdered Richard Burns."

Nick blinked at the ceiling for a few seconds before nodding curtly. "Murdered" was a strong word, coming from Ty.

Nick lifted his hand to wipe it across his face, but the motion came to an abrupt halt with a clang and a jerk. He stared at the handcuff around his wrist for a long time.

"I tried to talk to him down," Owen said, voice pitched low. He leaned closer and took Nick's hand, checking that the cuff wasn't too tight. His fingers were like ice against Nick's palm. He met Nick's eyes and held on to his hand, squeezing. "He's not listening to anyone, though, not even Garrett."

"Ty did this?" Nick gasped with another jerk at the handcuff.

Owen nodded sorrowfully. "He hasn't called it in yet. But he's going to. Soon. As soon as he decides whose jurisdiction it falls under."

Something fluttered in Nick's chest and then settled, heavy like an anchor, dragging at his heart. He'd known Ty would react badly, of course he had. But he'd expected more than a few minutes to plead his case before Ty shut him down. He sure as hell hadn't expected to be handcuffed to the fucking bed. Now he didn't feel so bad for bleeding all over their fancy memory foam mattress.

"How long was I out?" Nick asked after a few moments of trying to regain his composure. His words still came out shaky.

"Good part of the night."

"Is Doc here?"

"Not yet, but he's on his way. His flight was delayed."

"He can't see this, Johns. He can't."

"You want me to keep Doc out of here when he knows you're hurt?" Owen smiled ruefully. "I'm your brother, dude, and I love you. But I'm not suicidal."

Nick snorted, wincing as something in his side pulled. He craned his head, trying to get a look at the wound. "Did someone stitch me up?"

Owen pressed his lips together and frowned. "Digger."

"*What?*"

Owen raised a hand to fend off Nick's panic. "You were bleeding a lot, man. We had to close it up."

"And you let *Digger* do it? Oh my God, what did he use? It's not fishing line again, is it?"

"I don't know, it was in his go bag. And it was . . . green."

"Oh Jesus, it's probably alligator sinew or something, Johns! Get it out!"

Owen was very nearly laughing as he shook his head.

Nick was about to demand again for him to remove the stitching when the door shoved open and banged against the wall. Owen jumped at the intrusion.

"I told you to come get me when he woke up," Ty snarled.

Owen stood and turned to face him, squaring his shoulders. Nick could only see a part of his face, but he saw Owen's jaw jump. "Good thing I don't take orders from you anymore. He's not a fucking prisoner."

"Get out."

Owen hesitated, glancing over his shoulder at Nick. Nick nodded, and Owen waited a few more seconds, probably just to be ornery, before he brushed past Ty and out of the room.

Ty stood glowering in the doorway, his broad shoulders tensed, his head lowered. He took one step and kicked the door closed.

"Six," Nick whispered.

"Don't. Don't fucking call me that, not right now."

Nick gave that a few seconds to sink in, to burn its way through him. Then he set it aside and pulled at the handcuffs to force Ty to hear the noise they made. Ty should know exactly what memories that sound dredged up. "What should I call you, then?"

Ty's nostrils flared and he kicked the chair out of the way to pace beside the bed. "You fucking hypocrite," he said through gritted teeth. "You remember what you said to me about following orders? Do you remember?"

"I know."

"You broke my fucking heart!" Ty grabbed up a picture frame from the bedside table, whirling and chucking it across the room. Nick jerked at the handcuffs, trying to pull himself toward the headboard so he'd be a smaller target. Ty was just pacing, though, his hands bunched into fists.

"I know I did," Nick admitted, tears choking the words. "I had to tell you something I knew would hurt. I had to make sure you couldn't look me in the eye."

Ty whirled on him. Nick swallowed hard and pressed on before the look in Ty's eyes could wither his resolve. "I couldn't let you, you'd have seen right through me. You'd have known I killed him, and I needed more evidence for you before I told you."

Ty's hazel eyes had gone flat, like Nick's words had snuffed out something inside him, like Nick was a stranger who didn't deserve to see that light. Nick knew he deserved it. He'd known this was going to come down on his head the moment the NIA had tagged him for the hit. He'd known as soon as he'd taken his chance in Scotland, amid so much death. He'd known, even as he'd said the words, that Ty might never forgive him. But it had been a choice between killing an evil man or losing his best friend, and he'd chosen hope. Hope that his best friend could one day forgive him.

"Do you have more evidence for me?" Ty asked.

"No. It's not a two-man job, and all I've had was Liam."

Ty bared his teeth at the mention of the name.

"But I know how to get it."

Ty snorted angrily. "You're telling me you killed a man, a man I trusted, a man I *loved*, on the word of some NIA suit who pulled you off a military mission? Did it never occur to you to get the proof *before* you snapped his fucking neck?"

Nick fought down his anger. He knew how to handle Ty, and brute force wasn't ever successful. "I had all the proof I needed."

Ty eyed Nick up and down, and Nick could see his gears turning: he could tell Ty was trying to come to terms with so much betrayal, and quite obviously failing. Nick knew how he felt.

He pulled at the handcuffs again. "Are these really necessary? I came to you, Ty."

Ty's jaw jumped and he turned hard eyes on Nick. "That was your first mistake, I guess."

Zane stood on the front stoop of the row house, absently wiping the blood off the door, his phone hot in his hand because he'd been on it for so long.

He'd spent a full hour trying to talk Ty into *not* handcuffing Nick to their bed, but Ty had been beyond logic. Zane had rarely seen him like that, and he'd decided to let it go and live to fight another day. When Ty calmed he'd begin to see reason, what little there was of it right now. If the NIA had ordered the hit Nick had performed, who exactly did Ty plan on calling to report it to? He was just wounded and lashing out any way he could. Zane didn't blame him.

Owen and Digger had shown up not long after he'd called them, and Zane had forced himself to stay out of the fight that had ensued. It was fascinating, watching the way Sidewinder roiled with the controversy. Owen and Digger both seemed to be trying not to take sides and keep things calm, something Zane hadn't expected out of either man, and the argument twisted and turned like the very namesake of their team.

Ty was a force to be reckoned with, though, fueled by betrayal and pain and righteous anger. Neither man could make any headway with him, and so Nick had remained upstairs, unconscious and handcuffed to the brand-new bed Ty had bought Zane as a wedding present.

Ty'd been sitting on the back stoop, smoking a Cuban cigar and staring at stars ever since. Digger had informed Zane that peroxide would get blood out of everything, but hadn't felt the need to help Zane do it. Owen hadn't left Nick's side. And as soon as Zane had been certain Owen and Digger would keep the peace for a little while, he'd stepped outside and gotten on the phone.

The core of the problem here, and the only new information they'd been given, was Nick's claim about Richard Burns. At first Zane had reacted just like Ty, with utter disbelief and derision. But the more he thought about it, about the work Burns'd had him doing in Miami, about the secretive nature of the transmissions Zane had sent to him, about the way Burns had put Ty on him to watch him after he'd distanced himself from that case, the more suspicious Zane got.

He wasn't sure what to do about it, though, or who to go to for information. Who could he trust with that? He couldn't even put one of his own agents on it because he still had no idea who the fucking mole was in the Baltimore office.

As he'd pondered the problem, he'd fielded about ten calls from Kelly, who was flying in from Colorado to celebrate Ty and Zane's marriage with the others. Kelly had been diverted to DC and delayed, though, and as soon as he'd landed, he'd checked his messages and then called Zane in an absolute panic over Nick's condition. He'd immediately rented a car and was driving in instead of waiting for his connecting flight.

He'd called every ten minutes since, and so Zane was standing on the stoop with his overheated phone to his ear, speaking to Kelly even as he watched the headlights of the man's rental speed up the narrow street to their front door.

The wheels screeched on the damp road, and the engine had barely shut off before Kelly hopped out and jogged toward the house.

"What the hell?" Kelly shouted, even though Zane had filled him in at least ten times on the phone.

Zane turned his phone off and slid it into his back pocket. He put a hand out. "He's okay."

"What happened, what'd he say? Where the hell has he been? How long was he missing? Where is he?"

Zane couldn't help but smile. Kelly wasn't going to believe any of the answers Zane had already given him until he saw with his own two eyes, and Zane had made sure to keep the most interesting parts to himself so Kelly didn't go into a fit of rage and wreck the car on the way there. "We didn't really get a lot out of him, other than that he'd been with Liam Bell and something about Richard Burns and the cartel."

"Liam Bell? Why the fuck didn't you say that to start with?" Kelly shouted as he barged past Zane and into the house. Zane almost felt sorry for whomever he encountered first. "Where is he?"

Digger stood from the couch where he'd been drowsing, and pointed up the stairs, where Owen sat leaning against the banister and Ty was making his way down, probably coming to investigate the ruckus.

"Hold on, Doc," Ty said, blocking the way to the stairs and putting a hand on each of Kelly's shoulders.

"Zane said he was wounded, is he okay?"

"He's okay. Digger stitched it up and it's doing fine. No damage inside."

"I'm sorry, when did you get your medical degree?" Kelly demanded. "Why the fuck didn't you call an ambulance?"

"Doc—"

Kelly smacked Ty's hands away and shoved at him. "Dumbass. Move!"

Ty planted his feet. "Couple things you need to know first, okay? Calm down."

Zane glanced at the other two men, and Owen met his eyes from where he was sitting on the stairs and shook his head, looking grim.

"Listen," Ty said to Kelly, voice growing more heated as he spoke. "We don't know exactly what Nick was up to, or why. Okay? But one thing we know for sure is that he killed Richard Burns in Scotland."

"He what?" Kelly blurted.

"He confessed to it."

"No, he's got to be hallucinating from loss of blood or something."

"He's not, Doc," Owen said softly. "He's lucid. He killed him."

"I was with him almost the entire time in Scotland, no way he had the chance."

"We all know how Nick can operate, Doc," Digger offered.

Kelly paled. "Fuck that. Let me see him."

Ty made a "wait" motion, gritting his teeth. "Just be prepared, okay? He's handcuffed to the bed so he can't escape."

The room went silent, and even Zane found himself holding his breath as he waited for Kelly to react to that.

It wasn't an outburst when it came, but Kelly's dangerous murmur was almost more worrying. "You handcuffed him?"

"Doc, don't," Ty huffed. He sidestepped to prevent Kelly from getting past him.

Kelly wound up on the same level as Ty, and even though he was inches shorter, Ty backed away from him when he spoke. "You handcuffed him to the bed?"

"He admitted to murder."

Kelly gave that a derisive laugh, putting a hand on Ty's chest. "I hope whoever cuffed him has clean hands."

"What?" Ty asked.

"You got blood on your hands, Six? 'Cause I sure as hell do. Hard to cuff someone for doing wrong when your fucking palms are that slippery."

"Watch it," Ty growled.

"Fuck you!" Kelly shouted. He shoved Ty out of the way. "You think you're the only one who screams in his sleep? The only one who begs not to be tied down? Fuck you, Grady! You fucking fuck, get out of the way!"

Ty stumbled to the side, looking stricken as Kelly stormed past him and up the steps. Then Ty propelled himself after him. Zane had to force himself to move to make sure more blood wouldn't get spilled.

He was at the top of the stairs when Kelly shoved the bedroom door open, Ty right on his heels. They both skidded to a halt, though, and Zane hustled to see what the hell was going on.

The bed was empty. The bloody sheets were rumpled, and the pillows were askew. The handcuffs had been tossed into the middle of the sheets, gleaming accusingly in the low light.

"Fuck," Ty whispered.

Kelly stared at the scene for a few seconds, appearing calm as he took it all in. Zane slid past them both, since they seemed to be rooted to the spot, and moved carefully into the room.

"O'Flaherty?" he called, fighting the very real urge to reach for his gun. He'd seen what Nick could do when he felt threatened, when his reality began to slip. He didn't want to be on the receiving end of that.

Once he cleared the room he began to relax, but only slightly. Nick was gone. Gone and angry and feeling abandoned, betrayed, and cornered. He was not the kind of enemy they needed right now.

Zane looked all around the room again, noting the only thing Nick had left behind: a handwritten message on a piece of paper pinned to the wall beside the bed with a knife. Zane tried to pull the knife out, but it had been stuck with too much force. He gave up on it and yanked the paper instead, tearing it.

"What's it say?" Ty asked, his voice barely strong enough for Zane to hear.

Zane shook his head and glanced at his husband. He didn't want to read the note out loud, not when Ty looked like a puppy who'd just been kicked by his master, not when Zane could see that sickening realization sinking into Ty's eyes. The realization that his best friend had just escaped a trap he himself had put him in.

"Zane, what's it say?" Ty asked again.

"It just says . . . it just says twenty-three days, nine hours, and fifty-one minutes."

Ty took an involuntary step back, his hand going to his mouth as he lowered his head.

Kelly nodded, staring off toward the window. "With friends like you, who the fuck needs Liam Bell?" he said to Ty before leaving them alone with the note and the knife Ty had given Nick for his thirtieth birthday.

Nick was weaker than he would have liked while being on the run from his friends, but he didn't seem to have much choice in the matter. If Owen hadn't slipped him a key, he'd still be stuck in that fucking bed. Ty knew where Nick hid all his keys. Asshole.

It had begun to snow, and it was going to make getting to safety harder. Also, covering his trail would be impossible unless it got heavier. He'd stolen a sweatshirt from the bedroom closet, and he was pretty sure it was Zane's because it was actually too big. He hunched into it, still not warm enough to be out in this cold after losing so much blood.

He couldn't quite identify the feeling in his chest and stomach. Was it loss? Heartbreak? Anger? Guilt? Yeah, he remembered this feeling from Catholic school, and it was a hefty dose of guilt and anger. He trudged past the dark alley near Ty's row house, just barely smelling the smoke in time to realize that he was no longer alone.

Liam stepped away from the brick wall, flicking his cigarette. Nick stopped in the middle of the sidewalk, his hand on his newly stitched wound.

"Where's your knife?" Liam asked as his eyes traveled up and down Nick.

"Left it behind to make a point."

Liam nodded. "Did it?"

Nick just lowered his head. He'd been so sure Ty would help him.

Liam took a step toward him and slid his arm under Nick's, letting Nick lean on him. Nick wrapped his arm over Liam's shoulder and gripped the material of his coat, relieved when Liam took the weight. They began a slow shuffle toward the harbor, neither saying a word for nearly a block.

"So?" Liam finally asked.

"You were right. Ty's no good to us."

"Story of my life, love." Liam snorted, his breath puffing out in a crystallized cloud.

"Did you really have to stick me this deep?"

"It had to look real."

"Yeah, it's pretty fucking real."

"Walk it off, O'Flaherty." Liam paused to hitch Nick higher on his shoulder. "You stuck to the script?"

"Like Velcro. Told him you knifed me. I fucking begged him for help."

"That bastard. I told you not to admit you'd killed Burns."

"Oh my God," Nick grunted.

"What good could come from him knowing that shit, hmm?"

"None. But I had to tell him. I had to just . . ."

Liam huffed. "You convinced me this was the better plan."

"I know."

"Made me throw my frozen finger overboard."

"I know," Nick muttered. "What's Plan B?"

Liam's hand tightened on Nick's arm. "We don't have a Plan B."

"I don't get it," Kelly said for perhaps the fourth time in the last hour. "How the fuck could you do that, Ty? He's your best friend!"

Ty shook his head. "That didn't stop him from killing Richard Burns, did it?"

Kelly snarled, and Ty just shrugged like it didn't bother him.

Zane knew it did, though. He was working hard to keep his opinions to himself and trying to keep the remaining men of Sidewinder on track. And as far as he was concerned, on track was verifying what Nick had said.

He just didn't know exactly how to do that yet.

"I'm going after him," Kelly announced, and then he stood, grabbing for his coat.

"How?" Digger asked. "We don't know how long he was gone. And it's snowing like crazy, you can't track him in this."

Kelly raised his head, nostrils flaring. "Ty can."

Ty nodded for a few seconds, obviously deep in thought. Then he lurched to his feet. "He's right, we need to find him. He was hurt, he might be . . . it's too cold out there if he had nowhere to go."

"He *did* have somewhere to go," Kelly snapped. "You just drove him away!"

"Doc, give me a break!" Ty shouted. "If he'd told you he killed someone you loved, how would you have handled it? He fucking broke my heart!"

No one moved, and no one met Ty's eyes.

"Let's go find him first, and then we'll deal with the fallout," Zane finally said.

Owen snorted. "Only way I'm going out there to find him is if Ty promises he keeps his handcuffs to himself. Otherwise, I'm letting Irish have his way with Baltimore."

Digger nodded in agreement. "Man can wander out of the desert after three weeks, he can handle snow in the city with a little love tap in his side."

Ty sighed and put his hands together as if praying at an altar. "I promise. Okay? I promise. Let's go find him. Zane? Stay here in case he backtracks, please?"

"You got it. Be careful; he might strike first and ask questions later."

Ty merely nodded, looking sick as he followed Kelly to the front door.

Zane stood in the kitchen until the four of them left, then pulled his phone out and stared at his contacts list. He wanted to do some digging into Richard Burns. He just needed to pick the agent he trusted most. Or rather, the agent he suspected least. He pulled up Fred Perrimore's number and called him.

"What up, boss man?" Perrimore answered, the smile evident in his tone. "Working on your honeymoon?"

"Yeah. I have a favor to ask of you, Freddy."

"A favor? Not an order?"

"No, not this time. You up for it?"

Perrimore hummed, then sighed heavily. "Do you have bail money?"

Zane grinned. "If it goes well, you won't need it. I have faith in you."

"Great. Fill me in."

Zane tried to keep to the bare minimum, using the excuse of an ongoing undercover operation for not giving Perrimore all the details. Perrimore was a veteran, though; he understood that sometimes leadership meant compartmentalizing things. And sometimes granting favors to your boss meant not having the whole picture.

"So, when I find these account numbers, you just want a record of the transactions? I'll need a warrant for it."

"No, no warrants. This isn't to make a case, it's just for information. Do it fast, do it quiet, don't leave a paper trail. And only look at the time frame I gave you, okay?"

"You got it." Perrimore sounded like he was already on his computer, searching down the cartel's accounts.

Zane still had those numbers memorized all these years later. He hadn't even had to look them up.

"What's my turnaround on this?" Perrimore asked.

"ASAP. Life and death, here."

"Yeah. Hey, Garrett, you okay? You need more than account numbers from me?"

Zane held his breath, watching the door. "Not yet," he finally said. "But sleep with your gun, got it?"

"I really hate working for you sometimes," Perrimore claimed, but the grin in his voice told Zane another story.

He was smiling when he ended the call. For the first time, he'd tipped their hand to one of the agents at the office. And it felt good. It felt like he was finally on the offensive. If Perrimore was the mole—although Zane had just bet his life that he wasn't—things were going to start happening pretty fast now.

He checked that his gun was loaded, then slid it into his belt, just to feel better about his chances.

Ty knelt at the head of an alleyway near the row house. He'd found several cigarettes by the building, shielded from the heavy snow. Someone had waited here. Had someone waited for Nick? Unfortunately, there was no telling which way they had gone from here, not without guessing, and the snow had completely obscured anything else Ty might have been able to follow.

Kelly was standing on top of a fire hydrant, peering into the night. Owen and Digger were pacing back and forth like bloodhounds, but they didn't seem to be coming up with anything.

Ty examined the filter in his hand, turning it over with a frown.

His stomach dropped into his toes and he lurched to his feet. "This is Liam's brand."

"I thought Nick said he killed him," Kelly said. He hopped down and hunched his shoulders against the cold.

"He did, but then he said he didn't, then he said he killed Burns. I think he was just confused." Ty winced, head throbbing with stress and exhaustion. "Could be he thought he killed Liam and didn't hang around to make sure. Could be he was lying."

"Why would he lie about killing Liam when he copped to everything else?" Digger asked.

Ty shrugged helplessly. He was trying to think like Nick in this, but finding he just couldn't. He didn't understand any of it.

"Stockholm syndrome?" Owen asked tentatively.

"Bell always was good at psy ops," Kelly agreed. "If this was an attempt to make Nick think his friends had turned on him and Liam was all he had left to depend on, it was a damn good one."

"Lucky said he needed help getting evidence," Digger added. "Maybe he came here to feel you out. See how likely you were to work with him and Liam."

"Sounds like Nick," Owen agreed. "The bleeding was a little overly dramatic."

"The bleeding should have sold it," Kelly grunted.

Ty glared at him, but Kelly shrugged.

"How many times have you showed up on his door, bloody?" Kelly demanded. "How many times has he said yes without asking why? He still has holes in his boat!"

"But it still floats," Ty muttered defensively.

Kelly cursed under his breath.

"I've lost him." Ty ran his frozen fingers through his hair. Even without the snow to cover Nick's trail, he would be nearly impossible to track in the city. Guessing his destination and wandering around calling his name like a lost dog would be just as effective as tracking him at this point. They'd have better luck with educated guesses and phoning around to hospitals and marinas from the warmth of the row house.

"We should head back, start looking into the types of places he's gone to ground in before. Check all the marinas in case he has the *Fiddler* in town."

Owen and Digger fell in behind him as he trudged back toward the row house, but Kelly remained where he'd been, staring off down the street. Ty stopped and waited, but Kelly shook his head. "I'm not coming back 'til I find him."

"Doc," Owen started, but Kelly held his hand up and turned away.

"I'm not coming back," he said again, then started off in the opposite direction.

Ty glanced at the other two, waiting for them to make their choice. He wouldn't have been surprised, or even blamed them for it, if they followed Kelly into the dawn. But neither man budged. They finally gave Ty identical shrugs, and the three of them carried on toward the row house in silence.

Ty found himself facing down the barrel of Zane's gun when he opened the door. He stopped in his tracks, waiting while Zane stuffed the gun into his holster.

"Something happen?" Ty asked.

Digger shoved him inside when he didn't move. "Cold!"

Zane shook his head. "I put a call in to Freddy. You said Nick claimed Burns was stealing money from the cartel, so I figured I'd fact-check him. Freddy's looking up the accounts I sent to Burns when I was UC in Miami to see if money went missing from any of them."

"You trust him with that?" Ty asked.

Zane shrugged and patted his gun, a wry smile curving his lips. "Mostly."

Ty glanced around the room, at a loss now. Zane had been hard at work getting blood off the floor, the rug, and the few places Nick had put his bloody hand as he'd climbed the stairs.

"What now?" Owen asked.

"Where's Kelly?" Zane asked before anyone could answer the million-dollar question.

"He wouldn't come back," Digger answered.

Zane nodded, frowning. "Somehow I'm not surprised."

Ty glared at him.

"What?" Zane asked.

"I got enough pointed comments from him tonight, don't start with me too, Garrett."

"It wasn't pointed, Ty. I'm just saying . . . if that was you out there, I'd sure as shit still be searching."

Ty scowled, trying not to get upset and failing miserably.

"Kelly loves him, baby," Zane said. "Same way I love you. It's going to change the way the whole group operates. You get that, right? It's not just O'Flaherty you're standing to lose here."

Ty blew out a shaky breath, glancing back at Owen and Digger as Zane put a steadying hand on his shoulder.

"It'll be okay," Zane whispered into his ear, and Ty closed his eyes.

"Hey, if we're going to be plotting and shit, can we order pizza or something?" Digger asked.

"It's four in the morning," Zane said.

Digger checked his watch, nodding. "Pizza counts as breakfast, right?"

Zane looked thoroughly scandalized.

Ty fought the urge to wrap his arms around Zane's neck and demand a hug to make himself feel better. Then he pursed his lips and shrugged. "Might as well. I know I won't be sleeping any."

"Oh, yeah. The mattress?" Zane winced. "Yeah, it's not coming clean."

"Motherfucker," Ty huffed as he headed for the kitchen to grab the phone. "Now we got to hike *another* of those fucking things up those steps!"

"Karma," Owen shot at him.

Ty grumbled but didn't respond. They'd find Nick, they'd get the whole story, and he'd either apologize or he'd hit him. Maybe apologize and then hit him. Or hit him and then apologize. He was pissed, and Nick had crossed far over the line, but still . . . handcuffing him to the bed had not been the smartest move. Ty was going to have to pull a Zane and start thinking with his head and not his heart on this one. Or maybe just let Zane do all the thinking period for a while, until he got his mind around it all.

He didn't have to ask the others what they wanted on their pizza, so he just ordered as they talked in the living room.

"What do you think, Garrett? You think Burns could have been dirty?" Owen asked.

Ty averted his gaze, watching Zane in his peripheral vision and pretending not to have heard the question. Zane glanced in his direction, shifting uncomfortably. He leaned toward Owen, lowering his voice, but Ty still heard him.

"I think . . . yeah, he could have been. A lot of the things I was doing in Miami, they never drew blood and they should have. I never did figure out what Burns did with the information I culled down there. And I know for damn sure he had Ty doing things that no oversight committee would have approved of. Add it all together and . . . Jesus, I don't know. Nick's story makes sense."

Ty finished ordering, hung up the phone, and headed for the living room. They all shifted nervously. He threw himself on the couch and held his head in both hands. "What have I done?"

"He'll forgive you, man," Digger said after a few uncomfortable moments of silence. Ty didn't lift his head. "He always does."

"I think the question you're really struggling with, baby," Zane said as he laid his hand on Ty's back, "is: will you forgive him?"

Ty covered his face with his hands. "I need to see that proof he was talking about. I have to see it."

"So there's what we do," Digger said with a clap of his hands. "First we find Lucky. Then we get that evidence for you. Man, I love to have a plan!" He got up and strolled toward the kitchen, singing under his breath.

They all watched him, entirely baffled.

"Digger," Owen called after him.

"The man with a plan!" Digger sang, pointing at Ty before sticking his head into the fridge to find something to drink.

CHAPTER 4

"So you're telling me these people, these fucking people you spent half your life risking your arse for, the first hint you gave them that you weren't the fucking Boy Scout they thought you were, they turned on you?" Liam asked, his accent thickening into something Nick couldn't quite identify as the whiskey and the indignation settled in.

He'd started out intending to clean Nick's wound with the alcohol, but they'd swiftly turned to just drinking it.

Nick stared at him, trying to decipher the feelings Liam's words gave him. He knew on a basic level what Liam was doing, what he had been doing for almost two weeks now: psychological warfare. The best way to make an enemy your ally was to convince them their friends had abandoned them, turned on them, or just didn't care about them. Liam's methods were so subtle, Nick had caught himself falling victim to doubts even as he reminded himself of what Liam was trying to do.

And somewhere along the way, Nick had realized that, despite Liam's nefarious techniques, there was a lot of truth to his endgame. It had resulted in an odd sort of antagonistic camaraderie between them. Nick believed the man when he said he was after the cartel and the NIA was after him. Nick genuinely wanted to help him. Yet he still wouldn't hesitate to toss him overboard if given the chance.

"You're telling me you literally laid down your life for each and every one of those pompous fuckers, including Garrett! And they what? Handcuffed you to a bed when you admitted you aren't a fucking saint? Why? Were they afraid of you? Thought you'd go all homicidal maniac and kill them? Did they think they were actually going to call the police or some horseshit and arrest you for following through on a government-sanctioned hit?"

"I don't know. I guess. I don't know." Nick took a long drink from the bottle, then handed it off to Liam.

Liam waved it, and its contents sloshed. "Did they realize what would happen to you if the NIA discovered you'd been burned over that hit? The same fucking thing happening to me, mate, that's what! You'd have been taken to Gitmo and disposed of. Or found in some ravine or lake in a car with cut brake lines. Or hell . . . worse, you'd have been given a new identity and been their bitch until you got too slow to cut someone's throat."

Nick swallowed hard, trying not to let the stark fear filter through him. A lifetime of hits for the NIA? His soul was tarnished enough; that would be a fate worse than death for his conscience.

"Right." Liam nodded as his blue eyes stared into a distance Nick couldn't see. "This game, O'Flaherty, it's for people like me. You . . . it's not for you."

"Is that why you want back in?"

Liam handed off the bottle, then rested his hand on Nick's shoulder and leaned closer. "The world needs people like me. It doesn't have to like it. It doesn't even have to know it. But it needs me to do the things I do. And it helps if I enjoy them, hmm?"

"That's very altruistic of you," Nick grumbled, taking a plug from the bottle.

"Nicholas, you're not hearing my words."

"I'm barely *understanding* your words. You go all weird Russian when you drink."

Liam snorted, and Nick fought back a smile. "See," Liam whispered, and he pointed at Nick, pressing his finger against the tip of Nick's nose. "The world needs people like you and your mates, too. The good ones. If everyone was like me? What the hell would there be worth fighting for?"

Nick frowned, moving his nose out of the line of fire. Liam took the bottle from Nick, sighing as he looked it over.

"What the hell happened to you?" Nick asked him.

"Life," Liam spat out.

Nick cocked his head as Liam stared out the *Fiddler*'s windows.

Liam clutched the bottle to his heart. "I'm done. No more for me." He slid off the stool, tucking the bottle under his arm. "Good night, O'Flaherty. Let's never speak of this again."

Nick watched him head for the stairs, his path unsteady at best. "Hey," he called.

Liam turned and leaned against the railing, taking another sip from the bottle despite his claims that he was done.

"Have you been alone all this time?" Nick asked. "Since you left? The NIA, all that. You always work alone?"

Liam lowered his head, turning the bottle over. "My partner, she and I were together for a year or so."

"The one the cartel framed you for killing?"

"The very same. She was called Anna. She was quite lovely."

Nick searched for the right words, torn between wanting to dig for information and feeling sorry for the man. "I'm sorry for your loss," he finally said.

Liam cleared his throat. "I'm sorry for dragging you into this by force. I'm sorry . . . my life is such that the only person I could think to go to for help wasn't a friend, but rather an enemy." He laughed ruefully.

"I was a friend once. That counts, I guess."

Liam met his eyes, nodding absently. He was still nodding when he turned around and thumped down the stairs, calling out as he disappeared below deck. "Brace the mainsail, matey!"

Nick sighed and stared off at the harbor. He and Liam had swiftly run out of options and time. The cartel would be on Ty and Zane soon enough, the NIA would be on Liam and Nick, and then nothing would save any of them. Their only hope was to track down the money Burns had stolen and use it as leverage, offer it as a trade for Zane's freedom. That was what Nick had convinced Liam to do, anyway, instead of the original plan he'd been pushing.

He still had no idea how to clear Liam's name, but Nick wasn't losing sleep over that. If Nick had to let Liam crash and burn, he would.

He checked all their safeguards one last time before limping down to his cabin and crawling into bed. Kelly was in town. God, he was so close but Nick couldn't reach out to him, he couldn't risk any of his actions putting Kelly in more danger than he already was. And Ty . . . Nick's entire being ached at the very thought of the way Ty must hate him now that he'd come clean.

His oldest friend. His dearest friend.

Nick curled on his side, burying his head in the covers as the *Fiddler's Green* bobbed peacefully in the falling snow.

He woke later gasping for air around the hand that covered his mouth. His left wrist was pinned to the mattress in an iron grip, and there was a weight on his hips like someone had straddled him. There was also something dripping on him. It was too dark in the cabin to see much, but Nick struck out with his right hand, grabbing his assailant by the throat. If this was Liam in some fucked-up attempt at cuddling, they were both dying today.

"Nick, it's me. It's Doc."

As soon as that familiar voice broke the silence, Nick's fingers loosened their hold and his eyes widened. Kelly removed his hand from Nick's mouth, placing it on Nick's shoulder instead.

"Kelly?" Nick gasped. He could barely see Kelly's grinning, bearded face. "How did you find us?"

Kelly bent and kissed him, disregarding Nick's hand still at his throat. Nick pawed at him, desperate to feel the man and make sure he was real. It was apparent that Kelly had been in the water. He was shivering, and they were both breathless when Kelly finally broke the kiss.

"I knew you'd head for water, searched every marina until I saw the *Fiddler*."

"Jesus," Nick whispered, awe and sadness mixing in his tone. He sat up and wrapped Kelly in his arms, pressing his face against Kelly's chest despite how wet he was, squeezing until the man grunted. "God, it's good to feel you."

"You too," Kelly whispered, and he kissed Nick's temple.

"You're going to freeze, you need to dry off."

Kelly batted Nick's hands away as they tugged at his wet clothing. "Fuck that, we're getting right back in the water. I snuck past Bell to get down here. I kind of expected you to be tied up or something." He knelt back and patted Nick down like he was checking him for hidden restraints. "I watched him for a good hour from the dock; he's got no fucking pattern with his patrol. He's just weaving around up top like he's drunk. If we're going to get by him, we have to go now. Are there any more, or is it just Bell?"

"Kelly," Nick said, hesitating as nerves fluttered through him.

Kelly was crawling off of him, but he stopped and turned back to Nick, eyebrows raised. "You can run, right? Can you swim? They told me you'd been stabbed."

"Yeah, but . . . Kels, I can't leave."

"What?"

Nick opened his mouth to explain, but he couldn't force the words out.

Realization seeped through Kelly's expression as he studied Nick's face. He slumped back to the bed. "Oh my God." Kelly was breathless, as if the revelation had knocked the air from his lungs. "You're not a prisoner, are you? He didn't snatch you off the street after you left Ty's place. Did he?"

Nick shook his head. He couldn't pull in any air either, and the chill that ran through him made him light-headed. His heart pounded at his chest and his fingers pulsed with each beat as the silence stretched between them.

"You went with Liam Bell . . . by choice?" Kelly asked, his voice cracking.

"Kelly, no. He showed up after my surgery. He told me he'd be coming for my help, and if I refused . . . you'd be the one paying for it."

Kelly's shoulders slumped, and the water dripping off his nose into his scruffy beard made him look like some dejected cartoon character. "You're doing this because of me? You . . . you . . . you're with Liam Bell because of *me?*"

"No."

"Yeah, you are! You're working with Bell because of me. Why the fuck didn't you tell me? I could have helped you, I could have gotten you out of this!"

"I couldn't risk that he wasn't bluffing, and I couldn't lose you. We both know he strikes from a distance." Nick took a deep breath, nausea churning his gut. The look of utter betrayal in Kelly's eyes was almost too much for him. "Once I started actually listening to him . . . he's not on the wrong side of this."

But Kelly wasn't listening to Nick. "This explains why you babbled about wanting to kill him for two weeks when you were delirious." Then the frown deepened and he turned his changeable eyes on Nick.

"Wait . . . you *remember* being in the hospital? You remember after you woke up?"

Nick took a deep, shaky breath. "Yeah."

"You remember." Kelly gasped and looked away, swallowing hard. "You remember asking me to marry you?"

Nick reached for him, but before he could make contact he drew his hand back, lowering his head. He closed his eyes and clenched his trembling fingers into a fist.

"Why wouldn't you say anything? Why would you let me think . . ."

Kelly's words were like sandpaper against Nick's conscience. He stayed silent, unable to raise his head.

"You didn't say anything because you knew he was coming for you," Kelly realized. "You figured why marry me if you're just going to disappear and die on me."

"I'm sorry," Nick said without looking up.

"You son of a bitch!"

Kelly launched at him, flattened him to the mattress and backhanded him with a grunt. Nick bit back a cry of pain as Kelly's knee hit his stitches.

"What the fuck were you thinking?" Kelly demanded, barely managing to keep his voice down. "We're a *team*. We're partners, and I'm not some fucking possession of yours that can be threatened. That's *never* the way we've worked, and I refuse to start now just because you're fucking me."

"I—"

"Asshole!"

"I'm sorry."

"Fuck you, Nick. Fucking coward. You're going up against our own boys with a man who's tried to kill them, all because you thought I needed protecting. Do you get that? Do you understand that *you're* the bad guy now? You're a traitor."

Nick caught his breath. "Kelly."

"Hell, if what Ty says is right, you're a fucking murderer! All to protect other people who don't fucking need your protection in the first place!"

Nick nodded jerkily, the cold flowing through him again when he saw the disappointment and betrayal in Kelly's eyes. It was so much worse than waking up in handcuffs and finding out Ty had done it. Nick hadn't thought he could feel lower than that, could feel colder than he had then, but Kelly was proving him wrong.

He swallowed hard. "You're worth it," he managed to say.

Kelly waited a few heartbeats as Nick's words dissolved beneath the rhythmic thumping of the harbor's tides on the *Fiddler's* hull. Then he lunged and kissed Nick, biting at his lip, clacking their teeth together, scratching Nick's cheeks with his beard, as Nick groaned in surprise.

"Well," Liam said from the open doorway, and he flicked on the light to reveal a liquor bottle in one hand and a sniper rifle in the other.

Kelly rolled off Nick and came up flat on the mattress with a gun aimed at Liam. Nick tackled him before he could pull the trigger, and they both went tumbling off the bed.

Liam smirked and set his rifle against the doorframe, taking a drink from his nearly empty bottle. "Dinner and a show."

"Fuck you," Kelly snarled as he struggled to get his gun out from under Nick.

Nick rolled away from him and struggled to his feet, scurrying toward Liam to block Kelly's line of fire. He put both hands up, but then he had to hold one to his aching side. "Hear us out."

Kelly's lip curled mutinously, his eyes blazing.

"Please, Kels. Please."

"What are you doing, babe?" Kelly asked, his voice breaking. But he lowered the gun to his lap.

"I know how this looks, but we're not the bad guys. Not this time." Nick edged closer to Kelly and knelt. He placed his hand over the gun, squeezing Kelly's frozen fingers as he took the weapon from him. "Do you trust me?"

Kelly stared into Nick's eyes for several long, heartrending seconds. Then he looked over Nick's shoulder at Liam. His jaw jumped and his body tensed. "You know I do."

Liam cleared his throat. "Another man wouldn't hurt. If we can trust him."

Fire flared in Kelly's narrowed eyes, and Nick turned to sneer at Liam. "Could you . . . I don't know, keep your fucking mouth shut for one second?"

Liam shrugged.

Nick slid his fingers down Kelly's arm. "You can leave now, babe. Go back to Ty and the others and tell them everything. Tell them . . . tell them I'm working with Bell. Tell them where we are. We'll be gone before you can get back because we haven't finished what we started out to do. Or you can stay."

Kelly jerked his head, meeting Nick's eyes. His expression was unreadable, but his jaw was clenched.

"You can stay and help us save the others."

Kelly gave Liam one more slide of his eyes before returning his attention to Nick. "You know I'd follow you anywhere. Even if it's straight to Hell."

Nick brushed his fingertips over Kelly's cheek.

"I'll leave you to it, then," Liam drawled. "I'll be on watch."

"A lot of good that did you," Kelly snarled. "Are you drunk?"

"You think I didn't see your stupid frozen arse climbing out of the drink?" Liam chuckled. "Please."

He closed the cabin door as he left them, but neither Nick nor Kelly moved. Nick was pretty sure neither of them was even breathing.

"We should get you dry," Nick whispered, and he reached to pluck at Kelly's wet shirt.

Kelly shoved his hand away. "Don't fucking take care of me, man."

Nick bit his lip against an angry retort. Kelly had to get it out of his system, and Nick knew he deserved whatever Kelly dished out. "I'm sorry."

Kelly huffed. "I'm here with you, babe. I'll stand with you no matter how fucking stupid you are. And if we fall . . . we'll do it together."

Nick watched him longingly, fighting back the regret and shame and mourning that came with the domino effect of his decisions over the past year. If he'd stayed true to his own code of honor, they wouldn't be here right now. He'd never have taken the hit from the NIA, he'd never have wrapped his arms around Richard Burns's neck and snapped the life out of him, he'd never have said words to his best friend he knew would wreck him. He'd never have avoided Ty for the last year out of guilt and despair. He'd have married Kelly the moment he was able. He wouldn't be here now, begging for forgiveness from every person in his life he cared about.

"Ty's coming for you," Kelly said as he peeled out of his clothes. He still sounded torn, like he was trying to decide which side of the fence his loyalties would fall on. He gave a resigned sigh. "For *us*. He's not on the warpath anymore, but . . . we're going to need something to show him when he finds us. You said you had evidence that Burns was coming for him and Zane?"

"We may have enough to convince him. But Liam knows how to get more."

"Liam."

"I know," Nick said. "It's not easy trusting him, but . . ."

Kelly narrowed his eyes. "I don't trust him. I trust you. Only you. Regardless, we need that evidence when Ty finds us, or . . ." He shook his head and kicked his jeans to the side.

Nick had expected nothing less, but the news still hit him like a load of bricks being dropped on his heart. For a second time, he'd need proof to show Ty before the man would believe him. If he'd had it the first time they'd dealt with Burns, how different would their lives be now? Would Elias Sanchez still be with them?

He nodded and tried to catch his breath as he grabbed a robe out of his closet and handed it over to Kelly. He perched on the edge of the bed and dug his fingers into his knees as Kelly wrapped himself up. Ty hadn't taken Nick's word on the way he'd felt about Richard Burns ten years ago, and he wouldn't take him on his word now. Nick wasn't sure what part of him had expected that he would when he'd knocked on Ty's front door.

"Nick." Kelly knelt in front of him, putting a hand on top of Nick's. "You live on a boat and you're docked in the nearest harbor to Ty's house. He *will* find us soon."

Nick struggled not to fidget. The fact that Kelly was willing to stay with him after what he'd done was sinking in, and he met Kelly's eyes with a hint of awe. "You can really forgive this? Forgive what I did and stay with me?"

Kelly's nostrils flared and his eyes flickered away. "I'm not saying I'm proud of it. The whole time I was tracking you down, I kept telling myself you'd never kill Burns without . . . And if I got to you and found out I was wrong, I'd . . . But there was something in the back of my mind . . . I knew that wasn't true, that I'd stay with you no matter what. Even if you killed him just to see something burn, I'd stay with you. I'd . . ." He shook his head, cursing in disgust, then laughed ruefully. "Broke his neck righty so I wouldn't recognize it. That's some serial killer level shit, Nicko."

Nick's stomach churned. He took hold of Kelly's chin, turning his head so he could meet his gaze. Kelly was still angry, his eyes sparking. Nick didn't know if he was angry with himself or with Nick or maybe both, but the cold hard fact of the matter was that Kelly was ready to give up every good thing he'd ever done, ready to sell his soul just as surely as Nick had. All for Nick. He couldn't catch his breath, couldn't move. "I love you," he said desperately.

Kelly's jaw tightened. "You came to Ty's to feel him out, didn't you? See if he'd be willing to help you?"

"Yes."

"You let Liam stab you. On purpose."

"Yes," Nick whispered.

Kelly stood with a muttered curse, went to his pile of clothing to rummage through them, and came up with his dive knife clutched in one hand. "I'm going to initiate myself into the team, then."

"Kelly!" Nick called as Kelly stomped out of the cabin.

"It's okay, it's team building," Kelly answered, his voice fading as he jogged up the steps. A moment later Nick heard a squawk of alarm and a thump as Kelly and Liam introduced themselves.

Nick ran a hand over his face. "God help us."

Somewhere in the room, something began to vibrate. Nick straightened and looked around with a frown. His own phone had been tossed into the sea two weeks ago; not only had Liam not trusted him to somehow get a call off for help, but he'd also claimed the government could track them with the GPS. Nick had promptly made him a tinfoil hat with a little swan on top and then sulked on the flybridge for an hour.

Now, though, Nick was pretty sure Liam had been on the up-and-up. The cartel was after him. The NIA was after him. God knew how many other alphabet agencies were on his trail. Nick had no doubt they were tracking Liam down. He still missed having his phone, though.

The vibrating continued, and Nick picked up Kelly's jacket and patted the pockets. Inside he found Kelly's phone in an OtterBox. Nick turned it over to see the display. It was Owen.

He held his breath for a second, fighting with himself over whether to answer and what the consequences of doing so might be. Owen had slipped him that key in Ty's bedroom. Was he willing to pull Owen or Digger into this?

Before he could think the better of it, he slid his finger over the screen and brought it to his ear.

"Doc?" Owen said excitedly.

"No," Nick said.

Owen's breath caught, and then he cleared his throat. "So . . . you're okay then? We were getting worried when you didn't come back."

"We're on the *Fiddler*. Bell is here with us, but we're safe, you hear me? Safe."

"Yeah, good," Owen said, injecting a little upbeat tone into his voice. "I'll let the others know. You coming back to Grady's, or . . . we're at the Pier 5 hotel, near the aquarium. I left a key for you at the front desk when we checked in."

"Okay. We'll meet you at your hotel in one hour. Make damn sure Ty and Zane don't come with you, got it?"

"Okay, good. As long as you're safe. We'll see you when we get back. We'll find him, Doc, I promise."

Nick waited a heartbeat, then smiled sadly. "Thanks for the assist, Ozone."

"Hey, love you too, bud." He cleared his throat, and when he spoke again, his voice was further away. "No, he just hung up. He's fine, he gave up and he's going back to the hotel to shower and sleep. I told him we were pretty much done here, so we'd be there soon."

Nick was silent, waiting. It felt like hours before Owen whispered into the phone again. "Ty kills me for this, I'm haunting you for the rest of your life," he told Nick. And then the call was over and Nick was left to listen to the shouting drifting down the stairs.

Ty stood beside their bed, holding their bloodstained mattress pad in his hands. It turned out the pad had saved the mattress, but Ty didn't seem to care anymore. Zane watched him worriedly.

"Next time I'm about to do something stupid, try harder to stop me, okay?" Ty said, voice tired and thin.

"Me and what army?" Zane asked as he hung his shirt on the hook by the door to let it dry.

Ty snorted at him, still scowling at the bloody material between his thumb and forefinger.

"Ty, I . . ."

Ty shook his head. He let the mattress pad drop to the ground and crawled into bed, burying his face under Zane's pillow. He inhaled noisily, probably breathing in Zane's scent.

Zane smiled, trying not to be too amused. A miserable Ty was sometimes a ridiculous thing of beauty. A moment later Zane crawled in next to him, his hand on Ty's back.

"You did what your training told you was right," he said, stuffing his head under the pillow with Ty so he could be near him.

Ty shoved the pillow aside. "I reacted by the fucking book, Zane. My best friend was here begging for my help. What . . ."

"Ty," Zane said when Ty trailed off. "You have to forgive yourself before Nick ever will. And you're going to have to figure out if you want to forgive him. We'll find him. We'll figure out how to deal with this."

Ty laid his head back down, gazing desperately into Zane's eyes. "You know what scares me most?"

"Chipmunks?" Zane asked with a gentle smile.

Ty snorted despite looking like he didn't want to. He sighed. "I can't decide whether I want him to be right, or whether I want him to be wrong."

"I understand."

"Do you? 'Cause I don't. If he's right, then . . . a man who treated me like a son all my life was actually trying to *kill* me. I mean, imagine we adopted a son, okay? And imagine when he got older, after I'd taught him everything I knew, I *used* him for my own gain and then tried to kill him."

Zane was silent, struggling with the scenario and the anger that accompanied it. He ran his thumb over the bulldog tattoo on Ty's arm, the scar that marred it. "You were the tip of a spear," he said almost wistfully.

"But if Nick's wrong?" Ty continued. "He killed the man who gave us both a second chance in life."

"I know," Zane said, and gripped Ty's arm.

"Nick killed him. How do we deal with that?"

"You don't, not yet." Zane had begun to make slow circles with his palm against Ty's shoulder. "We're going to look into this as deep as we can. We're going to get to the truth and deal with it. Until then, Nick is a man who loves you, who's been loyal to you for twenty years, and who did what he thought was right in order to save you *and* me. That's how you deal with this right now."

Ty's eyes were welling as he stared past Zane's shoulder, at Nick's knife still stuck in the wall beside their bed. The note was sitting on the dresser.

"He told me I'd put a bullet in his head if someone ordered me to."

Zane's hand came to Ty's cheek, forcing him to meet his eyes instead of looking at that knife. "He was wrong."

"I need to get him back, Zane," Ty croaked.

"I know. And I'm here to help you do it, baby. Even if it's to handcuff him to the bed again." Zane gathered Ty up in his arms, rolling him until he was tucked safely against Zane's chest. Ty deflated, apparently allowing himself the luxury of wallowing for the night.

It was long minutes before Zane huffed against Ty's hair, a smile pulling at his lips. "Can I start calling you hubby?"

"Do it and die."

"Snookums, then."

Ty made a gurgling sound that might have been an attempt at not laughing. The warmth of it filtered through Zane's mind and body, and he began to settle as the house around them creaked and quieted.

But Ty couldn't truly rest. He was agitated in Zane's arms, keeping them both awake. Zane just held to him, trying to be a solid, steady presence. His mind replayed every moment of the day as Ty tossed and turned, details niggling.

Just an hour after they'd settled, he sat up and rested his hand on Ty's belly, shaking him awake. "Honest answer."

"Okay?"

"If I was in Nick's position, hurt, on the run, in the snow. Would you decide it was too late or too cold to keep looking for me?"

"Is that really a question you even have to ask me?"

Zane raised both eyebrows at his husband in the morning light. "So, do you buy that Doc called it quits and met Johns and Digger back at the hotel?"

Ty sat up beside him, sighing heavily. "No," he finally decided. They stared at each other, Ty's expression growing harder before he whispered, "They lied to us. Doc found him. Johns knew it."

Zane tossed the comforter aside and swung his legs off the bed. "Let's go, then."

Twenty minutes later, Zane flashed his badge at the receptionist as they entered the lobby. "I need the room number for Owen Johns."

The woman stuttered at him, obviously not aware of the legalities of such a request and shocked by their sudden appearance.

Zane slammed his hand down on the desk to take advantage of her confusion. "Now!"

She nodded and turned to her computer, typing shakily as she glanced at Ty and Zane. Ty bent over the counter to see the computer screen.

"Key," Ty said, waving his fingers at her in a "give me" gesture.

It took her three attempts to code the card for them, and Ty snatched it out of her hand as soon as she was done. They turned away from her before she could gather her wits or call for a manager.

Zane could feel Ty vibrating beside him in the elevator. He kept looking at him sideways to see if he was okay. But he also realized that this felt so fucking good, the two of them out somewhere, flashing badges, heading to confront someone with a gun.

"I miss this," he admitted.

Ty glanced at him, an eyebrow raised. He cracked a smile. "Me too."

"I want this back," Zane added before he could think the better of it.

Ty blinked rapidly, turning to face him. "Me too."

The door dinged and slid open, leaving them staring at each other in the open elevator. Zane's eyes drifted toward the gun at Ty's hip. "Should we call in backup?"

"They're my friends, Zane," Ty grunted, breaking the spell and stepping into the hallway.

"That why you have the gun?"

"I owe Liam Bell a bullet," Ty growled as he stalked down the hallway toward the door.

They set up outside the room, both of them putting an ear to the door to listen. Zane could hear voices within. It was impossible to make out words, though.

Ty held up the key. "On green."

Zane nodded and drew his gun, resting his other hand on the door handle.

Ty slid the key into the slot, and on green Zane shoved the door open. Ty burst into the room, gun drawn. Zane followed, seeking out targets in the room, counting how many people there were. Five men, all spread through the room. Impossible for Ty and Zane to cover them all.

Thank God they were Ty's friends, right?

Ty couldn't remember a situation where he'd been more nervous knocking down a door.

Owen and Digger were sitting on one of the beds, staring at Ty and Zane like they were insane. Kelly was cross-legged on the other bed, papers spread out in front of him, and Nick was in an armchair in the corner, a glass in his hand.

Liam Bell was lounging against the balcony door, arms crossed, head cocked. Not a man had reacted to the intrusion. No one moved.

"Everybody, hands on your heads," Zane ordered.

Ty's shoulders were tense, his body a bowstring waiting to be plucked as his aim settled on Liam. If Liam twitched, he was dead.

Nick finally moved enough to take another sip from his glass.

"Hands!" Zane shouted at him.

Nick stared at him for a few seconds, then dropped the glass to the floor, spilling its contents. He put his hands up, palms out.

"Come on in," Owen drawled. "No need to knock, complete open-door policy in this hotel."

"Shut up," Ty snarled. He jabbed his gun toward Liam. "What is he doing here?"

"Helping," Liam answered.

Ty reached behind him, and Zane placed a plastic zip tie into his palm. He took Ty's gun off him, holding it on Liam as Ty approached him.

"Turn around, hands on the glass," Ty ordered.

Liam did as he was told without comment or complaint. Ty secured his wrists with the zip tie, shoving his face against the glass for good measure before he yanked him around and forced him to sit on the end of Kelly's bed.

He hadn't yet made eye contact with Nick, who was observing silently. Ty almost wished he could just look at the man; he felt like it might ease some of the tension. But he couldn't make himself do it.

He pointed at Owen instead. "You lied to us."

"I didn't lie. I just . . . Yeah, I lied, whatever." Owen unscrewed the cap of his water bottle and took a long drink. "I'm too tired to be creative."

"Someone explain, now," Zane said, handing Ty his gun and then looking at each man in turn.

They all shared glances, and then Kelly sighed and rustled some of the papers in front of him. "We were trying to decide if we had enough evidence of what Burns was doing to show you."

Ty felt the blood draining from his face. He tore his eyes away from Liam to look at Nick, who met Ty's eyes unflinchingly. Nick seemed as desperate to say something as Ty, but neither was able to articulate it. The silence stretched on.

Zane cleared his throat. "And?"

Kelly shook his head. "It's enough for me. Maybe not for Ty."

"Is there more?" Zane asked.

"Perhaps. But we have to hit two places at once," Liam explained. "His home and his office. Irish and I couldn't do it alone, or we'd already have it."

"You don't know which location it's in? Or it's in both?" Zane asked.

"The former. Possibly the latter. But once we hit one location, the other will be unreachable."

Zane sat on the edge of the dresser beside the flat-screen television, crossing his arms and scowling. "Why do *you* need evidence about Burns? It's sure as hell not to help Nick out."

"That's none of your bloody business," Liam huffed.

Ty backhanded him so hard he almost rolled off the corner of the bed. He sprawled, kicking his leg out to keep his balance. No one moved to protest or help him.

Ty grabbed him by the shirt and yanked him back up. "It's our business now," he snarled. "Why are you here?"

Liam sucked air between his teeth, the only response he seemed willing to offer.

Nick stood, still showing his hands to Zane. "Let him go," he said quietly. "Ty, let him go."

Ty's grip loosened, and he stepped back.

Nick reached for the thick accordion file sitting by Kelly's knee, and he handed it to Ty. He seemed to be moving with extreme care, trying to prove he wasn't a threat. "Please, Six," he said, his voice still calm.

But Ty knew him too well. He could hear the fear in Nick's voice. The desperation and hope. He could hear the pleading undertone of an eighteen-year-old boy who didn't understand why someone would be his friend unless they wanted something from him.

Ty lowered his head as the memory flashed through his mind, and he gasped for air when he realized tears were threatening.

"Give me five minutes," Nick begged. "After that . . . you can do what you need to. With me, with him. We won't fight you. I just . . . Please."

Ty stared at him, his heart racing, his mind replaying what seemed like every moment of their lives together.

A stone-faced boy sitting on a bench at the bus depot with a set of bruised ribs and a black eye, ignoring the taunts of those around him.

A gentle, tentative smile that somehow *always* reached his eyes.

A hand on Ty's shoulder while he told him his brother would want him to be strong right now and everything would be okay.

A hand grasping across the narrow expanse between their medical racks, covered in blood while he begged for Ty to keep his eyes open.

An iron grip around his forearm, pulling him out of the mud as he ordered him to keep going because they were making Recon together whether Ty liked it or not.

Hunched over in a room too small for them both, holding Ty's head and shoulders in his lap and rocking for him because he knew Ty didn't have the strength to rock himself that night.

Green eyes Ty had been able to find across any room, anywhere when he needed a back to put to his.

His best friend. His brother. A man he'd have lain across a grenade for, and who would have done the same for him. A man he loved with every ounce of his soul. And all that Nick was asking for was five minutes.

Ty's chest tightened and twisted, and he took an involuntary step toward Nick with every intention of hugging him.

Nick flinched when Ty moved too quickly. He licked his lips like he'd always done when he was nervous, and he tried to pretend he hadn't moved. But Ty had seen it.

Ty froze. How had it come to this? He stared at Nick for a second longer, his heart split into shards that made it hard to catch his breath.

The room was silent, waiting. This felt like a crossroads, and Ty was the only one who could decide which way to go.

"Ty?" Zane finally said, breaking Ty from his memories, reminding him to take a breath because he was getting light-headed.

"Okay," Ty whispered.

Nick edged toward the bed, moving like he was trying to step away from a wild animal without scaring it. He sat on the bed next to Kelly, pulled several things out of the accordion folder, and laid them out. "This is where Liam and I have been the last two weeks, what we managed to steal from the NIA. These are the pieces they showed me," he explained. The hunted look in his eyes was agonizing, and it was several seconds before Ty could move to take the contents of the file.

He gave Nick and then Liam both careful stares as he walked over to Zane and leaned on the dresser beside him. He opened the file so they could both read it.

"What are these?" Zane asked Nick.

Nick cleared his throat, then did it again after trying to speak and failing. "That piece is the paper trail of a hit Burns ordered."

Zane waved a hand at it. "Is this where the whole thing starts?"

"No. It's where Ty was brought in."

Ty scowled at him. "It's a hit he ordered me to carry out?"

"No," Nick answered, sorrow engulfing his voice. "It's a hit he ordered on a Special Agent James Hathaway."

Ty's mouth went dry. "What?"

"Hathaway," Zane murmured as he scanned the documents. He turned to Ty. "Was that . . . wasn't that your old partner?"

"Jimmy," Ty croaked. "His name was Jimmy."

A lot of the file was redacted, but Ty could make out the high points. Or rather, the low points. He realized his fingers were grazing over the old scar on his hip where he'd taken the bullet that had gone through him and lodged in Jimmy Hathaway.

"You almost died trying to save him," Nick said to Ty, as if Ty might not remember it.

"You came down and stayed with me while I recovered." Ty's voice shook. "Spent two weeks trying to convince me to quit."

"What else is there?" Zane asked, hard and professional. He had apparently realized Ty's resolve was nonexistent.

"No," Ty said, shaking his head. "No, Jimmy's death wasn't a hit. That was a suspect we were after for . . ." He trailed off, clutching the file.

"For drug-trafficking?" Nick finished. "For the Vega cartel?"

"Yeah," Ty breathed.

"On the next page, you'll see that man's accounts received a hefty bonus the day before Hathaway was killed in the line of duty," Liam told Ty. He sounded almost apologetic. "Your drug trafficker was paid off by Burns. He used stolen cartel money."

"Burns made it look like a cartel hit if anyone examined it too closely," Nick added. They had either practiced this, or they'd spent enough time together that they could finish each other's sentences now. Ty sort of hated both of them for it.

Liam was nodding, working to free his hands from the zip tie as if no one would notice.

"No one did, though," Nick continued. "Because you killed the guy before he could talk. Case closed."

"Why?" Ty asked.

"Burns had to free you up, bud," Nick answered. "He needed you to be solo. He promised you you'd never have to have another partner, remember?"

Ty swallowed hard, glancing at Zane and back to the file. "This still doesn't connect directly to Burns, though."

"You're right," Nick said. He picked up another file and waved it.

Ty was rooted to the spot, so Zane moved to take the file. He opened it even as dread settled in Ty's belly. If they really did have even shreds of evidence, Ty had no idea how he was going to handle the fallout.

"Those are wire transfers made in your name, Garrett," Liam offered. "With the information you were gleaning in Miami. Burns was skimming money from cartel accounts, pushing it through an account he'd set up in your name in the Cayman Islands, and then transferring it to his own offshore accounts. I traced them to Switzerland, but lost the endgame to a Swiss stone wall. We're working on it, but neither of us have the know-how to follow Burns's trail. We're missing information we need."

"What information?" Zane asked.

"Access codes," Liam answered.

"Zane's name is in the trail?" Ty asked, voice going harsh.

"It's the start of the trail. We think *that's* why the cartel is after him," Nick told them. "Not because of Antonio de la Vega's assassination. Or, not completely because of it."

"His name on those accounts makes him complicit, Ty," Owen said. "If we can't prove Burns acted alone, you'll go down for multiple counts of murder, and Zane will go down for the money."

"If the cartel don't kill him first," Digger added.

"So Burns made it look like I not only stole millions of their dollars, but also killed their boss?" Zane asked, almost shrill.

"Hundreds of millions," Liam corrected.

"*Cabrón hijo de la gran puta!*"

"Zane," Ty grunted as the rest of Sidewinder gaped at Zane, wide-eyed.

Zane eyes blazed. "You remember when I said I'd hold him down so you could hit him?" he asked Nick. Nick nodded warily. "Let's dig him up."

"That's . . ." Nick shook his head.

Ty patted Zane's shoulder to calm him, nodding for Nick to continue.

"When it got too hot, he went in and pulled Zane out," Nick said. He was still shaky, but he seemed to be gaining confidence in relating the facts of the case to them, as opposed to when he was trying to justify his own actions.

"Why not just let Zane rot down there? Take the heat for him?" Kelly asked. "Why pull him?"

"Covering his own ass," Nick answered. "Cartel gets a hold of Zane, finds out he's FBI, they know where the money went. Cartel gets a hold of Zane, turns him, he has the information to maybe come after the money himself. Burns couldn't risk either scenario; he had to keep Zane on the straight and narrow." He glanced to Zane almost apologetically and dropped his voice. "Probably why he put you in rehab. That, and he needed you sober and predictable."

Zane laughed bitterly. "I never could figure out why he cared so much. Why he'd bother getting me clean. This is the first explanation that's ever made sense. He sent me back to Miami to die. He had so little faith in me that when I didn't fuck up and get myself killed, he thought I had to be on the cartel's payroll."

Ty squeezed his husband's shoulder. He knew how much of Zane's initial self-worth Zane had tied into Burns's belief in him, how much he'd looked to that as a reason he belonged in the Bureau. But Zane didn't need that now. He'd proven himself a thousand times over. Ty would make sure he remembered.

"Why'd he bring me in?" Ty asked after several moments of heavy silence.

"My guess?" Nick said. "He had to clean house. He used your loyalty, to him and your dad. He knew you wouldn't ask questions, knew you'd . . . you'd want to prove yourself worthy. Knew what you were capable of."

Ty nearly staggered as pain washed through him. He'd so blindly followed what he'd thought was right. He'd hurt so many people doing it, including himself. "This is why he recruited us in the first place," he said to Nick. "You, me, Eli. He only wanted us so we could clean up his messes."

"Makes you wonder if Sidewinder got pulled from active duty so we'd be free to use in civilian operations," Owen said. "NIA, FBI, the Corps. How high does this go?"

"We don't know," Nick answered.

Liam cleared his throat, looking grim. "I'd say high enough."

"You ever wonder why Sidewinder got sent off right before our time was up?" Kelly asked. "Right after we all survived a brush with the NIA in New Orleans?"

"You think the NIA sent us back to war?" Ty growled.

Kelly nodded, his eyes as gray and hard as steel.

"Why?"

"So they'd have unhindered access to one of us. They pulled Nick for this hit and then sent us home," Owen answered. "We were sent back over there just so Burns could be taken out of the game."

"It's free labor," Digger said with a shrug. "NIA tugs a string, Corps calls us back. They tug another string, Nick is sent to their door. Tug that last string, Burns is dead. They only lift a tiny finger and don't put out a cent for the trouble. Not a bad setup, if you're an evil bastard."

"Okay. Okay," Zane said, eyes wide. "But how was Burns such a threat to the NIA that they'd orchestrate all this?"

"We don't know," Liam said grimly. "I know *I'm* scared, though. Because whatever they wanted from him, they didn't get it. You and Garrett, and all of us, are next in line for their particular brand of borrowing."

"What about Eli?" Kelly asked. "Did Burns kill him?"

Nick shook his head. "Not that we've found. Eli was . . . he was just in the wrong fucking place."

Zane cursed quietly and raised one of the other pieces of the file he'd been reading over.

Ty almost didn't want to know what Zane had found. There was dread in his voice when he asked, "What?"

"Deuce," Zane croaked. "These are wiretaps from Burns's office. He was having Deuce report to him about us. Whether we were working well together, if we could be partnered."

"No," Ty gasped, and he snatched the transcript from Zane's hand.

"There's no evidence in there whatsoever to tie your brother to anything," Nick said quickly. "Burns was using him, just like everyone else."

"My God." Ty scanned the transcripts of Burns's conversations, his voice losing strength like a balloon gasping out its last bit of air. "He was like a fucking father to us."

"Ty." Nick stood quickly enough that Zane's hand went to his gun. Nick froze. He turned to Ty, hands still raised. "I wish he was the person you thought he was. I wish I'd been wrong."

Tears pricked at Ty's eyes again. Burns may have been like a father to him, but only because he'd been there when Ty was growing up. Nick . . . Nick was his brother, and he'd earned that with his blood being spilled across the sand.

Nick took a tiny step toward Ty before he seemed to realize he might not be welcome to do it and halted. He was so flustered that he probably didn't even know he was fidgeting. "I know what he was to you. I know what . . . a father . . . I would have given anything if it could have saved you from what this feels like. I would have been the bad guy."

"Nick," Ty choked out. He shook his head, gasping for breath. "I can't do this right now."

Nick didn't say anything further. His eyes were still on Ty's, though. He never looked away. That was the first thing Ty had ever loved about him.

"There's more," Nick told him, and Ty rubbed his eyes dejectedly.

Zane pulled out the next file, holding it up. He frowned, confused. "I don't get it, who is this guy? It says he was an undercover federal agent."

"Burns's last hit," Kelly answered. "Couple months before the boys were sent off."

"Who is he? How does he connect to us?" Zane asked as Ty took the file and read over it.

Ty's heart sank when he saw the picture attached. "I killed him," he said, feeling the heat drain from his face. "This man was a Fed?"

"ATF. Working undercover in the cartel," Liam told him.

"Was this one of the men Burns sent you to Miami to take out?" Zane asked.

"Yes." Ty felt ill as he looked at the file. He'd executed this man without question, thinking his death was vital to keeping Zane safe. Burns had lied to him at every turn, made him into a cold-blooded killer.

Liam continued talking even as Ty grew more distraught. "His death was the one that got the NIA involved, got me into this mess. He's the reason I was in New Orleans. Both the cartel and the NIA sent me looking for the man who ordered his hit, which is when I figured out there was a third party involved here. When I saw you, Tyler, I knew it had to be Richard Burns. You'd do anything for the man."

Nick slowly reached to the small of his back and pulled out a combat knife. He stretched toward the end of the bed, taking Liam's hands in his and slicing through the zip tie Liam had been struggling with.

"Thanks, mate," Liam said, rubbing at the red marks on his wrist.

"Tell them what you told me," Nick said, low enough that Ty could barely hear it.

Liam glared at Nick for a moment, then turned mutinous eyes on Ty and Zane. "When you two headed to New Orleans, it wasn't this mole you think you have that alerted the cartel."

"Who was it?" Zane demanded.

"I don't know. But I was embedded in the cartel for a year. You weren't on their radar until New Orleans. Someone put you there on purpose, and since Nicholas has convinced me it wasn't him, I now suspect it was Burns."

"Burns is the one who told us my phone was being monitored," Zane argued.

"Easy misdirect when he realized you weren't dead in New Orleans like you were supposed to be," Nick guessed. "When Ty called him, said he was still alive, Burns knew he had to cover his ass."

"But he came," Ty reminded them. "He came to help us."

"Yeah," Nick said bitterly. "Landed right after the action went down."

"You're saying he was done with us, and so he sent the cartel to go after us," Zane said slowly.

Liam and Nick were both nodding. Liam took a deep breath before speaking one last time. "Tyler took out every undercover agent placed in the cartel except me. Once he did that, Burns didn't need him or you anymore."

Ty's mouth worked, but no sound came out. Zane rested his hand against Ty's back, squeezing him gently. But Zane had no way to combat the betrayal and pain seeping into Ty's soul.

Ty sought out answers in his eyes that just weren't there. "He told me we were protecting your egress from Miami."

After a few tense seconds, Nick broke the silence. "He lied."

CHAPTER 5

Zane sat at his desk, staring at the paperwork in front of him but not seeing it. His mind was elsewhere, off with Sidewinder and his husband, who were either still in the hotel trying to decide how to gain access to Richard Burns's home and office, or off gallivanting around Washington, DC.

Every time his phone rang, he thought it was Ty calling to tell him they'd killed Liam and tossed him into the ocean, or they'd been arrested breaking into Burns's home or office in DC. Every knock at his door, he hoped it was Perrimore coming to him with something he'd dug up on those accounts, and not word of his brand-new husband involved in a high-speed car chase on the news.

He was so close to faking an illness and leaving the field office in the very capable hands of his second-in-charge. The only thing keeping him there was the knowledge that differing from his routine would alert the mole to something going on, and that was just one problem they did not need to be dealing with right now. So here he sat, useless and distracted and thoroughly exhausted.

A knock at his door had him straightening in anticipation yet again. "Enter," he called, and he almost deflated in relief when Perrimore stuck his head in.

"Got a second?"

"Yeah." Zane waved him in.

Perrimore looked apologetic, though. Not a good sign. "I hit a dead end on those accounts."

"What kind?" Zane asked, trying to keep his expression neutral.

"The government kind. My clearance isn't high enough."

"Which branch flagged it?"

"Us." Perrimore flopped a thin file on Zane's desk. "The Bureau flagged every single one of those accounts. I couldn't touch them without alerting someone."

Zane opened the file to the single paper inside. Perrimore had handwritten it, apparently not trusting the wireless printer in the office. Zane glanced up at him with a hint of admiration and appreciation.

Perrimore shrugged. "I know off the books when I see it. I wrote down the ID number of the agent who flagged those accounts. Figured that might help."

"Thanks, Freddy. I owe you big for this."

Perrimore clucked his tongue. "Offer's open, Garrett. You into something? You need help?"

Zane looked up guardedly, meeting Perrimore's eyes and holding his gaze. He considered himself pretty good at reading people. He didn't see anything but concern in Perrimore's eyes, but could he trust the man?

"I'm good, Freddy. Promise."

Perrimore lifted one eyebrow and nodded. "Okay. You on for Alston's party tomorrow night?"

"Party?"

"Yeah, his girl's doing some Valentine's Day shit."

"Oh fuck." Zane smacked his forehead with an open palm. "Oh God, tomorrow is Valentine's Day."

"Yeah," Perrimore drawled, his deep voice finding a whole new tenor as he began to laugh. He turned to see himself out. "Good luck with that, newlywed."

Zane waited until the door was closed, then had a brief moment to panic over having forgotten Valentine's Day. He and Ty had once been surprised when they couldn't find a restaurant on Valentine's Day, because they'd both forgotten what day it was. And they'd gotten married the week before the most romantic holiday of the year without realizing it. With Ty going through a little Sidewinder-induced crisis, Zane was pretty sure he didn't even know what month it was anymore.

Still, it was their first Valentine's Day as a married couple, so Zane needed to figure out something.

He set that aside as a problem to deal with soon, and instead examined the piece of paper again. There was no name attached, just a number. He didn't dare look up that number on his own computer; he'd have to find another way to access it. But the implications of an FBI agent blocking this information were pretty hefty, and it seemed to support what Nick had been trying to get at: that Burns had been up to something dirty. And who knew how far the corruption went into the Bureau? Zane had to tread more carefully and keep his head down.

If Burns wasn't the one who was dirty—and Zane was still on the fence about that—*someone* involved in the cartel operation had been. Someone who had worked that case with Zane had been stealing cartel money and orchestrating dozens of deaths. Jesus Christ. And whoever belonged to this ID number was either guilty, or had some information Zane was pretty sure Ty would want for Valentine's Day far more than a box of chocolates.

He unlocked the bottom drawer of his desk and dropped the file in there, then closed it and made sure it was locked again before going back to the report he'd been trying to read.

Since when did doing his job get in the way of the things he needed to be doing? He really was turning into Ty.

Another knock at his door had him tensing up all over again. "Enter," he called out, trying not to sound like he was terrified of whatever was coming next. He was the boss; he was not supposed to be afraid when people knocked on his door, they were supposed to be afraid of him.

The door opened, and Digger poked his head in. Zane sat up straighter, alarm streaking through him.

"What are you doing here?" he blurted. "How'd you get past security?"

Digger made an effort to look hurt, but he was still smiling when he pushed into the office. Owen followed after him, his expression a little less mischievous, and he closed the door behind them.

"Everything okay?" Zane asked.

"Yeah, it's fine." Digger threw himself into one of the chairs across from Zane's desk. "The others all headed down to DC for some sightseeing. But we missed you, so we decided to stay behind."

"Missed me?" Zane repeated, sinking back into his chair as if it could protect him from whatever plan Sidewinder had concocted while he wasn't there to supervise. "The office is clean, there's no bug here."

"Oh!" Digger grinned at Owen. "That makes this easier."

Owen huffed and sat beside him, remaining on the edge of his seat while Digger lounged with one leg tossed over an arm of his chair. Owen gave Zane a tired smile. "Six and the Doc are heading for Richard Burns's office. Irish and Bell went for his house. They've got six hours to check in before we follow if there's trouble. Until then, we're here to do a little digging on your vermin problem."

Zane raised an eyebrow at that. "What do you propose?"

Owen smirked and reached into his pocket, withdrawing a badge that he placed in front of Zane. Zane picked it up, meeting Owen's eyes with more than a hint of suspicion. "Caliburn Technologies. This is where you work?"

"Yeah. Weapons systems, government contracts. Stuff. We poach a lot of federal agents for security, and since I started out scouting talent, this wouldn't be the first time I snooped around an FBI office asking questions."

"You sneaky son of a bitch," Zane said with a smirk, pushing Owen's badge back toward him.

Owen grinned and gave Zane a wink as he stood. "It'll help sell it if you give it about an hour, then toss us out. Loudly."

Zane chuckled, biting his lip as he took in the utter glee on both their faces. "Toss you out on your asses. Got it."

Nick parked their stolen sedan in a shady spot along the sidewalk of a tree-lined residential street. The stately houses were situated on sprawling lots, with massive oaks dotting the landscape and overly obvious security systems with signs announcing their presence for good measure.

Nick didn't know a lot about DC or the surrounding suburbs, but this was obviously an upscale neighborhood. Hell, Richard Burns had probably put out more per month for his mortgage than Nick earned in a year.

Liam let out a low whistle. "Nice digs."

Nick nodded as he scanned the surroundings. "Richard Burns liked nice things."

"Says the man who lives on a yacht."

Nick shrugged. "At least it's not built on blood."

"I didn't know the man, but he was a piece of work, hmm? Anyone who can wrap Tyler around his finger must be."

Nick didn't respond. He was watching a vehicle parked facing them, roughly a block up. "Shit."

"I didn't do anything!"

"Cops." Nick nodded in the direction of the car, then ducked his head to look at his lap as if he were studying a map.

"Why would they be watching this house?" Liam asked. "Are you sure they're cops and not cartel?"

"Positive. Look up police reports for the last week. And grab me a map or something from the glove compartment."

Liam dug around and found a plastic folding map in one of the door panels. He set it on Nick's knee, then brought out his laptop and began typing. Nick watched the two shadows in the police vehicle, going over in his head how he would explain their presence if they were approached. Getting lost would be a viable excuse, because as soon as he started bickering with Liam as if they'd been stuck in the car for hours going the wrong way—something Liam was singularly good at—it would sell the story.

"Okay, here we go," Liam finally said, and Nick realized he'd been holding his breath as he waited. "They responded to a robbery at this address two nights ago."

"Robbery? Why the hell are they still sitting here, then?"

"No clue." Liam snapped his laptop shut. "This might fuck both operations right up the arse if security has been heightened. How the hell are we going to get into that house right under their noses? We don't have time for this shit; we have to be back to Baltimore by sundown."

"You got my shield on you?" Nick asked.

Liam didn't ask questions as he rummaged in the bags in the backseat. He handed Nick his badge.

Nick slid it onto his belt where it belonged. "Okay, I want you to walk right up to the front door and stand there watching me like you're impatient, okay?"

Liam nodded and popped the handle on his door, lurching out of the car and slamming the door without even offering a smart-ass comment. Nick got out and strolled toward the police sedan, one hand in his pocket so it pushed his jacket back and displayed his badge. He could only hope the shape and make of the Boston shield was similar to that of Great Falls. He had no idea what theirs looked like.

When he got closer to the two cops, he took his hand out of his pocket and waved, covering the blatant Boston PD written on his badge with his jacket.

The driver rolled his window down as Nick slowed. "Can we help you, Detective?"

"Detective Sullivan, how you doing?" Nick bent so he was at eye level with both men. The two men looked at each other, then back at Nick.

"New in town, Detective?" the driver asked.

"First week here," Nick said with a wide grin. "Moved down from Boston Robbery/Homicide. New everything, still getting lost at every turn."

Both cops gave him knowing smiles. The passenger, though, turned his head to watch Liam, who had stomped up the walkway to the Burns residence and was observing Nick with his hands on his hips. He had a badge on his belt, though Nick had no idea where he'd gotten it. Nick looked over at him and sighed.

"Still . . . working out the kinks on the partner too."

That got more genuine laughs from both men, and Nick breathed a little easier.

"We got tossed this one this morning, I saw you sitting here, wanted to come touch base, make sure we're not stepping on any toes. This your case?"

The driver groaned and rubbed his eyes. "There's nothing here to investigate, sir. Owner's a widow. Husband was some big shit in the FBI, got himself killed last year. We're babysitting, here. Sergeant's orders. Round the clock 'til the lady feels safe."

"Understood. We won't be long. I'll see what I can do about some coffee, huh?"

"You got my vote, Detective," the driver said, grinning.

Nick pounded his fist on the roof of their car, giving them both a wink before he sauntered away.

"What the hell, mate?" Liam said under his breath as soon as Nick came close.

Nick shrugged. "You said it yourself, we couldn't sneak past them."

"Brazen idiot." There was a hint of pride in Liam's voice as he spoke, though. "Are they legit?"

"I think so, yeah. Just the department looking after the widow of a high-profile politician." Nick eyed Liam up and down, then pushed his coat aside to get a look at his badge. It was plastic. "Junior firefighter?"

"No one ever looks at a badge, come on," Liam huffed, then knocked on the door.

When a woman answered, peering around the slit in the door, Nick held up his badge and then slid it back on his belt, keeping the words covered with his gloved fingers. "Mrs. Burns? Laura Burns?"

"Yes?"

"I'm Detective Black, and this is my partner, Detective Decker. Do you have a few minutes, ma'am?"

"Of course. This is about the robbery?"

"Yes, ma'am, may we come in?" Liam asked. He had assumed an accent and was giving Nick a sideways glare.

She pushed a stray lock of hair behind her ear and nodded, stepping to the side to usher them through the entry into a massive foyer. Nick stopped just inside, glancing around. There was a massive picture of Richard Burns, his wife, and two cocker spaniels above a table near the stairs. Nick stared at it, at the eyes of the man he'd killed, trying to find an ounce of regret in him.

He couldn't manage it.

The click of the door brought his attention back to Laura, and the sound of those cocker spaniels yapping somewhere in the house had his hair standing on end. He put on the professional, sympathetic smile he'd perfected over his years on the job. "Can you tell us what happened?"

Nick thought he heard her sniff, but she kept a stoic expression. "I was out of town, but the neighbor saw the lights of a flashlight through the window and called the police."

"What was stolen?" Liam asked.

"Nothing. The patrolmen came before they could get into it."

Liam raised an eyebrow. "Into . . . what?"

"The safe. I'll show you." She turned and gestured for them to follow, leading them into the formal dining room, where the hardwood floors had been ripped up and a safe in the floor had been exposed.

Nick and Liam circled the safe. The floors had been pulled up with a tool, but underneath were hinges where a section was supposed to lift with ease. If the robbers had known the safe was under there, why hadn't they known how to open the door to it? He realized that if the burglars had been interrupted and hadn't gotten into the safe, the patrolmen stationed outside made sense.

"Standard B rating, polyethylene casing, drill-resistant hardplate," Liam murmured. "Combination lock plus digital keypad. Wouldn't take long to get past those bolts." Nick stared at him until Liam met his eyes. He blinked a couple times and then looked at Burns's widow as if he was just realizing what he'd said. "Not long for a trained thief, of course."

She smiled politely, but her frown returned when she examined the safe.

"Ma'am, what was kept in this safe?" Nick asked.

"I don't know. I didn't even know it was there."

"Pardon?"

"My late husband worked for the FBI. He . . . must have had it installed to protect something from work, because he never mentioned it. We have a safe in the master bedroom upstairs for valuables, so I don't know why he needed another."

"I see. Who, besides your husband, might have known he had this safe?"

She shook her head, playing with a tiny gold charm around her neck. "He wasn't very close to many people. His oldest friend was a man he was in the Marines with. Earl Grady. And he never spoke about work when he came home. The only name I ever heard him say more than in passing was a man named Jack Tanner. He went through the academy with Richard. He came to dinner now and then."

Nick made a show of writing the names in a little notebook he'd taken from his pocket, but his mind was whirring. He gave Liam a glance and nodded before turning his attention back to her. "And you're sure nothing else was taken?"

"Positive. I had just gone over the entire house, categorizing everything for the estate after my husband's death. Richard's office is still just as he left it. I . . . I haven't been able to move anything. I would know if anything was out of place."

Nick fought the urge to turn away from her. He had taken this woman's husband, and now he was standing in her home, pretending to be someone who intended to help. Still, he couldn't manage more than passing guilt. Don't marry a monster, and you won't be as likely to become a widow.

"I see," he finally said.

"We're almost out of your hair, ma'am, but would you mind too terribly if we troubled you for coffee to bring our boys outside?" Liam asked after a few awkward seconds of silence.

"Oh! Yes, I meant to bring them something warm earlier. I could make a pot."

"That would be very nice, thank you." Nick forced a smile. "I'll help, if you don't mind. I have a few more questions."

She led him through the nearest door into the kitchen, and Nick asked a few more standard questions as he held mugs and pods of different coffee flavors for her. He raised his voice when she started toward the dining room again, and was relieved to find Liam pacing near the bay window at the front of the house, his hands clasped behind his back, instead of snooping.

He gave them a charming smile, taking two of the mugs from Nick. She'd made them both coffee as well, and Nick wasn't sure how to feel about that.

She smiled sadly. "Keep the mugs. Please. My late husband was the only one who used them."

They both murmured thanks, and she showed them out. Nick carried two mugs over to the men who were stuck watching the home, making good on his promise from earlier.

"Don't guess it's Irish coffee, is it, Detective?" one of them asked.

Nick clucked his tongue. "Maybe next time."

Liam picked him up, giving the cops a cheeky little salute as Nick slid into the car. They drove the opposite way they had come, making sure their stolen license plate wouldn't be noticed as the two cops sipped from the steaming mugs.

"Did you get into it?" Nick asked.

Liam handed him his mug. "Of course. What do I look like, an amateur?"

Nick gave him a dubious glance as he rolled down his window, the cold wind whipping at them and stirring the papers in the backseat. He tossed the coffee, mug and all, out the window, then rolled it back up.

"I would have taken that," Liam told him.

"Shut up. What was in the safe?"

"A book." Liam dug into his pocket and pulled out an SD memory card. "And this was in a cutout inside the pages."

Nick took the card and frowned at it, turning it over between his fingers. "Pictures?"

"Looks like."

Nick grunted. "Better be some super fucking state secrets on this thing."

Liam smirked. "Bigfoot or bust, right mate?"

Nick sighed and slid the SD card into his front pocket. "What book was it?"

"Pardon?"

"You said there was a book in there. What book?"

"I don't know."

"I thought you weren't an amateur. Why the fuck would you leave something like that behind?"

"What the fuck does it matter what book it was?"

Nick slammed his fist against the top of the car. "Everything with Burns mattered!"

"Well, I'm sorry. It was too fucking big to fit in my cleavage, mate. Deal with it."

Nick rolled his eyes.

"We can go back and tell her you dropped your mug and need more nummies," Liam said, his voice wavering with laughter.

"Just . . . drive." Nick fished his phone out of his pocket. He sent a prearranged text to let Ty and Owen know they'd made it in and out without issue. He didn't even have a chance to put the phone back in his pocket before it was ringing in his hand. It was a burner phone, so he had none of his ringtones or photos, but he knew it was Ty. "Hey," he answered.

"You got in?" Ty asked.

"Yeah, we—"

"We need help here."

"Where?"

Ty rattled off the address.

"You okay?"

"We'll see," Ty said, and the call ended.

Nick scowled at the phone, and Liam gave him a low whistle. "Holds a grudge, doesn't he?"

"Yeah, we'll just remind him about you shooting him and we'll be fine."

Liam smacked the steering wheel. "He shot me first!"

Nick snorted before he could stop himself. "Just drive."

It took Liam and Nick longer to find them than Ty had anticipated. He'd forgotten that neither man was all that familiar with DC.

He and Kelly were sitting at a sidewalk table, eating chips and waiting for the others. They weren't exactly being inconspicuous, considering it was just above freezing out, but Ty was beyond caring if they looked suspicious. It wasn't like they were actually doing anything wrong. Yet.

"You'd be okay if he did that to you?" Ty asked as Kelly sipped his tea. "Said something he knew would hurt you just so you wouldn't look too close at the bad things?"

"No, I wouldn't." Kelly leaned toward him. "I'm not okay that he did it to you, either, that's what I'm trying to tell you."

Ty eyed him warily, then watched two women walk by, all bundled up and struggling with their scarves in the wind.

"You know the soft spots, where to aim that it will hurt the most," Kelly said. "So does he. But you know deep down that you've never said anything to Nick without your best intentions behind it. And I'm sure the same can be said of him."

Ty chewed on the inside of his cheek, not able to look at his companion again as he thought back on all the rows he and Nick'd had over the years. They had indeed said some awful things to each other. When you'd known someone since you were a teenager, you were bound to hurt each other. "You hurt the ones you love, is that what you're saying?"

Kelly shrugged and sat back. "If it makes my point, yeah."

Ty was silent, watching passersby as if he could just push the pain to the back burner for a while. He desperately wanted to sit down and talk to Zane about this. His mind was a mess of confused emotions, and Zane was the only thought that seemed to keep him calm right now.

It wasn't long before two familiar figures were making their way toward the table, both men bundled against the cold. Ty had to tamp down on a flare of absolute rage as he watched them come closer. How the hell had he found himself working with Liam Bell *again*? The man had tried to kill him the last time Ty had trusted him, and now here he was, telling Ty to trust him one more time.

Nick and Liam sat at the table, winded from their walk in the cold. There was an outdoor heater nearby, and Liam turned toward it and put his hands out like it was a campfire. "Bloody hell," he muttered.

Nick seemed less bothered by the cold, but then Ty had been in Boston in the winter. He was pretty sure Antarctica was warmer.

"What'd you find?" he demanded.

Nick reached into his overcoat, fumbling at the pocket beneath the lapel for a few seconds before cursing and yanking his gloves off with his teeth. He kept digging for whatever he had in there.

"SD card," Liam told them as he watched Nick struggle. "Jesus Christ, man, do you need help?"

"Don't touch me," Nick grumbled. He finally pulled the tiny card out and held it between two trembling fingers, handing it to Ty without another word.

Ty scowled as he turned it over. "This is it? You broke into Burns's house and this is all you took from his files?"

Both men shook their heads. Liam's teeth were chattering as he spoke. "We didn't need to burglarize it. Someone did that for us."

Ty and Kelly exchanged a confused glance as Liam continued to explain what they'd seen at Burns's residence.

"What book was it?" Ty asked when Liam was finished.

Liam flopped his hands against the table.

"Told you," Nick muttered under his breath.

"I don't fucking know, okay!" Liam practically shouted. "It was a book. A big book. Get over it."

Nick slid his glove back on and hunched against the cold, leaning closer to Ty. "What's our play?"

Ty glanced up at the Federal Building, not a block away from where they sat. "I gave Nancy a call; she was Burns's assistant. She said they've moved all of his files to the archives."

"Can she get us access?" Nick asked.

Ty shook his head, sighing. His breath froze in the air and billowed in front of him. "She retired when he died. Hell, her information might be out of date at this point. We're going in blind."

"Forgive me for questioning your judgment," Liam said after a second of thought, "but why are we needed here? I'm kind of a big deal on the most wanted lists at the moment, if I hadn't made that clear."

"That's why you're here," Ty said with a smirk. "You need to get your face near the Bureau's cameras, get the facial recognition to kick in."

"You want to use me as a decoy?" Liam had the nerve to sound offended.

"Consider it the Grady version of switching a bullet," Ty snarled.

Liam huffed, turning to Nick as if Nick might stand up for him. Nick shrugged and shook his head.

"Fine!" Liam cried, and he crossed his arms and slumped in his chair. "But I get O'Flaherty as a getaway driver."

"Fair enough. We'll meet you back in Baltimore if you make it," Ty said, and then pushed his chair back to stand. Liam sat grumbling, but Nick was watching Ty with a look that could only be described as an abandoned puppy.

Ty turned and stalked off. He had a job to do.

It was almost dark when Zane slipped his key into the lock. He'd stayed late at the office, waiting for most of his staff to clear out so he could gain access to a computer that wouldn't leave a trail back to him. The upside to being the boss was not having to answer awkward questions about being where he wasn't supposed to be. The downside to being the boss was that when he stayed late, everyone else did as well.

He pushed into the dark row house and immediately tensed. Someone was there. He could feel it in the back of his mind, a sixth sense developed from too many years undercover.

His motions only halted for a second, and then he was moving normally again, closing the door behind him and tossing his satchel aside like he always did. He shrugged out of his overcoat, his hand on the gun under his arm.

"Relax, Garrett, it's just us," Owen said from the darkness of the living room.

Zane's shoulders slumped in relief. He hadn't been up for a battle royale tonight. And Ty would have killed him if he'd wrecked the furniture. "Why are you sitting in the dark? I could have shot you."

Digger chuckled. "You could have tried."

"You made a show of kicking us out of your office; we didn't want anyone seeing us with a key to your house," Owen explained.

Zane clicked on a lamp in the corner. "You have a key to the house?"

"Of course. Ty gave us all one when he bought the place."

Zane ran a hand through his hair, smiling wryly. "I basically married all of you, didn't I?"

Digger chuckled evilly and Owen rolled his eyes.

Zane sat on the end of the couch, struck by how odd this should have felt. Him and Digger and Owen, two men he'd never actually been alone with for any extended amount of time, not without Ty around. Or at least not without Nick around, if you counted that one time Ty had needed rescuing.

"What did you find out? Anything?" Zane asked.

"No one pinged verbally," Owen told him, sounding a little embarrassed about it. "I didn't get to everyone in your office, but I started with the team you used to work with and moved out from there."

Zane held his breath. "They're all clean?"

Owen winced. "I'm not going to say yes. The redhead gave Digger her number, so I'd fire her immediately for poor judgment."

"Hey!" Digger grunted.

"Clancy would eat you alive," Zane told Digger with a smirk. "Well, I ran the ID number of the agent who flagged the cartel's accounts."

"Was it Burns?" Digger asked.

Zane shook his head, sighing. "It was Ty."

Both men were quiet and thoughtful, frowns deepening. "What does that mean?" Owen finally asked.

"Either Ty did it himself, thinking it was part of a legit op, or someone—maybe Burns, but definitely someone in power—used his ID to do it."

"Or Ty's dirty," Digger offered.

Owen glared at him. "That might have been funny before O'Flaherty started killing people, dude."

"Sorry," Digger grumbled.

Zane rubbed at the tension between his eyes. "Either way, Nick was right. Someone in the Bureau hid something in those accounts, and there's no legal reason for that to happen."

Owen and Digger remained silent.

"Have we heard from Ty?" Zane asked. "The others?"

"Yeah, Irish checked in this afternoon," Owen answered. "He said they'd gotten in and out of the home with no problem and they were heading to Ty and Kelly, that Ty had called them for help."

"What kind of help?"

"He didn't say, but he didn't sound concerned about it. We haven't heard anything since. He uploaded the contents of an SD card to us as a backup in case something went wrong. He said we should get it to you ASAP."

"Why, what's on it?"

"Photos. D and I looked over it, but it's just photos." Owen stood and headed for a laptop on the dining table as he spoke.

Zane followed, watching over Owen's shoulder as he brought up the contents of the SD card Nick had uploaded to a cloud. There were other files on there, most of them labeled with trips Sidewinder had taken over the years by location or event.

"This where you guys share pictures and stuff?" Zane asked.

"Yeah, it's easier than relying on Digger or Doc to actually remember to send us copies," Owen said under his breath.

"I heard that!" Digger called from the living room.

Owen smirked and pulled up the right file. Zane leaned closer, scowling as an array of photos popped up. Nothing seemed abnormal about them. Burns and his wife on vacation in the Caribbean. Landmarks and scenery. A cocker spaniel with its tongue out. There were some older photos, as well, of Burns and Earl Grady as far back as Vietnam. Wedding photos. A very young Burns holding a baby Zane could only assume was Ty. He recognized the fireplace in the background as the one at the Grady home.

"What do you think?" Owen asked after letting Zane look over them for a few minutes.

Zane shook his head. "Why did Nick think this was important?"

"He said they found it in a safe in the floor that Burns's widow didn't even know was there. It was hidden inside a book."

"What book?"

Owen shrugged.

Zane hummed and clicked through a few more photos. Looking at picture after picture of Burns smiling for the camera, at moments of his life he'd caught for posterity, so important to him that he'd scanned them and kept digital copies in a safe, Zane felt a pang of mourning.

He'd been upset when Burns had been murdered, of course he had. He was human, after all. And he'd seen the way the loss had torn at Ty and his family. He'd suffered from sympathy and remorse. He'd never mourned the man, though. He'd never thought of Burns as anything but his boss who hadn't trusted him. He'd never thought of him as a husband, brother, or uncle. He'd never thought about the lifetime he'd left behind him.

"You okay?" Owen asked.

"Yeah, it's just . . . this is a side of him I never saw."

Owen laid a hesitant hand on his shoulder.

"This is the side of him Ty knew, though."

Digger spoke up behind them. "Six ain't ever going to get over Irish killing him. Is he?"

Owen and Zane exchanged uneasy glances. Zane looked back at the photos on the computer screen and Owen turned toward the kitchen, shaking his head.

Zane heard the others coming before they ever got close to the front door. They were bickering, berating each other for whatever had gone wrong. Zane couldn't hear the words, but he recognized Ty's "annoyed on a mission gone wrong" tone even through the door.

"I mean, how fucking hard is it?" Ty shouted when the door opened.

"You know me, Ty! I'm not a good liar!" Kelly slammed the door shut behind him. "I told you not to make me talk, I told you I couldn't do it, but no, go tell the girl you're in IT, Doc, people never ask questions when you're in IT."

"They don't!"

"Well obviously they do! How the fuck am I supposed to know how many megahertz is in the fucking Bureau processors, huh? That's not common knowledge!"

"I'll megahertz you," Ty grumbled.

Kelly dropped his coat and waggled his fingers at Ty. "Let's go then!"

"Hey!" Digger shouted. He stood with his hands outstretched, his eyebrows raised. "What happened?"

Ty and Kelly glared at each other for a moment longer before calming and separating. Kelly stomped to the kitchen, while Ty moved to the couch and sat next to Zane. He ran his hands through his hair. "We couldn't get the files. We didn't have enough time, and there were just too many to go through. We didn't know where to start."

"Where are the others?" Owen asked.

Ty raised his head, eyes scanning the room. "They're not back?"

No one answered. Kelly slammed the refrigerator door and cursed.

"We used Liam as a distraction to get into the building," Ty told them. "Nick was driving, I'm sure they got away. Probably had to dump the car, they'll be here soon."

No one argued the assertion. Zane observed the members of Sidewinder, wondering how they could fight like they did but still have so much faith in each other's abilities.

Actually, that pretty much summed up him and Ty.

"We need you to look at some pictures," Owen told Ty after a stretch of tense silence. "Nick uploaded an SD card for us, but we can't find anything that pings on it."

"It's all personal photos," Zane said. "We were thinking you might be able to catch whatever Burns thought was so important about them."

Ty nodded and got up to follow Zane to the dining table. He sat and began flipping through the pictures, going slowly, staring at each photograph for a long time. Zane wanted to comfort him, do something to ease the pain in his eyes, but no amount of coddling or cooing would ease the grief.

It took Ty nearly half an hour to page through every photograph, and then he sat back and sighed. "I don't know."

"No idea why he'd take such pains to hide and keep those safe?" Owen asked.

Ty shook his head. Then his lips curved in a smile. "You know, when they said it was inside a book, I half expected some sort of code that needed cracking. Dick loved replacement ciphers."

The fond smile on Ty's face brought one to Zane's. Then something struck him, and he stood so fast he almost toppled his chair over. Ty flinched. "He coded the photos!"

"Do what, now?" Ty asked.

"Digital steganography," Zane blurted. He shooed Ty out of his seat and plopped himself down in front of the computer.

"Can you figure that shit out?" Owen asked. "Doesn't it usually take a pretty advanced computer program to decode?"

"What the fuck is digital stego . . . saurus?" Ty asked.

"Steganography," Zane corrected. "It's the process of hiding information in electronic communications. Sort of a modern day invisible ink."

"Would Burns have been able to do that without leaving an electronic trail?" Ty asked.

"There are advanced ways of doing it that require equipment, which would have left a trail if he'd used them. But there are low-tech ways, too. A photo-manipulating program and some patience is all it would take."

"How so?" Kelly asked.

"The most common way, the easiest way, is to change the hue of the pixels according to a preset alphabetic code." Zane pulled up one of the photos as he spoke, zooming in on it until it was magnified by two thousand. It was no longer an image, just blocks of blurry color. He scanned along the photo, and couldn't help but grin triumphantly when he hit on a pattern of squares that were drastically different from the colors around them. "It's invisible to the naked eye, especially when the photo is printed out, but the more you enlarge the digital file, the more obvious it becomes. We just need to identify the pixels and figure out what they correspond to."

"Jesus. This is going to take forever," Owen said.

"It would," Zane said with a nod. "Luckily, I know a guy."

Ty felt stupid leading the boys into the Baltimore field office under the cover of darkness. This was the second federal building he'd trespassed on today; he was pushing his luck more than even he liked.

Owen, Digger, and Kelly followed him to the service entrance, keeping to the shadows and using the odd corners of the loading docks to shield them from prying video eyes. None of them said a word as they waited for Zane to meet them and let them into the building.

They took the service stairs to the fourth floor to avoid the telltale beep of the elevators.

The cybercrimes unit was dark and quiet, lit by emergency lights and the glow of several machines that had been left on. Ty waited in the stairwell as Zane moved out and checked that it was clear. If Zane was caught here at night, the only thing he could be accused of was being a workaholic. The rest of them, not so much. And if they were confronted by anyone from the cartel? Ty was confident the five of them could take care of it.

They moved out, the other boys fanning out behind Ty in a natural protective formation, falling back on all their years of training. They stayed low, confident in Zane to lead them through the floor without incident.

The room Zane took them into was lined with machines that gave off a soothing whir. It was cold in the room, too, cold enough that Ty didn't even bother taking his scarf off.

"We just need to load the photos into this one," Zane told them as he sat in front of a screen. "It'll take the program a few hours to run, but we should have what we need and be out of here before people start coming in."

Ty stood at Zane's side as he brought up the photos on the SD card and began loading them into the program that would identify and decode the pixels. Ty loved watching him in his element like this almost as much as he loved to watch Zane brawl.

"So we just . . . chill until it finishes?" Digger asked.

Zane nodded as he typed. "Break room down the hall has yogurt and crossword puzzles."

Digger muttered under his breath.

Ty turned to look over the others. Owen was standing by the door, keeping watch through the blinds on the window. Digger was touching things he probably shouldn't be touching. And Kelly was crouched against the wall, his phone in hand and a scowl lit by the device's glow.

"Still nothing from Nick," Kelly said when he saw Ty watching him. "We should have heard from them by now."

Ty nodded in agreement, but he had no words of comfort. He hadn't even thought twice about offering Liam up as bait, though he'd been a little surprised when Nick had agreed to help Liam. Maybe there was something to Kelly's theory about a sort of Stockholm syndrome going on. Nick wasn't easily susceptible to mind games, but two weeks alone with Liam and a gun would break anyone.

There was nothing to be done about their predicament right now, though, not until they heard something from one of the missing men.

"Isn't there something more worthwhile we could be doing than watching this computer do shit?" Kelly asked irritably. "Like looking for Nick?"

"Where would you start, man?" Ty sympathized with Kelly's desire to find the man. Hell, Ty wanted to hear from him too, and the more time that passed the more worried he got. But there was nowhere to start, and they had to trust in Nick and Liam to get out of a scrap on their own right now. "And if we run into trouble with this, we'll need you."

Kelly huffed, but he didn't argue.

"Movement on the elevator," Owen whispered, and he knelt below the level of the window in the door.

Ty and Zane shared a look as Ty reached for his gun, but Zane stopped him with a hand on his wrist, and stood. "I'll see if I can head them off. Y'all stay here. Keep quiet."

Ty nodded and slid his gun back into place.

Zane took his jacket off and draped it over the chair, then pushed the sleeves of his Henley to his elbows. He searched around the desk area, then grabbed a pen and slid it behind his ear. He held his hands out to Ty. "Do I look sleep-deprived and grumpy?"

Ty mussed his hair for him. "You always look sleep-deprived and grumpy."

Zane smacked him on the back of the head as he moved by him and slipped past Owen into the hall.

He closed the door tight behind him, but after a second Owen turned the handle and popped the door back open so they could hear. They crowded around, straining their ears to listen.

"Michelle?" Zane called.

"Garrett!" Michelle Clancy replied. "What the hell are you doing here? You scared the shit out of me."

Zane chuckled. "I was about to ask you the same thing."

"I was downstairs getting some work in, saw the elevator move. Came up to check it out."

Ty scowled and met Owen's eyes. Was it possible someone had taken this elevator up even as they'd been climbing the stairs on the other end of the building? Or was Clancy lying?

"The elevator?" Zane repeated, his tone more guarded.

"Get out there, Six," Kelly whispered. He patted Ty's leg as he listened from a spot on the ground. "Go go, give him backup."

Ty was already trying to get out of his coat and scarf and boots. He tossed his shirt aside as well, leaving himself in nothing but his jeans, socks, and a T-shirt with a picture of a piñata that said, "I'd hit that." He took off his holster and dropped it, sliding his gun into the back of his jeans and making sure his shirt covered it.

"Keep at that computer," Ty whispered. "If shit gets bad, you make sure you're gone before it ends, got it?"

They all nodded and moved aside so he could slip out of the room.

Clancy was standing by the elevators, and Zane was facing her with his back to Ty. They were eyeing each other with growing suspicion, neither of them speaking.

"Hey, Red," Ty said. Zane jumped when he spoke but he didn't turn around.

Clancy seemed to relax a little when Ty appeared, and then a slow smile spread across her face as she saw the condition of Ty's clothing. "Shit, I'm sorry. I didn't mean to interrupt . . . whatever you were doing." She turned half away and shielded her view with her hand.

Zane almost looked over his shoulder, his body twitching.

"Michelle, we came up the stairs," Ty said quietly. "You sure that elevator moved?"

Clancy's entire demeanor changed almost instantly. Her shoulders tensed and her hand hovered near the gun at her hip. Ty was stunned for the briefest of moments by the thought that Clancy might be about to draw on them.

Then she took a step to the side and put her back to the wall beside the elevator. "It was about ten minutes ago," she said, voice pitched lower. "Started at the ground floor and stopped here. Didn't move again."

Zane turned to meet Ty's eyes then, nodding. "Someone tailed us," he said, drawing his weapon.

Ty knocked on the door behind him, and the other three men poured out of the room. Owen and Digger fanned out onto the floor, sliding through cubicles and disappearing into the darkness. Kelly stayed behind, guarding the door to the computers.

Clancy watched slack-jawed. "Oh Christ. I'm going to get shot in the ass, aren't I?"

"Probably," Ty whispered. He moved to Zane's left, gun in hand.

"You two aren't here getting your rocks off on the equipment, huh?"

Ty shook his head.

"Thank God."

"You haven't seen anyone else here tonight?"

"No, just you assholes," Clancy grunted.

Zane scurried to the bank of windows at the front of the building and looked out. "Whoever they are, they parked out front."

"Means they're not worried about us knowing they're here," Ty said, brows drawn. "Why would they go years in the dark and then show themselves now?"

"What are you talking about?" Clancy asked. "Who's in the dark?"

Ty placed his back against the wall beside Clancy. "We've been tracking a cartel mole in the department for over a year and a half."

"And you thought it was me? You are so off the Christmas card list!"

"You don't send Christmas cards!"

"Guys," Zane snapped.

"Floor's clear," Digger called from the break room at one end of the floor.

"Clear!" Owen echoed from the other end.

Ty and Zane shared a confused frown across the room.

"What case are you doing overtime on?" Ty asked Clancy.

"Cut-and-dry gambling ring, nothing exciting. Alston's been kind of MIA on me; I've been covering for him, working late."

Ty turned his attention back to Zane, who was still hovering near the windows and watching the parking lot. "You told Garrett he's been gone?"

"No," Clancy admitted. When Ty frowned at her, she shrugged. "He's the boss now, man. You know how it goes. We all have stretches where we need time to get it together without a psych eval."

Ty nodded dazedly. He'd known Scott Alston for years. They'd gone to football games together, gotten drunk together, and been shot together. He'd helped Alston pick up girls and helped him dump them. Hell, he'd even met the man's mother once. The suspicion that he might be their mole damn near broke Ty's heart. "What's going on with Alston?"

There was a clang near the stairwell before Clancy could answer. The door creaked open, and by the time Alston stepped out of the stairwell, they had all positioned themselves around the entry, guns ready.

He held his hands high, eyes darting around at each of them. "I saw the accounts Freddy was looking up for you. I'm here to help."

"You got five seconds to convince me," Zane said.

Alston took a deep breath. "Richard Burns had me reporting on you. I thought it was a legit op at first, and by the time I realized it wasn't . . . there was nothing I could do."

Digger pulled the hammer back on his revolver, and the sound was like thunder in the quiet building.

"You could have told us," Zane growled.

"Easy," Ty ordered, holding his hand out to Digger. "Details, Scott. Now."

Alston hurried to answer. "Taps on your phones, and one in McCoy's office. That was all I did, I swear to you."

Zane holstered his gun and pulled a pair of handcuffs from his belt.

"Garrett, I'm on your side!" Alston insisted. "When I put it all together, I . . ."

"You what?" Ty urged, even as Zane took a step toward him with the handcuffs.

"After what happened in New Orleans, I . . . I think Burns was trying kill you two. He was the only one who had access to those taps, not even I did. He was the only one who could have known you were heading to Louisiana. He had to have been the one to tell all those people who were after you down there."

Ty and Zane shared a glance. It was the same accusation Liam had made. Was it possible Richard Burns had been the one bugging them? It had been a risky play to alert them to the taps, in that case, but it had worked. They hadn't once suspected him.

"When I found out he was dead, I thought you two had done it," Alston admitted. "I kept quiet to protect you."

Ty cursed under his breath. Fucking Alston and his loyalty. If what he was saying was true, then they'd been way off base on their mole issue. And Ty believed him.

Clancy stepped closer, gesturing to Zane to hold off on the handcuffs. She didn't get close enough for Alston to touch her, but she was blocking their line of fire. "Why didn't you come to me?" she asked him. "I could have helped you out with this."

"I was trying to protect my team. My friends."

Ty put his gun away, and the others reluctantly followed his lead.

"All you did for Burns was wiretaps?" Zane asked, taking no pity. "What about our house?"

Alston looked from Zane to Ty and then to Clancy, fear in his blue eyes that Ty had never seen in the man. "I haven't touched your house," he insisted, shaking his head violently. "Even when I was feeding those fucking evil cats, I went in, I fed them, and I left. I swear."

"Explains why no one ever replaced the bug in your office," Ty said to Zane.

"Yeah, but then who was listening at the house?" Zane countered.

"Why are you here now?" Owen demanded of Alston.

"I got a buddy in the Baltimore PD gang unit. Last night I met him for a drink, he was talking about a new crew in town. I put it together with those accounts Freddy was running, those cartel accounts. You guys are after the cartel, and you're doing it off the books. Thing is . . . the cartel's after you too. And Baltimore PD thinks they're here."

"This is why I never deal in places I haven't scouted first, mate," Liam was saying as Nick tried to pop the lock on a car nearby. It was an older model Dodge Charger, one he'd be able to hot-wire. They'd been forced to ditch their first car and run for it, barely making it to this long-term rideshare parking lot, where they'd finally shaken their pursuers.

"Be sure to file your complaint with the home office," Nick grumbled. He finally found the lock and popped it. He tensed, waiting for the inevitable alarm when he opened the door. It didn't come, though.

Liam chuckled. "No one installs alarms on restored cars anymore. People pay them no mind when they go off; they're a waste of resources when you could be putting seat warmers in there instead."

"Right," Nick huffed, and then ducked to take the plate off the dash to reach the wires beneath the steering wheel. He was shocked to find keys in the floorboard of the car, tucked under the seat. He plucked them up, staring at them in consternation before he showed them to Liam.

"Now I remember why they call you Lucky."

"Just get in." Nick eased into the seat and started up the car. "It's an hour drive to Baltimore if we're good on traffic."

"It's the middle of the night. There won't be any traffic at this hour."

The traffic in DC turned out to be a nightmare, which pretty much summed up their entire day of running and hiding and nearly getting caught. It took them more than an hour just to get out of the city proper, but as soon as they were on the interstate, Nick kicked it into higher gear. They'd both tossed their phones when they were being chased, more out of paranoia than anything, and Nick wasn't willing to stop long enough to put a call in when they were making good time. He also didn't know if Kelly or Ty were being monitored, and he and Liam had no idea if they'd been identified by any organizations yet. It was safer to stay dark.

Baltimore was calm and quiet when they reached the outer limits. Snow had begun to threaten once more, and the light of dawn was peaking over the water. Nick was exhausted by the time they reached the row house on North Ann Street. Zane's truck wasn't parked out front in its usual spot, and something about it being gone put Nick on high alert. He eased the stolen Charger into a spot a block away and turned off the headlights.

They sat in silence, both watching the front of Ty and Zane's house.

"Fuck I wish I'd taken a piss back there," Liam grumbled.

Nick glared at him, trying to figure out if he was starting to enjoy working with the man again or if he still kind of wanted to dismember him. He decided he would definitely enjoy dismembering him.

"Look there," Liam hissed a few minutes later. A vehicle was cruising up the street, going slow like the driver was scouting. "There, the car at the end of the row. Late-model white Honda Accord, guarantee you it's stolen."

The Accord stopped opposite the row house, turning the headlights off and waiting, just like they were doing.

"A lookout," Liam said. "That's the cartel. They'll sit here to see if the boys come home, and when they do they'll call in a strike team. The cartel is making their move; they're going to take them out tonight."

Nick didn't question it. Liam had spent enough time with the cartel to know the way they operated. "That means they'll have lookouts posted in other places."

Liam was nodding. "The division office for sure, the hotel if they know Garrett's been staying there. Anywhere they'd be likely to go. Even that old building Tyler bought last year."

"They'll only know about that if they've been following them for a while. It's not in Ty's name."

"If you say so."

"We have to warn them somehow, help them."

"It's too late, mate. There's no saving someone once the cartel has them in the crosshairs. You just fucking pray."

Nick popped the handle on his door and drew his gun. "I'm Catholic. I don't pray, I just ask for forgiveness after."

The only place they could take Alston and the information from the files they'd gleaned was the bookstore. There was far too much sensitive information sitting around Owen and Digger's hotel room, the row house was probably being watched, and the field office obviously wasn't secure. And the *Fiddler*, while arguably the most secure spot in the city, was the only place the cartel wouldn't know about, and therefore their only mode of escape if they needed to get out. They couldn't risk either Alston or Clancy finding out about it. Ty wanted to trust them both, but he wasn't stupid.

The bookstore, though, wasn't in either Ty's or Zane's name. It would be safe long enough for them to figure out their next move.

They split up into pairs and threes so their group wouldn't be quite so noticeable when they entered the old building. Ty hadn't had time to work on much lately, and the building had that abandoned-in-the-midst-of-a-project feeling to it. Alston only took a few steps before halting near the entry.

"Jesus, Grady. When Garrett said you guys needed help, he didn't mean just painting."

Ty snorted in annoyance. "The hole in the floor is an anomaly."

Alston gave him a dubious sideways glance.

"This is a no-judgment zone," Ty told him.

Alston held up his hands, which were restrained with one of Zane's zip ties. "Oh really."

The little bell above the door dinged as Owen, Digger, and Kelly walked in, and they all stood for a few seconds in an awkward silence.

"Still no word from Nick," Kelly announced.

"He'll show up," Owen said. He took a careful step into the building, craning his head to see the hole in the floor above them. "Jesus, Six."

"Right?" Alston said with a little laugh.

Ty rolled his eyes and led them to the hidden panel in the kitchen. He'd ripped most of it down in one go, so when they'd left he'd just rested the panel against the stairwell opening. With everything else in the building a mess, it wasn't all that conspicuous.

He made Alston go first, out of spite. The others followed with flashlights and a few portable work lights from around the space. Ty loitered at the top of the stairs until Zane and Clancy came through the back door with all the photos and information they'd printed from Richard Burns's SD card. Only then did he breathe easier.

His relief was mirrored on Zane's face. Zane took him by the elbow and kissed him on the corner of his mouth. Ty kissed him back for good measure, and Zane grinned almost impishly.

"Were you worried about me, doll?"

Ty barely restrained himself from rolling his eyes. "The stakes are kind of high on this one, Zane. I'm going to be worried about you until we bury the Vega cartel in a shallow grave."

Zane slid his hand into Ty's pocket and yanked him closer. "Likewise," he whispered. "Hey. It's past midnight."

Ty frowned. "Yeah? So?"

Zane's smile was warm, lighting up his beautiful eyes in the dim light. "Happy Valentine's Day, killer."

Ty snorted, lingering over another kiss. "Since when do you keep track of that kind of thing?"

"Since my brand-new husband revealed he's a hopeless romantic," Zane murmured into the kiss. He gave Ty a last peck on the cheek, then smacked his ass. "Get the front door, I'll get the back."

They locked up the building, both of them standing in the darkness and watching the exteriors for a few minutes to see if they'd been followed. Zane finally gave a low whistle. Ty turned to see his bulky shadow heading toward the stairs, and he moved to follow him.

He was halfway to the stairwell when he heard a soft, frantic tapping on the glass of the front door. He stopped, cocking his head to listen. The tapping came again, this time sounding even more urgent. Then the ancient doorknob rattled, and someone shoved experimentally against the door, like they were testing to see how easy it would be to break down.

Zane had already descended the steps, and Ty hesitated. He didn't dare call out and give away that the building was occupied. Instead he scooted silently to the front windows, peeking through a slit in the newspaper and grocery bags pasted all over the glass.

Nick and Liam were on the stoop. Nick was tapping at the glass and cursing quietly, while Liam had his back to Nick's, his gun out, surveying their surroundings like a hawk searching for a muskrat.

Both men were bloody. Ty reached for his gun.

"Break it down," Liam ordered, loud enough to carry inside.

Nick nodded, turning and dropping his shoulder. Ty knew exactly what kind of damage Nick could do to his fucking irreplaceable antique glass door if he put his shoulder into it.

"No, no, no!" he hissed. He threw the dead bolt and cracked the door open, lips parted to ask what was going on, but Nick reached through the crack and grabbed his shirtfront, then yanked him onto the stoop.

"What the hell, Irish?"

"Call them, get them out here," Nick demanded.

"What—"

"Six, get them out!"

Ty knew that tone of voice. He didn't ask another question, just snagged his phone and hit Zane's number.

"Are you seriously not going to come down here?" Zane asked when he answered the call, sounding both amused and exasperated.

"Zane, evac right now." Nick was nodding and rolling his hand through the air as if that might make the world spin faster. Even as Ty spoke, Nick took his arm and started pulling him away from the building, right out into the street. Again, Ty didn't question or argue, and he spoke over Zane when he asked what the hell was going on. "Nick's here. Get everyone out!"

If Zane responded, Ty didn't hear it. His world was encompassed by a wave of heat and sound, sound so loud it became nothing at all to his ears save for a high-pitched whine. He was shoved forward into the asphalt, his forehead hitting, pain blooming behind his eyes like white-hot pokers in his brain. Heat and debris blew over him. The sound faded, then came roaring back like some dragon sweeping down on them.

Ty pushed himself up, confused by the flames, the screaming, the panic. Little bits of debris littered the street, most of them on fire or steaming in the freezing night air.

He rolled until he was sitting on his ass, staring at what used to be the front door of the building. It felt like forever before he was able to process what had just happened. He blinked away the blurs in his vision and struggled to his hands and knees.

"Zane," he gasped. He pushed himself to his feet, wavering as the street beneath him seemed to tilt.

A hand grabbed his elbow, steadying him.

"Zane!" Ty cried again as the fire within the building raged. He took an impulsive step forward, wobbling. The grip on his elbow tightened, and he tried to jerk out of it.

"No, Six!" someone yelled, their voice so far away it might as well have been coming from Boston.

"Zane!" Ty shouted back. "God, no. No! It doesn't happen like this!"

He got free of the hand and struggled toward the ruined façade. Arms encircled him once again, dragging him away from the building. "I'll get them out, I promise!"

"He's in there!" Ty cried. Tears streamed down his face, and smoke filled his lungs as he gasped for more air to shout. "Let me get to him, I have to get him!"

"You'll kill yourself!"

Ty jerked away and pitched forward onto his hands and knees. "I don't care!" He scrabbled over twisted metal and heated bricks, his palms and knees taking the brunt of the punishment. The heat was so fierce it felt like the skin of his face was melting off. Sirens came from somewhere in the distance, but their meaning didn't register in Ty's mind.

"Not like this," he said, over and over, trying to make his way through the rubble and flame. "Please, Zane. Not like this!"

Hands wrapped around him again, strong hands, hands made of iron. Two men in firefighter uniforms picked him up off the ground. "Come on, man," one of them said, his voice distorted by the breathing apparatus on his face.

"No! Zane!" Ty sobbed as he tried desperately to get away from them. The fire filled his entire field of vision. It sounded like a banshee's wail as it ate through the old building like dry tinder. His knees went weak. He could get to Zane, he knew he could if they'd let him.

And if he couldn't get to him, at least he'd spend his last minutes knowing he had tried.

His vision began to blur and darken. His body was giving out on him, and the two firefighters were dragging him away.

"Don't make me leave him." His pleas fell on deaf ears, though. "Don't make me leave him like this!"

The inky darkness of unconsciousness finally blotted out the blaze. As Ty gave in, a part of him hoped—prayed—that it would be the last thing he ever saw.

CHAPTER 6

Nick sat on the flybridge of the *Fiddler's Green*, a beer in one hand, an ice pack in the other. He had slathered aloe all over his hands and arms, and used the rest of his little aloe plant on the survivors they'd pulled from the smoldering rubble of Ty and Zane's building. All that remained of the bookstore was a pile of bricks, and all that remained of his plant was a stub in a pot down in the galley.

The aloe plant would grow back. But everything else that had been lost tonight? It was lost for good.

He stared off into the night, but he wasn't seeing anything. There was nothing left of the bookstore but the foundation, which was a stroke of luck any way you looked at it. The rescuers had found the survivors in the basement, all but one of them still struggling for life. Nick had no idea who the unlucky body was, and no one had been able to tell him because they'd all been overcome by smoke by the time he and Liam had broken into the hidden basement.

Kelly. Owen. Digger. Ty. Hell, even Zane. A single bomb had almost taken out nearly everything Nick loved. He'd never felt this helpless in his life, not even when he'd been crouching on the basement stairs of his childhood home, disabling the light switch with a pilfered pocketknife.

A sound jolted him out of his spiraling thoughts, and he was almost to his feet before he even realized it. He held his ice pack out like it was his gun.

Liam put both hands up, his dubious gaze going to the ice pack. He had two bottles of beer between his fingers, and they clanked when he shook them. "Just me, mate."

"Is he awake?" Nick asked, still hovering half out of his seat and brandishing the dripping ice pack like an idiot.

Liam shook his head. He handed Nick one of the beers and threw himself into the seat across from him. They stared at one another for a long, tense moment, broken only by the slapping of the water on the *Fiddler's* hull and the whine of the cold wind as it whipped through the plastic that was supposed to protect them from the elements.

"Some crack rescue team we are," Nick finally muttered.

"You did what you could, mate."

"Don't." Nick popped the beer top on the table next to him. "At least one person is dead. Ty's missing. Johns and Digger were headed to a hospital burn unit the last time I saw them, and I've got two people unconscious downstairs that we *should* have let the EMTs take. Zane's going to be pissed when he wakes up. And Kelly . . ."

Liam waited for him to finish.

Nick jerked his head away. And Kelly might never forgive him. "There aren't words that make this okay, so don't try."

For once, Liam seemed to have no jaunty retort. He settled into his seat, curled up as if protecting himself, his chin resting in his hand. "Nicholas."

Nick forced himself to meet the man's eyes.

"With Tyler and Zane both gone, you don't have any stake in this now. The cartel is finished with them."

"But we're not finished with the cartel."

A slow, crooked smile spread over Liam's face. "What do you suggest?"

"I have some favors I can pull. Call in some backup."

"From?"

"Guy I helped out last year. Good in a fight. He knows Grady and Garrett, probably owes them his life. Might be up for some destruction if he's gotten bored enough."

"Might? We'll need more than that, what else do you have?"

Nick exhaled carefully, plucking at the label of his beer. "I . . ."

The scuff of a shoe on the stairs behind him had Nick lurching to his feet again. Liam stood with him, and Nick peered down the hatch into the main cabin, holding his breath.

Kelly sat on the steps, his head hanging.

"Kels?" Nick huffed, and he shoved his beer into Liam's hand and hustled down the hatch to kneel in front of Kelly.

He put a gentle hand on Kelly's cheek, but Kelly jerked away with a loud inhalation. "Don't touch."

Nick balled his hands into fists. "What are you doing?"

"I thought I could make it up there," Kelly muttered. "My head is pounding. Did I hit it?"

"No." Nick got his arm under Kelly's and helped him stand.

"Oh my God, don't touch it."

"Okay. Come on."

Kelly didn't fight as Nick helped him toward the sofa in the salon. "I heard you talking," Kelly told him. He shook his head and lowered himself carefully to the cushions. "The others?"

"Digger went with Johns to the hospital," Nick answered. "He had minor burns and a broken arm, Digger wasn't even bruised. He called not long ago, said they're about an hour away from discharge. They're coming here when he's out."

Kelly blinked at him, still looking dazed. Nick had sedated him as soon as they'd reached the *Fiddler*, and he appeared to still be fighting through it. "Grady and Garrett?"

Nick's stomach plummeted, but he managed to get the words out. Barely. "Ty's gone."

"Gone?" Kelly asked, voice going higher.

"He passed out trying to get back into the building. Two firemen carried him to an ambulance, and then Liam and I went in for search and rescue. When we came back out, Ty . . . He's not in any area hospital, he's not in any morgue. He's just gone."

"The cartel?"

Nick shrugged, feeling ill even as he thought about it. He'd seen those firemen carrying Ty away. He should have gone after them.

"What about Garrett?" Kelly asked. "And the two agents who were with us?"

Nick jerked his head toward the steps to the lower deck. "When you feel up to it, we'll go see Garrett. He hasn't woken yet. They only pulled one more person out, I guess she's one of the agents. Ambulance took her to the hospital, I haven't heard anything about her."

"Her name is Clancy," Kelly said as he used Nick's shoulder to pull himself to his feet once more. "I want to see Zane."

Nick nodded, despite wanting to protest. Kelly should rest and Zane wasn't going anywhere. But he helped Kelly down the steps into the corridor, and past the spare bunks to the closed door of the VIP cabin. "When you feel up to it, he needs looking over, okay? We got him out before the rescue team could, so he's listed as one of the victims."

"Why?"

"We couldn't let the EMTs at him. We had to make him disappear so the cartel would back off."

Kelly's brow was pinched in concern, and his eyes darted to the door before he gave Nick a single nod.

"We have him restrained until he wakes. He kept fighting us even when he wasn't conscious; we were afraid he'd hurt himself. Or us. Don't untie him until he knows where he is and who you are."

"Got it."

Nick turned the handle, but the door thumped open and knocked him sideways. He stumbled back as Kelly shouted.

Zane was crouching in the doorway, chest heaving, frayed ropes wrapped around his knuckles to protect them. The thick door was splintered where Zane had put his shoulder into it.

"Jesus!" Kelly cried. He had his back against the wall, eyes locked on Zane's hulking mass.

"Zane, stay calm," Nick urged as he stepped forward, but Zane lunged at him, leading with his shoulder and following with one of those vicious wrapped fists. He caught Nick under the chin and sent him to his back. Stars danced in Nick's vision, and darkness threatened.

Kelly stepped forward, but Zane shouted and hefted him off his feet. He tossed him toward the bunk nook, and the curtain tore as Kelly grabbed at it in midflight. He toppled into the bunks with a solid thump and colorful curses.

Nick was still bleeding and fighting for breath when Zane leapt over him, escaping down the hallway toward the stairs. Nick rolled over, trying and failing to push to his feet.

"Garrett, wait!" he called, barely able to get the words out through his gasping attempts for air. Jesus Christ, what had Zane hit him with?

A shadow loomed in the stairwell when Zane took the first step, and Zane veered away as Liam came to investigate the noise. He disappeared into the main cabin, slamming the door behind him.

The bunk curtain fluttered to the ground in front of Nick's face. There was a crash from the bunks as the top one gave way and the mattress fell. A fresh litany of curses came from Kelly, and he finally rolled out into the corridor, grasping at the wall as he tried to find his feet.

"What the bloody hell was that?" Liam shouted from the top step.

Nick gasped. "That . . . was a Zane."

Nick heard the pump action of a shotgun from within his cabin. He was going to have more holes in his boat by the end of this, he could feel it.

Kelly helped him to his feet, and they both stumbled sideways as Nick tried to shake the dizziness. A cut on Kelly's forehead was bleeding freely. Nick could taste the tang of blood on his lips, but he wasn't sure where it was coming from. He and Kelly both flattened against the wall beside his cabin door in case Zane started firing.

"Garrett," Nick called, and he had to clear his throat in order to speak again. "You're safe here, man, you're on the *Fiddler*."

Zane's answer was a blast of the shotgun. Nick and Kelly covered each other as debris from the thick door sprayed them.

"Jesus Christ!" Nick cried. "Don't shoot!"

"Wanker!" Liam called from above.

"If I'm safe, why the fuck did I have to cut through ropes with a fucking tiny nickel to get out of that room?" Zane shouted.

"You kept fighting us—"

"Why? Explain or I keep shooting until this fucking thing doesn't float anymore!"

"They were coming for you, Zane!" Nick said. He realized he sounded panicked and rushed; he didn't want to be taken out by friendly fire. "They had to think you were dead, we couldn't let them take you to the hospital!"

Zane shoved the shotgun out of the hole he'd made in the door and turned it so it was pointing toward them. Nick and Kelly both cowered against the wall, trying to shield each other. "Where is Ty?"

Kelly stood carefully, as if any swift movements would warrant another attack like the first.

Nick licked his chapped lips and remained on the floor, covering his head. How the hell could he explain this to Zane without getting shot in the face? "We don't know where Ty is."

"Why the hell isn't he with you?"

Kelly glanced at Nick and shrugged, helping Nick to his feet. Nick put a trembling hand on the door. "He went missing while we were digging you out of that basement."

"Where'd he go?"

"The whole point of 'missing' is we don't know where he is," Liam called from above before Nick could answer.

"Why hasn't he come looking for me?"

Liam snorted. "He probably thinks you're dead, darling, just like the rest of the world."

Nick gritted his teeth and turned his head away, wincing in anticipation of the shot that would follow. The barrel of the shotgun lowered, though, giving the impression that Zane himself was drooping dejectedly.

"It's only been half a day, Garrett. They don't think you're dead, just . . . missing right now."

"When do you get to the part where I'm *not* shooting you?" Zane asked.

"Put down the gun, let Doc look you over, and then we can start searching for Ty," Nick said as he edged toward the hole in the door. "We're on your side, Zane, we need your help."

Zane pumped the shotgun, his voice going lower. "Yeah, you're going to need help if you come any closer."

Nick put up both hands and stopped moving.

"First you fucking disappear on us. *Again.* Then you're conveniently the only ones absent when everything goes to hell! You want to tell me why that is?"

Nick swallowed against the tightening in his throat. He closed his eyes in a bid for calm, but it didn't even remotely work. "Look, dipshit! Cartel men were in Baltimore, they'd rigged the bookstore to blow to send you and Ty a message! We got it out of a man watching your house, and we came as fast as we could!"

"The bookstore has never been in play, it's not even in our names!"

Nick's jaw worked silently, his frown deepening. "So?"

"You saying the cartel blew up a building they didn't even know about?"

"Yes."

"What, on a fucking whim? Picked a random building and hit the jackpot?"

"I don't know, Garrett, they must've been watching you longer than we realized. Or they had inside information."

"No shit!"

"Are you honest to God telling me you think I'm the one's been narcing on you?" Nick gritted out, bristling at the thought of it. Kelly's fingers dug in to his shoulder to remind him to stay calm.

Zane was silent.

Nick waited a moment, then tried again. "We couldn't stop them in time, Zane, but we can take the opportunity it gave us, and . . ."

"And?" Zane said impatiently.

"And make you disappear. That's why you're here with us. It buys us time."

Zane began to laugh. The sound sent a chill up Nick's spine. Even Kelly's hand on his shoulder didn't help chase the shivers away.

"Buys us time?" Zane repeated, low and gruff. His next words were so loud they echoed off the hull. "Where the hell is Ty?"

Nick glanced up the stairwell, meeting Liam's eyes. "We think . . . it was either the cartel or the NIA. Either way, he's a prisoner, and we're the only people who even know he's still alive."

"Why the fuck were you digging around in the ashes for me when you should have been with him?" Zane shouted, his voice cracking.

Nick couldn't breathe at all. He tried to pull in air, but his throat was too tight and his chest hurt too much. He hadn't been digging around in the ashes for *Zane*. He'd seen two men dragging Ty's unconscious body toward an ambulance, and he'd let them take him away because the only thing Nick had been able to think about was Kelly in that building. He'd made a choice, a conscious one. And for maybe the first time since he'd met the man, his first choice hadn't been Ty Grady.

"Anything happens to Ty, and it's on your head!" Zane snarled, and he banged something against the wall. "You were supposed to have his back! He trusts you with his life, and you let him just disappear!"

"Bullshit," Kelly hissed.

Nick gulped a deep breath as he pressed a hand to Kelly's chest to calm him, forcing himself to keep at it even though he wanted to just bury his head in the sand until the storm passed. "You're right. It's on me right now. So help me make it right, Garrett."

The shotgun faltered again. After a few tense seconds, Zane pulled the barrel back inside. His face appeared in the opening, and he narrowed his eyes at Nick. "You got a plan?"

"Give us the gun and I'll give you more than a plan."

Zane's black eyes darted toward the stairs, then back to Nick. "Who else is out there? How many?"

"Three. All of us your friends."

"We'll see about that. I'm keeping the gun. Give me a phone and we'll talk."

Nick gave Liam a curt nod, and he disappeared for a moment. When he returned he tossed a cell phone to Nick, then ducked back behind the curve of the stairwell. Nick held the phone up for Zane to see. "Right now, you're a pile of ash in that basement," he told him. "Whoever you call—"

"Fuck you, O'Flaherty," Zane snarled. "Don't fucking tell me how to operate. You've botched this thing at every turn. It's time to do this shit my way."

Nick pressed his mouth into a thin line, staring through the hole in his cabin door. He waved the phone again. "Fine. Trade."

Zane nodded curtly. He showed Nick the shotgun through the hole. "Phone first."

Nick sighed and held the phone out in front of the bullet-riddled door. Zane snatched it through the largest portion of the opening.

"Gun," Nick said, beckoning with his fingers.

"Go fuck yourself," Zane grunted, and Nick could hear him moving away from the door as he dialed.

Kelly snorted, and Nick's shoulders slumped.

"Never trust a Fed," Liam called to them from the top of the steps. "Amateurs."

Ty had been in this room before. He'd been handcuffed to this table before. He'd been questioned by these agents before. Agents X and Y. He hadn't learned their names the last time the CIA had detained him, and now he just didn't care. His entire world seemed like a blur of grays moving too fast. His stomach churned. His head pounded. His pulse raced in his ears and he could hear nothing but a low whine.

He recognized the symptoms of shock, and a portion of his system that was compartmentalizing things looked on with a detached sort of interest. He'd gotten through this state of being once, but he'd had the advantage of friends, time, and loads and loads of therapy then. He'd also had the advantage of purpose back then, a reason to bounce back, something to live for, a mission in life he believed in.

This time? There was nothing left for his mind to latch onto. His job was gone. His freedom was gone. His friends were gone. His husband was gone. His mind might as well go with them.

"Special Agent Grady," Agent X said, more forcefully this time.

Ty tore his gaze away from the dull steel top of the table and made himself meet the CIA agent's eyes. "It's just Mr. Grady now."

The man cocked his head, sighing. "Tyler. We can help you."

"You dragged me away from the only thing I care about in the world when I still could have saved him. How the hell are you going to help me?"

"We're keeping an eye on the hospitals in Baltimore. Several people made it out of that building."

Ty straightened, his wrists pulling at the handcuffs. "Zane?"

"Not yet. Rescue is still ongoing."

Ty's shoulders slumped again. "You know as well as I do that it's not a rescue anymore. It's just recovery."

"You were unconscious before we got you in our vehicle; you couldn't have gotten to him. Your two friends who went in to help? They never came out. We saved you."

Ty laughed softly, closing his eyes. "From what?" He registered the exhaustion in his voice, but he was done faking any sort of bravado. He was done.

"The Vega cartel. The NIA. Anyone else who may be after the money Richard Burns stole and considers you an excellent source for finding it."

Ty opened his eyes again, a frown marring his brow as he stared at the tabletop.

"You hadn't considered that?" Agent Y asked. They were the first words he'd spoken. Ty met his eyes. "Why do you think *we* pulled you? Why do you think we've been listening in on you?"

"You were the ones who bugged our house?"

"No. We just piggybacked the signal already coming from it."

"Whose?"

"NIA."

"Wow. I haven't been this popular since high school."

"You'll be even more popular if you go back to that house," Agent Y told him.

Ty frowned, not quite catching his meaning. "Why?"

The man opened a folder and turned it around so Ty could see what looked like crime scene photos. Two men inside a vehicle, one with his throat slit clean through to his spine, the other with a bullet hole in his forehead. His fingers had all been broken. Someone had questioned him before the kill.

Ty stared, trying to pull anything from the photos that would connect these two men to him. The head shot was reminiscent of his work, quick and to the point, but the rest was messy and brutal. He hadn't done this. He finally shook his head.

"This car was found in front of your house," Agent Y said.

Ty eyed both agents suspiciously. "This wasn't me. I didn't go back home after . . ." He trailed off, staring at the photos as the realization hit him. This had to have been Nick and Liam. This was how they'd known to come after them and get them out of the building. Ty schooled his features. He certainly didn't want the CIA knowing that.

"Well. Considering the implements found in the trunk of that car, whoever is responsible for this did you quite a favor," Agent X continued. "Unfortunately, they didn't clean up after themselves, so your house is now attracting some attention. I hope you don't need to return anytime soon. For clues to Richard Burns's money, perhaps?"

Ty blinked at the photos, still reeling from the last twenty-four hours. Now his home was compromised too. His last vestiges of a normal life, of his life with Zane, were in that house.

Both agents sat quietly, watching him. Ty knew that tactic: just sit there and wait until he got restless and started rambling. He didn't have the patience for this, though. What was the point anymore?

"I don't know where the money is. I didn't know what Burns was doing. And I couldn't begin to figure it out now. Any evidence we had was destroyed in that fire. I can't help you even if I wanted to."

The two agents shared a glance, then looked to Ty again, studying him like he was the centerfold on a locker-room pin board. Ty returned their stares, unable to get himself to play the games he was normally so good at.

After a few seconds, both men stood as if by some silent cue. Ty clutched his hands together, trying to hide the nerves building in him. The CIA wasn't exactly a shining beacon of morality. If they thought he had something they wanted, he'd be on his way to Gitmo by nightfall. Ty wasn't sure he'd live through that again. Not again.

"There's someone who would like to speak with you," Agent X said, his tone almost gentle. "I have a feeling you'll be more comfortable with him."

They exited the room without further fanfare, and a moment later another suit stepped in and closed the door with a quiet snick. Ty recognized him by his shock of white-blond hair before he even turned around.

"Preston?" Ty blurted.

Preston unbuttoned his suit coat as he sat opposite Ty. He held up a shiny silver key and let Ty get a look at it before he took the chain between Ty's hands and freed him from the cuffs. "You look like hell, Tyler."

"You look like government."

"We do what we have to," Preston said with a hint of sadness.

Ty immediately regretted his words. He knew what Preston had done to end up with the CIA, and he certainly hadn't made the choice because he wanted to wear a suit.

"I'm sorry about Zane," Preston added, his tone unchanged.

The words hit Ty like a physical blow, stealing his breath. He ducked his head, trying to concentrate on getting air.

"We're keeping ears to the ground in case he turns up," Preston continued. "He's a smart man; he may have realized that the only way to escape the cartel at this juncture was to play dead."

"Zane wouldn't do that to me," Ty snarled.

"Even still. He's MIA, which means he may have made it out of that building. It's a shred of hope I'm trying to give you. Why don't you be a good boy and take it." Preston's smile was gentle as he spoke, the compassion in his eyes blunting the sharpness of his words. For some reason, the kindness from a trained killer was even worse than angry words would have been. "Along with that shred, we'd also like to offer you something else."

"What's that?" Ty croaked.

"Revenge."

When Ty closed his eyes this time, tears trailed down his cheeks. He wiped them away in surprise. "How?"

"Come work for us. We'll give you two weeks to . . . get your affairs in order. And the Company is willing to loan you my time to do it."

Ty's heart was racing, and he realized that despite his intense desire to just give up, it wasn't in him. The thought of revenge was a carrot dangling in front of him, and damn if he wasn't a fucking horse right now.

"You'd help me go after the cartel?" Ty asked, keeping his voice low like they might be overheard. Of course they were being overheard, there were probably a dozen people watching this interview.

Preston nodded grimly. "Off the books, of course. You fuck it up, it's all on you."

Ty nodded. He was used to working like that. "What do you get from me in return? The CIA doesn't just dispense favors out of the goodness of their hearts."

"They get a highly trained agent with nothing to lose. I don't have to tell you how valuable that is."

"Quit bullshitting me," Ty growled.

Preston smiled fondly. "The deal is dependent on you delivering Richard Burns's money to the Company's door."

"I don't know how—"

"Tyler. Understand me. The CIA is the only government agency in the world wanting to hold your hand on the playground. The rest of them, including your FBI, are waiting in line to push you off the monkey bars."

Ty was nodding almost unconsciously. When he realized it, he shook out his shoulders and straightened.

"You're nothing more than a hit man who got burned. No one cares that you didn't know what Richard Burns was doing. They want someone to fall, and Burns isn't around anymore to do it. But the CIA is willing to take that off your shoulders as soon as you walk that money through the door."

"But not before."

"All you get before is me. We'll do this right, and when it's done, you'll have a home here. A purpose."

Ty swallowed hard. "If you can't kill it, hire it, right?"

Preston huffed a small laugh. "Indeed. You don't belong in civilian life, Ty. I know you can feel that void. I hope Zane is still alive, I do. But if he's not—"

"Don't," Ty whispered.

"You'll need something to get you through to the other side."

Ty wrung his hands together, rubbing his thumb over the tattoo on his finger. Zane couldn't be gone. He wasn't. The hole in Ty's chest would feel bigger, would be a gaping maw of despair swallowing him. Ty didn't feel swallowed, did he? Not yet. Zane was still out there.

But if Zane was gone . . . if that building had taken everything Ty loved with it, then he'd need something solid to grasp onto, something to wake him each morning. Something to keep him going. He'd need revenge. He ran his thumb over the anchor tattoo on his finger. Something solid to hold on to.

He finally met Preston's eyes. "You'll give me a badge? A gun?"

Preston nodded.

"And all I have to do is bring you the cartel's money?"

Preston nodded again.

They stared at each other across the table, their dull reflections distorted in the stainless steel. Ty knew what sort of life Preston was offering him. He'd turned it down once, when the NIA had come calling. He'd had choices, then. Or he'd thought he did. Now? Well, yeah, he had a choice now, too.

"I'm in," Ty said before he could second-guess himself.

"What do you need?" Preston asked with a smile.

"I'll make a list. But there's one thing I'll need that you can't get me."

"I doubt that."

Ty smiled grimly. "It's in my house."

Preston rolled his eyes. "Never easy with you, is it?"

"If it was easy, everyone would do it."

Zane would have been pacing if he hadn't been so damn tired. After the adrenaline had worn off, he'd sunk down to the bed and hung his head, clutching the phone and the shotgun to his chest and praying Ty would answer his calls, trying over and over until he was mindlessly listening to the ringing of the phone on speaker. When Ty's voice mail message began, Zane would close his eyes and listen to Ty's voice, then end the call and start over.

An hour after he'd made his great escape and barricaded himself in Nick's cabin, Kelly worked up the nerve to knock and stick his head into the room.

"Ty's not answering his phone," Zane said.

Kelly slipped into the cabin and closed the door behind him. "You mind company?"

Zane shook his head forlornly, eyes fixed to the phone.

Kelly sat on the edge of the bed beside him, and eventually Zane realized that Kelly's hand was resting on his shoulder. Zane forced himself to meet Kelly's eyes.

"We'll find him," Kelly promised. "We're with you, Zane."

Zane tried to smile, but he failed miserably.

"Come up top with us? Help us plan?" Kelly asked. Zane could tell he was slipping into his corpsman mode. There was something soothing about it. "Let me look you over, make sure you're not hurt anywhere."

Zane nodded, pushing to his feet. He held the phone to his chest like it was a lifeline to his missing husband, and followed Kelly out of the cabin. He suspected Kelly wasn't actually concerned about his physical state; he was just trying to lure him out of the cabin. Zane was willing to play along for the Doc.

Nick and Liam were sitting at the banquette, watching him warily when he got to the top of the steps.

Zane gritted his teeth, feeling inordinately hostile toward Nick, and justifiably hostile toward Liam. He jutted his chin out and set the shotgun on the table in front of them. "I'm sorry about the holes in your boat," he told Nick.

Nick sighed. "At least it still floats."

Zane perched on the edge of the pilot's chair, and Kelly shone a light in his eyes. Then he checked all his reflexes by knocking his knuckles against Zane's joints, and then had Zane follow his finger as he moved it in front of him. Finally, he asked Zane a few questions and declared him fit. There were aches and pains in places Zane assumed had come from debris in the exploding building, but hell, at least he could still see this time.

Kelly went to the galley for glasses of water, and then slid into the banquette beside Nick.

"I need to find Ty," Zane said when it looked like no one else was planning to speak.

Nick and Kelly exchanged a look, and Liam cocked his head at Zane like he was studying an animal in a zoo.

"How?" Liam asked.

"I don't know! But I have to find him! Do you fucking understand? I'm going to find him, and if you stand in my fucking way you'll be the first to die!"

Liam waved a hand like a matador at an enraged bull. "You really want to start with me, mate?"

"Shut the fuck up," Nick grunted. He had his hand over his eyes, both elbows on the table. "One day you're going run your mouth at someone and they'll shoot you in the face just to shut you up."

"Like today," Zane growled.

Liam winked at him.

"We need to gather our resources," Nick continued, pointedly ignoring Liam and Zane's sniping. "When the boys get here, we'll set sail. If we intend to face down the cartel, we'll need weapons, and we'll need warm bodies. I'll call Julian Cross and see if he can help us."

"Cross?" Zane asked. "Why the hell would he help us?"

"Because he owes me," Nick said. "And he owes you and Ty even more. He'll help us with artillery if nothing else."

Zane sat back and took a deep breath, trying to stay calm. "So your plan is to just . . . sit and wait until more help arrives? Maiden in distress on a balcony?"

Nick glared at him for a few seconds. "Yeah, Zane," he said, and tapped Kelly on the arm. Kelly moved out of the bench seat, and Nick scooted out behind him to stand. He walked past Kelly and then Zane, yanking the phone out of Zane's hand as he went. "That's my fucking plan."

Zane almost followed him, but he took a deep breath instead and stayed put. Fighting with the few men still here to help him would not do him any good. The door slammed behind Nick as he left the salon.

"Fucker," Zane said under his breath.

Kelly threw himself back into the banquette. "None of this is his fault, Zane."

"Isn't it?" Liam asked with a laugh.

"Shut up," Zane snarled. "I'm so fucking sick of you and your stupid accent and . . ." Zane trailed off with an honest to God growl and made a throttling motion with both hands in Liam's direction.

Liam chuckled quietly.

"Why did you try to kill him?" Zane asked.

"Pardon?"

"Ty! You're here claiming you're helping us again, but the last we saw of you, you were trying to put an armor-piercing round in his heart."

"It weren't me, mate."

"Bullshit!"

Liam slammed his hand against the table, startling both Zane and Kelly with his sudden vehemence. "I didn't switch those bullets!"

"Why should we believe you?" Kelly asked.

"You weren't there," Liam snapped at him. "I had no reason to kill Tyler then, and I have no reason to lie now."

"Prove it," Zane grunted.

Liam barked a laugh, shrugging with both hands outstretched. "How?"

Zane raised an eyebrow. "Be creative."

"Look, I'm not discounting that I may have made a mistake. I don't make them often, and I don't think I mixed those bullets up. But I didn't mix them on purpose, and if someone did, I'm betting it was on your end."

"Our end?" Kelly asked, bristling at the implication.

"Only a few people had access to those bullets before I loaded my gun."

"Yeah," Zane huffed. "You. Me. Ty. Sidewinder. That's about it."

"You're right." Liam crossed his arms and sat back like he'd just proved his point.

Zane and Kelly exchanged a quick glance. Zane couldn't help but wonder if Liam was actually telling the truth. Not necessarily about a Sidewinder switching that bullet, but about him being innocent of it. He seemed to be genuine, but then, he could have declared the sky was green and done so with complete sincerity.

The door to the salon burst open before anyone could say more. Zane lurched to his feet, hand immediately going to his hip even though he wasn't armed.

Nick was holding the phone up, his green eyes wide and sparking. "Ty's alive."

Zane took an impulsive step toward him, his breath catching in his chest. "Who is that?"

"It's Cross," Nick said, and put the phone on the table.

"Gentlemen," Julian Cross said over the speaker.

Zane gripped the edge of the table and leaned in. "You know where Ty is?"

"I heard from Preston just an hour ago. Grady was taken to Langley."

Zane met Nick's eyes, confusion and relief and terror all sweeping through him. "The CIA has Ty?"

"He has accepted a position with the Company in exchange for their help."

Zane ran both hands through his hair and bent over the table, feeling ill. "Oh God, Ty. You idiot."

"Are you saying the CIA is declaring war on the Vega cartel?" Nick asked in disbelief.

"Not just the cartel, mate," Liam told them. "If they snatched Tyler up, they've declared themselves against the NIA as well. This just became a government pissing match."

"Why are they invested?" Zane asked Julian.

"I don't know. Preston said the Agency was on the lookout for signs of life from you. He knew if there was the slightest chance of you reaching out for help, I might hear from you, so he rang me up."

"Ty's okay?" Zane asked shakily.

"I'm not sure making a deal with the CIA could be classified as such."

"How do we find him?" Kelly asked. "Can you get a message to him?"

"That I don't know. Preston's gone dark so there's no reaching him again. I'll be flying into DC; don't be late picking me up, hmm?"

He ended the call before they could grill him further. Zane sank to the bench nearby, staring at the phone. "How long will it take us to get to DC?" he asked Nick.

"On the *Fiddler*? Three to five hours, depending on the Patapsco tides. We'll set off as soon as Johns and Digger get here."

"Good." Zane picked up the phone. "I got a few other people might want a piece of this too."

Ty went to the marina first, only to find an empty slip where the *Fiddler* had been. The harbormaster had no record of her leaving, and no idea when or where she'd gone.

That meant Nick had gotten out alive, if no one else. Ty had no way of reaching him, though, so he called Detective Alan Hagan of the Boston PD. He discovered that Nick's partner had put out a missing person's report on Nick and was tearing Boston apart trying to find him. Ty asked to be kept in the loop, then hung up, feeling guilty for not letting Hagan know Nick was alive out there somewhere.

Ty would give anything for a call like that about Zane.

Without anywhere else to turn, he headed for his row house.

He sat for hours in the driver's seat of a vehicle parked a block away, observing from a safe distance. The crime scene had been cleared surprisingly quickly. Either that was really good or really bad for him. There were two officers left guarding his front door, and probably one or two watching the back.

As he pondered where else they might be stationed, he realized it was a trap. The men on his front stoop were both smoking cigarettes. There were no cones to keep traffic away from the car where the CIA claimed Nick and Liam had massacred two cartel thugs. There were no flags denoting evidence, there was no crime scene tape. These weren't city cops. No. This was either the cartel or the NIA. They'd set two men out front like shining beacons for Ty to see, knowing he'd try to avoid them and sneak in another way.

God knew what awaited him inside.

But he had to get into the house. The CIA had provided him with *almost* everything he would need for the next two weeks. The last item was inside.

He glanced up at the sky. It was overcast and dreary, and the sun would be setting soon. Down the street, gaudy Christmas lights were hanging off one of the upper balconies. He was one of the only people in the neighborhood who didn't mind the frat boys who lived there. He'd spoken with them a few times, letting them know that if they stayed in line, he wouldn't rig their kegs to explode when they had parties. They were decent guys.

Ty smiled as an idea formed. When night fell, he'd be able to get into his house.

He wrapped his thin coat tight and hunkered down in the cab of his borrowed truck. When Preston had given him open access to Langley's fleet, Ty was pretty sure no one had expected him to ask for the landscaper's old Chevy. That was one thing he had to look forward to for the rest of his useful days: confounding baby CIA agents.

He snorted. As long as you did what the CIA told you to do, they were good employers. Of course, if Zane found out about this . . .

Ty cleared his throat, his eyes burning. Zane was alive. He would continue to believe that until he saw a body.

Warmth seeped in on Ty as he grew tired. Idle time was dangerous during missions. You let your guard down, allowed your mind to wander and your body rest, and the adrenaline died away.

His thoughts strayed to Zane again and he sniffed. All the things he'd said and done, all the lies he'd let blacken his soul. He'd never deserved something as good as Zane in his life, but somehow he'd managed to find it anyway. And Richard Burns, the very same man he'd always credited with giving him Zane, with giving him a reason to stay with Zane, was the man who'd torn him away, even from beyond the grave.

He was surprised to find his eyes burning when he closed them, and warm tears slid down his cheeks into his several days' worth of beard when he opened them again. He wiped at his face with his coat sleeve, shaking his head. He had to concern himself with trivial things like not getting killed before he could ponder Zane and what he would do if his husband was really dead.

He shifted and glanced down the street at the unmarked patrol car. It was a BPD car, not the standard-issue sedan or SUV most of the alphabet soup agencies would drive. Either the BPD was in on the hunt for him, or somewhere two poor patrol officers were tied up or dead.

When the darkness was almost upon him, Ty pulled away from the spot by the curb and watched in the rearview mirror as he drove away. The cop car didn't move, and Ty took the first turn. He headed for the ABC store several blocks away, and ten minutes later he tossed his haul into the bed of the truck and headed back toward his house. He parked as close to the house with the Christmas lights as possible. They were having a party, and Ty had come bearing gifts.

When the kid opened the door, Ty smiled widely and tapped the toe of his Converse against the keg he'd set on the stoop. "I need a favor," he told the kid, who was grinning at him, slightly glazed.

As two giddy pre-med students hauled the keg inside, the kid who'd answered the door led Ty up the two flights of stairs to the top floor. All these row houses were built pretty much the same. The kid was so buzzed he didn't even ask questions as Ty stepped out onto the rooftop terrace and glanced up the street.

"Thanks, kid," Ty said as he stepped closer to the railing.

"Hey, can I video this for YouTube?" the kid asked. He stepped up next to Ty and looked over at the next balcony, probably thinking that Ty actually planned to try jumping it.

"Sure, why not," Ty answered with a small groan. He didn't want the kid to get suspicious about why Ty was choosing to climb from rooftop to rooftop to get into his house instead of just calling a locksmith or something.

The houses along the street alternated between having a third-floor balcony and a rooftop terrace. Which meant to get from terrace to terrace, you had to climb over whatever partition the owners had chosen to put up. To Ty's relief, the way was mostly clear. A few potted plants and a privacy fence, and he would have access to his own home.

He didn't give the neighbor kid time to go back and get a video camera; he leaped over the partition and scuttled across the next terrace, keeping his silhouette low.

In a matter of moments, he was climbing down to the third-floor balcony of his home, three stories above the heads of the men loitering on his stoop. He tried to ease the door open, but it didn't budge. He scowled at it, pushing the handle harder. The latch moved, which meant it was unlocked. But it wasn't going anywhere.

Ty cursed as he remembered the warped doorframe he'd been meaning to fix. He'd put it off, and put it off, making excuses whenever Zane mentioned it, ignoring it like he had all the time in the world to address it. He gritted his teeth, his eyes watering as he shoved his shoulder into the door. It rattled, but it wasn't going anywhere.

"Really, Beaumont?" he said under his breath. He stared at the wooden boards of the balcony, at the flower pot where they'd discarded cigars and filters after smoking. He couldn't even break into his own house. How the fuck was he supposed to function in the fucking real world if he couldn't even break into his own god damn house?

He wiped his cheek on his shoulder, taking a deep breath. Then he pushed the handle, lifted the door so it would fit in the frame better, and pushed with all his strength. The door flew open, and Ty went tumbling into the attic room. He sprawled on the floor, blinking at the ceiling and wondering if just giving up was an option.

"You're okay," he whispered, and he hefted himself off the ground.

The first thing he did was move into the spare bedroom on the third floor and open up the wardrobe there. He searched through the array of boxes, some of them wooden, some of them metal, all of them antique and given to him as gifts. He kept all the odds and ends from his cases in them, a closet pack rat. It would serve him well now.

He found the box that held the makeup they'd used on him when he and Zane had been forced to assume the identities of Del and Corbin Porter on a cruise ship full of people who'd wanted to kill them. Inside was a leftover scrap of the synthetic skin graft they'd used to cover his tattoo. He smiled grimly as he palmed it and the glue that went with it.

He closed up the wardrobe and left the room, creeping down the stairs to the second level and their bedroom. He changed clothes quickly, but got stuck when he pulled out the closest T-shirt. He thought he was grabbing a plain drab-green shirt, but it had two panda bears wrestling on it, and under them in dramatic lettering it read WWF.

Zane had given it to him as a joke after Ty had forced him to donate a thousand dollars to the World Wildlife Fund so he could get a stuffed tiger. Ty put the shirt to his lips, closing his eyes and inhaling deeply, letting the ache settle low and hard. Then he shook the pain off and yanked the shirt over his head, grabbing his duffel that always remained mostly packed from the closet. Zane had stolen things out of it, damn him. Ty had never restocked it after Zane had taken it, and now he might pay for it.

He looked around at the bedroom, feeling cold all over. The sheets were tangled, the covers tossed aside. Was that the last time he'd ever be able to hold Zane? How could it be, when they'd done so little to make it special?

Again, he shook the thought off and took down the lockbox from inside the safe at the top of his closet, then opened it. His gun was gone. Fuck! Zane had cleaned him out. How had he gotten so complacent he hadn't made sure everything was back in order?

He stared at the empty indentation for a long moment before merely closing the box and replacing it. He pulled down another, smaller metal box and opened it, sifting through the random bits and pieces of things people had sent him over the years to find a set of handcuffs inside. He pulled the key from them, pocketing it. He replaced everything as quietly as he could, then made his way downstairs to the kitchen.

He weighed the key in his hand. It was heavy, but he thought the synthetic bit of skin would hold it. He only had enough for one attempt.

He went to the bathroom, closing the door carefully and stuffing a towel along the bottom to block the light when he turned it on. He laid out his haul and shook his head. "Pretty pitiful, Grady," he muttered as he wet a washcloth and wiped down his forearm, making certain he could reach the spot if his wrists happened to be handcuffed together. Then he went about covering the key with the false skin there.

It took more time than he'd expected it to, and by the time he'd finished it and wrapped a leather wrist cuff around it to secure it, he was getting antsy. He'd been here too long.

He gathered up his duffel, moving in utter silence. He held a penlight in his mouth and carried his half-empty bag over his shoulder, unsnapping it as he went off in search of his last item. The thing he'd really come here for. He stepped up to a framed photograph, the one of him and Zane sitting together on the porch of his parents' home in West Virginia. They both had their heads lowered, foreheads touching, in the middle of a fit of laughter that had wound up with Ty flat on his back, guffawing, and Zane watching him with a shining light in eyes.

Ty took the photo off the wall and carefully removed the back from the frame. Behind the black-and-white photo was a copy of the same picture in color. Ty took it, running his thumb over Zane's face before he slipped it into the front pocket of his shirt and put the frame back together. He replaced it on the wall, staring at Zane's handsome face for a few more seconds before he forced himself to move on.

He grabbed his bag and made his way back to the top floor of his row house.

If this was the last time he ever set foot in his home, well . . . he was okay with that now.

"I'm just saying, if you're going to blow shit up, you do it right!"

Zane rubbed his eyes. He didn't know if he could keep listening to this for the next couple hours as they sailed the last leg to DC.

Digger was ranting at Owen, who was sitting on the sofa and counting out his pain pills like he was considering taking them all at once.

"If it'd been me blowing that shit up? Ain't none of us would have crawled out. That's all I'm saying."

"Well, thank God for half-assed bad guys," Owen said, as if to appease him.

"Damn straight."

Zane was sitting opposite them, next to Clancy, staring at them with his mouth hanging open. It didn't matter how much time he spent with Sidewinder, he never failed to be terrified by them.

Owen narrowed his eyes at the two pills remaining in his hand after he'd counted off the rest and put them back in their bottle.

"Don't take those," Kelly said loudly, pointing at Owen from the banquette on the opposite end of the boat, like a mother shouting at her children in a grocery store. "Conserve."

Owen grumbled under his breath, but he dropped the last two in the bottle and put the cap on it.

Perrimore and Lassiter were both in the kitchen, watching Digger rant with much the same expression Zane had assumed when the Cajun had started in on why the bomb hadn't taken them out in the basement. The bottom line, Zane had deciphered, was that whoever had set the bomb simply hadn't known the basement existed. Ty's secret room had saved all of them.

Well. Almost all of them.

Scott Alston had made every move thinking he was just doing his job. He was no more guilty in all of this than Ty was, or Zane. He'd endangered Ty and Zane's lives, but certainly not on purpose. Hell, he'd even tried to cover for them when he thought they'd been the ones to take Burns out. Zane couldn't find it in him to be angry with him, and he mourned the man. Alston had died down there with them, prepared to atone for his actions, prepared to help them fight back. He'd died because he'd thrown his body over the satchel of evidence Zane had brought downstairs, to protect it from the flaming debris falling around them.

Zane had told Perrimore and Lassiter only that last part when he'd called them and explained what was happening. They would never know what else Alston had done. Zane and Clancy had both sworn to take that to their graves.

Zane had been shocked to see Clancy when she'd arrived from the hospital with Digger and Owen and the satchel full of photos and printouts Zane had thought they'd lost. She was beat all to hell, with a few broken ribs and a severe cough from all the smoke she'd inhaled. She'd looked determined when she'd stepped onto the *Fiddler*, though, so much so that Zane hadn't mentioned she shouldn't be there, as hurt as she was.

Alston had been her partner, she'd said. And Zane and Ty were her friends. If this was her last stand, at least she'd go down in a blaze of glory.

The thought sent a pang through Zane as he glanced around at the three FBI agents who were on the *Fiddler* simply because he'd called them to arms. They didn't have to be here. This wasn't their fight. They were risking far more than just their jobs by going rogue like this, and yet here they were. Zane had once told Nick that he'd never had friends like Ty had in Sidewinder, that he'd never known that sort of loyalty.

He'd been wrong.

"What's the plan, Garrett?" Perrimore asked as he sat on the coffee table in front of Zane.

Zane glanced around, taking a second to realize that everyone was watching him. Even Liam and Kelly, who were craning their heads to see into the salon.

Zane swallowed past the lump that had developed in his throat and sat up straight, trying to fake confidence he wasn't feeling. "My only priority right now is to find Ty," he announced. "And I'm going to operate under the assumption that his priority right now is to find me. He wouldn't accept that I was dead so easily; he'd keep searching until someone showed him a body."

Liam cleared his throat and shifted in his chair, grumbling something to Nick about a finger. Nick either didn't hear him, or pretended not to as he navigated the *Fiddler* in the dark.

"Okay, so you're both after each other. Do you have some sort of emergency backup plan you're supposed to follow in case you're separated like this?" Clancy asked.

Zane shook his head, blushing a little as the others complained.

"As obsessed as you are over the whole zombie genre, you don't have safe zone plans?" Perrimore teased. He smacked Zane's knee, chuckling like he hoped the light ribbing would raise Zane's spirits.

Zane's spirit didn't need to be raised, not right now. "I need to think like Ty," he declared. "Where he'd go next, what his next stop would be."

"What if you're thinking like Ty, and Ty's thinking like you?" Owen asked.

"Ty don't have the pictures from the SD card," Digger said. He lounged back into the sofa, putting his arm around Owen and patting him like he would to console a child with a scraped knee. Owen was either grudgingly allowing it or he was too drugged to notice.

"He'd need to pick up the trail," Zane agreed. "And he wouldn't know my satchel made it out of that building. He might be operating under the assumption that we'll need to somehow recover that information, pick up the trail another way."

"Where'd you get the originals?" Lassiter asked. He sounded like he was dreading the answer, like he couldn't possibly imagine what sordid ways Zane and Sidewinder had been operating under.

"Richard Burns's home," Zane answered with a sigh.

Laura Burns let Ty in with a watery smile and tight hug he wasn't sure he deserved.

"Tyler, it's so good to see you!" She ushered him into the house and gave him another hug. Ty had to look away from the oversized photo in the foyer of Richard Burns and his wife and dogs as she held on to him.

"How have you been?" he asked, forcing the words out through tightness in his throat that caught him off guard.

"Doing well, under the circumstances. To what do I owe the pleasure?"

Ty winced. "I wish this were just a social call, but I'm afraid I'm working a case."

"In DC? I thought you'd retired."

Ty smiled and glanced around, not willing to answer her. "Would you mind if I had a look at Uncle's Dick's study?"

She took a small step back, her brow furrowed. "Of course," she said after a few tense seconds where Ty thought she might refuse. She turned and gestured for him to follow her through the home. "You know, I've been meaning to ask you and Deacon here so you could go through his things. Your father, too. There's probably so much Richard had hidden away that he would have wanted you boys to have."

"Hundreds of millions of things, I bet," Ty muttered.

They walked past the dining room, and Ty stutter-stepped as he glanced in. The safe in the floor Nick had told him about was still a gaping hole near the bay window.

"Laura," Ty blurted, and she turned to face him. Ty felt almost guilty for playing dumb, but it was much easier than the truth would be right now. "What happened to the floor in here?"

She came closer and looked in, sighing. "Richard had a secret safe in there. Someone broke in, trying to get to it."

"Did they?"

"No. A few cops came by, but no one could get into it. I was hoping maybe your father would know what was in it, but I haven't gotten around to calling him."

"Could I try?" Ty asked.

"If you've got the time. It's going to cost so much money to get into it, it's not worth messing with. I'm going to have someone fix the floor over it before I sell the house."

Ty moved closer to peer into the hole.

"What do you need?" Laura asked.

Ty shrugged, raising an eyebrow at the safe. "Maybe a glass of water," he said as he rolled up his sleeves and sank to his knees next to the hole.

It took him longer than he would have liked to get into the safe, but he was still pleased with himself when he heard the telltale pop of the catch inside. Laura gave him a pat on the back when he lifted the lid, as if what he'd done was something any locksmith could have accomplished for ten bucks an hour instead of years of covert training.

Ty knew what he'd find in the safe, but he was still disappointed when he reached in and only pulled out a single book.

"Edgar Allan Poe?" Laura asked.

Ty shrugged. He wasn't sure if it was some random book Burns had chosen from his library, or if Burns had known on some level that Ty and Zane would end up here. It definitely sent a message, whether Burns had meant for it to or not.

Ty paged through it, shaking it to see if anything fell out. Then he sat back on his ass and stared at the cover. "Would you mind if I kept this?"

Her hand on his shoulder squeezed. "Sure."

Ty stared at it for a few more seconds, then climbed to his feet. He followed her to Burns's study, and she left him alone among Richard Burns's things.

Ty set the book aside, trying to decide where to start.

The sun had been down for hours by the time Laura returned. "Tyler?"

"Ma'am?" Ty said, and he popped his head up from behind the large walnut desk in the center of the room.

Her voice was shaky, and she had her finger twined around her necklace. "This may be my old lady imagination getting to me, but I think there's someone outside."

Ty clambered to his feet, flipping off the desk lamp next to him. "What'd you hear?"

"I saw a shadow in the backyard from the sunroom window. Heard a whisper. Should I call the police?"

Ty shook his head and drew his shiny new CIA-issue Glock. "Go to your bedroom and lock the door, okay? Stay away from the window. I'll take care of it."

Laura was already moving before Ty had finished. She'd been married to a Marine and FBI agent long enough that she knew when to question and when to take action. She turned off lights as she went, throwing Ty and the lower level of the big house into shadow.

Ty moved fast and low, going to the back to peer out the windows. Laura had been right. He caught glimpses of shadows moving. He had no idea who might be out there. Was it the cartel, coming to find information? Whoever had tried robbing that safe back to finish the job? Hell, it could even be the NIA making their move.

Ty watched out the window for a few more seconds, and then he headed for the kitchen and the back entrance to the home. He pulled his buff up onto his face to cover it, and slipped the hood of his coat over his head to blend into the darkness as best he could. Then he flicked the motion sensor lights off so they wouldn't flick on when he started moving around out there.

Once outside, he could hear whispers. It sounded almost like quiet bickering, and he had to pause and wonder if these weren't just neighborhood kids fucking around in the snow.

Ty began moving toward the detached garage, wincing with each footstep in the crunching snow. The voices hushed, and Ty moved several more steps before crouching at the corner of the house.

He checked his weapon, then peered across the expansive backyard at the tree line. They were out there, he knew, probably waiting until he gave them a target.

Out of the corner of his eye, he caught movement from the other side of the garage. A big man stepped halfway out of cover, wearing winter tactical gear, greasepaint, a scarf over half his face, and sunglasses meant to mute the glare off the newly fallen snow. He raised a gun and took aim at the security camera on the corner of the home.

Ty moved without thinking, knowing this was his only chance to pick this guy off. He didn't want to make noise by firing his Glock, and the angle was useless for throwing a knife. He wanted to take the man alive to question him, maybe even use him against whoever else was out there.

He rushed the big guy, tackling him to the snow. They both rolled and popped up in an instant, squaring off against each other. Ty took in the size of the man and sort of wished he'd realized how big his opponent was *before* he'd tackled him.

Ty kicked the gun from his opponent's hands and raised his own, but the guy was fast, ducking and viciously swinging one leg against Ty's calves, knocking him off-balance. In the seconds gained, the attacker pulled wicked-looking knives from sheaths strapped to his thighs, flipping them in his hands to thump against the fingerless leather gloves that covered his palms.

Ty fought through the deep snow to his feet, stumbling back and falling on his ass again as the man slashed at him. He scrambled backward through the snow, his fingers going numb, barely staying far enough away to keep the knives from drawing blood.

The man kicked Ty's head before he could get out of reach. Ty's ears rang, drowning out everything but a buzzing sound in the back of his head. He drove one heavy combat boot at his attacker's knee with every intention of breaking his kneecap, but a well-muscled forearm smacked his leg to the side, and the knife came down fast, glancing off the butt of Ty's gun as Ty tried to shield himself.

A husky voice swore in crude Spanish.

Ty bared his teeth and took advantage of the momentum of his opponent's arm swing to hop to his feet, pulling his own knife from the sheath at his thigh. The oversized blade flashed in the moonlight. He goaded the man on with a curl of his fingers, then swung the hilt of his knife, hitting the man in the ear and sending him staggering sideways.

Ty came at him again, determined to incapacitate him so he'd be easy to question. The man righted himself and flipped his knives so the blades faced down. Ty's free arm shot up and stopped a punch, and then he wrapped his arm around the man's elbow and used the leverage to jerk his shoulder up and out. They were entangled as Ty tried with all his strength to break the man's arm, but they were at a standstill. The man snorted at him, gritting his teeth as he fought against the pressure Ty was exerting. He was bigger than Ty, and maybe even stronger. The struggle brought them so close that Ty could see the reflection of his own eyes in the man's sunglasses.

"Only *pendejos* wear sunglasses at night," Ty ground out, voice strained thin with effort.

The guy's head turned toward him. "Grady?" he said, his voice garbled amidst the ringing in Ty's ears.

Ty shouted and shoved at the man's wrist. He heard a crack, but the man just growled like an angry bear Ty had poked with a stick.

He dropped to one knee without warning, using the momentum to drag Ty over his shoulder and flip him to the ground. Ty cursed as his back hit the hard-packed snow. Son of a bitch, he'd just finished teaching Zane that move, he should have been able to defend it better.

Off-balance with one foot stuck in the snow, the cartel thug fell over along with Ty, one of the knives flying away into the night.

Ty caught his foot and trapped the heavy winter boot against his chest. He twisted the toes to the side and forced the man's entire body to contort in the snow, wrenching a pained scream from his opponent as he kicked at the small of his back. Ty managed two hard, sharp kicks and then rolled on top of him. He slapped a hand across the man's mouth so he couldn't call for help from the rest of his team.

"Say *hola* to de la Vega when you get to Hell," Ty growled as he straddled him, raising the knife for the final blow. This guy was too fucking big to take prisoner; Ty would have to try to pick off one of the others instead.

The man scrabbled at Ty's arm and hand, thrashing his head back and forth as he tried to free his mouth. Ty struggled to keep him silent, unable to get a grip on his knife for the killing blow. The guy managed to grab at Ty's buff, pulling it down to reveal his face.

Ty snarled at him, flipping the knife over his fingers. But the guy was still struggling, desperately fighting for his life. He whipped his head again, sending his sunglasses skittering to the side and dragging his scarf off the lower half of his face. Ty raised the knife even as the man looked up at him with dark, familiar eyes and gasped Ty's name.

Ty's arm stuttered in its arc. "Zane?"

Zane's response was lost in the blast of a suppressed round. Ty was thrown backward, sliding across the salted driveway on his back.

Stunned, Ty lay spread-eagle in the salt and snow he had dredged up, trying to breathe as time slowed. He couldn't pull air in, and his attempts sounded like Darth Vader having an asthma attack. He wasn't wearing a vest, but it didn't feel like there'd been any penetration. Something had stopped the projectile, but it hadn't stopped the explosive impact.

The yard became a mess of flashing and shadows as lights in the neighboring houses flared on. Snow fell peacefully through the beams. Sounds didn't quite reach Ty's awareness, and there was an undercurrent of rushing in his ears he knew was his blood through his veins. Everything had that "you almost died again, you asshole" sheen to it that made it seem like a dream. There was hissed whispering, and finally a shout or two, and it all mixed with the clamor in Ty's ears.

The next thing that registered was a shadow falling across his face and someone crouching next to him.

"Ty!" Zane cried. He cut Ty's buff away from his face so he could breathe easier, and pawed at Ty's heavy coat. He turned toward the trees and shouted, "Hold your fire!"

"Did you shoot me?" Ty uttered, dazed and incredulous. "You dick."

"Come on, baby," Zane growled as he gripped under Ty's arms and dragged him toward the shelter of the garage. He stretched above his head to flick on the work light attached to the garage opener, bathing them both in a sickly yellow glow. "Are you hurt?"

Ty fought to get off his back, finally taking Zane's hand to sit up. It was difficult with the burden of the pain in his sternum, and even more difficult to look down and see what sort of damage the bullet had done to his chest. Ty patted weakly at his jacket as he shook his head, trying to think clearly and catch his breath. His hands were shaking. He didn't care who you were, if you took one in the chest, adrenaline was going to have its way with you.

"It's just a beanbag, baby," Zane whispered, and he took Ty's face in his hands. "You're okay."

He looked up at Zane, who was running his trembling fingers through Ty's hair and over his face and neck. Ty tried to catch his breath as he stared. "Are you alive?"

Zane waited a few heartbeats before pressing his forehead to Ty's. "I am now."

"You shot me, Zane."

"Baby, if I'd shot you, you wouldn't be alive complaining about it," Zane said, then leaned sideways to check the backyard.

"Well, someone shot me. It's upsetting."

Zane glared at him before rolling his eyes. "Kelly had the beanbags, you can talk to him about it later."

"It's very upsetting," Ty repeated, pressing his hand to his chest.

Zane jammed Ty's gun into his waistband and went down on one knee next to Ty. He slid his fingers under Ty's chin and tilted his face up, though Ty knew he wouldn't be able to see much in the yellow wash.

Ty let him look for a moment, gazing into eyes he'd been afraid he'd never see again. "Help me up."

"Stay down for a minute," Zane murmured. He smoothed his hand over Ty's face, his hands lingering.

Ty reached for him, taking a single tendril of Zane's damp, curly hair and twining it around his finger as he gazed into Zane's eyes, so dark and calm. His mere presence was as soothing to Ty as a warm breeze on a fall day. "I thought you were dead," he whispered.

Zane was silent, nodding, his brow furrowing as Ty clutched at his hair and pulled him closer to cling to him. Zane's arms wrapped around him, and he buried his face in Ty's neck. "I thought I'd lost you."

"I told you I'd always find you, Zane," Ty choked out. He held to him, clutching at his wet jacket. He could hear the others talking and moving in the earpiece Zane wore, but for the moment, Zane was his whole world.

Zane slid an arm around his back and carefully levered Ty to his feet. "I was hoping we'd find you here. Meeting could have gone smoother, but still."

"Tell me about it. You hit me. Hard."

"You called me a *pendejo*."

"You are a *pendejo*," Ty grunted, voice strained. "I had to pick up the trail you were following if I had any hope of finding you. This was the only lead I had."

"That's why we came here. Hoping to find you. Julian Cross said you joined the CIA." His voice went softer as his arm tightened on Ty's waist. "You fucking idiot."

"Hey, save the lecture for later, Garrett. I need a hug."

Zane pulled him into his arms and kissed him. Even with the greasepaint on, it was probably the most delightful kiss Ty had ever been given.

They were still clinging to each other when footsteps crunched in the snow. He gripped his gun, which was stuffed in Zane's pants. Over Zane's shoulder, he saw two men come around the edge of the building, guns raised. They both lowered them, though, and glanced at each other. They were dressed just like Zane, in tactical winter gear, scarves over their faces and tinted ski goggles or sunglasses. The taller of the two put his hand to his throat and said, "Doc just shot Grady."

The shorter man smacked the taller one in the chest and yanked his goggles off. "Like no one's ever wanted to do that before!" Kelly huffed.

Another man came jogging up, and Ty would have recognized Liam Bell's voice anywhere. "You literally bagged you one," he told Kelly, chuckling.

The taller man muffled a laugh.

"No, wait wait. Yanks say 'you beaned him,' right?" Liam said, and both men began to snicker.

Ty growled and lunged toward him, but Zane caught him, holding on to him so tight that Ty yipped with the pain in his chest. He kept fighting to get at Liam, shoving away from Zane, his feet sliding on the icy concrete. "You son of a bitch!" He pointed at Liam and bared his teeth. "I'll kill you. I'll fucking kill you!"

Liam raised an eyebrow and glanced at the others, leaning further away from Ty and Zane. "I'll just be in the car, shall I?"

The tallest of the three nodded wordlessly, and as Liam disappeared from sight, the man removed his protective headgear to reveal his face.

Ty came up short, cocking his head at Julian Cross. "Where the hell'd you come from?"

Julian arched an eyebrow, not even offering him a smile. "Cameron made me come. Something about being a good person," he said as he walked away, shaking his head.

CHAPTER 7

Ty had never seen the *Fiddler* with so many people on it. Part of him, the part that was afraid of small, dark spaces because of the thought of the earth crumbling over him, was sort of worried about the fucking yacht sinking under the weight.

The yacht wasn't the only thing feeling heavy. On the ride to the harbor, Zane told Ty about losing Alston in the explosion at their bookstore, and everyone who'd been in that basement was beat all to hell. Even Liam and Nick were in rough shape, with Nick's hands and forearms bandaged, and Liam's forehead neatly stitched.

"They saved us," Zane had told him in the car.

"And now, no one knows if you're still kicking or not," Ty had added amidst the flashing from the headlights of oncoming traffic. "That advantage won't last long."

"No, it won't." Zane had kept his hand in Ty's as Ty drove, clutching it as if he never intended to let go. Ty was ambidextrous, so he supposed he could afford to lose that arm if it meant never ever going through this kind of pain again, thinking Zane was gone.

They'd managed to disengage by the time they'd reached the boat, of course. They were given the VIP cabin, and frankly Ty would have taken it by force anyway. He saw the shotgun spray in the door to Nick's cabin as they passed, but Zane didn't even bat an eye at it, so Ty followed him without pausing to examine it. When they got to the VIP cabin, Zane tossed himself face-first onto the bed without a word.

Ty stood at the door, though, looking at the ruined casing and the splintered wood and frowning. "Did Liam keep Nick locked up in here?"

"No, that was me," Zane answered, his voice muffled by the covers. He was smearing greasepaint all over the quilt, but Ty supposed the *Fiddler* was beyond caring about its façade. It had so many holes in it now Ty really did wonder if it would keep floating.

"Poor *Fiddler*," Ty murmured, running his hand along its hull and patting it as if in consolation. He heard a thump behind him and turned to look down the corridor. A shadow moved in the main cabin, as if someone had come down the stairs just fast enough for Ty to miss them. With so many people on board, though, Ty wasn't exactly expecting privacy. He patted the *Fiddler*'s hull again, heading toward the bed.

Zane grunted, but didn't comment.

Ty tossed his coat at the bed, stretching out sore muscles and wincing when he found a few scrapes and bruises he hadn't noticed earning. Zane had pretty much beat the shit out of him.

"It's entirely possible I'm too old for this shit," he said, and Zane nodded. Ty snorted and stared at him for a few long seconds.

Zane finally pushed himself up and started trying to get out of his gear. He seemed to be having trouble with the Velcro and the straps, so Ty helped him out of his flak jacket. He let his fingers linger against Zane's muscles.

Zane rewarded him with a smile, albeit a weary one. "You okay?"

Ty shrugged, nodding.

"Have you forgiven him?"

Ty's breath caught, and he glanced around the cabin, looking for Nick through the open door again. The rift in their friendship pulled at him just as viscerally as the scars on the *Fiddler*'s walls. Then Ty noticed the white noise of running water coming from down the corridor. His nerves tumbled when he thought about going in there.

"You need to. For your sake and his." Zane patted Ty's cheek and shrugged out of his shirt.

Ty lowered his head and shook it, hooking his fingers in Zane's belt loops. "I'm not letting you out of my sight right now."

"I need to shower to get this stuff off me," Zane argued. Ty sighed as he searched Zane's eyes. He wondered which Sidewinder had put the camo paint on Zane's face, and if there was photographic evidence he could see later. Zane smiled, even though the expression was mostly marred by the greasepaint. "You need to talk to him, I need to clean up. I'll be right here when you're done."

Ty could take a hint that loud. He grudgingly headed out, leaving Zane to take his shower. But when he stepped into the main cabin and peered through the door of the head, he stopped short, watching as Nick hung his head over the sink and splashed his face with water over and over. He apparently hadn't heard Ty's quiet approach with the water on.

A towel was slung over Nick's bare shoulder, and he was trying to rub the greasepaint off his face with the tips of his fingers, but it wasn't working very well. He'd only gotten about half of it off. His actions were slow and deliberate, his eyes never rising to meet his reflection in the mirror. He finally gave up and straightened. The crisscrossed scars on his back stretched across tense muscles, the large Celtic cross flexing like severed wings against his shoulder blades.

He wet the towel, then scrubbed at his face. It was a routine Ty was well familiar with. How many times had he and Nick stood side by side at a mirror, wiping off the greasepaint in a heavy silence? Or more often, wiping themselves clean as Kelly bitched at them from the doorway to let him stitch them up.

Nick cut the faucet off and looked up. His eyes met Ty's in the mirror, and he froze. "Hey."

"Missed a spot," Ty said with a small smile.

Nick turned his head from side to side to find the remaining paint. Ty moved closer and took the towel from him, holding it up to ask for permission. Nick turned to him and cleared his throat uncomfortably. Ty ran the towel over his nose and cheeks, forcing Nick to squeeze his eyes shut as he removed the remnants of the paint.

"Every time, man," Ty said, smiling sadly.

"Thanks." Nick took the towel from him, folding it even though it was sopping wet and covered in paint that would likely never come clean. He seemed to force himself to meet Ty's eyes, steeling himself for whatever he thought Ty had come in here for.

"I see you got more holes in your boat," Ty finally said.

Nick nodded, trying to remain stoic. But Ty could tell he was barely holding himself together. "It still floats," he managed.

Ty found himself smiling gently.

"I should have come to you," Nick blurted.

Ty winced and shook his head. "How could you have?"

Nick's brow creased and he cocked his head, his shoulders tensing.

"I made it impossible for you to come to me with this. You tried to warn me about him ten years ago, and I didn't listen. Your gut never let us down all those years, and I still didn't hear you when you tried to tell me."

"Tyler."

"No. You earned that from me. You earned my trust when you said something didn't feel right. And I didn't listen when you tried to bank it."

Nick averted his gaze, pressing his lips tight. Ty couldn't tell if he was upset or relieved.

"It wasn't about you," Ty continued. "It was because I didn't want to hear you. And I didn't want to hear you this time, either."

Nick opened his mouth like he was going to speak, but he closed it again without making a sound. He met Ty's eyes, wincing like he was looking at something too bright.

"Anyone but Richard Burns, and . . . I would have listened to you," Ty said. "Anyone but him."

Nick nodded and swallowed hard, not even trying to speak now.

"Maybe you should have come to me, man, I don't know. But we would have wound up right here no matter what path we took to get here." Ty ran his teeth across his lip to keep from saying more, and chewed on the inside of his cheek as he waited for Nick to say something. Anything.

"I don't like the path I took," Nick admitted.

Ty had to concentrate on the signet ring on his finger. The one Nick wore was different than his, but they meant the same thing: semper fi. Ty swallowed around the lump in his throat. "Neither do I."

They stood in awkward silence for a few more seconds, and then Nick moved past Ty, into the cabin again.

But Ty wasn't done. He couldn't let it hang like that. He followed Nick, and after sparing a moment to think about it, he practically tackled Nick from behind to hug him.

Nick stumbled, grunting as Ty's body hit him, then looked over his shoulder like he wasn't sure what Ty was doing. Ty just held on to him, resting his cheek against the back of Nick's shoulder, locking his wrists so Nick couldn't get away.

Nick reached up hesitantly and patted Ty's hands.

Ty distantly registered Zane and Kelly watching them from the corridor, and Digger and Owen contorting themselves in the stairwell so they could see. He didn't care, though.

Nick was trembling under Ty's embrace, his breathing ragged. He laughed weakly. "What are you doing, Beaumont?"

"Something I should have done a long time ago," Ty whispered, so only Nick could hear him. "Forcing you to love me again."

Nick snorted and lowered his head. Ty could just make out the barest of smiles.

"I can live with Richard Burns being a monster," Ty said. "I can even live with knowing he used me, and God knows how many innocent men I killed." Ty sniffed, squeezing his eyes shut as Nick began trying to disentangle himself.

Ty let him go, and Nick turned to face him.

"But the last year?" Ty said, choking on the words. He swallowed past it and pushed on. "Thinking you didn't trust me, thinking I'd lost you? I don't want to live in that world. I don't want to live that life. I can't."

Nick was visibly fighting back tears, his nostrils flaring, his lips trembling and his jaw tight. His eyes were still on Ty's, though, filled with sadness and hope.

"I love you, brother," Ty whispered, and when he tried to take a breath to say the next words, his lungs failed him. His throat tightened, and what he'd intended came out an unintelligible huff. He gripped Nick again and pulled him into a proper hug instead, resting his chin on Nick's shoulder.

"I love you too, Tyler," Nick managed to say. "God, I'm sorry."

Ty gasped as relief swept over him like a cool breeze in the desert they'd once walked through together. "I need you to be my brother again," he said against Nick's bare shoulder. "I don't know how to be me without it."

Nick's arms tightened around Ty, his fingers grasping at Ty's shirt.

Someone behind Ty sniffled. He and Nick laughed weakly, still clinging to each other.

"Fuck all y'all," Digger finally blurted. "I'm getting in on this."

A moment later Digger wrapped his arms around Ty and Nick, squishing his face against Ty's. In mere seconds, the others had joined them, piling into a hug that had been a long time—years—in coming. Ty reached out blindly and found Zane's shoulder as the man hovered near them, pulling him closer until he was forced to join in.

Nick rested his forehead against Ty's shoulder, and his entire body seemed to slump in relief. "Thank you," he said. He repeated it several more times, until it became so soft it blended with the whirring of the yacht's heating system and faded into the darkness.

Zane couldn't quite place the relief he felt as he slid under the covers that night, waiting for Ty to finish showering. It was obviously a relief to have Ty next to him again; he wouldn't have survived another spiral like the one he'd suffered previously. But what he was fixating on tonight was the way he felt lighter, and Ty felt lighter, and the yacht felt lighter. Perhaps it was relief that Ty's sanity would still be intact by morning, because as much as Zane *was* for Ty, he couldn't be everything.

Zane was Ty's anchor, a way to keep him from floating away. But Nick was Ty's seashore, always in the distance, visible, comforting, and harkening to home. And Zane was relieved Ty could spot the shore again.

The shower turned off, and a few minutes later Ty was crawling into bed next to him. They wrapped around each other without a word. They didn't need words. Their mouths met, the kisses hot and hard. Zane ground against Ty, hands on his hips, both men demanding and almost violent in their desire to assure themselves they were really there.

Ty threw the covers off them, kicking them down to the bottom of the bed, and then got to his knees, scooting until he was perched on the edge of the bow-shaped bed. Zane sat up to watch Ty in the moonlight that weaved through the portholes.

"Remember the last round bed we tried?" Ty asked, his voice gone low and intimate.

Zane grinned. "Should we just start this on the floor, then?" He was almost shocked when his voice came out in a predatory growl. He got to his knees and crawled closer.

Ty reached for him, sinking his hands into Zane's hair. "Let's see."

Zane dragged him to the side of the bed, until his back was pushed against the curved shelf that encircled the mattress and he was bent against the hull. He kissed him possessively, yanking at Ty's legs until he'd settled between them. Ty banged his head on the hull, cursing even as he squeezed Zane with his knees.

"God, yes," Zane growled. He dug his fingers into Ty's thighs and dragged him into his lap.

He slid one arm behind Ty to keep it out of the way. It was the wrist that still throbbed like he might have broken it during their fight, but he was determined not to let Ty know that. He'd have to figure out how to keep that arm out of play for a few days. His other hand, though, it was just fine. He let it roam over Ty's naked body. He wanted more kisses, more contact.

Ty hooked his ankles behind Zane's thighs and clutched at his neck, dragging his blunt fingernails down Zane's back and over his shoulder blades, setting Zane's skin on fire. He was either forgetting Zane's bumps and bruises and tender places, or he didn't care if Zane burned. In fact, Zane thought that was exactly what Ty wanted him to do. Burn.

Ty sighed against his lips and shifted his hips forward, legs tightening around Zane's waist, forcing the head of Zane's leaking cock against his ass.

"I don't think you can fuck me right here tonight," Ty said between heated kisses, sounding decidedly upset about it.

Zane put one hand on Ty's chest and pushed him until he thumped against the hull, getting up on his knees to loom over him. "Why not?" he asked roughly, and leaned in to lick and bite his way across the exposed skin of Ty's belly. Ty was beaten and bruised from their fight, since he hadn't been wearing armor when Zane had taken his shots. His body was covered in the sordid tales of his life and the battles he'd fought. The battles he'd fought to get to Zane.

Zane brushed his palm over some of those bruises, his fingers going from gentle to rough as he yanked at Ty's hips.

Ty groaned again and rested his head back on the porthole behind him. "Because we don't have any lube and I won't be able to walk. We kind of need me to be able to walk, baby."

"You can't tell me there's not lube on this boat," Zane grunted as he played his nose over Ty's skin.

Ty chuckled.

Zane sighed and wound Ty's pliable body around him, grinding his hardened cock against Ty's. "That could be a problem," he whispered, trying to steady his breathing.

"God, I want you inside me," Ty hissed as he flattened his hands against Zane's skin.

"You're sending some serious mixed signals right now," Zane snarled. Ty shrugged unapologetically, and Zane pushed away just enough to shove the pillows and blankets around beside them. He yanked at Ty's legs, rubbing against him, then picked Ty up and slammed him into the mattress. He wanted to make damn sure they started in the middle of the bed this time.

Ty lifted his hips, the action tightening his grip on Zane's waist. "Zane," he moaned.

"God damn it, Ty, work with me here," Zane grunted as he slid his hands between Ty's thighs, palm and fingers cupping his hard cock. "You won't let me fuck you, I'll just have to do something else."

Ty groaned, writhing under Zane's touch. "When have you ever listened to me before?"

Zane kissed him and bit at his lower lip. "Just don't scream," he warned. Seconds later, Zane had Ty's cock in his mouth.

Ty's fingers gripped the edge of the shelf surrounding the bed, and he cried out Zane's name in something like outrage after he banged his knuckles on the rim. He arched his back and thrust his hips, his feet seeking purchase against Zane's body as Zane wrapped him up. "You're going to fucking kill me."

"Eat you alive, maybe," Zane rasped, one hand pumping Ty's cock before his lips closed around the head, tongue swirling and lapping.

"Oh God," Ty groaned. His grip on the shelf tightened until his knuckles went white. Ty's cum was leaking onto Zane's tongue as he worked for more. Each gasp and groan and curse drove him on. He was so hard it was almost painful, but he wouldn't spare a hand for himself. Ty was still trying to find leverage as he attempted to thrust his hips. He settled his heels in the center of Zane's back, and Zane hissed at the pain.

He grazed his teeth over Ty's shaft in warning, and Ty cried out and bucked his hips, cupping the back of Zane's head in a trembling hand as he struggled to put his feet anywhere else. He was obviously trying hard not to just grab Zane's head and fuck his mouth, but Zane was determined to make Ty lose what little control he was exerting.

Zane's cock ached almost as much as his injured wrist. He slid his fingers between Ty's legs and behind his tightened balls to rub, trying to throw Ty over the edge. It spurred Ty into moving, but not like Zane had intended. Ty scrabbled at his shoulders, pushing him, pulling him, urging him to move until he was turned around and they wound back together. Zane was still on his knees with Ty in his mouth, but now he had Ty's body beneath him, Ty's tongue on his cock.

Zane took a few thrusts just to appreciate how talented Ty was in this position, then returned his attention to making Ty come. It wasn't long after all his attention before Ty curled in on himself and tightened his fingers on Zane's ass. He was still sucking Zane off even as he thrust up into Zane's mouth. He gave a moan that traveled through Zane's body, and he bucked his hips, emptying himself into Zane's mouth with a plaintive whimper.

Zane swallowed and sucked as Ty shuddered under him, until Ty was struggling. "Please!" Ty finally cried, squirming away from the overstimulation.

Zane licked his lips, sucking in deep breaths as he fought his own need for release. He rolled over and looked Ty up and down, all flushed and shaky and gasping. Zane just groaned. He turned around, crawling up Ty's body.

"Next time I have you naked," he growled.

Ty was still trembling under Zane's caresses, and he spread his legs wider so Zane could get to him. "Come on."

Zane shook his head. Ty had been right; if Zane got at him now without lube, he wouldn't be at full physical capacity, and Zane would never hurt him. But that didn't mean Zane didn't want to just skewer him on his cock and pound him until he cried for mercy.

Ty huffed when he realized Zane really wasn't going to fuck him. He wrapped his arms around Zane's neck, kissing him messily. "Come up here then," he said, giving Zane's ass a little tug.

Zane crawled up his body, pushing the pillows and sheets aside as he did so. Ty laughed quietly as the edge of the bed loomed near them. They readjusted their position. Zane refused to lose this opportunity to a round bed. He absolutely refused.

He slammed his good hand down on the shelf, holding on so they wouldn't fucking roll off, and watched as Ty took his cock between those full lips of his. Ty gave him a cheeky little wink. Zane had to bite his tongue. He cradled Ty's head in one hand, trying not to wince as it throbbed, and braced himself on the other. He started with slow, careful thrusts that soon became the same ruthless rhythm he would have hit if he'd been fucking Ty.

Zane spent long, torturous moments watching the sordid little show and letting that pleasure curl in his gut, letting Ty bring him closer and closer to the brink. It wasn't enough, though. It was never enough when he couldn't have all of Ty wrapped up in his arms. "Ty," he whispered, his breaths shuddering.

Ty grabbed for his hips and encouraged him to go harder. His hazel eyes were sparkling. Zane's hand tightened in his hair as he wondered what the hell Ty had up his sleeve to put that look in his eyes. "Oh, doll, don't be mean."

Ty winked, his tongue sliding along the underside of Zane's straining cock.

"Oh, Jesus, Ty," Zane whimpered. He pulled out just enough that Ty had to chase after him, and Zane completely lost what little control he'd had.

He held on to him and pounded into his mouth. Ty's hands came up to clutch at his hips, but Zane didn't stop. He couldn't stop. He closed his eyes, getting lost in the pleasure as he used Ty's mouth, thrusting deep until Ty's nose brushed his belly, until Ty's fingers were burning scratches into his skin, until he could feel that elusive flutter just on the edge of his senses.

Ty grasped at Zane's chest, sliding around to rake his nails across the small of his back. He didn't try to slow Zane's punishing thrusts, though. He pulled Zane's ass toward him, encouraging him to continue. When Ty began to moan, Zane could feel it in his cock, feel it making its way all the way to his toes, his tongue, into his very heartbeat.

He cried out Ty's name as his orgasm rushed up on him.

Ty gave a muffled groan, scratching at Zane's hip as he struggled to take all of Zane in and swallow, and Zane was desperately trying not to close his eyes. When Ty began trying to squirm away, digging his heels in to push further into the mattress, Zane closed his eyes and pulled out. He fell to the side, gasping for breath.

Ty chuckled, and Zane glanced at him, squinting as if Ty was simply too bright to see.

Ty threw himself down beside Zane, wiping a thumb over his bottom lip like he might have missed a bit.

"You're dirty," Zane told him, his voice cracking.

"You love it."

Zane barked a laugh. Ty rolled over and straddled him, grabbing both wrists to press them to the mattress. Zane didn't have time to prepare for the pain, and he gasped and winced away from Ty's touch. Ty released him like he was hot, holding his hands in the air, eyes wide.

"What'd I do?"

Zane shook his head, trying to grin about it. "Sore wrist. It's nothing."

Ty's eyes darted to the wrist Zane was cradling against his chest and then back to Zane's eyes. "That where I got you?"

Zane shrugged noncommittally. "Let's go back to the postorgasm cuddling we were about to do, huh?"

But Ty gently took his arm, frowning at his wrist as he turned it over. "Is it broken? It looks broken."

Zane pursed his lips, trying to be nonchalant.

"Did I break your wrist?" Ty asked, his voice going higher. Then he was just flat-out shouting. "I broke your wrist!"

Zane tried to hush him, patting at his chest, still shaking his head. "It's just a sprain, it's okay."

"I broke your wrist!" Ty repeated, his voice cracking. "Why the hell didn't you say something?"

"Probably to avoid this," Zane muttered.

A knock on the cabin door interrupted them before Ty could work himself up further.

"It's open!" Zane called, expecting Sidewinder and an amused FBI agent or three.

But it was just Kelly, and he had a hand slapped over his eyes. He took a tentative step into the cabin, then tossed a handful of medical supplies on the bed and retreated without ever saying a word.

Ty and Zane stared at the supplies as the door shut. They included a flexible wrap, some popsicle sticks, one length of metal that could be bent and molded, and a little tube of lubricant.

"Asshole!" Ty called after Kelly.

"You're welcome!"

When Zane popped his head over the stairwell railing to sniff at the smell of hash browns in the air, he found Nick sat at the banquette, a bottle of Gatorade at his elbow and a stack of papers in front of him.

Zane wondered how he was taking all the people on his boat. He hadn't handled it well last night. He and Kelly had taken the main cabin because, "Fuck all these people." And no one had argued. Zane had destroyed the bunks on his rampage, so they'd just thrown the mattresses on the floor of the salon, leaving the others to fight over space between watch shifts. Owen and Digger had somehow wound up in the banquette by morning, their heads on a shared pillow in the corner, Owen's feet dangling over the edge of Nick's lap.

"Hey," Zane greeted under his breath. Everyone else was still asleep, and Julian must have been up top, on watch. Zane stood awkwardly for a moment, and Nick stared at him, waiting.

"You do coffee in the morning?"

"Yeah, I'd love some," Zane said in relief.

"I don't have coffee," Nick answered, looking immediately amused and apologetic.

Zane just rolled his eyes.

"I have tea?"

"You got more of those Gatorades?"

Nick nodded at the refrigerator. "Don't drink the orange one, it's spiked."

"Of course it is," Zane mumbled as he retrieved a drink and some cold hash browns. He slid into the banquette at Digger's feet, struggling with it for a few seconds, then finally surrendering and picking Digger's bare feet up to set them on his knee.

Nick watched him silently.

"What are you doing?" Zane asked him once he'd settled.

Nick studied the files. "I got these out of your bag," he admitted. "Are these from Burns's memory card?"

Zane nodded as he ran a hand over his face. His wrist was wrapped in the bandage Kelly had brought him last night, but he kept forgetting it would hurt when he poked it.

"Ty break your wrist?" Nick asked after popping a hash brown into his mouth.

"I'm not sure. If he did, it's just a crack."

"Watch it close. If your fingers start doing weird, we need to get it set right."

Zane nodded. "You've probably dealt with broken wrists before, huh?"

Nick frowned at him carefully.

"Ty told me about your dad, how he knocked you around. Fractured wrist is pretty common, right?"

Nick raised one eyebrow. "I used to wait 'til recess, fake a fall off the slide or something. Football or hockey practice, when I was older." He popped another hash brown in his mouth and returned his attention to the photos. "Johns said this was a digital steganography code. You pegged it?"

"Yeah. We ran it through the Bureau computers; it spit out what you're reading now."

"You make sense of this?" Nick asked dubiously.

"I haven't looked at it." Zane shrugged. "All I could see was Ty."

Nick returned his attention to the messages Richard Burns had hidden in the photos. "It's all numbers. It's a simple replacement cipher." He winced. "God, I'm so fucking sick of replacement ciphers."

Zane snorted. "When do we get to hear what you and Doc got up to over the summer? How did you get a favor from Cross?"

"Kelly tells the story better than I do," Nick answered. He set the paper on the table. "To solve this, we need to find the cryptovariable Burns used, or it's useless."

Zane nodded, staring at the pages. Then he grinned up at Nick. "He hid it in a book."

Nick smiled slowly in return. "There you go."

"What book was it?" Zane asked.

"I don't know," Nick answered with a sigh. He glanced into the salon, and Zane followed his eyes to an armchair where Liam was sleeping under a furry throw blanket. "He might, but he claims he doesn't."

"I don't," Liam answered without moving or opening his eyes.

Nick grunted.

"We'll have to go back to the house," Zane decided.

A moment later, something thumped belowdecks, and Ty appeared a few seconds after. He gave everyone a suspicious once-over, probably wondering how Zane and Nick had come to be sitting there together, sharing a plate of hash browns as they acted as footstools for sleeping Sidewinders.

But Ty just shrugged and moved beside them, nodding at the papers. "Anything?"

"We need the book the memory card was in," Zane said. "We think it's the key to the replacement cipher."

"Edgar Allan Poe," Ty said as he slid the hash browns closer and stole one.

"How do you know that?" Nick demanded.

"I had it last night," Ty said through a mouthful. "I forgot to go back and get it after Doc beanbagged me."

"We need it," Zane said. "Has to be the right edition or it's useless."

Ty nodded, going to the refrigerator to get a drink. "Easy fix, I'll just go back and tell her I forgot to take it with me." He popped the refrigerator open.

"Don't drink the orange one," Liam told him, still curled up with his eyes closed.

Ty straightened and glared at him, then turned to Zane and Nick. "Is it spiked?"

Nick nodded, sighing as Owen kicked him in his sleep.

An hour later, Ty took Owen with him to retrieve the book, and while they were gone, Zane went about trying to organize his thoughts so they could plan their next move. He sat up top with Clancy, Lassiter, and Perrimore, writing in a notepad he assumed had once been the one Nick used on the job.

"We have three leads, right now," he was telling them. "The accounts I had you hunt down, Freddy, they're still out there. We have to find them. And then O'Flaherty said Laura Burns gave him two names of people who may have known about that safe in her floor. A man named Jack Tanner, who still works at the academy in Quantico, and . . . Earl Grady."

"Is that . . . Ty's dad?" Clancy asked.

Zane nodded.

"Is he a suspect?" she asked, sounding even more tentative than before.

Zane shook his head, but he couldn't say no with any confidence. The only person he trusted implicitly right now was Ty.

"So what's our play?" Lassiter asked.

Zane licked his lips. "I want you three to follow those accounts."

"What?" Perrimore boomed out. "You mean you're going off to storm the fucking beaches with all those assholes downstairs and you want us to go skiing in Switzerland?"

Zane smiled fondly and nodded. "Yeah, that's what I mean."

"Garrett, come on, we can keep up with those Recon guys," Clancy spat.

"It's not about being able to keep up. Those guys down there, they know how to blow holes in things. But you, you're trained federal agents. You know how to follow a lead, and you know how to handle red tape, and I need you."

They all stared at him mutinously.

"If we don't find that money, we have nothing. And I go down for it. Ty goes down for murder because the CIA made it damn clear they'd only help if he brought the money in. Without that money, it doesn't matter how we handle the cartel, Ty and I go down."

They shared glances, shifting uncomfortably.

"I'm not sending you after those accounts because I don't believe in you, or because I don't think you can handle the heat," he stressed, and was surprised when he got choked up over it. He scrubbed his hands over his face, taking a moment to compose himself. "I'm sending you out there to save us. Because I don't think anyone else can do it."

When he raised his head, they were all meeting his eyes. Perrimore was nodding. Clancy had clenched her teeth and looked frighteningly determined, and Lassiter's eyes were shining like they were about to water.

Zane gave them all a weak smile. "I love you guys," he said impulsively. "You're the first family I found in a long time that took me for what I am. And now I need you to go save me."

Clancy nodded curtly, then lurched to her feet and threw her arms around his neck. "We can do that."

Zane held her tightly. "I know you can."

An hour later, Ty returned from retrieving the book and accosted Zane with questions because he'd noticed one of their vehicles missing from the marina parking lot. Zane understood. When Liam Bell was involved, Ty worried about everything.

"They're on their way to the airport," Zane informed him.

"What, why?"

Zane explained what he'd done, and Ty was visibly distraught over the realization that Clancy, Perrimore, and Lassiter were gone.

"I didn't get to say good-bye."

Zane patted his shoulder. "You'll say hello when this is over."

Ty tried to smile and nod, to fake that confidence for Zane. He didn't quite manage it.

"The only other lead we have is the safe," Nick informed the others after they all gathered in the salon. "We need to get eyes on that house in case whoever got after it comes back. Six, have you heard from your CIA contact?"

Ty shook his head, obviously still struggling internally, judging by the tempest in his hazel eyes. "Some beanbag destroyed my phone."

"I'm sorry, Mr. Snuffles, would you rather I had let you stab your husband in the eye?" Kelly snapped. "At least it was me with the beanbag and not Bell with an armor-piercing tank cutter again!"

"Hey!" Liam shouted. "I already told you, that was an accident."

As the salon devolved into a mishmash of shouting and confused questions, Nick crossed his arms and sighed, staring at the coffee table like he was thinking about bashing his face into it.

Ty put two fingers in his mouth, whistling to get everyone's attention. The others quieted, all of them grudgingly turning toward him.

"Past is the past," Ty growled. "Whatever happened before we set foot on this boat, it's over. It's done. From here on out, we live and die with the actions of the man next to us. Get a fucking grip on it."

Sidewinder looked ashamed, and Liam and Julian were both wearing eerily similar frowns. Zane smiled serenely at his husband.

Ty waved at Nick. "Gunny."

Nick said nothing for a few seconds, probably thrown by Ty's use of his new rank. He cleared his throat, though. "We have two names to check on: Ty's dad, and a man named Jack Tanner. Both of them knew Burns well and might have known about the floor safe. If we can find the person who tried to get into it, we may pick up a lead on the money itself. And we all know finding that money is the key for Grady and Garrett."

"I think it should be added that Burns wasn't the only one close to Jack Tanner," Zane said when Nick paused. "Ty and I both knew him well when we went through the academy. He . . . he made a huge impact on me. He's a good man."

Everyone remained quiet.

"Will that be a problem?" Nick finally asked.

Ty bit his lip, glancing at Zane and studying the deep furrow in his brow.

"No," Zane answered after a few seconds. "We'll go in two groups. We have to assume that both the Vega cartel and the NIA are onto the fact that we didn't die in that fire. No one goes anywhere alone from here on out. Watch your back and your front."

"How do you want us to split?" Owen asked.

"We're down to eight, now," Zane answered. "Four and four."

Digger huffed. "Who gets stuck with Bell?"

"Hey, I have feelings," Liam said, pressing his hand to his chest dramatically.

"Bell stays with me," Nick declared, and Ty almost did a double take. "I'll take him, Cross, and the Doc to take a first run at Tanner," Nick continued as he met Ty's eyes. "If he's cagey, we'll hit him a second time with the two of you."

Ty nodded.

"Hold on, do we really want Ty interrogating his own dad?" Zane pointed out.

"Do you really want to walk into Mara's house without her son?" Nick countered.

Zane shook his head violently. "West Virginia it is, then."

"You know how I always complain about having to trek my ass up here for Christmas?" Ty was saying as he drove the rambling old landscaper's truck over the icy, treacherous roads to his parents' place in Bluefield.

Zane was trying hard not to grip the handle above him, focusing instead on Ty's words and keeping his aching wrist from being jarred.

"Well, trekking my ass up here to tell my dad his oldest friend was a horrible human being, that's worse."

"Are we just discounting the possibility that your dad might have been horrible-human-beings-in-cahoots, then?" Owen asked from the cramped backseat.

"Hey! That is my dad you're talking about, jackhole."

"I think Grady might need to sit this one out," Owen said to Zane.

"Agreed," Digger offered.

"Fuck you both!" Ty shouted.

"They're right, Ty," Zane said regretfully. He winced when Ty shot daggers at him. "Please watch the road."

"I *am* watching the road, *you* watch the road!"

Zane finally grasped at the handle.

"I am not sitting anything out. I'm not going to drive you assholes up to my dad's front porch and then let you go in and accuse him of being . . . evil!"

Zane tore his eyes away from the road to face Ty, and he sighed as he glanced over his shoulder at the two men in the backseat. They were both shaking their heads.

"Tyler," Zane said sternly. "You're going to stay outside until I let you come in."

Ty gaped at him, almost sending them off into a snow-filled ditch before he got control of himself and the truck. He snorted angrily. "Fine."

Zane nodded, pleased with himself.

"You're wearing my boots," Ty grumbled a few minutes later.

"What?"

"My go bag boots. You stole them. Asshole."

"They're nice," Zane acknowledged, grinning instead of offering an apology. "Do you want them back?"

Ty glared at him, then shook his head. "Keep them. They might save your life one day."

Ten minutes later, the truck had managed the climb up the side of the mountain, and they sat with the engine off, the freezing night seeping into the cab. Zane was fighting the bubbling of nerves as he stared at the dark porch. What if he went in there and told Earl what they knew, and the man never forgave him? What if this was the moment he lost the new family he'd so recently earned a place in? Maybe he'd been wrong, maybe they needed Ty in there to keep things smooth. But then, would they really get answers in an atmosphere charged with grief and emotion?

No. No, they wouldn't.

"You guys know we don't have doors back here, right?" Owen finally said as he rested his chin on the back of the front seat.

Ty snarled and turned to Zane. His eyes were blazing, and he'd obviously been going over an inner monologue that had gotten him worked up. He looked absolutely livid.

Zane took a deep, soothing breath. "Okay," he said quietly. "We'll go in, ask a few questions. I'll flash the porch light when it's clear for you to join."

Ty sat silent, glaring.

Zane didn't linger further, just popped the handle and slid out of the cab. He pulled the seat forward so Owen and Digger could follow, and they left Ty sitting in the cold.

Ty seethed as he watched them walk up to the unlit door and knock. A few seconds later, his mother answered, her face morphing into a pleased smile as she pulled Zane into a hug.

She seemed to recognize Owen and Digger, probably placing them as Ty's Recon team even if she might not recall their names. As soon as she saw Ty wasn't with them, concern filtered into her expression. Zane's motions seemed to be aimed at calming her, and she ushered them inside. Zane glanced over his shoulder at Ty before shutting the door behind him.

Yes, Zane was right. Ty didn't need to be the one asking his own father if he might happen to have been involved with stealing millions from a Colombian cartel. That didn't mean Ty couldn't sit and sulk about being left like a dog in the car with the windows cracked.

He waited until his knee began bouncing, and then he realized he had far too much energy to just sit there. He pulled on a pair of gloves, then got out of the truck and closed the door with a quiet snick. He checked that his gun was loaded and the safety was off, and then he slunk into the woods to perform a perimeter check so he could feel useful.

He'd grown up on this land and he knew this mountain like the back of his hand. He traveled through the trees with a fluidity normally reserved for wild animals. There wasn't much snow on the ground here because the canopy was far too thick, so he traded crunching on snow for trying to avoid the snap of twigs as he moved.

When he came around the small gully that behaved as a natural barrier for the property, he turned south and headed toward the back of the house. He could see the lights of the kitchen between the trees, see the smoke rising from the chimney. He stopped and smiled wistfully at the peaceful scene straight from his childhood.

Then a shadow moved amid the trees, blocking out the light.

Zane hadn't realized he was nervous until he'd tried to move his hands from where they were clutching his jeans, and his fingers throbbed as they started getting blood to them again.

Earl was sitting across from him, on the edge of the sofa. Mara and Chester had joined them, which seemed to make Owen and Digger uncomfortable, but Zane knew the Gradys. Mara wasn't exactly the little woman puttering around the kitchen.

She didn't seem as distraught as Earl did right now.

"That can't be," he was insisting. He was shaking his head, staring at the table. "I knew him too well."

"Sir," Owen said gently. "We wish it weren't true, but we have too much evidence."

Earl glanced up at him, then turned his attention back to Zane. He looked so wounded, Zane wasn't sure how to handle it. He had expected Earl to rail at them, to deny it, to get violent and protective like Ty had when Nick had tried to tell him. But Earl was none of those things. He merely seemed broken and sad.

"I'm sorry," Zane whispered.

Earl shook his head. "Don't apologize, son, this ain't your doing. Where is Ty?"

Zane winced, glancing at Owen and Digger to make sure they had his back. They both nodded. Zane licked his lips and took a deep breath. "He's in the truck," he answered carefully.

Mara sat up straighter and peered out the window, scowling. "Why didn't he come in?"

But the dawning realization in Earl's eyes told Zane that Earl knew exactly why Ty had stayed in the truck. He blew out a noisy puff of air.

"I have to ask you a few questions," Zane told him, trying to keep the professional mask that had served him so well for so long.

Mara turned back around, her brow still furrowed. She looked between them and put her hand on Earl's knee.

"Of course you do," Earl said, and he was astoundingly calm. Fuck, he was making Zane nervous! "Go on, boy. Get it over with."

"Were you aware of Richard Burns's activities?"

"No." Earl's answer came out soft and sad.

"Were you aware of the safe he had installed in the floor of his home?"

Earl shook his head. "No."

Zane licked his lips, steeling himself. "Were you aware that Richard Burns was planning to murder myself and Ty so we'd take the fall for his crimes?"

Earl looked up sharply, eyes flashing. His breath seemed to leave him, and he stood. "Is that true?" he asked, barely audible since he still hadn't caught his breath.

Zane nodded. "We believe so, yes."

Earl covered his face with both hands, and Zane could see he was trying to calm himself. It obviously didn't work, because he snatched a round decorative candle off the coffee table and chucked it at the nearest wall. It smashed into a picture, and glass shards crashed to the ground.

Zane stood, and Owen and Digger were both tensing, waiting. Earl didn't move again, though. He stood with his hands on his hips, his entire body shaking.

"Earl?" Zane tried.

"Can't believe that bastard got himself killed before I could do it," Earl growled.

"Zane," Mara said shakily. "Can you call Tyler in now?"

"Yes, ma'am." Zane nodded for Digger to flash the porch light like they'd discussed. "He'll be just a second."

Ty saw the old yellow light on the front porch flash on and off, bathing the yard in a kinetic sort of energy for a few brief seconds that seemed entirely too fitting with the arm wrapped around his neck.

Ty reached out toward the light, then went back to trying to pry the arm full of solid muscle away from his windpipe so he could call out for backup or, hell, breathe. Breathing would be just fine right now.

He kicked at the man holding him, aiming for a kneecap, or maybe even a nice tendon, but his bootheel hit with a solid *thunk*. The guy was wearing body armor.

That was why Ty's initial attack had failed so miserably. You can't hit a pressure point that's under a protective layer of Kevlar. Ty lurched forward, then threw himself back with all his strength. He heard Under Armour's head hit the tree behind them, and it stunned him enough that Ty could break the hold around his neck and duck away. He turned with a wheelhouse kick toward the side of the man's knee, where the body armor was weakest.

A twig snapped behind him, and he spun in time to see the attack, but not to defend it. The second man leveled him with a fallen tree limb.

Ty found himself staring at the moonlight through the trees, trying to shake off the whirling queasiness of an impending blackout. He slid his hand into his pocket and got a grip on his gun as the man came into his view. He pulled the trigger without even taking the weapon out of his coat.

The man fell away, and Ty lay there on the frozen ground, fighting to stay conscious. If there were two men on this side of the house, there were definitely more. He sure as hell wasn't safe, and neither was his family inside.

In the clear cold of the night, Ty heard the screen door screech open and slam again. The floodlights he and Deuce had spent one Easter installing all snapped on, bathing the backyard and the edges of the forest in light.

"Ty!" Zane called.

Ty turned his head, blinking away the sprinkling of floating lights on the edge of his vision. He saw Under Armour trying to stand on his newly ruined knee and bringing his assault rifle up.

Ty tugged his Smith & Wesson out of his destroyed pocket and pointed it at the man. "One chance," he said to the guy, who was caught with his head turned toward Ty but his weapon turned toward the house.

They stared at each other for long seconds as Ty's family and friends called his name and fanned out. Someone was coming closer to them, calling. Under Armour turned, aiming the assault rifle at whoever was approaching.

Ty pulled the trigger, and no armor in the world was a match for a head shot. The man coming toward them dropped to the ground at the sound of the gun.

"Six?" Digger called.

"I'm here." Ty's abused voice was hoarse, so he swallowed and tried again. "Here! Incoming!"

He could hear Digger skittering through the undergrowth toward him, and soon enough he'd found Ty in the darkness.

"You hit?" Digger asked him.

"No. Got me with a fucking stick in the head."

Digger's hands came to his head, checking him over. He could feel what seemed to be a split on his cheek, but Digger didn't seem concerned. "You'll live."

He got Ty up without a word, letting him lean on him as they struggled their way toward the edge of the forest. They stopped right on the periphery of the light, crouching down.

"How many?"

"I got two," Ty answered. "It's an NIA strike team; they travel in packs of six to eight. They either tailed us, or they were sitting on my parents, waiting for us to show."

"Why the fuck they after us?"

"They must think we have the money."

"Well, fuck."

Ty nodded as he strained to spot Zane or his dad, both of whom had probably come out in search of him. Owen was out there somewhere too, and between the five of them they could be pretty fucking lethal. They just needed a plan.

"Got a plan, boss?" Digger asked.

Ty huffed a laugh. "I was about to ask you that."

"You knew Richard Burns well, didn't you, Agent Tanner?" Nick asked the grizzled man who'd let them into his living room in Stafford, Virginia.

"Just call me Jack," he told him with a wave. He'd offered them all drinks when they'd filtered into his home, but they'd declined. Tanner hadn't, pouring himself a bourbon right out of a flask in his back pocket.

Nick glanced sideways as the man drank, meeting Kelly's eyes dubiously. This guy was the one Ty and Zane both spoke so highly of?

"You boys say you're friends with Tyler Grady?"

"Yes, sir," Nick answered. "Laura Burns asked him to make some inquiries after her husband's death."

Tanner nodded, glancing at the others.

Julian had remained outside, and Liam was standing and restless, walking around the living room. Nick knew he was looking for anything that might help them, but he was still making Nick edgy. Nick was fighting against telling him to just sit the fuck down.

"I knew Richard," Tanner said with a sorrowful nod. "He was a good friend. Good man. They made any progress in finding out who killed him?"

Nick didn't blink. "Not that I know of," he said evenly.

"Well, I hope they hang the bastard by his nut sac," Tanner said before taking a long swig from his glass.

Liam coughed behind Nick to cover any sound he'd been about to make.

"That's why we're here," Nick added.

"Sir, did you happen to know about anything Burns was keeping hidden?" Kelly asked Tanner. "A hiding spot he had from even his wife?"

"You mean the safe he put in his floor?" Tanner asked, his keen eyes narrowing.

Kelly and Nick shared another glance, surprised it was looking like this lead might pan out.

"He had that thing put in a few years ago. I made fun of him. 'What you going to do with a safe in a floor, put your wife's heart in there?'" Tanner smiled weakly. "Ain't so funny now."

Nick realized he was scowling at the man, and he worked to school his features again.

"Did he ever say why he needed it?" Kelly asked.

Tanner shook his head. "I figured it had something to do with the ops he ran on the side."

"Can you tell us about those?" Nick asked. Ty and Zane had told them that Tanner helped Burns recruit for his side jobs, but it never hurt to play a little dumb.

Tanner sighed. "He'd have me single out promising candidates, wine and dine them, groom them for special tasks. He shut it all down a few years ago, 'round the same time he put that safe in. I just thought he took all the evidence he gathered and put it in there. Second coming of J. Edgar Hoover or something."

Nick was frowning again when he asked, "Who else would know about that safe?"

Tanner raised both eyebrows, tapping a finger against his glass. "Well, his son came by here not two weeks ago. I told him about it."

"His son?" Nick repeated.

Tanner hummed. "Yeah, estranged or something. Trying to find his daddy's will, he said."

"Can you tell us what he looked like?" Kelly asked, trying to sound nonchalant.

Tanner pursed his lips. "Must have been a fling 'cause he didn't exactly look the part. Latino, if you ask me."

Zane and Earl crouched in a depression running through the backyard, squinting into the woods. They didn't dare fire, because they'd heard Ty's voice coming from out there.

"Who's after you?" Earl asked.

"Who's not?" Zane grunted. "NIA, cartel, maybe CIA, we're a little iffy on whose side they're on right now."

"God damn, son."

Zane almost laughed.

"If we can get back to the house, we can get to the big guns, some high ground and cover," Earl whispered.

Zane peered over the lip of the ditch they were stretched out in. "That's a lot of open ground," he said as he stared at the back porch in the distance. Not only did they risk exposing their silhouettes to the moon and becoming easy targets for whoever was out there, but also their own men might not know it was them and think they were attacking the house. He didn't know where Owen was, other than the general direction he'd gone in. Zane could only hope Digger had found Ty out there so he wasn't alone.

He shook his head. "Too risky, they'd cut us down."

Earl shivered next to him. He'd run out into the cold night in just his jeans and long-sleeved shirt. He wasn't even wearing shoes. Zane looked him over, hoping Earl was as fucking tough as Zane thought he was.

Movement off on the periphery of the light drew Zane's eye, but it was difficult to tell what was real and what was a play of the lights and falling snow.

"That them?" Earl asked breathlessly.

"I saw it," Zane told him. They both strained to see. A moment later, Zane watched two men scampering over the driveway and climbing into the back of the truck. He would recognize the roll of those shoulders anywhere. "It's Ty."

"The hell are they doing?"

Zane shook his head. Bullets pinged off the truck. One hit a tire, and it hissed as it flattened. Whatever Ty and Digger had gone in there to do, their movement had created one advantage: Zane turned right and aimed for the muzzle flashes in the woods, offering a spray of covering fire. From somewhere to their left, they heard a bloodcurdling scream.

"Johns," Zane breathed, praying to God that hadn't been Owen out there. He was alone with a broken arm, and that had been the scream of a dying man.

Earl grabbed the back of Zane's shirt and hefted him off the ground. "Come on, boy," he growled, and they both ran toward the house, staying low, using the distraction Ty and Digger had offered.

They made it up the porch steps, only to be met with a rifle in their faces as they tried to get through the door.

Mara lowered it and waved them in just as a shot pinged off the metal doorknob.

"Oh, the hell you are!" Mara shouted into the night. She shouldered her way past Earl and raised the rifle, sparing the briefest of moments to take aim before she fired. A dark figure out in the yard stopped in its tracks, propelled backward by the shot.

"Damn it, Mara, now ain't the time!" Earl cried, and he picked her up with an arm around her waist and dragged her inside. "Keep your head down when you take that shot!"

Zane could hear commotion outside, and he headed for the stairs. Mara handed him her rifle as he went, then headed for the study where the rest of the guns were kept locked up. He took the steps three at a time, shoving into Deuce's old bedroom, and went to the window, turning the crank with one hand as he tried to pry the screen loose with the other. From here he could see Digger and Ty in the truck, lying prone and doing something with the tools that were in the bed.

Then Zane understood. That was Digger down there, and the landscaper's truck was full of bags of fertilizer. They were making bombs. Zane grinned and set the rifle on the windowsill, snugging it against his shoulder. Through the sight he tracked the men approaching the house. The light from the spotlights filtered out into the forest, landing accusingly on anything that moved.

Zane took a shaky breath, lining up the first figure he saw wearing bulky black armor, and pulled the trigger.

Another scream rent the night in the echo of the rifle, a plea for mercy to God and mother, cut short by a sudden silence.

Zane's breaths were hard and fast to his own ears as he stared into the woods. What the hell was making these men scream like that? Was it Owen? Please let it be Owen. Actually, Zane almost hoped it was a mountain lion. Would serve them right.

A road flare burst to life near the truck.

Zane lined up another shot, taking it and missing as his target hit a hole in the ground and was suddenly too low. The bullet whizzed past him, and Zane cursed. He pulled back, readjusting. A streak of fire arced its way toward the woods. It hit high up on a tree and stuck there for a few seconds, and just as it began to slide to the ground, it burst open. Shards of the tree and flaming debris spread out, and someone screamed.

Two more fertilizer bombs flew into the woods, both exploding a few seconds after they hit.

Zane panned the rifle around the periphery of the woods, but he couldn't find anyone. He pulled back, heading to Ty's old bedroom and the window facing the backyard. When he saw no movement outside, no one approaching, he headed downstairs to find Mara sitting on the bottom step with a shotgun across her lap. "I think we pushed them back for now," he told her.

Earl came into the large foyer from the living room, nodding as he heard Zane's last words. Zane headed for the front door, opening it carefully to stick his head out. "Ty?"

"Clear?" Ty called from the bed of the truck.

"Stay frosty, baby," Digger called to him, laughing delightedly.

Zane was almost as disturbed by that as he'd been by the screams out in the woods.

Ty and Digger both vaulted over the back of the truck, scuttling across the driveway to the cover of the porch. Movement to the left caught Zane's eye, and he raised the rifle until he could make out Owen carefully approaching.

Ty and Digger ducked inside to safety, and Zane covered Owen until he joined them.

"Was that you?" Ty asked Owen.

Owen's eyes were wide. "What?"

"The screams. Was that you?"

Owen jerked his head. "I got one, but he died quiet. I was hoping it was one of you. Almost pissed myself with the first one."

Ty paled and met Zane's eyes. Zane sort of felt sick, realizing none of them had been responsible for the dying pleas of the men in the woods.

Earl set his rifle down, glancing around the house. "Where's Dad?" he asked Mara.

The back screen popped open before she could answer, and everyone who was still armed raised their weapons again, waiting breathlessly for the heavy footsteps to draw near. Chester came around the corner, a rag in his hands, wiping them clean. His shovel was held in the crook of his elbow, the shaft resting on his shoulder. Blood dripped from the sharpened tip of the blade.

"Got me a couple," he said with a pleased grin.

CHAPTER 8

Kelly threw himself into a chair in the corner of the living room of a ratty, old safe house just outside Charlottesville, where they'd agreed to meet the other team. Nick watched him surreptitiously as he rolled his head around and made his neck pop.

"This shit is getting on my nerves," Kelly finally said. "I liked it better when they showed us a picture, and we went in and killed it."

Nick raised an eyebrow.

"What? It was sort of fun."

"If it was only sort of fun, you were doing it wrong," Liam offered.

"I've decided I like you," Julian said as he passed through the living room to the kitchen.

Liam frowned as if that didn't sit right with him. "It took you *this* long?"

"I don't make rash decisions."

Nick sat down hard and stretched his aching legs out in front of him. The cold never did good things to the shrapnel in his thigh, and tension was adding to it. His eyes closed and the voices of the others faded.

Liam's hand landed on his elbow, and Nick had his gun against Liam's chest before he even realized he'd been asleep.

Liam put both hands up slowly. "Mate. Not cool."

Nick flicked the safety on with his thumb, lowering the gun to his lap and eyeing the room. Julian had gone off somewhere, but Kelly was standing nearby, shoulders tense, watching with wide eyes. He either hadn't expected Nick to wake like that, or he'd fully anticipated Nick shooting Liam in the face and was disappointed it hadn't happened.

"You okay?" Kelly asked carefully.

Nick nodded, glancing up at Liam. From the look in the man's eyes, he knew he'd almost died.

"The others are here, looks like they ran into some trouble," Liam told him.

Nick hefted himself out of the chair and peered through the front window. The landscaper's truck Ty had been driving wasn't out there, and the old SUV they'd acquired was sporting West Virginia plates.

Nick went to the door as they trudged up the walk. "What happened?"

"NIA," Ty answered.

Zane was halfway grinning when he added, "Digger got to blow shit up."

Nick shook his head in confusion as he stepped aside, letting them file in.

Once they'd locked up the safe house again, Ty related what had gone down in Bluefield. "We sent my family to Texas."

"Texas?" Kelly asked.

Ty nodded. "Zane's ranch. I got in touch with Preston, he convinced the CIA to put agents from Austin down there to keep an eye out."

Julian perked up at the mention of the name. "Is Preston joining us?"

"He'll be here any minute. He said he has a job for you."

"Excellent," Julian said with a huge grin.

"How'd Tanner pan out?" Zane asked.

"He knew about the safe," Kelly answered. "Said a man claiming to be Burns's son came to him, asking about hiding spots. He told him where the safe was."

Nick was wincing and shaking his head as Kelly spoke. Something about Tanner's story hadn't settled right, but he wasn't sure what.

"Irish?" Ty asked.

Nick raised his head, surprised to find all of them looking at him. He sighed heavily. "I think he was lying as a misdirect so we'd think it was the cartel."

Nick had a hard time looking at Kelly, who had difficulty concealing his surprise. Nick wasn't used to playing his cards this close to the vest, and he could see it driving a wedge between him and Kelly with every passing minute.

"Something he said, about the safe in the floor. He made a joke."

"Jack Tanner was nothing but a big walking joke," Zane told him. "He was always really sarcastic. Maybe he hit you wrong?"

Nick shrugged. "It was a reference to 'The Tell-Tale Heart.'"

"So?" Owen asked.

"The book we found in the safe," Ty answered. "It was a collection of Edgar Allan Poe stories."

"Why the hell didn't you point this out earlier?" Liam demanded of Nick.

"Because I hate you, shut up," Nick grunted. He rubbed his eyes.

"If Tanner suspected you weren't who you said, he could have been playing with you." Zane sounded almost hopeful. He glanced at Ty. "Damn it, we should have gone to him, he would have known us."

Ty didn't respond, and his frown deepened.

"What's the plan now?" Digger finally asked.

The room was silent, everyone uncomfortable and tense without a solid answer.

Without a viable next step, the group decided there was no time like the present to gather their resources and get some sleep. They'd taken many extra hours making sure they hadn't been tailed to this location. They were safe here, for now. Ty couldn't shake off the sense that something was fundamentally wrong, but he supposed sitting here and staring at Liam while his chest throbbed from the beanbag he'd run into was bound to make him inherently uneasy.

Preston showed up not long after they did. He brought a folder with him that he silently handed to Ty.

"What's this?" Ty asked.

"The information you asked for," Preston told him, then turned to Julian, a smile spreading over his face. The two men embraced, holding on to each other for a long time.

Ty left them to their reunion, taking the folder over to Zane and sitting beside him at the card table in the kitchen.

"Is that the replacement cipher?" Zane asked, sounding impressed. They'd sent Preston copies of the printouts from the photos, and told him what book he needed for the key. It paid to have the CIA breathing down your neck, apparently.

Ty laid the papers out, and he and Zane bowed their heads together to study them.

"This is bank routing information," Zane said almost immediately.

"Send this shit to Clancy, tell them to get their hands on that money!"

But Zane was shaking his head, deep furrows in his brow. "We're missing information."

"What information?"

"This is what's called a numbered account at a Swiss bank," Zane told him, tapping the information. "Basically, the name of the account holder is shielded from all but the highest bank officials. You have to give them a code word to get into the account. Without that word, this information won't even tell us what bank it's at."

Ty rested his head in his hands, watching Zane through his fingers.

"And look at the file names of Burns's photos," Zane continued. "They're in numerical order. Three of the numbers aren't here. I think he erased those three photos, and whatever was in them, that's what we need to get into that numbered account."

"God damn it. So, he used this to keep his name off the radar."

Zane nodded, sighing as he crossed his arms on the table. "We're doing this ass-backwards. Usually, we're trying to find the name on the account. We already know it was his."

"What if it's yours?" Ty asked before he could stop himself.

Zane met his eyes as he ran a hand through his hair. "Then I'd go down for everything."

Ty lowered his head, closing his eyes.

"But if it is my name . . . all we'd have to do is figure out the code word, and I'd have access to the money. We get to it first, get it to the CIA, then this all goes away. We're in the clear."

Ty nodded, leaning closer until their shoulders brushed, until Zane's warmth was seeping into him. "We could take this to the CIA now. Let them handle it with what we've gleaned."

"And if they don't?" Zane posed. "They have no reason to go to bat for us, they could throw us under the bus just as easily as Burns did. Hell, *more* easily. And if it's my name on there, they wouldn't even have to work to put me away."

Ty nodded, fighting the constriction of encroaching panic in his chest. Over the last few years, basically every person in power Ty had ever trusted had turned out to be a horrible person who'd been trying to kill him. He wasn't about to take what they had to anyone until they were damn sure he and Zane would both come out the other end unscathed. He was beginning to realize that he'd never been out there on the wire without a backup. He'd always trusted Burns to do whatever was in his power to save him, and now, without that safety net, the world felt a lot bigger.

"The only way we're truly going to be safe is if we have that money in hand," Zane whispered. "We have to give the CIA what they asked for."

"Okay. So what do we need?"

"We need the code word."

"Word!" Digger said as he walked through the kitchen, heading toward the hallway where the bedrooms were.

Ty and Zane watched him, nonplussed. Owen came into the kitchen a moment later, smiling at their confused faces. "Cross and his CIA buddy left."

"What?" Ty blurted.

"He said they'd be back. Cross said he had a couple hides he could clear out, bring back some major ammunition and cash so we can stay off grid."

"Good," Zane grunted as he rubbed his eyes.

Owen sat across the table from them, backward in one of the cheap folding chairs, and leaned his elbows on the back of it. "Have you been watching Nick?" he asked Ty.

Ty scowled. "What do you mean?"

Owen shrugged, pressing his lips tightly together. "He's bent."

Ty blinked at Owen, his mind whirring, trying to deal with far too many problems at once.

"Bent?" Zane asked.

Ty took a deep breath. "It was something we used to say, back in service. It's . . . kind of hard to explain, but it's not good."

"Try."

Ty huffed. "See . . . there's a bond that can't be broken when you've fought together, and bled together, and cried together."

Zane slid his hand into Ty's lap, grasping his fingers and squeezing. He nodded.

"That bond is the only thing that keeps people like us from going insane," Owen added. "But when that wasn't enough, when one of us started losing it? We called it bending."

"You'd push and you'd push," Ty practically gasped. "And you'd fight and kill, and you'd see things no man should ever have to see. Do things no person should ever be forced to have on their conscience, and your mind would start to bend. You'd get to thinking that was just how life was."

"Did you ever bend?" Zane asked quietly.

"Hell yeah. It happened to each of us. Sometimes it was slow, we could see it coming, do something to head it off."

Owen rested his chin on the back of the chair, looking melancholy and distant. "A few nights of leave would help us realize there was a world out there beyond . . . sand and bullets and blood. But sometimes it'd just hit with no warning, one of us would go off the deep end. Hurt people we didn't need to."

Zane didn't speak, and Ty was kind of glad for it. His grip on Zane's hand tightened.

"Being cruel for no reason other than to see fear in someone's eyes," Ty whispered as he met Zane's eyes with a sad smile. "The thing was, your mind would bend and bend and bend, but it had to break to go back to normal. If it didn't break, you just bent until you got all twisted inside."

"We saw that happen too; evil, twisted bastards on both sides of the fighting."

Zane was frowning so hard it was almost painful to look at him. He rapped his knuckles on the table. "And Nick? Is he . . . bent? Twisted?"

Ty shrugged, his chin still resting in his hand. He moved his water glass around on the table.

"He was usually the one pulling us back from it. He always knew what we could and couldn't do if we ever wanted cosmic forgiveness," Owen explained.

"He was . . . like our moral center. I think it weighed heavy on him, but it was his way of anchoring himself. I saw him break once." Ty fell silent, staring at the water in his glass, lost in the memory somewhere.

"Ty?" Zane whispered.

"He was a scary motherfucker on his way down," Ty whispered, as if he'd never paused. "You remember how he was in Scotland?"

Zane swallowed hard, nodding. "Are we in danger? Will he hurt one of us if he snaps?"

Owen winced, meeting Ty's eyes. But Ty shook his head, jarring himself out of the funk. "I don't think so, no."

Someone cleared his throat from the doorway, and Ty tensed in expectation of it being Nick eavesdropping. He was almost relieved when it was just Liam. "I wouldn't be so sure of that, mate."

"I'm going to bed," Owen told them, and he stood with a quiet good-night, glaring at Liam in passing.

Liam slid into the chair that Owen had vacated.

Ty straightened, his eyes going hard. "What?"

"I know you think it was me switched those bullets out in New Orleans," Liam said solemnly. "But I've never tried to hurt you, mate, not before, not then. Not now. Someone switched those casings on me, someone who wanted you to die ugly."

"Are you really accusing Nick of that? *Again*?" Zane snapped.

"What?" Ty blurted.

Liam held up a hand. "I'm saying, how many people had access between the time you made up that fragmenting round, and when I loaded it into my gun? You two. Me. Sidewinder. And for the briefest of moments, my handler."

"Who was your handler?" Ty demanded.

"Her name was Anna. And the cartel killed her shortly after she left New Orleans. They framed me for her murder, and that's why the NIA is tracking my arse down like a dog. If she'd been working for anyone who wanted you dead, she'd still be kicking."

"Nick didn't switch those bullets," Ty declared.

"If you say so, mate." Liam sounded almost sad. He certainly looked it. "I'm just trying to tell you . . . watch your back. Take it from someone who knows. Friends and enemies? They sometimes wear the same clothes."

Zane was sitting in the middle of the sparsely furnished living room, helping to assemble their supplies. Cross had checked in a couple times during the night and the following morning, and he sounded certain that he and Preston would be bringing enough firepower to take over a Caribbean island by nightfall.

Until then, they were sorting the supplies they did have, and each of them had been studying Burns's cipher code, trying to figure out what the missing pieces might be.

So far they'd all come up empty.

Zane watched absently as they divided up and repacked their supplies. He found his eyes following Ty's hands as his nimble fingers folded, loaded, stacked, and packed. He'd always loved watching the way Ty's long fingers moved when he worked, and it didn't matter what Ty was doing for it to get Zane's attention.

"Need help?" Ty asked Nick, pulling Zane from his wandering thoughts.

Ty frowned as Nick muttered a reply, and Zane switched his focus to Nick's hands. They were trembling. He was so unsteady, in fact, that he had to try twice to insert an extra magazine into the elastic catchall on the side of one of the duffel bags.

Ty's words had drawn Kelly's attention as well. He craned his neck like a curious prairie dog, scowling at Ty and Nick from where he was sitting between two chairs. "Why do you need help?"

"I don't need help," Nick insisted, and he continued his packing, rolling up a piece of clothing so he could stuff it into the bag to cushion whatever explosive goody he'd just packed in there.

"Why are you shaking," Ty asked him. "I thought that medicine you had took care of the tremor."

It was obvious Nick had been hoping they'd all just drop it, and he glared at Ty before glancing at Liam, who was sitting on the arm of the couch, loading and checking their few weapons.

Liam looked up when the silence became oppressive, and he narrowed his eyes at each of them. "What?"

"What'd you do?" Kelly asked him. Zane could tell Kelly was getting angry and trying to keep a lid on his temper. He'd been angry ever since he'd arrived in Baltimore, though. He was angry at everything and everyone, including Nick.

Liam scowled, and he seemed confused when he glanced around the room again. He obviously hadn't been listening to them.

"Why's Nick shaking?" Kelly asked Liam. "What'd you do?"

"Hey!" Nick shouted. "I didn't fucking answer the question, means I don't want it answered!"

Kelly hopped to his feet, but it wasn't to confront Nick or yell at him. His brow creased in concern.

"Drop it," Nick grunted, and he went back to his packing, stuffing several bottles of Gatorade into his bag.

Zane realized he was holding his breath, and he met Ty's eyes across the room. Zane shook his head minutely, then tipped it toward the door. Ty pretended he didn't understand the gesture, though, and he stood and stepped toward Nick instead. He grabbed Nick's hand as Nick was reaching for the next Gatorade he intended to try to stuff into that duffel.

Nick's eyes were wide. Zane could see the tremor in Nick's palm, the unsteadiness in his fingers, and looking closer at him, Zane could see his jaw tensing, see the exhaustion and fear in his eyes.

Nick had been a Scout Sniper, the best in his class and, according to Ty, the best in their platoon. Snipers didn't get far with a tremor like the one rambling its way down Nick's arm into his fingers.

"How long's it been this bad?" Ty asked.

Nick yanked his hand out of Ty's grasp. "Don't worry about it. I can still shoot fine."

"Where's your propranolol?" Kelly asked him. His voice had lost that angry edge for once; he'd spoken in low, soothing tones designed to put injured men at ease and convince stubborn patients to trust him.

Nick's eyes darted back toward Liam, and he said, "It got misplaced."

They all shifted their attention from Nick to Liam.

"I tossed it overboard," Liam admitted. "First night on the *Fiddler* with him."

"You what?" Kelly and Ty blurted almost in unison.

"Nicholas isn't exactly a mewling kitten in the rain, gentlemen," Liam insisted. "Once I was on the boat with him and he knew I couldn't reach the Doc as a threat, I needed to find a weakness so I'd be able to handle him."

"A *weakness*?" Kelly tilted his head toward Liam as if he hadn't heard him correctly, and turned his body to the side like a man about to strike, offering less of a target by showing his profile. "Did you have any idea what it'd do to him to go off those meds like that?"

"I knew enough," Liam admitted. "I certainly regret the action now that we need him and his aim, but it's none of your concern either way. Irish and I have made our peace with it."

Zane looked back down at Nick, who had his hands resting on his knees, his tongue pushing against his upper teeth. Even with something under his fingers, they were trembling to the point that he looked like he was shivering with cold or nerves.

"What happens if you can't get more of the stuff?" Zane asked him.

"Nothing," Nick answered quietly. He held up his hand to show them, palm facing the floor. There was so much movement it seemed like Nick was doing it on purpose, exaggerating it until it looked fake. "I've been off it for almost three weeks; this is what happens. It's just a tremor."

"You told me it felt like your whole body was unsteady, that your *mind* was trembling!" Kelly growled. "You told me before that medication, it felt like you were standing on a vibrating platform. Is that what you're back to?"

Nick didn't answer. He wouldn't even meet Kelly's eyes.

"Maybe it's a mental thing, and you'll be nice and cured of it by the time this all ends," Liam said cheerfully. "Intestinal fortitude and all that rubbish." He snapped the cylinder closed on one gun and set it aside, reaching for the next.

Kelly chucked a shoe at him, hitting him in the temple. He teetered off the edge of the couch and toppled to the ground before he could catch his balance, then shouted a curse as he bunched his fingers in the edge of the couch to pull himself up. When his head popped up again, his eyes were wide. "What the hell, mate?"

Kelly dove over the arm of the couch, tackling Liam back to the ground. "Smug son of a bitch!"

Nick and Zane both hurried to their feet, and Ty rounded the couch in time to witness a wicked uppercut that laid Liam out like a cartoon boxer. Kelly straddled him, grabbing for him again as soon as his head hit the floor, fingers tangling in Liam's shirtfront.

"Piece of shit! Let's take something vital to your daily functioning and toss it over the edge of the boat!" He unholstered the knife on his thigh with one hand and grabbed the shell of Liam's ear with the other.

Ty and Nick shouted in alarm and lurched into action. They each grabbed one of Kelly's arms so he couldn't cut off Liam's ears. Or any other protruding parts. Kelly fought against their hold, nearly slipping through Ty's grasp before they were able to yank him off-balance and throw him to his back.

Nick held his forearm with both hands, wrapping his elbow around it to keep it immobile. Kelly was still clutching the knife, though.

"A little help here, Zane!" Ty said through gritted teeth as they struggled to keep Kelly from slipping past them. He was smaller than both of them, but he was wiry and trained and determined.

Zane stood a few feet away, arms crossed. "If I help anyone here, I'll be helping Doc loose so he can finish what he was doing."

Nick finally sank his teeth into Kelly's wrist, not breaking skin but biting just hard enough to warn. Kelly dropped his knife, but his usually placid eyes were blazing when he glowered up at Nick. "Why do you keep defending him?" he shouted. "Don't you fucking see what he did to you?"

Ty was on his hands and knees, breathing hard. Zane felt more than saw Owen and Digger come running in, both armed and ready for whatever mess had started. Ty held his hand out to stop them from coming closer.

"He isolated you, exploited your weaknesses!" Kelly was shouting "Exacerbated them by taking away the few things that you actually allow yourself to help you, and then he tried to convince you that *he* was the one who needed *your* help!"

"Doc, calm down!" Nick yelled, trying and failing to raise his voice over Kelly's ranting.

"Fuck you!" Kelly tore his hands away from Nick and Ty's holds and skittered backward. He lashed out with his foot, landing a solid kick at Liam's shin before he rolled to his stomach and pushed to his feet. He gave Nick a shove, snarling, trapping Nick's legs against the arm of the couch.

"Doc," Ty tried, resting his hand on Kelly's shoulder.

Kelly shrugged him off, pointing his finger at Nick's chest. "He stole you from us," he hissed. His expression crumpled, his breath catching when he inhaled. The loss and betrayal in his eyes was infinitely sadder when he spoke again. "He stole you from me. And the only thing you can do is sit there and defend him."

Nick was breathing harder, his lips parted as he stared at Kelly. He touched Kelly's arm, but Kelly slapped his hand away.

"I know how that tremor made you feel," Kelly whispered. "You told me once, remember? Back when you still trusted me. You told me once."

"Kelly," Nick repeated. He looked around at all of them, then at Liam on the floor. He seemed at a loss for how to handle Kelly when he was filled with what frankly seemed like savage rage and sorrow. Everyone seemed at a loss.

Kelly shoved away from them and stormed toward the doorway. Owen and Digger parted like the Red Sea to get out of his way. Liam groaned on the floor, holding his head.

Nick watched Kelly leave, a longing in his eyes that Zane hadn't known Nick was capable of feeling. But then to Zane's shock, Nick turned and reached down, offering his hand to help Liam off the floor.

Liam climbed to his feet, using Nick's arm and holding his jaw. "God damn."

A second later Zane saw a flash of movement and shouted a warning. Ty flinched as a knife flew past his ear and embedded itself in the wall next to Liam's head.

"Jesus Christ!" Liam shouted, stumbling back into Ty and flailing a little.

Nick ducked and covered his head, one hand reaching for the knife at his belt. Ty whirled around, hand on his gun.

It was Kelly at the door, though, chest heaving.

"Doc, what the fuck?" Ty cried.

Kelly wasn't looking at him. Or even at Liam. He was staring at Nick, his changeable eyes blazing. "Next time, I won't miss him," Kelly promised, then turned and left them.

More than a day after being cooped up with Sidewinder, Zane sat with his hands over his eyes, listening to them argue over dinner. Dinner! They argued over *everything*!

"Shut up!" he finally hollered.

Everyone froze, staring at him in shock.

"Pizza," Zane grunted, pointing at Owen. "Order it. Just cheese. Now."

The silence lasted a few more seconds. Then without a word, Owen shrugged and took out his phone to search for a pizza place, and the others all dispersed to go do whatever the hell Sidewinder did when they weren't trying to kill each other. How the hell had these men all lived in one house for years?

Ty patted Zane on the shoulder as he passed by, giving him a wink. Zane had to just roll his eyes. No fucking wonder the Marines had ousted these yahoos.

He was still sitting on the couch when he saw Kelly standing at the end of the hallway, his head cocked like he was listening to something. Then Kelly moved down the hall, out of sight. Zane glanced around, but no one else was around. He hefted himself off the plastic-covered couch and followed the man, peeking around the corner to see what he was doing.

Kelly was standing at one of the closed bedroom doors with his hand on his gun. Zane cocked his head just like Kelly had done, listening. He could hear voices now.

He'd seen Nick disappear this way earlier, slinking off with a shake of his head as the others argued about dinner. And Zane knew who else had missed the dinner discussion. Liam Bell. That meant Liam and Nick were in there talking. What would they have to talk about that they needed to sneak away like this?

Zane moved closer, and the creak of a floorboard under his boot had Kelly tensing and turning toward him, his gun halfway out of the holster. Zane held up his hands, then put a finger to his lips. He moved closer, and stood by Kelly's side as they listened to the conversation within.

It made Zane's fucking blood boil to hear Liam's quiet, soothing tones as he spoke to Nick. How much fucking with Nick's head had he managed before Nick had knocked on their door? What the hell was Liam's endgame here, anyway? He seemed to be aiming at simply driving Nick insane. The hell of it was, it was working.

The door was cracked, and Zane could just barely distinguish their words. Liam seemed to be trying to convince Nick that his friends would never forgive him. Kelly met Zane's eyes, and Zane wished he could comfort the man somehow. He looked so angry and distraught. Zane wondered if Kelly might actually kill Liam in his sleep soon, just to get his prongs out of Nick.

Zane might, if Kelly didn't.

Kelly angled his chin toward Zane, indicating he should move away. Zane ducked into the bedroom across the hall to watch, and Kelly silently eased the door open.

Inside, Nick was crouching with his back to the wall, even though there was plenty of furniture to sit on. Liam was on the edge of the bed, his back turned to them. Nick was gazing up at him, listening intently to whatever Liam had been saying.

Liam's final words reached Zane's ears. "It's not something you go back from, mate."

"It's not something *you* come back from," Nick snarled. "I'm not you."

"You could be," Liam said. "Lay your head down every night with no guilt on your conscience. You'd kill for that alone."

"The killing would only add more guilt," Kelly said. He sounded so livid, it made the hair on Zane's neck stand on end.

Nick looked up sharply, meeting Kelly's eyes with a distinct lack of emotion.

Liam, though, gave Kelly a crooked smirk over his shoulder and stood. He patted Nick on the head as he stepped past him. "I see it's time for the devil on the other shoulder," he drawled as he strolled past Kelly. "Don't put him up wet, hmm?"

Zane backed further into the dark bedroom as Liam went past.

Kelly took a step to go after Liam, but Nick barked, "Doc!"

It halted Kelly in his tracks, and he met Zane's eyes, nostrils flaring, eyes blazing. He finally turned back to Nick, shoving the door closed so Zane couldn't see or hear anymore.

Zane peeked around the corner to make sure no one was at the end of the hallway, then ducked across the hall, stretching himself out flat and peering through the gap under the bottom of the cheaply hung door. He could see Nick still sitting there, and Kelly's feet as he stood near the door, spread wide in a combative stance.

"I won't lose you to him. I won't," Kelly growled. "I refuse to see you go this way."

"Kels," Nick said tiredly.

Nick didn't make a move to stand or even get off the floor. He just sighed and hung his head, rubbing at his eyes.

Kelly moved toward him, dropping to his knees at Nick's feet. He gripped both Nick's ankles. Zane could still see Nick's face thanks to the extreme low angle of peeking under the door like a creeper.

"You know what he's trying to do," Kelly hissed.

"Of course I know what he's trying to do," Nick grunted, his green eyes flashing angrily. "You really think less than a month with him and I'd be cracking? Think, Doc. Use your head instead of your heart for once."

Kelly sat back, shoulders slumping. He was silent in the face of the anger roiling behind Nick's eyes. "You're playing his game," he realized, keeping his voice low. "You're trying to make him think he's winning."

Nick's expression softened. "I've gotten more information out of him in the last three weeks than we did in a year of working with him. He's trying to *recruit* me. He's scared. He thinks he'll be flying solo if he lives through this, which means he's either lying about wanting to clear his name with the NIA, or he knows his case is too hopeless for redemption and he pulled us in for another reason."

"What do you think?" Kelly asked.

"At first, I thought he was just after the money. But now . . . I think he's square with us. I think he was just desperate for someone to trust."

Kelly was beginning to tremble, but Zane wasn't sure if it was from relief that Nick wasn't as broken as they'd all thought, or from dread. "You . . . What do we do?"

"Just leave him be. Try to trust him like we used to."

Kelly was silent, his shoulders rigid. Zane took that moment to check his surroundings again, because he had absolutely no story for why he was on the ground in the hall watching Nick and Kelly talk if someone found him. When he peered under the door again, Nick had his hands on Kelly's shoulders.

He shook Kelly gently. "Can you *lie* about trusting him?"

"You know I'm no good at lying."

A smile tugged at Nick's lips. "Yeah, I heard about the IT thing."

Kelly snorted, but the laugh that followed was watery at best. He didn't say anything else; they just looked at each other for several seconds, communicating in that silent way Zane had observed. All of Sidewinder seemed to be able to do it, but Ty and Nick, and then Nick and Kelly, they seemed to be best at it.

"Just . . . will you give me back the man I know? Come back to me?" Kelly asked.

Nick nodded, moving his hands to Kelly's face. "I never left."

Kelly shook his head.

"I love you," Nick said. "You can't lose me. Not to him. Not to this."

Kelly kissed Nick, then threw himself on the floor beside him, leaning against the wall with him. They sat side by side, silent, their fingers curling together.

Kelly finally tilted his head, frowning at the door. "What's down, Garrett?"

Zane planted his face into the hardwood floor, blushing hotly. "Nothing. Just . . . lying around," he answered, and Nick and Kelly chuckled at him from within the bedroom.

CHAPTER 9

Zane sat on the front porch. He'd been caught spying, and though Nick and Kelly had laughed it off, he still felt awful about it. He'd expected to find himself eavesdropping on a fight, not a tender moment. He was still blushing even as he held his phone to his ear, listening to Clancy report on what they'd found in Switzerland.

So far they were striking out because they had absolutely no authority there, and opening up international channels would be impossible without tipping off the entire intelligence community to what they were doing. Zane told her about the numbered account and missing code word, and with the information her team had already culled, it only took her a few minutes to find the right bank and even the right contact at the branch they needed to visit. Clancy was good at her job, Zane had always known that. He was more impressed than ever with her now, though. He knew whose name he'd be submitting to replace him when he left his post.

Without the code word, though, even Clancy was at a dead end. She insisted they had to find those three missing pieces. They needed them, and for the first time Zane wasn't sure if they'd be able to get to the money at all.

What the hell were they going to do if they had nothing to trade the CIA for their freedom? The Company had made it quite clear to Ty that he was only useful if he brought that stolen money in, despite the fact that they probably had enough information to prove they were innocent. They even had enough information to give to the CIA and tell them to figure it the fuck out on their own. But without the money, there was no guarantee the CIA wouldn't burn them. And if they'd learned one thing over the years of dealing with men like Randall Jonas and Richard Burns, it was that they couldn't trust anyone.

What the hell were they going to do?

He thanked Clancy and hung up, taking a deep breath of the cold night.

The creak of a floorboard behind him was the only indication he was no longer alone. Ty sank to the step beside him.

"Bad news?" Ty asked softly.

"We need those missing pieces. Without them, we're dead in the water. We may as well start figuring out which alphabet agency we want to kill us."

Ty nodded and sighed. "We'll powwow one more time, see if we can't brainstorm something new. And we still have Cross and Preston out there, they may come up with a miracle. If nothing else . . . we'll head to Miami. If we can't bring the CIA money, maybe we can bring them de la Vega as the next best option. He'd be a huge win for whatever agency we take him to. It might work."

Zane nodded, watching Ty sympathetically. Ty's mind must have been reeling if he thought they had a snowball's chance in Hell at getting to de la Vega.

Ty glanced at him, smiling gently. "Nick told me you were pulling a Peeping Tom in there. What's wrong, love life not exciting enough anymore?" he teased, pushing his shoulder into Zane's.

Zane blushed, ducking his head. "I thought they were going to fight."

"It's Nick and Kelly. They never fight."

Zane nodded. He had to admire Nick's fortitude. Not only had he withstood Liam's mind games, but he'd actually managed to use them to his advantage.

"If only everything was as easy as that," Ty said, staring off into the distance.

Zane scooted closer and slid his arm around Ty's waist. He kissed Ty's shoulder, then rested his chin there as he held on to Ty.

Ty sighed out a puff of air and rested his cheek against Zane's forehead. "First Jonas, now Burns. I can't help but feel like my family is tearing itself apart."

"It'll be okay," Zane whispered. He nudged his face closer, holding Ty tightly. "We'll make it. You, me, family. We'll make it."

Ty didn't respond, merely sat there nuzzling Zane in the darkness, both of them swaying gently as Ty began to hum a tune. Then he straightened suddenly under Zane's hand, gasping, "Oh my God."

"What?" Zane asked, raising his hand like Ty was hot to the touch.

"Family. Three missing pieces. Three photos, right?"

"Probably."

"Before we left for Scotland, Dick gave me, Deuce, and my dad each a framed photo for Christmas. It was weird, he didn't usually go for that kind of stuff. It was him and my dad in 'Nam, him and Deuce at his college graduation, and him and me at Parris Island."

"That could be it, doll. Where are they?"

"Mine's at the house. Dad's is somewhere, Ma probably hung it up. Who the hell knows with Deuce."

"Call them. Call them now."

Ty scrambled to his feet and hurried back into the house to retrieve the brand-new, secure phone Preston had brought them. Zane stood as well, staring after him, hope burgeoning in his chest finally. A shadow moved in the corner of his eye, and he pulled his gun, aiming at the intruder without making a sound.

"Put it down, babe," Kelly said.

Zane lowered it with a roll of his eyes, sliding it back into the holster.

Kelly stepped out of the shadow of the building, glancing through the windows to check that the others were all inside. Then he looked back at Zane, silent and still.

Zane fought the urge to shuffle. "What?"

Kelly smiled slowly. "You heard me and Nick?"

Zane sighed, blushing yet again. "I told you I was sorry for spying."

Kelly nodded minutely. "You think Nick's right? About Bell?"

"No," Zane whispered.

"Why?"

Zane took a deep breath. "Bell's tried twice to convince me Nick switched the bullet that would have killed Ty in New Orleans. He's still playing sides, sowing seeds. I don't trust him. I *won't* trust him."

"Yeah," Kelly replied, hanging his head and twisting his fingers together. "As long as we all know."

"I got your back, Doc," Zane promised. "We won't let Nick slip away."

Kelly gave him a sad smile and a lazy salute. Zane heard the door thump, and he turned to see Ty coming back out with his phone to his ear. When Zane glanced back at Kelly, the man was gone.

Zane put his back to the darkness, just a little unsettled, and indicated for Ty to turn the speaker on his phone higher.

"What do you mean, where's my picture?" Deuce was saying. "Dude, you have *got* to remember that people can't read your brain waves."

"The framed photo that Uncle Dick gave you last Christmas," Ty clarified. "Do you still have it?"

"Yeah, it's in my office." Deuce sounded suspicious. "What's going on?"

"You still out of town?"

"Yeah, why?"

"Anyone know where you are?"

"What?"

Ty huffed impatiently. "Is there a trail that someone could follow to find you?"

"I guess, but we're on a yacht in the Caribbean, so . . . Ty, what's going on?"

"I need to break into your house."

Deuce sighed loudly. "Again?"

Zane left Ty to it, hurrying inside to roust anyone who might be sleeping. Most of them were gathered in the living room already, and Zane rounded up the stragglers, including Kelly, who had somehow made it back inside. Ty came in a moment later, shoving his phone into his pocket.

"What happened?" Nick demanded.

"Figured out where the missing pieces are," Ty answered. "One in Philly, one in Bluefield, one back in Baltimore." He glanced at Zane, breathing out shakily.

Zane nodded. "We can't hit all three places, stay under the radar, and keep ahead of the NIA on this. We have to split up."

"Is that our only option?" Owen asked.

"It is, yeah," Ty answered with an apologetic tilt of his head.

"We'll go in three pairs," Zane said. "One man waiting in the wings as backup."

"You already know you've got trouble in Bluefield," Kelly argued. "Take the third man there."

"Okay. Doc, you're coming with us." Ty waggled his finger between himself and Zane before he headed for the hallway to get their supplies.

Kelly opened his mouth as Ty walked away, but he didn't get a chance to voice an argument. He looked at Zane, his brow furrowed. "That's not really what I was aiming for."

"Ain't it a bitch?" Zane asked, following after his husband.

"Surprised they let us go at this alone," Liam told Nick as they moved toward Ty's row house in Baltimore.

"I promised them I'd kill you and throw your lifeless body into the ocean on the way home."

Liam gave Nick a sideways glance, narrowing his eyes like he was trying to determine if that was true or if Nick was just fucking with him.

Nick took the key from his pocket as they waited in the shadows at the corner of the block, watching the row house.

"Figures," Liam grumbled. "We get the place we *know* was being watched."

"More chance of losing you in a scuffle," Nick muttered.

"Sorry?"

"I said, front door or balcony?"

Liam shrugged, wincing as he glanced up at the moon. It was shining bright on the newly fallen snow, and that didn't exactly do them any favors. It was too cold for them to stand there with their thumbs up their asses for too long, and there was no darkness for them to hide in, no way to conceal their entry into the house from the pure white snow.

"Rather not deal with the neighbors and all that. Now or never, eh mate?" Liam finally said with a sigh that billowed out in front of him.

Nick just nodded, and they crossed the street together at an angle, both of them tense and wary. Liam was an absolute son of a bitch, but even Nick would admit he made a good wingman on nights like this. He always had.

They didn't encounter anyone on their way in. Getting into the house was easy too, since Ty'd given them his key. They both stood in the entryway, listening. The house was silent, but something didn't feel right. Nick glanced over at Liam, frowning. Liam nodded. He could feel it too.

Nick pointed at Liam with two fingers, then gestured toward the stairs.

Liam nodded and started silently up the steps. He managed to avoid most of the creaky places, but it was an old house and he wasn't a fucking magician.

If there was someone lying in wait, they'd know Nick and Liam were here. Nick began to rummage through the kitchen loudly, working as a distraction to give Liam time to find the photo. All they knew was it was on the third floor. All they had to do was take a picture of the thing, out of its frame, and send it to Zane. He'd said the photo would serve better than the print itself.

After a few minutes of making noise with the kitchen drawers and stealing two of Ty's cigars from under the sink, Nick headed up the steps, taking them two at a time. There was no need for silence now.

He stopped short in the hallway outside Ty and Zane's bedroom, attention caught by a photo on the wall. Ty's house was full of photos. This one was of Ty and Elias Sanchez on the day they'd graduated from the academy at Quantico, standing with Richard Burns and smiling for the camera. Nick had to shove down the anger he still grappled with every time he thought about Burns and the way he'd lured them into the Bureau, into whatever ring of corruption and evil he'd been running. Now wasn't the time to linger over things he couldn't go back and fix.

The ceiling above him creaked, the noise almost lost in the ambient sounds of the building. Nick's head jerked up, his body tensing. Liam was up there, of course. Nick had one hand on his weapon, regardless.

He'd spent plenty of nights in Ty's bedroom or the guest room on the third floor, listening to the house creaking, to the neighbors talking. It was always weird, coming from the solitude of his boat. He waited a few more seconds, just to be sure, but no other sounds came from above.

He gazed at the picture of Sanchez, Ty, and Burns and then forced himself to move away. He had to focus on the people he could help now. He wiped his eyes with the back of his sleeve as he headed for the top floor. The stairs were silent under foot, so he cleared his throat when he found Liam up there. Liam's phone was out, and he was watching the screen with a frown.

"Got it?" Nick whispered.

"It's going slow, the bastard." Liam winced, glancing up at him. His eyes widened. "Irish!"

Nick ducked instinctively, and whatever had been swung at him from behind grazed the top of his hair.

Nick turned on his assailant, pulling his gun and kicking out at the same time. The man tumbled backward down the stairs, crashing into the wall and knocking all the framed photos off their nails to clatter on top of his head.

"O'Flaherty," Liam hissed as he took the photo and stuffed it under his jacket. He ran for the balcony, yanking the stubborn doors open. "Come on!"

But Nick stood at the top of the stairs, eyes on the man who lay at the bottom in a heap. He was groaning and trying to get back to his feet.

"Go on, get that photo to transfer," Nick told Liam. "I have a few questions for our friend."

"Irish," Liam said urgently. "He is not the mission. Hear me? And if I go back without you, the Doc will kill me."

Bonus. Nick nodded, then started down the steps. He heard Liam curse, and then slip out onto the balcony.

Liam knew when to carry on with a mission, and his mission right now was to make sure that picture went through to the others. Nick had a new endgame tonight.

He got to the bottom of the steps, his gun trained on his attacker. The man was still sprawled on the ground, holding his head.

"Name," Nick demanded.

"Fuck you."

Nick snarled. The anger was just enough of a distraction that he didn't see the shadow in the doorway to the bedroom until it was too late.

A third dark form materialized in the bathroom door, flanking him as he put his back to the wall. The man on the floor took advantage and kicked Nick's gun from his hand. It clattered through the banister and down the stairs, dropping to the hardwood floor of the first level. Nick reached for the spare gun at the small of his back and shoved a shoulder into the nearest man, sending him crashing against the wall. But the second man wrapped him up from behind before he could draw his weapon.

Nick used the narrow hallway to his advantage as he slammed the man against the wall, cracking the plaster. He bent forward as the assailant's arm snaked around his neck, rearing back to slam him into the wall again. The plaster crunched beneath them, a crack skittering up to the ancient ceiling and showering bits of it down on them.

The man didn't let go, though, merely tightened his grip around Nick's neck. The second man picked himself up off the floor, pulled out a gun, and held it to Nick's head.

"Hello, Detective O'Flaherty. Long time, no see."

Nick stared at him, seeking out his shadowed eyes in shock. "You," he gasped, struggling for air as he yanked at the arm around his neck. He was getting light-headed.

"You sound more surprised than I'd thought you'd be."

"You son of a bitch!" he snarled, and he lunged at Jack Tanner, heedless of the gun at his head or of being outnumbered three to one. The man restraining him grunted, fighting to hold on. He was smaller, and the way he moved told Nick he wasn't extensively trained. Nick could take him if that gun wasn't on him.

"Money talks, Detective O'Flaherty," Tanner said almost sadly. "Money talks."

Nick growled like a tormented pit bull in a cage, the sound turning into one of anguish even as he gained the advantage on the man who held him. He put all his strength into turning, picking the man up, and swinging him around, practically throwing him and toppling Tanner and the third man into the banister as they collided. Nick reached again for the gun at the small of his back, but Tanner kicked at his hand from where he was sprawled against the cracking wooden spindles, sending that gun flying into the darker reaches of the bedroom.

Nick shouted as pain shot up his fingers and arm. He retaliated with a badly aimed kick that caught the first henchman in the thigh as they writhed in a pile of tangled limbs. Tanner was struggling to his feet, raising his gun.

Nick tackled him again, driven by blind rage. They rolled across the landing floor, and wound up teetering on the top of the stairs as each man got in some impressive punches. Then Tanner caught Nick under the chin with his elbow, and his balance went as the stairs opened up behind him. He wrapped an arm around Tanner, intent on taking the man with him.

They toppled down the stairs, the bricks opening up bleeding scrapes, the railing cracking beneath solid limbs. Something snapped like a handful of dry kindling, and Tanner cried out in agony.

Nick hit the ground floor and rolled, trying to fight the dizzying disorientation so he could scramble to his feet. He hit his head on one of the barstools in the kitchen, then got caught in it. He wound up picking the stool up off the ground and chucking it at Tanner.

Tanner cowered at the bottom of the steps as the barstool sailed over him. Nick set himself to defend, crouching low as he desperately searched for either of his lost guns. Tanner wasn't grinning anymore, but as his two henchmen hustled down the stairs, he seemed to gain a little of that confidence back.

One guy pulled a knife, lunging toward Nick. Nick strong-armed him, twisting to the side as he did so and pulling the kid with him. He threw him off-balance, and then slammed him to his back using his twisted arm. The floor shook with the impact and the knife went sliding off into the darkness.

Nick smashed his boot into the kid's face, then threw himself at Tanner as the man raised his gun to fire.

Both of them went sliding through the narrow dining room as they clawed and punched and fought for Tanner's gun. Tanner kept hold of it and rolled away, diving behind the chair in the living room for enough cover to take a shot. Nick leaped on the oversized armchair, heedless of what should have been an obstacle, and batted the gun from Tanner's hand. Tanner backpedaled, his eyes wide, but then lowered his shoulder and rammed into Nick, sending them both backward and upending the chair with them.

Nick hit the floor hard, kicking Tanner up and over his head. But he lay stunned for a moment as Tanner scrambled after the gun he'd dropped. Nick grabbed for his leg and tripped him up, scrabbling for the knife at his own thigh. He'd kill the bastard if he had to cut him a thousand times to do it.

One of the other men, whom Nick belatedly realized must have been Jack Tanner's newest prize pupils from the academy, kicked the knife from his hand before he could land a blow. Nick rolled to his feet, only to be kicked backward again before he could get his balance. The upturned chair behind him sent him head over heels, and he crashed into the coffee table.

He lay amid the wreckage of broken glass and shards of iron, stunned and trying desperately to convince his body to move before they came after him again.

But Jack Tanner and his two lackeys soon stood over him, guns retrieved and breathing hard. Tanner nodded to one of his men, who handed his gun to Tanner, yanked Nick up by his hair and throat, and held him by his elbows as Tanner threw a punch right into Nick's gut.

Nick doubled over, unable to make a sound as the stitches on his already bleeding wound failed and pain lanced through his midsection. Anger followed, white-hot anger so powerful it was almost as painful as his physical wounds. They were going to kill him anyway; he'd be damn sure to make a mess of it.

He threw his head back, ramming it into the rookie agent's nose. The kid gave a bark of pain, but he didn't let go. Nick kicked up and out at Tanner's head, and though he caught him in the chest, it wasn't enough.

Tanner staggered back, then returned even angrier to kick the side of Nick's knee so viciously it made an audible crack.

Nick howled in pain, his legs going weak. The rookie's arms were now the only things holding him up. The other one grabbed Nick's other arm, shoring him up between the two of them.

"Now, Detective, perhaps you can make this quick with some . . . interdepartmental cooperation," Tanner drawled as he picked up Nick's gun. He was trying to put up a calm front, but he was still panting, and his bruised fingers were shaking. Nick hoped that whatever he'd broken on the fall down the stairs would get gangrene and kill him nice and slow.

Nick was also gasping for breath, but he was unable to catch his. He closed his eyes, trying to will the pain away. He had to at least kill one of these bastards before they started talking. He just didn't have the patience for a monologue, not when his friends were out there fighting for their lives.

"You were so close ten years ago, you know that?" Tanner said. He glanced down at the floor, squatted to pick up a photo from a pile of broken glass, and stood, studying it. Then he squinted at Nick. "You didn't think I recognized you when you knocked on my door, did you? But Richard wanted all three of you. Wanted you desperately. The things he could do with a trained unit like that. When he realized you were going to refuse, he wanted you killed."

Nick's body flooded with ice. He hoped the pain covered his reaction.

"He decided to spare you, mostly because he knew your death would devastate the other two and make them useless to him. But if you'd convinced Grady not to join, I was supposed to take you down." He paused, flipping the photo so Nick could see it. It was of Ty and Nick, grinning, arms around each other, faces covered in greasepaint and blood. "So much potential," Tanner mused as he looked back at the picture.

Nick sneered at him, but he was fighting just to stay aware.

Tanner examined him speculatively. "I can't decide if you're worth keeping around, or if I should leave you for Tyler to find. I'm not sure we want to put that fire under him. Not yet."

Nick sagged against the men holding him, his vision blurring as the pain began to win the battle for his consciousness. "They'll kill you. He'll kill you."

Tanner narrowed his eyes.

Nick's strength gave out. He had no more fight in him. His knees buckled. His vision darkened and he cursed himself for giving in, for letting them win. But his body was broken and his mind was tired.

"What should we do with him, Wilkins?" Tanner asked one of his trainees.

"Kill him, sir."

Tanner smiled at Nick. "He's the best student I've had since Tyler came through."

Ty sat in the passenger seat, eating a chicken sandwich he wasn't entirely confident in, staring through the falling snow at the expanse of deserted parking lot around them.

They'd used a map to pick a town that seemed like it might be halfway for everyone, deciding to meet up in Winchester, Virginia, at a place called Apple Blossom Mall. It was big enough that their group wouldn't look too suspicious, and Ty and Zane had managed to find a corner of the parking lot that was out of the way of the security cameras.

"Heard from Cross yet?" Zane asked after a few minutes of silence.

Ty had to fight to swallow, and he shook his head. "I told him we were scattering, we'd be in touch when we hit the ground again. So I called him when we left the house, told him to meet us here. He should be here soon with a shitload of supplies."

Zane nodded, eyes on the moonlit parking lot. Ty wrapped up his questionable sandwich and stuffed it into his bag, placing it on the floorboard. "If I die, the chicken did it," he grumbled, earning a snort from Zane and nothing more.

Kelly sat in the backseat, bundled in a coat with a furry lining he was apparently having issues with, because he'd been threatening to hack it off with his knife all day long. "Told you to skip the fast food."

Ty rolled his eyes, sighing heavily. Kelly had been damn near impossible to deal with on their trip to Bluefield, and Ty just wasn't used to him being like this. Owen, sure. Hell, even Nick sometimes. Himself? Yeah, Ty was usually the one sitting in the backseat making people murderous with his comments. But he didn't know how to handle Kelly like this. They needed him, though. The house is Bluefield was a proven risk. Ty had made the call and Zane had backed him.

Ty glanced at Zane. He had assumed a position of leadership with their ragtag little band, whether it was giving orders himself or backing Ty's, and that suited him beautifully.

Zane obviously felt eyes on him, because he turned and winked at Ty, a smile flitting across his lips.

"They uploaded the photos, right?" Kelly asked. "Both teams?"

"Yeah, and we don't have any distress signals. We're okay, Doc," Zane assured him.

Nearly an hour later, headlights pierced through the snow, aiming toward them. The car came into view and pulled up beside theirs. Ty rolled down his window, raising an eyebrow at Owen and Digger. "You good?"

Both men nodded. "You?" Digger asked.

"We ran into leftover issues, but we handled it."

"Damn," Digger snarled, and he dug around in his pocket, pulling out a twenty-dollar bill and slapping it into Owen's waiting hand. "Why can't you assholes ever do nothing easy? God damn, son."

Ty grinned, glancing over to find his husband with his head lowered, rubbing his eyes with one hand.

Digger and Owen both got out of their car and climbed into the back of the SUV with Kelly, huddling in the chilly night.

"We get all three?" Owen asked.

Zane nodded, holding up his iPad. They'd forwarded the photos to Preston's contact at the CIA, and they were being graced with a live stream of the decoding so they could run with it if they figured it out before it was done.

"This fucking code word of his better not be 'password' or some shit; I'll throw down," Digger grunted. Kelly snorted as he huddled between them, arms crossed, looking mutinous.

"So far, we know it's six letters. That's as far as they've gotten," Zane told them.

"Hey Six, you knew the guy. You got any ideas yet?" Owen asked.

Ty shook his head forlornly. "I didn't know him at all."

Headlights blinked from several sections over, and Ty could feel Kelly shifting around in the backseat, peering through the window. The car came to a stop on Zane's side, and he rolled down the window so they could see past the ice accumulating. Liam was in the driver's seat, his head lowered. He was alone.

"No," Kelly snarled. "No!"

Liam rolled his window down, sighing as he shook his head. "There were men waiting in the house," he told them. "We thought it was one, I went outside to get the transmission through, Irish stayed in to handle it. Turns out there were three."

Ty's breath left him in a rush so painful he had to grab at his chest.

"I saw them carry him out," Liam continued solemnly. "He wasn't fighting."

The backseat was as quiet as a crypt. The only sound in the car was Zane breathing.

"I had no clear shot, so I followed them. But I lost them in the city," Liam admitted. "I'm sorry."

Zane took a deep breath before he glanced at Ty, expressionless.

"Six," Digger whispered. "We got to go after him."

Ty nodded, but he wasn't actually hearing anything but the blood rushing through his ears.

"Ty," Zane finally whispered.

As they sat in the heavy silence, Zane's iPad beeped at them. He picked it up, catching his breath. "We have three of the letters."

Ty's skin pricked as he realized he had to make the decision. Go after the money, save himself and Zane, prevent the CIA and NIA from going to war, and get the Vega cartel off Zane's back for good. Or go back for Nick, who may well have been dead before he left that house.

He swallowed hard, looking over the backseat at Kelly.

"No!" Kelly shouted, and began struggling to get past Owen and out the door. "Fuck you!"

There was a lot of tussling in the backseat, and Kelly finally managed to get out of the SUV, taking Owen with him as he did. He rounded the car, slamming both fists against the hood of Liam's sedan. "You came to him for help! He was the only one who trusted you to have his back, and you left him alone!"

Ty was leaning over the console, watching Kelly, eyes widening the more Kelly shouted. He huffed angrily and moved to join Owen, who was standing behind Kelly, watching him rant.

"He trusted you!" Kelly shouted at Liam, who was still in his car. Kelly pointed at him, turning to Ty. "He's after the money, nothing more. Everything he's told us, we can't fucking believe it. Anything he's told you, anything, you fucking forget he ever said it!"

As they stood in the beams of Liam's headlights, another car approached. The crunching tires and Kelly's heaving breaths were the only sounds in the snow.

Julian and Preston got out, both men warily examining the scene. Finally, Julian nodded at Kelly. "What's up, Doc?"

Kelly turned to Ty and Owen defiantly, as if that had been the absolute last straw. Ty put his hands up to ward off whatever Kelly had in mind, but Kelly moved to Owen, palm out.

"Keys!"

"Where's the detective?" Julian asked.

"He was taken," Ty answered.

"And I'm assuming the Doc is going to go rampage after him," Julian said. "Well, then."

"Doc, stop!" Owen cried as he tried to fend Kelly off, who was patting him down to find the keys to the other car. "We're going with you!"

Liam opened his door, but Zane reached through the window and shut it in his face as he tried to get out. "Stay."

Kelly turned on Ty then, jaw set, eyes flashing. "You have to go find that money to save the man you love, I get that." Then he pointed to his own chest. "But I've got to do the same thing. I'm going to find Nick. I'm done."

Ty felt the world spin a little as he tried to come to terms with the fact he was considering letting anyone else go rescue his best friend without him. "Fuck this!" he finally huffed. He brushed past Kelly, heading for the driver's side door of the SUV. "Zane."

Zane was nodding. "Let's go get him."

Ty's heart clenched. "Are you sure?"

Zane smiled softly. "What good is it to save ourselves if we sacrifice who we love along the way?"

Ty puffed out a relieved breath.

"I'm not coming with you, though," Zane added.

"What, why?"

"I want to go to Quantico, talk to Jack Tanner. I think I can read him better than Nick. A day out of the way, then I'll join you."

"But going alone—"

"Ty, I'll be okay for twelve hours."

Ty was skeptical, but he nodded. "We'll find Nick. You question Tanner. We'll meet in the middle."

A face swam above Zane's vision, blinking in and out as he fought his way back to consciousness.

"First lesson I ever taught you, boy," Jack Tanner said with a shake of his head. "Never trust *anyone*."

"What?" Zane whispered, and he squeezed his eyes closed to fight back the nausea and confusion.

What the hell had happened? He remembered leaving the other boys to their search for Nick and driving toward Quantico. He vaguely remembered trying to find the right address to talk to Jack Tanner, and he remembered being excited to see the man again. The one man in the academy who'd believed in him, who'd seen something in him to push for. He wasn't ashamed to admit he was looking forward to Tanner seeing him now, seeing what he'd made of himself.

But after that, he had no memory of anything. Had he been jumped? Had he had an accident? Why the hell did his head hurt so much?

"I hit you in the head, son," Tanner told him, sounding almost amused. "Wilkins. You two idiots come hold him before he gets his senses back."

Rough hands dragged him off the ground. Zane was battling to remember, to understand. He'd been welcomed into Tanner's home and offered coffee, and then . . . This was not how he remembered Tanner's coffee.

He shook away the confusion and the blurriness, meeting Tanner's eyes as two other men held his arms and propped him up on wobbly legs.

"Always did have a hard head, didn't you, Zane?" Tanner asked. "Where's Dick's money?"

"What?"

Tanner waved a photo in Zane's face. It was the one of Ty and Nick that had been hanging in their living room. There was blood smeared over the corner of it. "I know you and your boys are looking for the money Dick stole. You got into that safe, didn't you?"

"You were the one after it?"

"Neighbors called the law on me before I could get it open. Richard and I were partners. The information in that safe is rightfully mine. What was in it?"

Zane struggled to pull in breaths, trying not to react too violently to the photo or to Tanner's betrayal. Pain burned through him, making things hazy, blurring his vision. Blood was pounding through his head at warp speed, and he could feel it trickling down his neck.

"Why not just kill them when they came to you?" he asked Tanner roughly, though deep down he knew the answer. If he could stall, though, maybe Ty would realize he was in danger, or he'd find an opening to attack. "Why the act?"

"Because when your idiot friends showed up at my door, I realized you and Grady knew where the last pieces of Richard's little puzzle were hidden. He tried to screw me." Tanner stood up, shoving the picture of Ty and Nick in Zane's shirt pocket. "And really, Garrett, I just need you. Not Grady. Certainly not any of your friends. All I need is the information from that safe. And I know you can get it for me."

"Fuck you."

"I thought that might be your answer." Tanner held up one of Zane's knives in a hand with a brand-new cast. "I can get it from your husband."

Zane couldn't hide the stark fear that came over him. He tensed his shoulders and yanked at the men holding him, almost pulling the smaller of the two off his feet.

Tanner laughed and then hit Zane with a sharp left hook, leaving his cohorts to shore Zane up. Zane used the leverage and kicked out with both feet, hooking one ankle around Tanner's neck. When Tanner ducked and bowed his head under the weight, Zane got the other foot against his neck and tightened his feet together like a vise.

Tanner flailed and pushed ineffectually at Zane's foot, hitting his leg with the plaster cast. A little more torque and Zane thought he might be able to snap the man's neck. He pushed his toes against Tanner's chin. Tanner gasped and motioned wildly at his lackeys, who both simply stepped back and let Zane go, removing his leverage. But Zane refused to release Tanner, even as he lost the support from behind.

The thin rug didn't do anything to pad his fall, and the hard landing stunned him once more as pain lanced through every joint in his body. He lost his grip on Tanner's neck, and a heavy, booted foot pressed down on his throat before he could recover his senses. He gasped and grabbed at the ankle, receiving an angry kick to the ribs for his trouble.

"Always were a persistent little shit," Tanner hissed breathlessly. He was on his knees, and he gestured to his men as he climbed back to his feet. "Get the bastard up. And hold him this time!"

The rookie agents bent obediently to haul Zane up, cursing at him under their breath.

Tanner took a syringe from his back pocket, holding it up as they struggled with Zane to bare his arm. Zane twisted and fought, even biting down on an arm that came too close to his mouth. But the needle burned into his skin, flooding his body with ice.

Tanner sneered at him as his vision wavered. "We'll see how fucking tough you are when you're watching your friend bleed out in front of you."

"I'll kill you," Zane whispered.

"You can sure as hell try, boy."

CHAPTER 10

Zane woke so fast it stole his breath. It was dim when he opened his eyes, and what little he could see in the room was blurry.

He blinked the haziness away, trying to focus on something. It was long, painful minutes before he truly trusted what he was seeing. An old ceiling fan was spinning lazily above him, and Zane's eyes followed the waffle-knit pattern on the stained blades.

The motion of the fan began to make him queasy, and he turned his head before he could think better of it. He hadn't meant to alert anyone until he could discern where he was, but he'd fucked that up. He must have been hit harder than he'd thought.

Movement in the room made him tense, and he kept his eyes shut, trying to fake sleep. Chains clanked.

"Garrett?" someone whispered.

Zane's eyes popped open.

Nick was hunched across the room, watching him. He breathed out in relief when Zane revealed he was conscious. "Thank Christ."

"O'Flaherty?" The word came out slurred and mangled. He closed his eyes and tried to clear the cobwebs left in his head.

"You been out a long time. Take it slow."

"How long?"

"Twelve hours. Maybe longer."

"Shit. Oh God, my head." Zane tried to reach up to check for a knot or blood. Neither hand moved.

"You apparently have a habit of fighting in your sleep. Didn't bother with handcuffs after you decked him."

Whoever had tied him up had wrapped a nylon rope around him, securing his hands behind him. He looked across the room at Nick. "Tanner?"

"He's after the money."

Zane blinked, and Nick nodded, smiling grimly.

"*Hijo de puta*," Zane snarled. He remembered now. He remembered everything. "Why the hell didn't we make that connection earlier? I walked right into his fucking house and asked for coffee."

"Too much shit blowing up."

Zane tried to turn so he could see Nick's condition better. His face was bruised and bloodied. He'd ripped his shirt into long strips and tied them around his ribs and his knee like he was trying to stabilize a break or dislocation. He was in awful shape, but he was alive. "We thought you were dead."

Nick shrugged one shoulder and looked pointedly around the room. "Close enough. Don't eat the food, by the way. It's drugged."

They stared at each other, and Zane could guess what was going through Nick's mind: flashes of a tiny cell and orders shouted in Pashto like Ty had told him about.

"O'Flaherty."

"Don't worry about it, Garrett, I'm okay." Nick smiled tiredly, tapping his temple.

Zane returned the smile with a glimmer of hope. Between the two of them, they'd be resourceful enough to get out of here. Right?

"How far have you gotten?" Zane asked him.

"Made it to the front door. One of his little cockmuppets took me down with a Taser."

Zane had to smile. Of course they had Tasers. "What's the structure?"

"Trail cabin, maybe. Definitely in the middle of nowhere. No one to hear you scream."

"Jack Tanner had a hunting cabin in northern Virginia."

Nick adjusted the way he was sitting on his thin mattress. A bed just like Zane's had obviously once been there. Zane wondered what Nick had done to get it taken away. He leaned against the wall with his hands in his lap. He was handcuffed and chained to a bolt that appeared to have been hastily drilled into the subfloor beneath the hardwood.

"Can you get out of those?" Zane asked, hope sparking in his chest.

"Yeah, Garrett. I've just been sitting here wearing them because they bring out the stainless steel in my eyes."

Zane glared at him. He knew Ty had a knack for escaping from handcuffs, and he had no doubt Nick knew the same tricks.

"I used my only lockpick the first attempt," Nick said. "I got nothing left. You still got that nickel?"

Zane sighed and shook his head. "Gave it back to Ty when he started whining about me stealing his toys."

Nick nodded.

Zane studied the room for anything to aid in their escape. There was one window, possibly large enough for them to slip through, but it would be tight. Nick had tested the door already. But hell, they had to get out of their restraints first.

Nick inhaled noisily as Zane pondered their situation. "Did you steal Ty's go bag boots?"

Zane glanced at him distractedly, nodding. "Yeah. I told him he could have them back, but I'm a dirty liar. They're like walking on clouds."

"Garrett!" Nick's handcuffs clanked when he moved. "The laces on those boots, the plastic thingies have modified handcuff keys on them."

"The aglets?" Zane asked. He squirmed around, trying to loosen the ropes enough so he could see his shoes.

"The what?" Nick asked, sounding an odd combination of desperate and exasperated.

"Aglets. Plastic thingies."

"Why do you know what those things are called?"

"*Phineas and Ferb*."

"You watch cartoons?"

Zane laughed hoarsely. "Kind of judgy for someone who can sing the country song from *Animaniacs*."

"Damn you, Tyler! Can't keep a fucking secret!"

"I know all sorts of things, O'Flaherty," Zane crooned, grinning as he squirmed.

Nick grunted, taking a deep breath. "Garrett, just . . . can you get your foot this way?"

Zane gauged the distance between them, estimating it was perhaps ten feet, maybe less. There was no way he could get his foot to reach Nick, even with his long legs.

"I can try kicking it," Zane decided. He tried to work his boot off with his other foot, struggling with the tightly tied laces. While he worked at the boot, Nick stretched across the expanse between them. It was a standard-sized bedroom, but suddenly it seemed like a football field. With his arms straining above his head, pulling the chain of his handcuffs so tight they cut into him, Nick could just manage to brush his bare toes against Zane's boots.

They could do this. Zane could get the boot close enough that Nick could pull it in and free them both.

He just had to get the damn thing off. "The laces are too tight," he said through gritted teeth.

Nick huffed and felt for the end of one of the laces with his toes.

Zane couldn't help it. He started to laugh.

Nick sighed, staring up at the ceiling. "I don't know who's worse to be held captive with, you or Ty." He grunted when he was able to get a lace between his toes and tug it free.

Zane was still laughing when he managed to get his boot off and kick it over. It landed on Nick's stomach, muffling any sound made in the exchange.

Nick winced and gritted his teeth against a cry of pain. Then he looked down at the boot, one eyebrow raised. "Bravo."

"It's been a weird week."

Ty knelt in the living room of the little house near the Marine base at Quantico, his eyes trailing over the mess, his body tense.

The others were fanned out, some of them keeping watch, some of them helping Ty search.

They'd scoured Baltimore for clues to where Nick had gone, starting with the scene in the row house and then following the trail until Ty had dead-ended at a road where Fell's Point tourists often parked cars.

The trail he'd followed had been nothing but evidence of a body being dragged. He'd tried to prepare himself, and the others, for not finding Nick alive. Or at all. His body might be in the harbor right now. Or in some swamp down south. Ty didn't know. He couldn't know.

Owen had tapped into the local police database, searching for security camera feeds to give them a hint of what type of vehicle they were after, or whether Nick had even been alive. He'd gotten nothing.

Their twelve hours had run out on them with nothing but heartache to show for it, and they'd gone to meet with Zane. When he hadn't shown up, Ty had driven them to Quantico.

And they'd found this disaster.

"At least it don't look as bad as your house," Digger tried. They all stood around, listless, shoulders slumped, looking like they'd lost already.

They *had* lost. And now they'd lost Zane, too.

Ty felt a sort of calm coming over him, much like the one he'd experienced at Langley while being questioned, but this was a little different. There was an edge to it, one that made him want to see fire on the horizon.

He'd find Zane, or he'd burn this place to the ground.

"I got Zane's service weapon," Kelly called from the kitchen. He stood up, holding the gun up by a pen through the trigger guard. "Wedged under the cabinets, like it slid in here."

Ty looked from him to the drag marks in the carpet. Next to them was a granite block that appeared to be a set of coasters in a holder. The top coaster had a war eagle on it, with the words Ranger Up written on it to make a decorative seal. There was blood on the corner.

Jack Tanner had been a Ranger.

If Zane had walked in here, he'd been caught entirely unaware. Digger was right, there'd been no struggle, nothing like the one at the row house. That meant Zane had been attacked by someone he trusted.

Someone like Tanner.

Ty stood, taking a deep breath as he his body ran with ice. "I know where they are."

The others stopped whatever they were doing and moved closer.

"Jack Tanner. He worked with Burns, and he must have known about the money. He's after it. He took Nick. And now he's taken Zane. I know the way he works, he'll use one to make the other talk."

Kelly closed his eyes and turned his head away.

"You can find them?" Owen asked.

"Tanner had a cabin. A hunting cabin. He'd take them there."

"Can you find it?" Liam asked.

Ty merely nodded, returning his weapon to its holster and turning for the door. "We have to hurry. They'll be dead by nightfall."

Zane crouched behind the head of the bed, trying to make himself small. They'd shoved the window open, and though Zane was fairly certain he could get his shoulders through it with a little creativity, Nick was too injured to manage it, even with help.

He'd told Zane to run, but Zane would be damned if he left the man there. The only way they were getting out of this place was together, and the only way they were doing that was by fighting their way out.

Nick lay curled on his mattress, his cuffed hands held to his ribs, rocking rhythmically, much like Ty always did when he was miserable.

Zane worried about the internal damage Nick may have suffered. He'd taken a look at Nick's torso, and the bruising looked like a Rorschach test. Not only that, but once they were free of the room, Nick wouldn't be able to run. He claimed his knee wasn't dislocated, but Zane wasn't going to bet their lives on him being right.

That left them only one chance at getting out of here: kill everyone they encountered, and walk out.

After what seemed like hours of waiting, there was a thump at the door, and the metallic slide of a hefty lock. Nick didn't cease his rocking. Zane shrank further into his hiding spot, forcing his mind to calm, his body to steady. They had exactly one shot at this.

A man stepped into the room, halting when he saw the ropes on the ground and empty bed where Zane was supposed to be. "Shit!" He dropped whatever he'd been holding to dart toward the window and look out. "Wilkins!"

The man then turned to Nick with a snarl. He lunged toward him, grabbing his hair to pull him out of his curled position.

"How long's he been gone?" he demanded.

Nick moved fast, going from hurt and lethargic to lethal in a blink of an eye. He brought an elbow against the man's neck, laying him out, and then he whipped the handcuffs off his wrists as he pounced the felled jailer. He slung one of the rings open with a flick of his fingers and drove the dull tip into the man's eye.

Zane shot forward, stripping the twitching guard of every possible weapon even as Nick, one hand over the man's mouth, tried to pull the curved bit of the handcuff out of his eye socket.

Zane put the guard out of his misery as Nick held him down. Then he tapped Nick's shoulder with the dripping knife blade and handed him the gun. When he looked up, a man was standing in the doorway, stunned into immobility. Zane stood and tossed the knife, but the man ducked out of sight.

Zane dove for the door, grabbing up the plastic tray full of spilled food the guard had been bringing them, and then shoving it into the frame as the heavy door slammed closed. The tray snapped, but it prevented the door from latching, and Zane kicked it open.

A gun wavered toward his head. Zane smacked it away with what remained of the tray in his hands, and it went flying. The guard, who was nothing more than a kid, grabbed for the knife at his thigh.

Zane yanked his knife out of the doorframe and then flipped it in his hand so it was snug against his forearm. He lunged, grabbing the kid by his shoulder and slicing the knife across the side of his neck, then coming back and embedding it into his spine. When he pulled the knife out, the kid dropped like a stone.

Zane wasn't even breathing hard when he crouched and got eyes on the cabin. He'd never been here; he'd merely heard Tanner talk about it a few times. It was one large room with a kitchen and dining area on one end, a living space on the other. There was the bedroom they'd been kept in, and what appeared to be another bedroom next to it.

Tanner was nowhere to be seen.

"Garrett?" Nick was out of breath and getting worse. They couldn't linger or Zane might not be able to get Nick out at all.

"Tanner's not here," Zane answered, keeping his voice soft.

"Let's book it, then, bud," Nick grunted, and Zane glanced over his shoulder to find Nick right there behind him.

"You moving okay?"

"Enough to get the fuck out of here."

Zane offered his help anyway, and Nick wrapped an arm around Zane's neck, leaning on him as they limped out of the room. Zane led them as Nick kept his gun up, watching the other bedroom for movement.

They were almost to the front door when Nick fired a shot, then cursed.

Zane dropped low, pulling Nick with him. But they had nowhere to take cover in the wide-open room.

"Missed him," Nick grunted as he checked the sight on the gun they'd taken from one of the dead men. "Off by an inch. Motherfucking federal rookie doucheclowns!"

Zane stared at the open bedroom door, bringing Nick to rest with his back against the sofa. "Cover me."

"Garrett, either this gun's off or I am," Nick warned.

Zane didn't take his eyes off the doorway. He just nodded, patting Nick on the shoulder. "You'll figure it out when I need you. Cover me," he said again, and he slapped the bloody knife against his forearm, creeping closer to the open door. "Jack?"

He heard a loud sigh from within the room. "You really could have been something, Zane."

Zane tried to find an angle or a reflection, anything to get an idea of where Tanner was and how he was armed. "I do okay."

Tanner laughed. "Millions of dollars, Zane. *Hundreds* of millions. And you had to go turn honorable on me. You and Grady. Never pegged you for the type. Him, yeah, I pegged him. So fucking eager to bend over and take it."

Zane gritted his teeth, telling himself to ignore everything the man said and keep his eye on the prize here.

"I'm going to kill you, Zane," Tanner said, his tone conversational. "Right after you tell me where that money is."

"How do you figure?"

"Class fuckup, couldn't even make it up the rope," Tanner drawled, chuckling. "Thinks he can take down Teacher. You remember who taught you to use those knives?"

Zane narrowed his eyes, adjusting his grip on the handle of the knife. All these years, Jack Tanner had been a bright spot in his memory, the only person besides Becky who'd ever believed in him. Losing that memory to Tanner's betrayal brought sharp grief barreling back into him, like he was standing in the damp and watching his beloved wife's casket being lowered into the ground all over again.

He bared his teeth, unwilling to lose one more piece of himself to anguish from the past. Tanner was about to pay for every moment of Zane's suffering, every turn of his spiral. Finally, Zane could avenge himself on someone who fucking deserved it. "Let's play, then."

"Garrett!" Nick said from behind him. "Don't be fucking stupid, man."

Zane just shook his head. Tanner appeared in the doorway, two small blades in his hands. Zane motioned with one hand for Nick to hold his fire, and was rewarded with a string of curses.

Tanner raised an eyebrow, shrugging at Zane. He was grizzled, with more wrinkles on his leathery face and more gray hair than the last time Zane had seen him. But he was still wiry and spry, still capable. He rolled his head from side to side and shook his shoulders out. "All grown up, now, Zane."

Zane eased back into a defensive stance, bringing both hands up and flipping the knife so the blade faced out. Tanner didn't offer more conversation. He lunged, aiming for Zane's knees. Zane dodged and swiped at his head, coming back on the return to nick the meat of Tanner's upper arm. Blood sprayed, and he retreated, circling, arms up and ready.

"Garrett, I got him," Nick called, but Zane shook his head.

"This one's for me."

Tanner attacked again, and this time Zane stepped to the side. Tanner's thrusting knife went past his torso, and Zane brought an elbow up, smashing his chin. He jammed his ring finger under Tanner's nose, forcing his head back, and threw him to the ground headfirst.

He kicked Tanner's knife away, then jammed his blade in Tanner's wrist, pinning his arm to the ground.

Tanner screamed and dropped his other knife.

Zane bent over him with a sneer. "My husband taught me that one," he growled, and then he straightened and smashed his boot into Tanner's face.

He backed away, knowing better than to take his eyes off Tanner even though he was pretty sure the man wasn't getting up again. He put out a hand, and Nick placed the gun in it, then Zane took three long strides back to Tanner, looming over him.

He gurgled when he breathed, and his eyes were fluttering as he fought with consciousness. "Zane."

"Go straight to Hell," Zane snarled, and put a bullet in the man's forehead.

Zane stood over him for a moment, letting the pain leak out of him along with the blood pooling on the floor.

He was done losing things from the past.

"Garrett," Nick finally said, and Zane turned to him. He was holding to his side, breaths ragged and eyes glassy.

Zane nodded, then bent to search Tanner's pockets for keys. He took the time to go through Tanner's desk too, but there was nothing in the cabin they didn't already know, and Zane wasn't willing to spend more time searching. If Nick didn't get help, Zane would lose him.

He gathered Nick up, and they struggled to their feet. Zane handed him the gun again so he could cover them while Zane got them to Tanner's car.

"That was pretty," Nick croaked.

Zane merely nodded as they shoved through the front door of the cabin. They stumbled into the dirt driveway, the setting sun blinding them both.

Something broke the tree line to their left and skidded to a halt. When Zane turned Nick toward it, Nick squeezed the trigger.

The shot whizzed past Ty's ear before anyone even realized he was almost dead.

Nick hung off Zane's shoulders by an arm, both of them staring at Ty with wide eyes. The gun was still clutched in Nick's trembling hand, wavering in Ty's direction.

Ty breathed out slowly. He patted his chest to make sure he was okay.

"I'm going to throw up," Nick grunted. He pulled off Zane's shoulder and turned, falling to his knees. The gun clattered away from him.

Zane took a few careful steps toward Ty before jogging to him and grabbing him.

Ty clutched to him, digging his fingers in his hair. "I swear to God, I'm never letting you leave my sight again," he hissed in Zane's ear.

Zane buried his face in Ty's neck. "I'm good with that."

CHAPTER 11

The drive to Texas from Virginia was harrowing, to say the least. It took them a solid day to get there.

They had to worry about Digger strangling Liam every time the man spoke. And the way Nick's eyes went distant when he thought no one was watching him, the way he favored his injuries when he thought no one saw. And Owen taking a couple of those pain pills for his broken arm and waxing poetic about a girl he'd been dating named Riley that none of them had heard of before, and Ty wasn't sure whether to think she was real or a figment of Owen's drugs.

When they rolled into Austin, Ty was driving the Mustang, with Kelly following in the SUV. Ty'd seen the car swerve a few times in his rearview mirror, but no alerts had come over their two-way. He sort of imagined a fight in the backseat that wound up with Kelly threatening everyone with a flyswatter as he drove.

Zane, apparently, had seen the last swerve as well. "Not exactly the elite fighting force we were hoping for, huh?"

"They'll settle when it's time," Ty assured him. He could feel Zane watching him, and he glanced over with a weak smile. "How's the arm?"

"It's fine," Zane assured him. "I can go."

Ty knew his husband well enough to see a lie when Zane told one.

Nick lay in the backseat of the Mustang, sleeping off whatever shot Kelly had given him. His ribs were bound and they had wrapped his knee as tightly as he could stand it. Ty shook his head; the two men he trusted most in the fucking world to have his back during a fight, and neither was well enough to get into a fight.

An hour after hitting Austin, they were stopped at the front gate of the Carter Garrett Ranch. Zane got out and opened it, holding it for both cars to drive through before swinging it shut and latching it. He jogged toward the Mustang and hopped back in, and Ty continued on toward the main house.

He was surprised to see how different the ranch looked from the last time they'd visited. A few of the buildings that had caught fire had been rebuilt. New fences stretched as far as the eye could see. Even the main house had some additions: repairs from the attack it had suffered several years ago.

Ty wasn't sure why he was surprised. Of course they'd rebuilt the place. He got out of the Mustang, stretching. Nick was still asleep in the back, and Ty left him to rest.

The chase car turned off, the engine clicking in the peaceful silence of the ranch. Then both of the driver's side doors popped open and Kelly lunged out of the car, grabbed Liam through the open window of the door between them, and punched him in the face. The only reason Kelly didn't go after him again was because he got caught in the window.

Ty and Zane stood side by side, watching as the others tumbled out of the vehicle to break up the fight.

Ty finally shrugged at Zane. "I don't want to know," he grunted, and they turned in unison toward the front porch.

Harrison met them on the porch, a tired smile hidden halfway under his handlebar mustache. He gave them each a hug, patting them both on the back and then the head like he was making sure they were really there.

"Hey, Dad," Zane said.

"You okay?" Harrison asked, pointing to the hand Zane had in its makeshift cast.

Zane nodded. "It'll be fine."

"Sir, are my parents here?" Ty asked.

Harrison nodded. "Got in two days ago. They're settling in. Got them staying in the house instead of the guesthouse, reckoned it was best to have everyone close."

Ty breathed a sigh of relief.

A moment later, Zane's mother stepped into the doorway. She looked frailer than Ty remembered. He nodded to her as Zane said a stiff hello. Beverly held her chin high for a moment, then brushed past Harrison and pulled Zane into an awkward, clumsy hug.

Ty gaped, and Harrison stepped closer to him, smiling as Zane tried to figure out what to do.

"Your mama and my wife have spent the last few days discussing things," Harrison told Ty under his breath. "Been real … enlightening."

"Yes, sir."

"What's the plan?" Harrison asked when it appeared that Beverly didn't intend to let Zane go.

Ty glanced over his shoulder at the others. They were all loitering by the car, watching. Nick had roused and somehow dragged himself out of the back of the Mustang to lean against the hood, his head hanging.

"We've got two days tops before the NIA catches up to us," Ty said. "We can't risk staying longer than that. We were hoping to stay here for a day, though, and rest. Maybe leave our wounded when we go?"

Harrison looked between Ty and the others and frowned. "Your boys could use the bunkhouse, if you want them close by."

Ty glanced at Zane for his opinion. He had wrapped his arms tightly around his mother, his head resting atop hers. His eyes were closed, but somehow he knew Ty had looked to him for an answer. He nodded.

Ty found his throat tightening at the expression gracing Zane's face. He tore his eyes away and nodded at Harrison. "Thank you, sir," he croaked. "That'll be perfect."

Harrison gestured at the small army Ty and Zane had dragged with them to Texas, waving them over as he thumped down the front steps. "Let's go, boys," he called to them. "I'll show you the accommodations."

Ty followed so he could give Zane a moment alone with his mother. The others fell in behind them, with Nick taking up his usual spot on point even though he was limping, and the others fanning out behind them.

"That car looks to be in mighty fine shape, Ty," Harrison said as they headed for a rustic little building across the yard from the main house and beside the barn that had nearly burned down several years before. He smiled at Ty. "I'm happy to see I wasn't wrong in thinking you'd do her right."

"Thank you, sir. I'll be expecting the keys back when this is all done."

Harrison chuckled. He gave the other men a pointed look. "These boys your team?"

"These are my brothers."

Harrison glanced back at Sidewinder and nodded, smiling sadly. He unlocked the bunkhouse door and led them inside. They filed in obediently.

The bunkhouse had only one exit because it was all one room, but for a section built into a corner by the kitchen that Ty assumed was a bathroom. There was an old apron sink with a curtain to cover the lower cabinets, and a beat-up fridge and range. The only electric light appeared to be mounted over the sink. Ty supposed ranch hands went to bed and rose with the sun. A long wooden table that could seat at least twelve sat in the center of the pine plank floor. A couple old sofas were situated around a scuffed coffee table in the corner near an old wood stove, and the right half of the room was lined with sets of bunk beds.

"Built these myself," Harrison told Ty, beaming.

"Thank you, sir," Ty said.

The boys all moved to the bunks and set their bags down. Ty smiled wistfully when he noticed that Sidewinder had aligned themselves in the same way they'd slept a decade ago. Some habits died hard. The bed Elias Sanchez had always claimed, the bunk above Kelly, remained untouched. The bunk beside that, the one over Nick, was where Ty had always laid his head. Ty stared at both empty beds, his stomach churning.

Harrison was silent. He could probably tell that Ty had too much on his mind to take the full tour right now. He gave Ty a gentle pat on the shoulder and left them alone.

Ty stood in the middle of the big room, frowning at the door. The others were murmuring to each other, rustling around as they got settled. Finally, Ty moved to sit on the edge of one of the nearby racks. He leaned his elbows on his knees and stared without really seeing.

The bunkhouse had the same feeling the desert camps always had, and Ty was surprised by how hard that feeling hit him with the other boys here. It was something almost like homesickness: the feeling that something was simply missing.

The bed opposite him creaked and Ty straightened in surprise, feeling the heat creep up his face at being caught off guard.

"Doing okay?" Owen asked.

Ty nodded. "Feels like Eli's here."

Owen was still for a few seconds, but finally he nodded. "Yeah, it does."

Neither of them had moved when the door creaked open and Zane stepped inside. He shut it again, turning the dead bolt.

"Hey," he greeted.

The others all quieted, waiting for Zane to speak. Ty lowered his head, fighting an ache in his head and in his heart.

Zane sat down on the bunk beside Ty. "Your family is settled in. Safe." Zane looked over the others and raised his voice. "Clancy called. They couldn't get to the money."

Ty breathed out uneasily. Plan A had been to simply give the fucking money to the CIA and let *them* deal with everyone else who was gunning for the millions. Without the money, though, they were stuck with Plan B. And Plan B was the one where they all died trying to kidnap the head of the Vega cartel so they could trade him for the protection of the CIA.

"What happened?" Liam asked.

"Clancy said they hit too much red tape. Even with the code word, it would take a year or more to get to that money without the account owner. Not only do we not have Burns, all we've got is six random letters."

"What are they?" Ty asked. They'd been so caught up in trying to find Nick, and then Zane, that no one had even looked at the final transmissions from the CIA.

Zane retrieved his iPad, flipping until he found it. "An A. Two H's. Two O's. And an R."

Nick coughed and curled onto his side, holding his ribs. Ty and Zane both turned to him in concern. Nick was glowering, his green eyes blazing as Kelly sat on the bunk next to him and rested a hand on his shoulder. "Oohrah, boys," Nick said through gritted teeth.

The word hit Ty hard, and he met Zane's eyes as molten rage filtered through him. Burns had used the word as his code, his way to get into all that blood money.

"Who's sorry he's dead, now?" Nick asked as he settled his cheek against Kelly's leg, pulling a blanket over his head.

Ty tried to fight back the anger so he could think. Zane's hand came to rest on his back, gentle and soothing.

"I'll call Clancy. See if I can catch her before they get on a plane."

The others were silent as Zane flipped through his phone. He sniffed as his phone rang. He perked up when Clancy answered, and he quickly told her the code word they'd uncovered and what to do. "We have no more than forty-eight hours to move before the NIA catches up. If you can't get it done in twenty-four, we need you here. Then we head to Miami. Finish this." He ended the call after another moment, glancing around. The news felt woefully inadequate.

Ty wrapped an arm around him, hugging him close. "It's going to be okay."

Zane met Ty's eyes solemnly. "That's a lie."

"I'm always lying about something, Zane," Ty said softly.

"I know," Zane replied just as softly. He smiled, though, squeezing Ty's knee to soften the blow of the words. "We going to sleep down here?"

"That was the plan."

"My old room in the house is empty." Zane glanced at the bunk behind them, where Kelly was holding Nick's head in his lap. "There's spare rooms too."

Kelly nodded. He gazed at Owen and then Digger, then at the bunk above him and finally at Nick, who had fallen asleep as Kelly stroked his hair. "This feels like home enough."

Zane's eyes went soft and sad. Ty leaned forward and ran his fingers through Zane's hair, brushing across his skin when Zane turned his head. When Zane stood and headed for the door, Ty trailed after him.

"Well, fine then!" Digger shouted after them as they left.

Dinner was a solemn affair, considering how many people were involved. Sidewinder ate in the kitchen to give the two families time alone.

Mara, Earl, and Chester were all there safely, and Zane could see relief in the more relaxed lines of Ty's shoulders. He'd insisted he hadn't been worried the last few days, but Zane knew his husband.

Something he let slip out loud without thinking as they ate.

"I'm sorry, husband?" Mara asked, her voice reaching a pitch that made the dog raise his head and growl. Silverware clinked. All conversation stopped.

Ty blinked at her with his mouth open.

Zane cleared his throat and reached to pet Mara's arm. "Just the civil ceremony," he said quickly. "We'll do the rest whenever it's a good time. We . . . we were tired of waiting."

"And you can't call your mama and tell her you got hitched?" Mara shouted at Ty.

"She gon' beat his ass," Digger observed from the kitchen.

"Well, Ma, I'm sorry, but I've kind of had a rough week!" Ty yelled back.

"Tyler," Earl growled.

Ty glanced at him, looking mutinous, but he bit his lip and sighed. "Sorry, Ma."

"Mara, stow it 'til later, huh?" Earl added. He went back to cutting his steak. After taking a bite, he nodded. "Congratulations, boys." He gave Zane a wink and said nothing more about it.

Harrison, though, got up from the head of the table and came over to him. When Zane stood, his father embraced him tightly. He didn't say anything, just hugged him. Zane realized he'd actually been more concerned about what the Gradys would say than his own parents, but this small gesture from his dad meant the world to him. Zane held on to him for a few extra seconds, then released him and sat back down, trying to conceal the grin bubbling up as his father forced Ty to stand and hug him as well. Even Beverly managed to offer them a smile. Zane held a tiny flicker of hope in his heart that she would come around. If they lived out the week.

When dinner was over, the Sidewinder boys and Liam all flowed out into the courtyard, disappearing right before Zane's eyes in all different directions. "What are they doing?" he asked Ty.

"Perimeter check. It's not the first one they've done." Ty watched them go as he pushed through the screen door and held it open for Zane. Zane thanked him quietly, his mind still elsewhere and his body moving mostly on autopilot. He was trying to pick out the figures in the night, but Sidewinder was gone. He heard one loud yip from the left and then cackling laughter.

He glanced at Ty, who was smiling off into the darkness.

Chester was already easing into one of the numerous rocking chairs on the front porch. He'd apparently claimed it as his own almost immediately upon arrival, and no one seemed willing to argue with him or his shovel.

Since landing in Texas, he'd also acquired another object to carry with him everywhere he went: a pump-action 12-gauge shotgun from Harrison's gun case.

No one seemed willing to argue with that, either.

He cleared his throat as the screen door squeaked, spit a wad of tobacco into a paper cup, and pulled his shovel and his shotgun into his lap without saying a word. Zane was a little wary of the man after what he'd witnessed in West Virginia, but he also had even more admiration for him, if that was possible.

Zane was basically looking at Ty's future, right now.

Ty flopped into one of the chairs beside the old man and threw his feet up onto the railing. Earl was right behind them, and he pulled two more heavy chairs across the wooden boards of the porch. Zane sat in one of them with a murmur of thanks.

Harrison settled in beside Ty and propped his feet on the railing as well.

Zane grinned as he watched the other men. This was his family. His husband. His father. His father-in-law. Chester had even told Zane to call him Grandpa. Zane leaned back in the chair and extended his long legs, crossing them at the ankles. It felt weird to be relaxing when the world seemed to be burning out there, but if he had learned one thing from Ty, it was to take what fate gave you in that moment and not question it.

There was a long moment of comfortable silence as they settled in, taking in the deepening cool in the air accompanying the setting sun, and the growing sounds of the ranch as darkness fell: The horses in the distance, the dog off barking at his shadow. The hoots of nonindigenous owls that Zane soon decided were some sort of communication between Sidewinder as they made their perimeter.

"I miss my tiger roaring," Ty finally mused.

Zane and Harrison both chuckled. "I don't," Harrison said with a huff.

The screen door squeaked again, and Mara and Beverly both came out to join them. Zane was so surprised to see his mother that he stood, awkwardly offering his chair to her as if there weren't five other empty ones sitting around.

"Thank you, Zane," she said, and she sat primly on the edge of the rocking chair.

Ty got up and rearranged some things, making room for Mara. She was holding something in her hands that Zane hadn't noticed at first glance, and after she sat, she handed it to Ty. It was Annie's old practice violin.

Ty took it in both hands, holding it gently. He looked pained as he ran his fingers over it.

Beverly cleared her throat, displaying her discomfort through her stiff shoulders and rigid spine. "Mara was telling me you can play, Tyler," she said. "I was hoping you might do us the honor of a song or two."

Ty stared at her for a long moment, until even Zane was uncomfortable with the silence.

"I . . . I would be glad to, ma'am, but I'm afraid I may not be able."

"Why not?" Mara asked, her brow creasing in concern.

Ty grimaced again. "The way my hand's been all beat up. If it requires me to stretch, it won't do it too well."

"You can't play anything?" Earl asked, sounding almost sad.

"I haven't gotten up the nerve to try," Ty admitted. He was stroking the old violin, not raising his head. Zane watched him, frowning. He wondered if Ty was telling the truth or if he shied away from the instruments he had been known for in New Orleans just like he shied away from singing now. The loss of that talent seemed such a tragedy.

"Will you try?" Zane asked.

Ty looked up at him in surprise, and his worried frown faded into a gentle, sad smile. He took the bow in one hand and settled the violin against his chin. He began to tune it by ear, and the sounds of the strings whining their way to the right pitch brought back memories of Zane's childhood, of sitting in his room reading while Annie practiced down the hall, of the musicians warming up before his wedding to Becky.

Zane smiled serenely as Ty started a slow, melancholy waltz.

He was a little rusty. So was the violin. But the tune filtered through the night with an otherworldly oddity, taking over the music of the wind and giving the evening an eerie, haunting sway.

When he was finished, the world once again fell into silence, and to Zane everything seemed darker and sadder for the loss. He gazed at Ty like the man could rope the moon.

From the darkness came a round of clapping and a few whistles.

Ty was smiling crookedly. Earl and Mara sat with their hands clasped together, and Chester appeared to be asleep. Harrison was nodding as if in approval, and to Zane's surprise, Beverly had her fingers over her lips, watching Ty as if she might be seeing him for the first time.

"That was lovely, Tyler," she whispered after a few moments. "Thank you for sharing."

"Thank you for asking, ma'am," Ty whispered, like he was afraid his voice would destroy the peace the music had created.

Beverly stood and wished them all a good-night, then retired into the house. Silence threatened, but the wind chimes tinkling down the porch and Ty's ever-fidgeting fingers idly plucking the strings of the violin battled against it.

"I had an idea," Zane told Ty after a few seconds. Ty raised his head. There was strain around his eyes and mouth, tension in his shoulders, that spoke of exhaustion and fear. Zane's heart broke as he met Ty's eyes, but he smiled anyway. "Brick & Mortar."

Ty blinked a few times. "What?"

"The store. That's what we'll call it. Brick & Mortar."

Ty peered at him for a long moment, not quite able to smile, but obviously trying. He nodded, the sadness in his eyes almost unbearable. "I like it," he choked out. He nodded again, then looked down at the violin in his lap.

Zane jumped when his burner phone rang, and he dug it out. "Clancy?"

"It'll take two weeks to get that money moving."

Zane's heart sank. "We won't last two weeks with the NIA on us."

"We got it rolling here. We're coming home to help you."

Zane's nostrils flared as he concentrated on keeping outwardly calm. "We'll see you in Miami. And Clancy?"

"Yeah?"

"Excellent work."

Clancy was silent for a long time. When she answered, it was a choked, "Thanks, boss."

Zane hung up and lifted his gaze to Ty, who was watching him with that same wistful sadness. It seemed to Zane that Ty had known all along it would come to this.

"You boys leaving in the morning?" Harrison asked.

"Yes, sir," Zane managed to say. He was still staring raptly at Ty, and he had to tear his eyes away. "Staying longer will just put you all in more danger. The longer we wait, the worse it'll be."

"I wish it was anyone but you," Harrison said, and his voice wavered.

Zane fought to swallow past the lump in his throat. "It has to be us."

Earl's chair creaked against the floorboards as he rocked. "I couldn't hope for a better man to be at my son's side in a time like this," he said, and Zane was shocked to see his eyes glistening. Their eyes locked, and Earl gave him a nod. "Not a better man."

Zane couldn't manage to respond.

Someone cleared his throat from the bottom of the stairs, and they were all surprised to see Nick standing there. He'd been too quiet approaching, even with his ribs tightly bound and his knee in bad shape. "Perimeter's clear, Six. We're heading in."

"Aye," Ty managed, and they watched Nick melt back into the moonless night. Another figure silently joined him, helping him limp away.

Earl stood and took a deep, unsteady breath. "Early morning coming. Best to get a good night's sleep." He gave both Ty and Zane a long, tight hug. Mara did the same as she followed him. "Good night, boys. Harrison."

Harrison was nodding like he just couldn't manage to find words. Zane knew how he felt. He supposed "good night" was so much easier than "good-bye."

"Night, Dad!" Earl shouted to Ty's grandfather.

Chester gave him a modified salute, his gnarled fingers waving through the air before gripping his shovel again. It sat on his thighs as he rocked.

Harrison took a last couple sips of his coffee before standing. "I guess I'll turn in too," he said, and he waited only a few seconds before giving Zane a fierce hug. He added a kiss on the cheek that caused his mustache to tickle Zane's ear, and then he did the same to Ty. "You boys . . . you boys come back, now. You hear?"

Zane's smile was watery at best. He nodded obediently. Harrison patted him on the cheek, then gave Ty's shoulder a squeeze before he disappeared into the house.

Ty and Zane were left on the porch with Chester, listening to the ranch go to sleep as the screen door snicked shut.

Ty's gaze lingered on Zane. Zane knew what he was thinking without having to ask or even ponder too hard. This was their last moment of peace. The calm before the storm. The otherworldly silence before the fire.

"Oohrah, kiddo," Chester said quietly.

Ty smiled and squeezed his eyes shut as tears trailed down his face. "Oohrah, Gunny."

Nick sat on the side of his bunk, staring but seeing very little. It wasn't until Kelly sat beside him that he roused himself.

"You okay?"

Nick shook his head. He wasn't okay. He wouldn't be okay. It was time he stopped pretending. "Everyone we love is going to die in a few days," he said. "And I feel like I started it, instead of finishing it like I hoped to."

The rustling from the others ceased, and Nick realized everyone in the bunkhouse was watching them, listening. He glanced around. His friends. His brothers. Men he'd spent half his life loving and sacrificing with. And then there was Liam, but he'd get a pass tonight, because Nick was finally coming to terms with being at death's door.

"I thought I could save all of you," he told them. "My soul for your lives."

"Nicko, that's not the way it works," Kelly whispered.

Owen and Digger came closer, sitting on Kelly's bunk across from them. Liam leaned against the end of the bunk, his arms crossed and his head lowered. He had a black eye where Kelly had slugged him earlier, but even Liam had admitted he'd deserved it.

Nick stared at Owen and Digger, remembering the day both men had joined the Force Recon team that would later be christened Sidewinder. That had been a good day. All their days had been good days.

"Do you remember that little village south of Kabul?" Owen asked. "I cleared a room but missed a trapdoor, guy popped out and had me in his sights."

Nick nodded, frowning.

"You stepped in and got him with a knife, got him before he could get me."

Nick shivered violently, nodding again.

"Do you regret that?" Owen asked.

"No," Nick answered immediately.

"You don't stay awake and mourn the life you took that day? The life of the man who was pointing his gun at me?"

Nick hesitated, frowning at Owen. "No."

"You think that makes you a bad person?"

"What?" Nick asked, feeling his chest tighten.

"You killed that man. But you don't regret it. Do you think that makes you a bad person?"

Nick was silent, searching himself for the answer. He found himself shaking his head. "No."

"This is no different, Irish," Owen said. "Burns had a gun to Ty's head. You stepped in and got him before he could fire. It's no different at all."

Nick glanced at Kelly, who was nodding. Digger was silent, but he finally huffed and leaned closer. "It was dumb luck you got sent back with that message, Rico, we all know that. But I guarandamntee you if it had been me, I'd have smoked the fucker too. So you take that fucking wreath of thorns off your head and come back to us. Only way we die out there is if you let us. And you sitting here mourning your soul ain't going to stop a bullet to my head. Your knife? Your hands? Your aim? Those will."

"My aim," Nick started.

"Fuck that medicine shit," Digger snarled. "You said it wasn't important enough for us to track some down. You'll be you when we need you. We know it."

Nick swallowed hard as Digger and Owen both got up and moved away. His eyes followed them back to their bunks, and then his gaze landed on Liam as the man leaned against the bed. Liam shrugged. "I've been trying to tell you, mate."

"Tell him what?" Kelly growled.

"Maybe you see him through rose-colored glasses now, Doc, but I remember what he was, what all of you were, and it was god damned beautiful. Silently psychotic." Liam inclined his head, raising an eyebrow at Nick. "You coming to terms with the fact that *no one* can be as good as you try to force yourself to be is the only way you'll ever be okay again."

Nick was still frowning at him, wondering why the hell Liam was trying to help him now after weeks of playing mind games.

"Once you realize you *are* the thing in the dark, you sleep easier at night. Hell. Your hands don't even shake like they were." He pointed to Nick's hands, then moved away, leaving Nick and Kelly sitting there.

Nick watched his fingers tremble as he laced them together. They hadn't risked trying to get him more medication, but Liam was right. His tremor had begun to ease up. His eyes sought out Kelly's.

"You're not a thing in the dark," Kelly said under his breath.

"No." Nick clutched his fingers tighter. "But I can be."

Kelly stared at him for a long time, nodding, blue-gray eyes turning to quartz granite. "Then we'll be things in the dark together."

"I feel like I need to go talk to them," Ty said as he stared out the window of Zane's bedroom at the dark bunkhouse. Zane wasn't sure what was drawing Ty there, but the pull was as strong as the one Zane had offered here.

"Go do it, then," Zane said. "I need Kelly to wrap my arm again; I could go with you."

Ty scowled at him. "I thought you said it was okay."

Zane shrugged, beginning to unwrap the immobilizing bandage on his arm. He spread his fingers, wincing.

Ty rounded on him, anger seeming to bubble up from somewhere he'd been storing it for too long. "How the hell are you supposed to shoot a gun? Throw a knife? You couldn't even crank the fucking car this morning."

"I'm not willing to hurt myself to turn a key, Ty, but I'll be okay when the fighting starts."

"Prove it," Ty challenged.

Zane huffed a laugh. "How? You want me to kill Tanner *again*? Want to try and kick my ass now that we don't have anyone else to fight? Just go and get whatever you need from Sidewinder and let me deal with this. Go give Nick hell for getting himself beat up too, make it fair." He held up his hand. "I'll be here when you're done."

Ty narrowed his eyes.

Zane turned away to dig into his duffel bag for fresh clothes. When he straightened up once more, Ty was behind him. He wrapped his arm around Zane's neck, kicked at his heel, and upended him easily, slamming him to the floor with a thud that rattled the bedside table next to them. Zane cried out when he hit.

Ty knelt over him and pressed his knee into Zane's chest to keep him down.

"Son of a bitch! You trying to break my fucking back?" Zane ground out, both hands trying to dislodge Ty's knee. He really didn't want to hurt Ty, but he was on the edge of losing his temper. "Get off, Grady!"

Ty raised an eyebrow, obviously contemplating refusing. But he removed his knee and stood fluidly, then offered his hand. Zane not only didn't take it, he batted it out of the way as he struggled to his feet.

"What the fuck was that about?" Zane snapped, grabbing his sweatpants and yanking them on. He was barely keeping it under control. It would hurt to get into another physical fight with Ty—a lot—but he was about to do it anyway.

"You really think I should be able to do that to you, Garrett?" Ty asked.

"Why the hell would I be on alert in my own bedroom with no pants on when the only threat is my husband stomping around in a shitty mood?" Zane snapped as he dug into the duffel with his left hand, holding his right arm against his body. "You're an idiot."

"Never stopped you from being on alert before," Ty pointed out. "You're hurt."

"Yeah, I am now! Everything hurts." Zane pulled a T-shirt over his head, forcing himself to quit favoring his injured arm.

"Your face looks like you went three rounds with a kangaroo."

"If you want to call yourself a kangaroo, fine." Zane gave him a sideways glance. Man had a lot of nerve, bitching at him for being beaten up *by him*.

"I did all that?" Ty asked carefully.

"Tanner never got a swing in."

"You fucking idiot," Ty hissed. "Fighting him like that when Irish could have just taken the shot."

Zane sat on the side of the bed, calming himself, prepared to let Ty rail at him now that he understood where this anger was coming from. Ty needed to rail at *something*, and Zane was okay with being the target. For a minute.

For some reason, the patient silence and acceptance made Ty even angrier, though. "You could have died, you realize that? You could have died because you're stubborn and stupid, and the last kiss we shared would have been with questionable chicken sandwich on my breath!" Ty shouted, fluttering his fingers in front of his mouth and sneering.

Zane nodded, pressing his lips together tightly so he wouldn't laugh.

"It's not funny!" Ty cried. "What were you thinking?"

"I was thinking about Becky," Zane admitted. Ty came up short, his mouth snapping shut. "I was thinking about how damn much I loved her. I was thinking about how I spiraled after I lost her. I was thinking about sitting at the dinner table with her hand in mine, and Jack Tanner across from me eating steak."

Ty nodded minutely as he appeared to try to compose himself. When he looked back up, his eyes were full of grief and fear. "I hadn't . . . seen that angle. I'm sorry."

Zane closed his eyes. "She'd have really liked you, Beaumont."

Ty chewed on his lip, looking torn. "She helped you be the man I fell in love with. I owe her everything I have."

Zane stood and took a step toward him, placing the tips of his fingers against Ty's cheekbones.

"Please stay here when we leave," Ty whispered. "Stay with Nick."

Zane's lips curled and he backed off, anger welling again. He turned away from Ty, cursing as he returned to his duffel.

"Zane."

Even through the anger, that soft plea was enough to get Zane's attention. He stopped his jerky motions and waited.

"Zane," Ty repeated, and his hand came to rest on Zane's back. "I love you. I trust you. I know you can do anything I can do, and you can do it just as good or better. But you're *hurt*. Too hurt to come with us."

Zane closed his eyes, surprised when they burned with the threat of tears. He turned his head, and he found Ty gazing at him, his hazel eyes gone dark with sorrow.

"Zane," he whispered again, seeming to linger on the way the name sounded on his tongue. "I don't want you to die because you're stubborn."

The tightening in Zane's chest relaxed and he was able to take a breath without forcing it. "I love you, Tyler Grady," he said. "And I'm too stubborn to let you die without me."

Zane knocked on the bunkhouse door, head lowered as he listened to the guys moving inside. The door opened enough for the barrel of a gun to appear. Zane held his hands up. "I come in peace."

Digger shoved the door wider. "You're not the newlywed I thought I was about to shoot."

"I get that a lot," Zane deadpanned.

Digger gestured Zane in with his gun, which he then shoved under his belt at the small of his back.

Owen was leaning against the kitchen counter, talking on the burner phone. From the tone of his voice, Zane assumed he was speaking to his girlfriend. Nick and Kelly were both sitting on the couch, examining a framed map on the table in front of them. Zane recognized it as the ranch. He wondered where the hell they'd stolen that from, and if his mom would notice before they could get the fuck out of Dodge.

Liam was lounging in his bunk, smoking a cigarette. Zane was surprised to see Nick with an unlit cigarette behind his ear, and another being used as a pointer.

Zane followed Digger to the couch, sitting opposite Kelly and Nick. "What are you doing?"

Nick sighed, eyes darting between Kelly and Digger before returning to the map again. He swallowed nervously, which made the butterflies in Zane's stomach start up. If Nick was nervous, then *everybody* should be nervous.

"We're looking for a landing strip on the property," Nick admitted.

"What, why?"

"Egress for the families, in case we don't come back."

The implication hit Zane hard. Sidewinder was sitting here planning how to keep the Gradys and Garretts safe for when they all died in Miami.

"What the hell?" Zane blurted, lurching to his feet. "What? Sitting out here all 'be careful, we might get hurt'? There's no way to go into this but knowing we come back."

They all watched him impassively. Finally, Kelly sighed. "You haven't lived in the same world we have. You *never* assume you come back."

"And when you do, it's a goddamned miracle every time," Digger added.

Zane stared, his mouth hanging open. "Wow." He shook his head and aimed for the door, refusing to sit in on this conversation. "No wonder Ty's fucking nuts."

When he jerked the door open, Ty was standing there, a bag over his shoulder, fist raised to knock, eyes wide. "Hey," he said awkwardly.

Zane sighed and hung his head, stepping aside to let Ty in.

Ty gave him a good once-over, then glanced around at the others. "What's going on?"

"They're planning the fucking funeral out here," Zane spat.

Ty didn't look angry or shocked, merely confused. He took in the map on the table and the grim expressions of the others, then pursed his lips, nodding.

Zane stared at him, unable to comprehend that sort of backup plan. "What's the fucking point of this if we don't think we're coming back?"

On the other side of the room, Owen was eyeing them, his ear to the phone. "Honey, I have to go," he said without taking his eyes off Zane.

Ty reached for Zane's arm, but Zane jerked out of his grasp and paced away.

"I thought you were supposed to be this mythical fucking creature or something. *Sidewinder*," he intoned sarcastically. "This bunch of invincible, crazy warriors, up for anything. You're just scared little boys sitting in a tree house, trying to figure out how to sneak back inside once your mama turns off the lights!"

"Rude," Digger huffed. None of the others spoke, though.

Zane turned to Ty, his heart racing, anger and helplessness coursing through him.

Ty smiled sadly. "This is the way we've always done it, Zane. It doesn't mean we intend to die out there. It just . . ."

"If we do, it'll be with no regrets," Owen offered when Ty's explanation faltered. "You say good-bye first. When the bullet hits, you won't wish you'd told anyone you loved them one last time."

"Bullshit," Zane snarled. "You're all bullshit."

"It's part of going in prepared," Ty tried.

"I don't fucking believe this," Zane muttered.

No one else spoke. They didn't seem willing to try to explain it further to Zane, and his rant had made no mark on any of them. Zane stomped over and threw himself onto the couch beside Digger, crossing his arms and huffing.

"I came to get my arm bandaged."

Kelly nodded and went to get his med kit.

The others watched Zane, obviously uneasy now. Nick took a long look at the cigarette he was holding, then slipped it in his mouth. No one made a sound as he lit it.

"Broke your streak," Kelly said as he sat beside Zane and started working on the new bandage for his arm. "Twenty years."

"Even condemned men get one last smoke," Nick said, blowing a stream of fragrant smoke into the air.

"Just wait until Ty gives you his 'you're too hurt to fight' speech and tries to leave you behind," Zane snapped.

Nick looked from Zane to Ty, expression unreadable.

Ty shrugged, moving closer. He gestured for Liam to join them as he took a bag off his shoulder. He held up a bottle of orange Gatorade and set it on the table, then a stack of shot glasses that he spread out on the wood, and he smiled almost shyly.

"Your dad rid the house of all things alcohol," he told Zane. He handed Zane a bottle of green tea from the bag of stuff he'd obviously stolen from the kitchen, then glanced around at the others. "No matter what happens tomorrow . . . I figured Nick's spiked Gatorade was the best we could do."

"Uh," Nick said uncomfortably, glancing around the coffee table at everyone. He turned his head to blow smoke away from them. "That's not a great idea."

"Why not?" Ty asked, frowning.

"It's . . ." Nick glanced at Liam and rolled his eyes. "It's not alcohol."

"What?" Liam asked.

"I spiked it with my spare bottle of propranolol," Nick admitted. The others barraged him with questions, and he shrugged. "You think I'm stupid? Of course I had a spare bottle on the boat."

"What would that have done to me?" Liam demanded.

"In large doses, it behaves sort of like Rohypnol. It makes you extremely suggestible and causes memory loss. It was my backup plan."

"You wanker!" Liam cried. "I'm starting to feel very victimized by my time with you!"

Nick sat unfazed, blowing smoke toward Liam's face. "Come at me again, see who winds up on his ass."

Zane just opened his green tea and took a sip, shaking his head. "You're all idiots."

Ty carefully closed the door to the bedroom behind him. He set his gun on the low table by the door and then moved toward the bed.

He stood studying Zane for a moment, then put one knee on the edge of the mattress and leaned over his husband. Zane's eyes blinked open to meet his.

"Morning, sunshine," Ty rumbled with a crooked smile.

A few more blinks and Zane made a soft sound of disagreement and tried to roll over. "It's not morning. Heifer."

"You awake?" Ty asked as he poked gently at Zane's ribs.

Zane shut his eyes and grunted. Without warning, he lurched over to yank Ty off-balance, tugged him down on the mattress next to him, and then secured him by curling around him. "Sleepy."

Ty didn't bother struggling. He'd been cuddled too many times to even try anymore. Instead, he slid his hand over Zane's waist and pulled him closer.

"It's pretty damn useless, us fighting right now," he murmured against Zane's cheek.

Zane was quiet long enough that Ty thought he might have actually gone back to sleep. But then he drew a deep breath. "We're good at it."

"I'm good at juggling, too. Don't mean I have to do it all the time," Ty countered.

Zane cracked one eye open. "You do not juggle."

Ty pulled back enough to see Zane's face, "Do too."

Zane sighed and slid one arm under his pillow. "Don't leave me behind, Ty. Don't make me live with that."

"I was wrong," Ty said before pushing at Zane's chest and rolling on top of him.

"Yeah, you were," Zane slid his hands up Ty's back under the T-shirt.

Ty brushed his nose and lips against Zane's cheek. "I'm sorry. I wasn't thinking about anything but you being safe. It was selfish. And it was wrong. Everything I did was wrong."

The smile playing at Zane's lips grew wider as he pulled up one of his legs, their bodies touching from ankle to chest. "And now?"

"I want you with me. 'Til the end. That may be selfish too, but I don't care."

"The world out there is burning, Ty."

Ty ran his finger down Zane's cheek, nodding. "But we were born in a kiln."

Zane grinned. "I'm game."

"I think the word you're looking for there is prey," Ty growled before smashing their mouths together. How many times could he fuck up and still gain Zane's forgiveness? He clamped his hand in Zane's curls, which were damp for some reason. "How did you get wet?"

Zane inhaled through his nose and let out a shaky sigh. "Showered," he said, sounding oddly nervous. "Needed to cool off."

"Because of me?"

"Because of you. Because of your crazy fucking Recon guys. You know what they were doing out there when I walked in?"

"Smoking, drinking, orgy?" Ty guessed.

"Planning on how to get people off the ranch if no one survives Miami."

Ty nodded, sighing. "We tried to tell you, that's what we do, Zane. But we've always come back."

Zane clapped his hand over Ty's mouth. "Just . . . don't jinx it this time."

Ty raised his hand in a silent promise.

"That's the Girl Scout pledge, Ty."

The sun was barely up when Zane blinked open his eyes. It was still dark in the bedroom that had once been his, and the morning air was cool on his face. It would be chilly when he got out of bed, but for now he was content in a bundle of quilts and sheets and body warmth, and that was how he wanted to stay.

Ty had his head tucked under his pillow. It was his default sleep mode. Zane watched him for a few more minutes, enjoying the fuzzy half-awake feeling of contentment as he stretched out beside his husband.

Finally, Zane rolled closer under the heavy quilt and slid his knee over Ty to rest his leg against the back of Ty's thigh. He threw an arm over him as well, soaking in the warmth, pressing his nose and mouth against the side of Ty's shoulder. He could almost fool himself into thinking this was a moment they could afford to enjoy.

Fuck it, though, why couldn't they grasp for happiness in the midst of all this? The bomb that had taken their bookstore, that had burned down their future, had been reminder enough that happiness could go up in a spark, be gone in an instant. It had also reminded Zane that the only thing in this world that mattered to him was Ty, and he still had him right now. Why the hell not enjoy this quiet, peaceful morning while they could?

Zane closed his eyes, snuggling closer and sighing. Ty smelled vaguely of smoke, leather, dirt, grass, and the frantic, desperate sex they'd had last night.

Zane would never get tired of the feeling Ty gave him, that spark of life he had reignited deep inside him.

Ty raised his head, causing the pillow to fall away, and squinted at Zane. His hair was an insult to humanity. Was it possible for Zane to love this man any more than he did right now?

"What time is it?" Ty grumbled, looking at the window. Dawn was just now stretching toward it. They didn't have long before the others would wake and they'd need to start moving. Zane's eyes followed Ty's. The light was infused with the gloom of winter, even in Texas. It made the warmth they'd created within the blankets that much more inviting. When Zane returned his attention to his husband, Ty was gazing down at him, his magnificent hazel eyes warm and shining.

He lifted his head enough to press a gentle kiss to Ty's chin. "Morning."

Ty's hands glided up Zane's sides and along his arms until they were pressing Zane's hands into the mattress. Zane groaned, but he didn't try to pull away. Instead, he licked his lips and shifted his hips.

He loved waking up like this. He intended to wake up like this every day for the rest of his life, no matter how long or short it might be. Even if today was the last.

He smiled crookedly and kissed Ty. "I love you," he whispered, voice so low it was almost a breath of air. "So much."

Ty's smile filtered into his eyes, even in the dim light. "I love you too. I thought I'd lost you, you know? For real, this time. I . . ."

"You didn't, Ty."

Ty swallowed hard, gazing into Zane's eyes with a swirl of emotions Zane couldn't begin to understand. "Just those couple of hours, thinking you were gone . . . and you went five years with that feeling."

"Ty."

"You'll never know how strong you are, Zane," Ty whispered vehemently. He brushed his fingers over Zane's forehead, swiping a few stray curls aside. "You did something I would never have been able to do."

Zane's eyes darted over Ty's face.

"You're so much stronger than you could ever know."

Zane's hands tightened around Ty's. "Thank you," he finally managed. He squeezed Ty hard. "Let's just agree never to find out if I can do it again, okay?"

Ty nodded earnestly, then schooled his features into something even more serious. "On a less romantic and life-affirming note, if we were at home, I'd already be fucking you by now. Just so you know."

Zane snorted, trying to keep it low so they wouldn't wake anyone. "So romantic," he crooned. He spread his arms to his sides, inviting Ty to proceed. "But this is still awfully nice."

Ty entwined his fingers with Zane's again. "This will all be over soon. And then every morning can be like this."

Zane smiled, trying to keep the concern at bay and almost succeeding. Ty rolled back again, bringing Zane with him until they both lay on their sides facing each other. He threw his leg over Zane's hip and drew them flush together.

"I've been trying to figure out how to get out of the deal I made," he said, his words measured, his brow creasing deeper.

Zane licked his lips, adjusting his head against the crook of Ty's arm. "With the CIA?"

"With the devil."

Zane scowled, his eyes on Ty's.

"I don't know how," Ty whispered.

"Then don't, Ty."

Ty jerked his head back. "What?"

"Don't get out of it," Zane repeated. "We both know we missed it. Us. A gun and a badge and having each other's backs."

"Yeah, but . . ."

"CIA Special Agent Grady." Zane smiled mischievously. "It fits you."

"Zane." Ty drew out his name.

"CIA Special Agent Garrett," Zane added with another quirk of his lips. Ty had been trying to be retired for a whole year. He had failed miserably. This was Ty's second chance, and Zane was willing to take it with him. "Yeah. I could get used to that."

"A-are you saying you want to join the CIA?"

Zane exhaled loudly and rolled in Ty's arms, putting his back to him. Ty tugged him close again. "They said the offer was open way back when we were dealing with Cross. I think it's time we get back to what brought us together in the first place."

Ty held his breath for a few seconds. "Murder?"

Zane thought of the rubble in Baltimore that had once been their future, and of the face of the man in Miami who'd tried to take Ty from him. "That too," he growled.

Ty still seemed confused. He buried his face in Zane's unruly curls. Zane snuggled close, fitting his ass in the curve of Ty's groin.

Ty grunted. "If you're trying to keep me from being turned on, this is not the best way to do it."

"Why would I try to do that?"

Ty kissed the back of his shoulder, and Zane's heart rate picked up. This was, bar none, his favorite position no matter which one of them topped. Being able to drag his hand up and down Ty's hard body as he fucked him. Feeling his impressive muscles flexing as Ty moved. Every part of them touching and rubbing from the tip of his nose to the tips of his toes. Being forced to go slow because they were on their sides and there was little leverage to be found when Ty worked his way inside. The way he could turn his head in a desperate plea for a kiss over his shoulder . . . It never failed to do the trick.

Merely the thought of making love like this was getting Zane uncomfortably hard in record time, just like it always would. And Ty loved it just as much as he did.

Ty inhaled deeply. "You're an evil, evil man."

Zane shimmied his hips. "Consider this payback for disappearing on me and making me think you were dead."

"That wasn't my fault!" Ty hissed. "And hey, you did it to me too, so we should be even!"

Zane's eyes fluttered as Ty touched the tip of his nose to Zane's neck. He grumbled as he glanced over his shoulder, and Ty pushed onto his elbow to kiss him. His hand began to slide toward Zane's hip, dragging against his muscles, and Zane hummed longingly into the kiss. He had fucked Ty last night, going hard as Ty wrapped around him, going until they were both sweating and panting and Ty was laid out and begging in the most debauched ways possible.

That didn't mean they couldn't do it again this morning, nice and slow this time.

Ty was hard against Zane's ass by the time Zane tossed his leg over Ty's knees, opening himself up a little more. Ty gasped.

"How long do you need?" Zane finally rumbled against his lips.

"Minutes," Ty hissed. He was already shoving down his boxers in anticipation of the go-ahead. The head of his cock pushed at Zane's ass.

Zane stretched and sucked in a breath to steady himself. "You've got ten."

It only took two for Ty to accomplish everything Zane loved about being taken from behind. Ten minutes after his ten minutes were up, Ty was buried deep inside him, clutching at him, rocking into him, fucking him as they kissed over Zane's shoulder, when someone knocked on the door.

Zane's fingers dug into Ty's hip so he wouldn't move. "Yeah," he called out, his voice remarkably normal for someone who was about to be caught in a very precarious position.

Ty dragged the heavy quilt up to their shoulders and buried his face against Zane's neck, rotating his hips just enough to make Zane gasp.

The door creaked open and Owen poked his head in. "You guys up?"

"You could say that," Ty answered wryly.

Zane tightened his muscles around Ty's cock, and Ty grunted.

"Irish said to tell you we're gearing up," Owen told them. "Wheels up in half an hour."

"We'll be down," Ty told him, somehow able to make it sound casual and sleepy.

Owen nodded and shut the door behind him, and Zane almost immediately began to snicker. Ty rolled him until he had him squished into the mattress, and Zane was still laughing when Ty found his rhythm again.

Zane clomped down the steps. He'd settled for one of his knives in his boot, his sheaths on his wrists, and his gun and a backup under a very light canvas jacket. He'd pretty much stuffed weapons everywhere they could be stuffed, actually.

Ty shuffled after him, dragging his feet and buttoning up his shirt.

"My shades are toast, man," Ty said as he held the brown aviators up and examined them critically.

"You shouldn't have sat on them," Zane said, distracted by the heavenly smell of sizzling bacon and fresh bread wafting through the house.

"Well, I didn't mean to. These things lasted me three freaking years, and *one day* in Texas and they're all, 'I give up.'" He waved his hands through the air.

Zane chuckled. He stopped at the doorway to the kitchen and motioned for Ty to go ahead.

Ty stepped past him, glancing up at him with a small smile as he slid his broken sunglasses onto his face. "I expect more fortitude out of my inanimate objects than that."

Zane raised an eyebrow. "I am not inanimate."

"Sometimes you're not."

"You boys come get breakfast," Mara said. They'd sent all the ranch staff home for the week to keep them out of danger, and Mara had made herself at home in the gourmet kitchen.

"Yes, ma'am," Ty answered without taking his eyes off Zane. He winked. "Come on, Lone Star."

Zane followed, buoyed by Ty's good humor. If this was their last bit of peace, then he would be content. Mara had laid out a full breakfast, and she was still standing at the stove.

Beverly was sitting in the breakfast nook with a cup of coffee. She gave them both a stiff, almost nervous smile. "Good morning, boys," she offered.

They both responded in kind. Was this what a normal family felt like?

Ty took his sunglasses off again, gently bending the rims, trying to tweak them back into shape.

"What'd those cost you, Ty?" Zane asked him. "Ten bucks? Fifteen?"

Ty glanced up at him distractedly before going back to it. He had his tongue out of his mouth, tip between his teeth, and his brow was furrowed. Zane smirked, watching him surreptitiously. Ty slid them on one last time to test his work and gave Zane a triumphant grin.

Zane offered him a sarcastic thumbs-up. He sat with a jar of *picante* sauce and pulled the bowl of scrambled eggs to him, then tried to twist the top off the jar with his hurt hand.

Ty watched in abject horror, not saying anything.

"It's good!" Zane told him, still trying to get the top off.

"Zane," Ty grunted with a shake of his head. He gestured for the jar.

Zane frowned, but extended his arm. Ty reached across the table and gripped the lid of the jar with his left hand, twisting hard as Zane held the bottom. The lid popped off with a wet sucking sound.

Ty held up the lid, gave it a sniff and a grimace, then set it down on the table.

Zane rolled his eyes and grabbed up his spoon. "Thanks."

Ty pointed his fork at Zane as he chewed. "Teamwork."

Zane winked and started back on his *picante* sauce and eggs.

"The other boys been in yet?" Ty asked through a mouthful of breakfast.

"They probably went back to sleep," Zane muttered. "Assholes."

"Love you too, Garrett," Nick said as he entered the kitchen, the others trailing in after him. He flopped a legal pad on the kitchen table between Ty and Zane. "Those are your times. Don't miss your flight."

Ty picked the pad up and scowled at it. "You boys did a lot of planning after I left you last night, Gunny."

Nick shrugged, a smirk on his lips. "That's what the gunny does."

"We get in an hour before you do so we don't have all the balls in one basket," Owen told them as he stole a spoonful of Ty's eggs.

"Balls?" Zane asked.

Owen held up Ty's spoon. "Eggs."

The others were moving through the kitchen, loading up on what appeared to be a mobile breakfast. Their bags were sitting in the foyer. They were preparing to leave.

Owen continued to speak as he chewed. "We'll meet at Cross's safe house. Anything goes tits up, it's every man for himself."

Zane nodded, committing the information on the legal pad to memory.

Ty stood, giving each man a hug. Even Liam received one, and he looked both surprised and suspicious when Ty let him go. Zane had to take a bite of toast to hide his smile. Ty held Nick tightly, saying something in his ear. He patted Nick's cheek, smiling as Nick nodded. "I'll see you on the other side, brother."

Nick held up his hand, and Ty grasped it. "Not if I see you first," Nick murmured, and then Sidewinder melted out of the kitchen, leaving a stillness behind that enveloped those remaining.

Zane gave his mother and Mara both a reassuring smile. Beverly stood suddenly, hurrying across the large kitchen toward Zane. Her eyes glistened as she reached both hands out to him, and Zane stood in shock to take her in his arms.

She clung to him, frail and trembling. "You come back from this, Zane," she hissed against his chest. "Then we'll tend to that wedding you boys promised us."

CHAPTER 12

"I'm not freaking out. *You're* freaking out. Shut up." Liam was, though, and they all knew it.

Nick rolled his eyes and banged his head against the back of the freezer.

He would have thought that waking up on a horse ranch in Texas and getting stuck in a restaurant freezer in Miami by late afternoon would be a long story, but it turned out that it was very short.

The NIA had been waiting for Liam when they'd landed in Miami. Apparently, Preston's CIA-created ID hadn't been quite as foolproof as they'd expected.

They'd been bagged, tagged, and transported to this building with hoods over their faces. Nick knew it was a restaurant from the sounds and smells alone.

And good *God* he hoped the slabs of meat hanging in here with them were beef and pork.

Owen was standing in front of Liam, a hand on his shoulder as he tried to calm the man. They had spent long minutes seeking a way out of the locked freezer by the lights of their useless phones, and now they were all shivering, their teeth chattering.

"There should be a safety latch on the inside," Kelly grumbled.

"Dude, the NIA just threw us on ice. Literally. They're going to kill us and leave our body parts scattered around town when they get all that money," Nick drawled. He and Kelly had perched on one of the shelves to keep off the freezing floor. "I don't think they're too worried about safety."

"I'm from Louisiana, man, I ain't built for this weather," Digger told them.

"It's not weather! It's a freezer!" Liam shouted.

"Shut up!" Digger shouted back.

"God!" Nick squeezed his eyes closed. "Sack up and rejoin the Regiment, dude! Jesus."

"How can you be so calm?" Liam demanded. "Do you know how much air we have left now?"

"Probably like twenty minutes," Nick answered, deadpan. "Maybe ten."

"Bell, calm down," Owen said. "Breathe."

Kelly flicked his flashlight app on and waved it in their direction. They'd been left their phones. They couldn't get service here anyway. Liam winced away from its glare, and Owen held up a hand to shield his eyes. Kelly's face was impossible to see, but there was concern in his voice. "Dude, you don't look so hot."

"That's because I'm stuck in a freezer!" Liam shouted. His voice echoed off the walls.

"Do you want someone to put you out of your misery?" Kelly asked, suppressed laughter in his voice.

Nick lounged beside Kelly with his back against one of the shelf supports, massaging the bridge of his nose. "Talk it through, man," he grunted to Liam.

"No, you dealt with Tyler, and you know I have the same issue, okay? Stop being a bag of dicks!"

"He's rocking," Nick said.

"T minus five minutes to meltdown," Kelly added.

"Shut up," Liam snarled.

Owen rested a hand on Liam's back, glaring at Nick and Kelly. "As much as I'm secretly enjoying it and trying to pretend I'm not, you two aren't actually helping the situation right now."

"It's fine," Nick told him. "Just like we used to do to Ty. He'll panic for a couple minutes, he'll hyperventilate, he'll pass out. It's easier that way than trying to keep him calm."

Kelly laughed again.

Liam covered his head with his hands. "You're both arseholes."

"Yeah, well so are you," Nick said. "So it all works out."

Liam raised his head, glaring through the low light. "I'm getting fucking sick of your shite, O'Flaherty. I swear to God."

Nick slid off the shelf and straightened. "What are you going to do, Bell? Threaten my boyfriend? Break into my boat? Drug me and take me hostage?" Kelly took his arm to calm him but Nick yanked away. "Force me to try to get my friends killed by making the guilt from the past too much to bear? You going to try all that *again*? 'Cause I didn't see it working too well for you the first time, son. Second time's a charm?"

Liam clambered to his feet, shrugging off Owen's hand when he tried to stop him.

"What am I doing?" Owen asked, holding his hands away from Liam. "Yeah, just kick his ass."

Kelly remained where he was, the light wavering in his grip. Nick took a step toward Liam, rolling up the sleeves of his shirt.

"You got something you've been wanting to say to me?" Liam snarled.

Nick turned a little, rolling his shoulder. "I'm going to do you a favor, bud. One old friend to another."

"Oh, really? 'Cause your last favor got me shot!"

Nick's jaw tightened and he nodded, glancing at Kelly before he met Liam's eyes again. He moved quickly, too fast for Liam to react even though Liam really should have known it was coming. It was a classic O'Flaherty haymaker, and it knocked the lights in the freezer right out for the man.

"What the fuck are you doing?" Digger shouted. "What if we need him?"

Nick stood over Liam, huffing and rubbing at his knuckles. Kelly was behind him, a hand on his elbow. "Goddamn your stupid face," Nick muttered, cradling his hand.

Owen and Digger were both eyeing Liam like they weren't sure whether to help him or leave him down there to freeze.

"He's just like Ty in small spaces, remember? If you make him angry, he forgets to panic," Nick explained, his voice soft and calm again.

Kelly squinted at him through the glaring light of his phone's flash.

Nick shrugged. "If I'm wrong, at least I got a lot out of it."

Kelly knelt at Liam's hip, taking his pulse and checking his pupils. "He's okay," he told the others, sounding sort of disappointed about it. "Let's get him off the floor."

"Put him down with one swing," Owen finally said, grinning. "Damn I wish we'd recorded that."

Nick held up his right hand, displaying a fist full of scars and mended fingers and one slightly bloody, gold claddagh ring. "I learned from a champion."

The freezer fell into tense silence after they laid Liam out on a shelf next to the truffles and bacon. Kelly climbed onto the shelf next to Nick and extinguished the light, throwing everything into pitch-black. It was getting colder. They'd come to Miami prepared for battle and muggy warmth, not below-freezing temperatures. They probably weren't going to freeze in here, but Nick was sort of wondering how much oxygen they had left.

He also wondered why the NIA hadn't just taken care of them when they had them, instead of literally putting them in cold storage. It all seemed such a waste. The NIA as an organization had been living off handouts ever since Sidewinder had been one of the elite active Recon teams. They'd had to scavenge spec ops from the military, they'd had to pull military officers for their jobs just like they had with Nick, they'd had to scrape and scrounge for their resources. Those hundreds of millions of dollars of cartel money would go a long way toward making them a true power in the intelligence game again, and not just the toothless old aunt in Uncle Sam's basement.

But that money wouldn't last long in this game. So why the desperate hunt for it? Why the willingness to kill decorated American veterans in the pursuit? Nick still didn't understand. Did some suit with three degrees riding an NIA desk somewhere think Ty and Zane possessed the knowledge to get more money out of the Vega cartel? Did they think the information they'd been seeking would somehow siphon off more? Was that what this boiled down to?

It made sense. It was the only thing that did. Nick supposed, if he was right, that they were a backup plan, there to be used as spare parts to make Ty and Zane talk.

Hell. Those agents would probably be back to fetch them before they had to worry about freezing or suffocating. Then it'd be knives and guns and maybe a little boat ride to Gitmo they had to fear.

He snuggled up to Kelly, trying to keep them both warm. Kelly's breath was shaky. Nick pressed his forehead to Kelly's and closed his eyes. "I'm sorry," he whispered. "For all I've done. I . . ."

Kelly turned his head, his nose brushing Nick's cheek in the dark. "You did it out of love, babe. That's all you've ever done."

Nick was silent, the weight of Kelly's limitless forgiveness almost as oppressive as the cold. All he had left to him was to hold on as Kelly began to rock.

"Any ideas?" Kelly finally asked everyone.

"Stay calm, stay still. Conserve our air and keep warm." Nick said.

"All we can do is last until someone lets us out," Digger added. "Then we take our chances with the guns."

"We should be able to hear them coming," Owen said. "There's enough frozen meat in here to use as weapons. If we stay limber enough, we may be able to rush them."

"You want us to attack the NIA agents with frozen meat?" Digger asked, his voice trembling and his teeth chattering. He snickered. "Literally hit them over the head with our big meatsacks?"

"Oh my God," Owen grumbled.

It felt like hours, but Nick's watch proved it was only thirty minutes before there was a clank outside the freezer door and then a sliver of light. They were as prepared as nearly frozen men could be, armed with anything hard or sharp they could find.

When the door opened, the overhead light popped on. Nick had to close his eyes against the glare, and then he squinted at the two men in the doorway. The blond man had his hands on his hips. The big man had an Irish accent.

"Hey, iceholes," Julian greeted a little too cheerfully.

Nick dropped the frozen meat hook he'd taken from the ceiling, gaping at the two men.

"You boys turn up in the weirdest places," Preston said as he stepped aside to usher them out into the blessed warmth.

"What the hell are you doing here?" Nick demanded.

"A very pleasant woman named Agent Clancy called, said you'd been unable to perform when you reached the airport," Preston explained. "I hear there's a medication for that problem, sir."

Nick glared at him for a second, then turned to Julian.

ABIGAIL ROUX

Julian arched an eyebrow. "We tailed your captors from the airport. Place was being guarded by two agents. From what we heard, they're after Garrett, and Garrett alone. They were holding you until they got to him."

"What the hell did they think this was, cryogenic suspension?" Owen spat as he rubbed at his arms and tried to shake off the bone-deep chill.

"Where are they now?" Nick asked.

"They weren't quite as durable as we had thought," Preston drawled with a frightening grin.

"We really must be moving on; we have to get to the airport before these wankers pick up Grady and Garrett. They've got their faces plastered all over the place, legitimate and not quite so. Everyone in Miami with a gun and a pair of handcuffs will be looking for them."

Nick nodded, gesturing for them to lead the way.

Preston pointed the tip of his sniper rifle toward the freezer. "Forgetting something?"

Nick glanced back inside at Liam, stretched out on the shelf where they'd left him. It took him a long moment to decide whether to go back in and get him or just fucking leave him there to get what he deserved.

The others seemed to mostly disapprove of his decision to retrieve the man.

"He'd 'a been a dickcicle if we'd left him," Digger told them, chuckling as they dragged Liam's limp body out of the freezer.

Nick grunted and looked down at Liam as Digger and Owen dragged the man between them.

"You still think we can trust him?" Kelly asked Nick as they stepped out into the sunshine.

Nick closed his eyes and lifted his face toward the sun, warmth seeping into him. "I don't want to think anymore. It's about feeling now."

Kelly was nodding, watching as they loaded Liam's unconscious body into the back of a big, red Ford Excursion. He sniffed. "What's your gut say?"

Nick let Kelly's words sink in. "I think . . . I think I might trust him."

Kelly grimaced as he turned to Nick. "Me too."

"You gents coming?" Julian called from the passenger side of the Excursion. Preston was in the driver's seat, starting it up.

Kelly wrapped a hand around Nick's waist, helping him limp across the street and climb into the back of the car.

The radio was on in the front, the telltale static of a police band whining away. Preston and Julian both looked grim. "We're too late," Julian informed them. "Local PD picked Grady and Garrett up at the airport. They're transporting them now."

Nick shrugged, smirking as he met Julian's eyes. "So let's go bust them the fuck out of jail."

"Now you see why I hate Miami?"

Ty was sitting beside Zane in the back of the police cruiser, his hands cuffed behind him just like Zane's were. Ty shrugged. Or sort of shrugged; it was hard with the cuffs. "I don't know, I'm kind of digging the whole 'mix of glitter and sweat in my ass crack' vibe it's got going. Locals are a little unfriendly."

"What do you think?" Zane asked. "Are they really local PD, or are those stripper outfits?"

Ty pursed his lips and shrugged again. "I don't know, dude, they look a little light on the donut to be real PD."

The two officers in the front seat were trying valiantly to ignore them, both of them stone-faced, eyes on the road as they navigated toward what Zane could only assume was a nice, neat, bottleneck trap where the NIA could pick them off. Zane hoped Ty had a plan, because he'd followed Ty's lead when they'd submitted to being arrested instead of fighting their way free. Ty usually had a plan. Right? Please God say Ty had a plan.

"I can't believe we managed to get picked up by the two dumbest sentient beings in the universe."

Ty snorted. "Well, how were we supposed to prepare for *this*? I mean Jesus Christ, what kind of fucking Barney thinks it's legit when they're issued an arrest order for the Agent in Charge of an FBI field office because a rival government agency wanted them to?"

Ty was chuckling as he spoke, and the sound kicked Zane off into a laughing fit as well. God *damn*, how fucking unlucky could two people be?

"Shut up, both of you," the passenger snarled over his shoulder.

"Son, I hope you had a heavy lunch," Ty drawled. "'Cause you ain't making it home to dinner."

"Are you threatening an officer of the law back there?"

"No, sir," Ty said, elongating the syllables until the simple words sounded like yet another insult. "I'm just telling you. The people who put that alert out on us? They're not exactly wearing patches with the thin blue on them, you feel me?"

"I don't think he feels you," Zane offered.

Ty suddenly looked alarmed. "I hope he won't feel me. My heart belongs to the TSA."

The cops went back to ignoring them, and Ty and Zane met each other's eyes. Zane frowned and ducked his head toward Ty's hands, and Ty winked. He was scratching at his wrist with his fingernails, and to Zane's horror it looked like he was actually raking off skin in swaths, leaving little curled bits of it on the seat behind him.

Then the scratching revealed something dull and gray beneath, and Zane realized it was a key under some type of synthetic skin.

"You fucking beautiful bastard," Zane murmured. There was Ty's plan. Get loose and steal the cop car.

"Can I use the flashy blue lights?" Ty drawled. He got hold of the key between two fingers, grinning widely. Zane was still gazing at Ty's pleased expression when the impact came, throwing them both sideways, knocking the key out of Ty's grasp and sending the police cruiser and all its occupants into a sickening spin.

Nick was leaning between the front seats, watching as a GPS dot blinked on the tablet in Julian's hands. It was showing their location and the location of the LoJack system on the PD unit that had picked up Ty and Zane at the airport. They were closing in.

"Where'd you get that?" Nick asked.

"Best Buy," Julian answered flatly.

Nick gave him a sideways glance, but Julian was frowning at the screen.

"Take this next left, then gun it," Julian told Preston. "We can cut them off."

Preston smirked as he weaved through traffic at breakneck speed. "Yes, sir."

He took a hard left across the oncoming lanes that made even Nick want to cover his eyes, and then the Excursion screamed down a one-way street that was definitely not meant to be traveled in this direction.

Nick ducked his head. They roared past stunned drivers trying to get out of the way, but he couldn't take his eyes off the road. It was like some sort of morbid dance, the way the man drove. Nick found himself wanting to geek out a little about it.

Preston yanked the emergency brake, turning the wheel smoothly as they took a hairpin turn onto another main thoroughfare, and Kelly tumbled across the bench seat into Nick. His ribs burned and he gasped, holding on to them.

"Sorry," Kelly whispered.

Nick just shook his head, unable to speak though the pain.

"Dude!" Digger cried from the back.

"I think I'm going to yark," Owen added pitifully.

Nick and Kelly both edged closer to the front, away from the backseat. They remembered the last time Owen had been in a helicopter a little too vividly.

They came up on an intersection, and Nick pointed ahead of them at the white, green, and yellow Miami-Dade police cruiser. "There they are."

They were just in time to see a big, black Denali, with its reinforced grill guard, lumber through the intersection and plow into the front driver's side of the cruiser.

"Welp," Preston said as he slowed the Excursion.

The Denali sat there, crumpled and steaming, as the cruiser spun away and threatened to tip. Four more black SUVs were closing in on the intersection, and Nick fumbled for the door handle. "Stop those fucking cars from reaching that cruiser," he ordered, and they all toppled out into the street.

The police cruiser rocked up on two wheels, creaking and groaning as it threatened to tip. Zane slid toward Ty until the seat belt stopped him, choking and cutting into him. He ducked his head and curled, but the handcuffs prevented either of them from shielding their heads or faces as the car rocked back and slammed onto its tires.

Ty gasped, fighting the seat belt, fighting his handcuffs. The two cops in the front of the car were both either unconscious or dead.

Zane coughed and gagged, struggling to right himself. "What happened?"

"Car rammed us," Ty answered. He was short of breath, taking in the chaotic scene outside the window. He finally managed to hit the release with his elbow, and the seat belt popped free.

Zane's arms were stuck in the mangled cavities behind the backseat meant to allow handcuffed prisoners room for their hands, and he had to fight out of it, ripping at the skin of his arms to get loose. He slid his hands under his ass and legs until they were in front of him. The key Ty had just managed to free from the synthetic skin on his arm was nowhere in sight.

Zane scooted closer to the window. The car that had hit them was a black Yukon Denali, and it was sitting like a wounded leviathan about fifty feet away, blocking the quiet intersection.

"Oh shit."

"What?" Ty asked. He was still struggling to get out of his cuffs. "What is it?"

"It's them."

The driver of the Denali stumbled from the SUV. He turned, straightening and chuckling when he saw they were trapped.

Even if they got out of the handcuffs, they were still locked in the back of a police cruiser. It would be like shooting fish in a barrel. Unless of course the NIA wanted to question them first, in which case it would be like torturing fish in a barrel.

The driver stalked through the debris, heading for Zane's side of the police cruiser. He pulled a gun from his jacket. Ty turned in his seat, lying flat and kicking at the window.

"Ty," Zane gasped.

Ty didn't stop. A tiny crack appeared under his heel.

"Ty, I love you," Zane said quickly. "I love you. If we don't get—"

"No!" Ty shouted. He kicked furiously at the window. Zane could see the impact jarring his ankles. "We're not dying today, Zane, not like this."

"Ty!" Zane cried when he looked back out his window.

"Not like this!"

Zane gripped Ty's hair and yanked so he'd look out the window. The driver of the Denali was right there, the gun in his hand and a tattooed, bandaged arm wrapped around his neck. His face contorted as his body arched and flailed. He gritted his teeth, shouting and trying to point the gun behind his head, but then the arm around his neck jerked, breaking his neck and draining the life from him.

The gun fell from his hand, and his body dropped out of sight. Nick was standing behind him, breathing hard and sneering down at the dead man.

"Fuck, man, you have the best timing ever!" Ty shouted as he struggled to sit up again. He leaned over Zane's lap, pressing both hands to the window.

Nick knocked on the glass. "You assholes can't even get arrested right."

"You beautiful fucking bastard," Zane whispered.

"Get us the fuck out of here, Irish!"

Nick tried the door, but as Zane had expected, it was locked and probably jammed shut. Nick knocked the shards of glass remaining from the window of the front door and leaned through to check the driver's pulse as he reached in for the car keys. "He's dead," he told them, then searched the man for the keys to the handcuffs.

"Come on, Irish, double-time it, man," Ty urged.

Nick fit the handcuff keys through the wires so they could get themselves loose, then pushed the unlock button that should have released the back door. Nothing happened.

The squealing of tires drew Zane's attention to two more black SUVs tearing up the sidewalk several blocks away. The traffic from the wreck and the crowded, chaotic streets were slowing them down, but they would be here in minutes. Gunfire went off somewhere, which meant Nick wasn't here alone. They had a chance if they could get out.

"Come on, O'Flaherty!" Zane shouted. He banged on the glass.

Nick fumbled with the keys and came back to the door. Ty watched him, leaning over Zane's lap. Zane caught sight of movement behind Nick and shouted at the same time as Ty banged a warning on the glass.

Nick turned and blocked the first slash of the man's knife with his forearm. He swung with his left, wrapping the man up and kneeing him in the kidney. Then he pounded the man's face. Nick's gun clattered away from them, and they grappled until Nick finally got him in a choke hold. He held on long after the man had lost consciousness, ensuring he wouldn't wake up.

Nick let him drop to the ground, then took one step toward the car before someone grabbed him from behind.

"No!" Ty cried. He banged on the glass, futilely pulling at the handle. "No!"

Nick's body contorted and his mouth fell open as a knife drove into his side. The attacker twisted it, and Nick screamed.

Ty echoed the anguished cry and threw himself against the opposite window, slamming his fist into the already cracked glass over and over in a desperate bid to get free. He left the glass bloody, but couldn't get out. He jostled Zane when he returned to his side, tears streaming. Nick was on his knees, head bowed, still being held around the neck by the man with the knife. His attacker yanked the knife out of Nick's side and plunged it in again.

Nick screamed again, his back arching, his eyes tightly shut. But he reached into his boot as he arched his back, and came out with a dagger, flipping it in his palm and jamming it into the killer's throat.

Blood spurted, and both of them fell to the ground.

"Jesus Christ," Zane whispered.

He and Ty pressed closer to the glass. Nick was still on his knees, holding to the wounds at his side. The black SUVs were drawing near, full of more NIA agents with guns and knives who no doubt wanted to ask them some very pointed questions. Sidewinder was retreating under fire to a big red SUV in the middle of the street.

Nick began crawling for the cruiser, keeping low as the rattle of gunfire from further down the street got closer. His fingers reached the gun he had dropped during his tussle. He collapsed in the debris, holding to the handle of the knife in his side. He met Ty's eyes through the glass, then reached out with a trembling, bloody hand and aimed the gun he'd taken off the first agent he'd killed.

Ty nodded hastily, grabbing Zane by the shoulder. "Get down, down!"

They shielded each other, flattening in the floorboard of the cruiser. The shot was deafening, and glass sprayed them as the window collapsed in a nearly solid sheet, freeing Ty and Zane from their impromptu prison.

Zane shoved at the remaining shards, and Ty crawled over him to get out of the car. He thumped gracelessly to the ground, then scrambled over to Nick, heedless of the debris shredding his hands and knees, favoring his shoulder as if the wreck had dislocated it. Zane hurried out of the cruiser.

Ty grabbed Nick to help him up. Nick tried to get to his feet, but he collapsed in Ty's arms; and Ty fell to his knees again, holding Nick to him. Zane cast around for the gun Nick had dropped.

Nick stared up at the sky, taking shallow, quick breaths. Tears trailed from both his eyes. He focused on Ty and nodded. "Okay."

"It's okay," Ty whispered. His fingers tightened in Nick's shirt, cradling him in his lap. "We'll get you all patched up and you'll be fine. Zane, help me!"

Zane knelt at Nick's other side, shaking his head as he placed a palm over Nick's chest. He was alarmingly cold. Even his clothes were cold. The gunfire was closer, and Ty hunched defensively.

"Run, Ty," Nick murmured.

"We're not leaving you here."

Nick's mouth barely moved when he spoke. "I'm already dead, babe. Go."

"No!"

Nick closed his eyes. "See you on the other side, brother."

"No," Ty hissed. He shook his head, wrapping Nick's arm over his neck so he could deadlift him into a fireman's carry.

Zane gripped Ty's shoulder to halt him. His hand was covered in Nick's blood. "Ty, you can't move him, it'll kill him!"

Nick had gone limp, and his weight seemed to be too much for Ty's injured arm. He couldn't lift his friend. He sank back down, holding tighter to Nick as he laid him on the hard asphalt.

Zane watched, speechless, trying to decide what to do. Ty shook his head again, fighting back tears.

"We have to leave him, Ty," Zane urged brokenly.

Tires screeched as a set of black SUVs trapped the red one in the intersection. The driver gunned the red Excursion, and it plowed through the smaller vehicles, disappearing out of sight. Sidewinder had been forced to retreat. Ty and Zane were on their own.

"They're coming, Ty."

Ty gripped Nick's hair and hugged him to his chest, tears falling against his forehead. "I'm not leaving him here."

"He's dead if you move him and so are we!" Zane tugged urgently at Ty's uninjured shoulder as he struggled to get him up.

"I can't leave him here," Ty said, almost panicked as Zane pried him away.

"Look at that knife, Ty! You'll kill him!"

Nick lay in a slowly spreading pool of blood, his green eyes closed to the brilliant blue sky, his skin unnaturally pale and cool. Ty struggled as Zane wrapped him up and pulled him to his feet.

"Don't make me leave him here!" Ty sobbed.

It broke Zane's heart, but he wasn't going to lose Ty on this street. "We have to go. He died for us, Ty, we have to go now!"

"He's not dead! I can't leave him like this. I can't leave him like this! Please!"

"We'll come back for him." Ty didn't take his eyes off Nick or stop struggling as Zane dragged him toward a little, blue Prius that had been abandoned by its owner in the chaos. "I promise," Zane tried again breathlessly. "I promise! But we have to go!"

Ty sat on the couch and rocked, unblinking. Zane watched him, worrying, mourning for him and the others, who were all sitting quietly with much the same distant expressions on their faces.

Zane met Julian's eyes across the room. It was hard to judge the man, but he seemed sad as well. Even Liam, who'd done his best to drag Nick and the rest of Sidewinder into his own brand of Hell, was sitting with his head lowered and his eyes closed.

Zane had managed to get out of the chaos and find his way to the safe house by his memory of the city's streets alone. Ty had held his head in his hands the entire way. When they'd gotten out of the car without Nick, Owen and Digger had been forced to drag Kelly away to prevent him from tearing off into the city alone.

An hour after leaving Nick's body in the street, Preston was the only one still up and moving, reloading all their weapons and laying them out on the cracked laminate countertop. Zane had contacted Clancy and her crew to update them. They were on their way here, but Zane wasn't sure if it mattered. Sidewinder was broken.

"He could have made it," Kelly said suddenly from where he was crouched against the wall, curled into a ball under the window. "Someone on the scene could have gotten him help, right? He could still make it. Right?"

No one answered him. No one even looked at him. Zane ran a hand through his hair, watching Kelly with heaviness in his heart he wasn't sure he could shake. "Yeah, Doc," he whispered. "Yeah, he could have made it."

Kelly bowed his head, tears falling onto his folded arms.

"I am truly sorry for your loss," Julian said. He let out a slow breath, squaring his shoulders. "But I need to know if this mission is still viable. My favors only extend so far past their expiration date."

Ty's eyes snapped to Julian with the sudden light of murderous intent. Zane lunged to his feet, getting between them before Ty could launch himself at the man.

"Expiration date?" Ty shoved at Zane, heedless of his dislocated shoulder or any of the bumps, scrapes, and bruises they shared. "Son of a bitch!"

Julian put both hands up. "I had the greatest respect for Detective O'Flaherty. I am simply asking if the rest of you intend to sacrifice yourselves on this altar as well."

Ty trembled in Zane's arms, his breaths shaky. "Yeah, I do."

Zane nodded in a silent show of support. He and Ty had no choice. This was their altar to bleed on. Nick had thrown himself in their path, maybe slowed down the knife. But it was still coming. His death meant nothing. Not yet.

"Very well, then," Julian said quietly.

Preston accentuated Julian's statement by slamming a magazine home.

"What's our play, Six?" Owen asked. He'd been crying, and he hadn't made any effort to hide it. His eyes glistened and his voice shook, but he looked angry and determined.

Ty was still shaking, anger and grief warring in his eyes. "We can't take on the NIA, not the eight of us."

"Fortunately," Preston drawled as he screwed a large suppressor onto the end of a sniper rifle. "They overplayed their hand out there, showed willingness to assassinate not only US citizens like dogs in the street, but also officers of the law. Let's just say the Central Intelligence Agency is now highly perturbed."

"Will they help us?" Zane asked.

Preston shook his head, jaw tight. "They still expect you to uphold your end."

"Which we can't do for another two weeks," Zane said. "We'll all be dead by then."

Ty nodded. "That leaves the Vega cartel."

"Is this revenge now, Tyler?" Julian asked.

Ty gritted his teeth, breathing hard. "With the cartel still out there, Zane and I are dead men even if we do get cleared. Anyone who wants out is free to walk, but we're going. With or without help."

"And what, pray tell, do you intend to do with them?" Liam asked. For the first time, Zane thought the man sounded defeated.

Ty met Zane's eyes, and he nodded minutely. They couldn't blame everything that'd happened on the cartel. They couldn't even say that Nick—their friend, their brother—had died because of the cartel. No, that blame rested solely on Richard Burns's shoulders. Ty would have the rest of his life to mourn that loss, and no one left to seek revenge on. Zane could feel the pain flickering on the edges of his own consciousness like a forest fire bearing down on him. He could imagine what the other men were feeling. He could see in their eyes, too; they wanted revenge.

The cartel had come after them. Burned down their bookstore, tried to take them all out with it. But they'd risen from the ashes with vengeance and mourning in their hearts. And someone had to pay. For them. For Nick. Someone had to pay.

Zane smiled slowly, nodding at his husband. "We burn them. We burn everything."

Ty crouched at the perimeter of the Tuscan-style villa nestled on Star Island. The sand on this fucking island was probably worth more than gold.

They'd performed a solid day of recon, complete with having Zane and Owen track down digital blueprints from the architect and Kelly finding the hours of the moon and the tides. They'd set charges in all the possible places on the island they could reach without tipping their hand, and Preston's sole job during the attack would be to litter more of them throughout the compound.

One press of a button at the end of this, and the Vega cartel was going to become intimately acquainted with the meaning of crash and burn.

Zane had dubbed their plan Wile E. Coyote Phase 4. They were doing everything but painting a getaway tunnel on the side of the house.

Ty shielded his wristwatch with his hand and lifted the cover to check the glowing dial. It was time.

"Go," he whispered, the word sharp in the humid night. His men broke the perimeter. Within two seconds, a siren began to wail. Searchlights clanked on, probing the shadows of the vast estate. Dogs bayed and barked from somewhere uncomfortably close.

To Ty's left, an explosion rocked the compound. The shock wave blasted over them. Buffs and scarves protected their faces against the heat. At least Digger's discount C4 worked.

Their primary goal was to take Juan Carlos de la Vega alive. He could either be leveraged for the cartel's bounty on Ty and Zane's heads, or he could be turned over to the government in exchange for pardons. Hell, Ty didn't even mind pitting the cartel and the Feds against each other, as long as he and Zane weren't part of it anymore.

Their secondary goal, of course, was to cripple the cartel to the point that they'd be forced to retreat from Miami altogether. You can't kill what you can't catch, and since Ty and Zane didn't plan on vacationing in Colombia anytime soon, Ty would be just fine if the cartel stayed the fuck down there.

Tertiary goal? Well. Like Zane had said: flame and ash. Fire and brimstone.

But even if they didn't manage to accomplish anything they were setting out to do tonight, they had just used a homemade rocket launcher to blow the shit out of the building their intel indicated was the main distribution point for all the cocaine flowing from this operation. All in the name of distraction.

So, there was that.

Ty dove to his elbows and knees, firing at the sentries stationed on the roof of the mansion. The sound of gunfire was deafening. Men shouting, screaming in pain and panic, dogs barking, minor explosions following the major one. It was chaos. Pure hell raining down on upscale Miami.

Julian had been given a sniper rifle and the detonators, much to Digger's dismay, and he seemed to be enjoying himself from his perch atop the western wall.

Zane was sticking to Ty's side. He knew the compound intimately, and their job was to find de la Vega.

Clancy, Perrimore, and Lassiter had gone left, Owen, Digger, and Kelly right. Their jobs were to kill everything they found. Everything. Liam claimed he still needed proof the cartel had killed his handler in order to clear his name, and he'd gone off alone.

"Burn it to the ground, boys," Kelly growled through their earpieces. "Burn it so high Nick can see."

Tears tracked down Ty's face. *One last time into the fray. See you on the other side, brother.*

There was a familiar whistle off to the left, and Ty watched the graceful arc of a rocket-propelled projectile fired from a shoulder launcher. It hit an outer building of the compound with impressive results. He could hear Julian snickering in his earpiece.

Ty and Zane moved toward the main building, clumps of well-manicured grass kicking up around them as they scrambled through heavy fire. They'd advance several steps at a time, then kneel and return fire at intervals as they crept closer and closer.

Finally they crouched at the corner of the main building. So far, so good.

"Where's the entry point?" he asked Zane, who was kneeling beside him, breathing hard. His eyes were hard black, reflecting the flames as if they were coming from within him instead of without. Ty's phoenix, come to life.

"Keep up," Zane rumbled, and he took off at a lope into the smoking shadows.

"Keep up," Ty muttered. He found himself smirking as he jogged after him.

Zane led them through a maze of corridors deep into the house, moving quickly and quietly, dispatching anyone they encountered with frightening indiscrimination.

He took a turn and Ty nearly ran over him when he stopped short. He was blinking at a painting hung in an alcove.

"Garrett," Ty hissed. "This ain't a museum, come on."

"This . . . used to be a hallway. They must have remodeled."

Ty stared at him.

Zane shrugged and moved off again. After a few more twists and turns, he finally stopped at a corner and held up his hand to halt Ty. He pulled an aerosol can from his flak jacket and stretched his long body, reaching up and around the corner to disable what Ty assumed was a motion sensor. They crept around the corner and crouched outside an ornate set of double doors, where Zane cocked his head to listen.

Some of the gunfire outside let up, and Zane inhaled deeply. "This is the command center. Security system, files, maybe even el Jefe himself if he's trying to hole up."

"Can we take it just the two of us?"

"Only one way to find out," Zane said with a grin, his eyes shining with mischief.

Ty shook his head. "So this is what it's like being partnered with *me*, huh? Is that what this is? Is that what you're doing?"

Zane chuckled. When he spoke again, he lowered his voice even further. "This may seem hypocritical, but there are a few things I just didn't want you to know about me." He pulled his scuffed Glock out of his waistband, checked the clip, and held it at the ready.

"Is this really the right time for this conversation?" Ty asked with a raised eyebrow.

Zane winced. "I just need you to know . . . I . . . I hate baseball."

"You shut your whore mouth!"

Zane snickered as he pulled a knife from its sheath.

Ty cradled his assault rifle with practiced ease, but he had a feeling he might not need it if Zane was about to go get his freak on in this room. "But you *do* actually like baseball, right?"

Zane's mouth quirked, but then he nodded. "You've always thought I was a better man than I am. I'm about to prove you wrong." A bark of angry Spanish from inside the room interrupted him. He nodded curtly and turned toward the door.

Footsteps coming from the smoky corridor had Ty dropping to his knees, gun up and ready. The man approaching put a hand up, though, tugging his scarf down.

Ty stood again, motioning Liam forward. "Did you find what you were after?" Ty asked.

Liam shook his head. "I don't know why I hoped I would. I came to help you take de la Vega. Perhaps . . . make some amends."

Ty nodded, looking Liam up and down, battling within himself over whether to finally just fucking trust the man. He held his fist out, the leather of his gloves squeaking in the hefty silence.

Liam waited a breath, then pressed his fist to Ty's, nodding. "For old times' sake?"

"Oohrah," Ty agreed with a small smile.

They set up on either side of Zane, who turned his back to the door and mule-kicked it at the weakest point. Ty and Liam streamed in, Zane following them, their weapons popping in short bursts as they cleared the room of the few people inside.

It lasted just seconds, and then they stood in the center of the room amid the dead. One wall was covered with a bank of security feeds. On another, rows and rows of file cabinets.

"Cartels keep receipts for taxes?" Liam asked as he moved toward the cabinets.

Ty stepped toward the screens, though, peering at the grainy videos. He was distantly aware of Liam opening and closing the file cabinets.

"Got eyes on de la Vega?" Zane asked as he came up behind Ty. He pressed his back to Ty's, facing the door.

"I don't know what de la Vega looks like." Ty's eyes darted over the screens, though, almost obsessively looking for their people to make sure no one else had been lost.

Liam grunted as he opened one of the cabinet drawers.

"What's in there?" Zane asked.

"Uhh . . . more like *who's* in here?" Liam answered as he shut the drawer.

Zane made a sound Ty wasn't sure he'd ever heard before. Ty tapped at Zane's arm, and Zane turned to the screens. "I can't see any of our guys," Ty said with a scowl.

A horrible scratching sound echoed through the room, a hidden door scraping on concrete, and Liam put his back to Ty and Zane's as they tried to cover every wall.

The left side of the room opened up, revealing an impeccably dressed woman, her blonde hair cut in a neat bob, a gun at her hip. She was surrounded by men, all of them with their firearms pointed at Ty, Zane, and Liam.

"Anna," Liam blurted.

The blonde winked at him. She was quite stunning, but Ty wasn't sure if it was physical or if it was more in her attitude. Either way, she had them by their figurative balls.

She graced them with a sly smile. "You could have knocked."

"I'm curious," Anna said as she marched her captives into a large holding tank that appeared to have once been part of a water tower. It echoed with her amused tones as Ty and the others stepped inside. "What exactly was the plan here? You didn't expect to get out of here, did you?"

In addition to himself, Zane, and Liam, Anna and her men had also rounded up Owen, Clancy, and Perrimore. Ty didn't know where the others were, or if they were even alive.

He stood between Zane and Clancy, his jaw set.

"You faked your death," Liam said to Anna, and he had the audacity to sound wounded by it. "They hunted me down like a dog for your murder."

Anna's brow creased, and she shook her head, appearing sympathetic. "That certainly wasn't my intention. My intention was to get *paid*. And Juan Carlos pays better than any other player on the board right now. It was never personal."

"It felt pretty personal to me," Liam growled.

She made a clicking sound and shrugged. "Them's the breaks, kiddo. Now! Listen carefully, I know this will be a difficult concept to grasp for a group that thought they could just walk in and blow shit up and walk out. But this is a once in a lifetime offer."

A man came up to stand beside her, loading a nickel-plated Walther PP semiautomatic. Ty could see the gun clearly, but it was hard to see the man's features with the light from the doorway framing him. From the way Zane tensed at Ty's side, though, Zane recognized the man.

Zane had probably known a lot of the lower-level thugs in the cartel, and it had been long enough that some of them may have worked their way higher. What the hell would they do to Zane if they recognized him as the man, the traitor, they had all known as Xander so many years ago? Energy came off Zane in waves. Ty could feel him coiling, either to attack or defend, but he had to know there was nothing they could do, cornered and unarmed. Any move from them would be suicide. Ty didn't even risk reaching out to touch his husband. The others were all restless, sneering at the cartel lackeys, thrumming in place.

A basket full of snakes.

"The first person to join us will get quite the astonishing signing bonus," Anna said. "Meaning you will get to live, and you will tell us everything you know. Then you'll get a nice finder's fee that will aid in alleviating your guilty conscience. Then you'll either be sent on your way or offered a job, depending on how you handle the first steps. The rest of you? You'll be dying tonight after some festivities."

Ty looked down the line at Liam. If anyone would turn on them to save his own skin, Liam would. And he'd do it now. But Liam stood with his arms crossed, his shoulders rigid and his chin raised high. He seemed to feel eyes on him, and he glanced toward Ty and Zane, smiling sadly when he met Ty's eyes. "We all die someday, mate," he said quietly. "I intend to do it well."

"Offer's going once," Anna called. She held up her hand, one manicured finger raised. "Twice!"

Ty sniffed. Someone else cursed in the damp. No one moved.

"Last chance."

Owen huffed somewhere to Ty's left. It drew Ty's attention, and out of the corner of his eye he saw Zane lower his head. Then Zane turned to Ty and took his face between his hands, kissing him carefully.

"I'm sorry." Though his words were whispered, they seemed to echo off the rusting walls. "But I told you I'd disappoint you."

His hands dropped away from Ty's face, and he backed away a few steps, moving toward Anna and the cartel men. Ty and the others watched him tensely, right up until he turned his back on them and what he was doing hit home.

"Garrett!" Perrimore and Clancy cried in unison.

"Zane," Ty gasped. He shifted his weight, but the guns kept his feet rooted to the spot.

Zane kept moving, hands out as the cartel henchmen grew warier. They patted him down, and then to Ty's growing astonishment, Zane took the cartel man's hand and shook it, speaking in rapid Spanish. The man laughed, patting Zane on the shoulder.

He handed Zane the nickel-plated semiautomatic.

Zane ejected the magazine to check it as he spoke. "I'm sorry, Grady. You weren't the only one who went into this with ulterior motives." He shoved the magazine back in place and tapped the gun against his palm.

"Zane, what are you doing?" Ty asked breathlessly.

"When Burns told you he suspected I'd been turned down here?" Zane sounded calm, almost conversational. "Well, he was right."

"No." Ty swallowed hard. "No, this isn't happening."

The words trailed off, echoing in the cavernous room. No one even breathed, and Zane almost smiled as he cocked his head at Ty. "It was a pretty good con, though, huh?" he said, then pointed the gun at Liam and fired.

Ty heard screaming in his mind as Liam fell away from them. He registered the others moving, rushing the cartel men. Zane fired three more times, downing Clancy, Perrimore, and Owen in rapid succession. Ty stood in the middle of the room, his friends bleeding and dying around him, and stared at Zane.

Zane moved closer to him, the gun still raised, his eyes hard as obsidian. "Seven bullets left, Ty," he said softly. It was an almost intimate whisper. "Where do you want them?"

One of their captors said something in impatient Spanish. Ty couldn't understand it, but Zane glanced over his shoulder in annoyance and said a single word that shut both men up instantly.

Ty could have taken that moment to rush him, to wrestle the gun from him. But he blinked at Zane's profile instead, emptiness engulfing him. Like it was no longer real, he was merely watching it play out in front of him on a stage.

Zane gestured to the two cartel men, and they both chuckled and exited the room. Anna remained, and Zane gave her a pointed look. "I'm about to become a widower for the second time," Zane told her. "I'd like a minute alone with my grief."

She raised both eyebrows, shaking her head as she left them. Ty heard the door lock from the outside after she closed it.

"Zane," Ty whispered.

Someone on the ground moaned.

"Shut up," Zane hissed at Liam, and he used his foot to roll Liam over to his back. Liam had his eyes closed and both hands pressed to his side, blood leaking through his fingers. Zane looked him over, then kicked him back onto his side.

Zane met Ty's eyes, and the darkness seeped out of them, replaced by that familiar warmth Ty knew so well. "You're either earning an Oscar right now or you really believed me."

"What?" Ty blurted.

Zane pounced on him and slapped a hand over his mouth, shushing him. Ty jabbed him in the stomach and grabbed for the gun.

Zane let it go without a fight, and he stepped away from Ty with his hands held up. "I have to shoot you, Ty. Or they'll come in and do a better job than I did." He waved a hand at the others, who were all still breathing, still moving, trying to stop the bleeding from each of their wounds. The Walther was a .22, and none of those wounds were center mass. None of the shots were fatal.

Ty knew Zane didn't miss when he aimed at something.

"What exactly is your plan here?" Ty hissed. He shoved the gun back in Zane's hands. "Asshole!"

"These guys are just low-level grunts, they have no idea who I am. Once I get to the lieutenants, they'll know I wasn't turned when I was UC, and they'll probably kill me."

Ty stood unblinking, his jaw slack.

"Awesome plan, Garrett," Owen growled.

Ty shook his head at Zane. "There are no words for how stupid you are."

Zane nodded in agreement. Ty realized he was shaking his head almost frantically and he forced himself to stop. He plucked the black-and-brown buff from his head and fisted it, then used the buff to slick Zane's hair back off his face and hold it there. Then he surveyed him with a satisfied nod. "There you go."

"Thanks." Zane grasped Ty's hand and threading their fingers together for a short squeeze. He dropped his voice even lower. "*Te amo.*"

"*Je t'aime, mon chéri,*" Ty said brokenly.

Zane kissed him. "You have ten minutes," he whispered, and then he took three long strides toward the door. He banged on it, then turned and raised the gun, giving Ty only enough time to squeeze his eyes shut before he fired.

The bullet hit home with the force of a dump truck slamming into him, laying him out on the cold cement. The sound in the enclosed space made Ty feel like his very insides were vibrating, and excruciating pain burned its way down his side and filtered through him as Zane exited the room.

The door clanged behind him, but the lock didn't sound. Ty waited a few seconds, stunned and trying to fight through the pain, then struggled to his feet as the others all bitched and moaned.

"What good's this done us now?" Liam gasped. He was trying to wrap the bullet graze on his torso, but he couldn't seem to manage it without help. "We're still unarmed, now we're all bleeding to death, and he's out there alone."

"Not alone," Ty said. "Not for long."

Anna stood with her arms crossed, smirking as if she found the whole thing amusing. Zane pointedly shoved the Walther in his belt, raising an eyebrow in challenge.

"You work for Juan Carlos?" Anna asked dubiously.

"I worked for Antonio. No one else knew me."

"Antonio de la Vega is dead."

Zane turned his head carefully, smiling. "I guess that makes me a free agent."

Anna looked him up and down, considering him. "I suppose you'll do," she decided with an impish little glint. She switched to flawless Spanish and told the others to follow.

The four men formed behind her and Zane. They each held an M4 rifle in their hands, and the array of backup knives and handguns on them made fighting back pretty unlikely.

"I'm sure Juan Carlos is interested in hearing what you have to say."

Zane followed her silently, wishing he had his knives, wishing he had one of those M4s, wishing he had more than six bullets in a shitty little nickel-plated semiautomatic from the '60s.

His only hope of making it out of this alive was Ty and the others regrouping at Mach 4 and finding the remaining members of their team—without the benefit of the earpiece—then getting more weaponry, and finding Zane within the rabbit warren of the compound in time to save him.

Zane was starting to rethink the validity of his plan.

They progressed from the dingy corridor into a shining marble hallway that swiftly led to a curved staircase. Zane had spent plenty of time in this house, and though the décor had changed, its bones were the same. He'd given Preston some pretty effective pressure points in which to place the explosives. Zane wondered if Preston had been able to get them all planted.

He wondered who else was out there still alive at all.

"Did you destroy all their earpieces?"

Anna glanced at him. "No. They've gone silent, though. I assume the few who escaped us realized we were monitoring the frequency."

"How many escaped?"

"How many did you have?" she countered.

"Eight," Zane lied.

She nodded. "Well, then. No one," she said with a pleased smile.

Zane nodded, trying to hide the stark fear flooding him. That math meant at least two people were dead. There'd been eleven of them; did that mean three were still out there kicking?

His mind whirred, trying to calculate anyone's chances at survival if everyone was either dead or weaponless and lost in a maze.

Anna led him to a heavy, wooden, hand-carved door and pushed it open with a flourish.

Zane steeled himself to walk in confidently. Like Ty always told him: fake it 'til you make it, darlin'.

Juan Carlos de la Vega was sitting behind a large mahogany desk. He stood when Zane entered, buttoning his suit coat. "Hola, Xander," he said, not sounding very surprised.

Zane nodded, desperately seeking the skin in which he'd lived for so long in the Miami heat. "I was sorry to hear of your brother's death," he told Juan Carlos, slipping into Spanish. "I mourned him."

"Did you?" Juan Carlos jutted his chin at Anna, who closed the door behind Zane, leaving him alone with the head of the Vega cartel and just two of his bodyguards.

Zane didn't move.

"I understand you wish to come back into the fold. Is this true?"

"No," Zane answered. "I'm retired. And I have been since Antonio's death. I'd like to stay that way."

"Is that why you are here on my doorstep, wielding automatic weapons and explosives?"

Zane cocked an eyebrow. "Have you ever been married to someone with a bit of a temper?"

Juan Carlos chuckled. "I suppose I know what you mean."

They stood facing each other, both of them silent and trying to pretend they weren't tense. Finally Juan Carlos turned to one of his bodyguards and nodded, and the man brought a hand to his mouth and whispered something. A hidden door at the far end of the large office opened, and two men marched through, dragging a third between them.

Zane frowned at the shock of blond hair, the stoic expression on the captive's face.

"You know this man?" Juan Carlos asked, waving his hand at Preston.

Zane stared at Preston, who raised his head regally and stared back.

"Yes," Zane answered without looking away.

"You know what he was doing in my house?"

Zane fought the urge to swallow or lick his lips.

Juan Carlos pushed a button, and static filtered in from artfully concealed speakers in the ceiling.

"Go for Cross," a voice said quietly. It was met with utter silence. Zane's heart thudded in his throat. Was Julian the only one still out there?

"Please speak to this hanger-on," Juan Carlos requested, pushing a button that cut into the feed from their mics and allowed them to speak without a headset.

Zane monitored the bodyguards for movement, keeping Preston and his two very new friends in his peripheral vision. He cleared his throat and raised his voice. "Go for Garrett."

"I think you're the only one still alive in there, mate," Cross said quietly. "Do you have eyes on anyone?"

Zane met Preston's clear blue eyes, feeling his heart drop and the world slow.

"I'm here, sir," Preston said, his voice strong and unwavering.

One of the men beside Preston brought his gun up, jabbing it under Preston's chin.

"No!" Zane cried, reaching for his gun.

The man fired, and Preston's head jerked back, then his body fell forward like a puppet whose strings had been cut. Zane was still shouting, but the roaring in his ears drowned out everything, even his own words. Preston's body hit the ground hard enough to jar something lose from his grip. A grenade rolled away from his hand, the pin left behind, snug around his middle finger. Of *course* Preston would find a way to sneak that past the guards—one last parting shot from Preston to the world.

Zane fired at the bodyguards, then drove hard at de la Vega and tackled him, shoving him all the way toward the broad window behind him. They both crashed through the paned glass, de la Vega's body taking the brunt of the punishment as Zane's power sent them sailing out into the open air.

The blast of the grenade followed them down.

Ty and his bleeding, complaining, really pissed-off crew had just found Kelly and Digger skulking through the passages below the compound when the anguished scream came over Kelly's earpiece.

Ty's breath caught, and they all froze, listening to Julian's almost animal shout of rage and pain, followed in seconds by an explosion that made plaster trail through cracks in the corridor's ceiling.

"Preston," Ty murmured, trying to catch his breath and shake the chills that ran through him.

"Anyone still alive in there?" Julian asked, and he sounded like the fucking horseman of Death calling them all home. "If you are, you won't be for long. I'm hitting every one of those explosives in exactly ninety seconds."

Ty met Owen's eyes, and after a second to let it sink in that Julian was about to kill them all to avenge Preston's death, they bolted into action, racing down the corridor after Kelly and Digger, who claimed they knew the way out.

When they reached the main house once more, Kelly turned right to lead them out. But Liam hesitated, and Ty slowed, shaking his head.

"Six, come on!" Digger shouted.

"I have to find Garrett. Go." They waited the briefest of seconds, and Ty shouted again, "Go!"

They all turned and fled, leaving Ty and Liam there, counting down the seconds. They met each other's eyes.

"If I don't bring Anna out, I'll be hunted all my life," Liam said. He pursed his lips. "It's not worth the fear of running."

Ty nodded. "They're probably in the same place."

Liam raised his fist, and Ty knocked it with his own before they sprinted in the direction of the screams and destruction.

Smoke roiled from the top of the staircase. Ty and Liam stood at the bottom, trying to find any way humanly possible for them to climb.

Zane had been up there. Ty took a deep breath and started up the burning steps.

"Grady!" Liam called. "What the bloody hell . . . oh fuck it." Ty heard him follow. Soon his face was burning and his eyes were watering. They both pulled their scarves up to protect their lungs, but it didn't take long for that to fail. They couldn't make it to the landing.

Ty squinted through the flames, then pointed at a bright-white spot amid the destruction. "Anna!"

Liam edged that way, wincing away from falling bits of the burning ceiling.

Ty turned away from him, trying to make it to the doorway at the top of the grand staircase. He could see the inside well enough to know that was where the explosion had happened. That was where they'd had Preston. That was where they'd taken Zane.

"Grady!" Liam was waving at Ty from further down the stairs, pointing up frantically. When Ty craned his head, he saw a burning ceiling beam breaking apart.

His feet were rooted to the spot, though. He looked down at Liam through the smoke. "Go!" he shouted. "My guys . . . they'll testify you died in here with me!"

"Tyler!"

"Tell them I love them. Tell them . . . oohrah."

Liam took a few steps up, but the debris of the swiftly failing roof stopped him from coming closer. Ty turned away from him, ducking his head and forging his way up and into the heat.

In the distance, Ty heard the first detonation. Cross had finished his count and he was taking out anyone still in the vicinity. Ty had no way out. No way down, no way up. No way out.

He had to walk on nothing but beams as he made his way into what remained of the office. It was a complete ruin, barely recognizable as a room at all. He was getting light-headed, his lungs filling with smoke.

The beam below his feet shook, groaning under his weight. And then he saw it: The same thing Zane had probably been able to see through what had once been a beautiful set of windows. The swimming pool right outside.

Ty pushed off the failing beam, sprinting along it recklessly as it swayed and gave under him. He ran full speed at the flaming edge and launched himself over it, turning in the air in case he didn't have enough behind his leap to make the pool. If he missed and hit that concrete, he really didn't want to see it coming.

CHAPTER 13

Ty stared at the ceiling.

His arm was in a splint and bandaged from elbow to hand, he was hooked up to enough pain medication to kill an elephant, and he couldn't reach his leg to scratch a mosquito bite that was driving him insane.

He couldn't roll over, and he couldn't sit up because the last time someone had come in to check his vitals the bed control remote had dropped down the side of the mattress and he couldn't reach the damn thing with his arm in a sling. Worst of all, he had no idea what had happened to his boys. Alive, dead, trussed up in the next hospital room in a coma. He had no idea.

He cleared his throat and forced himself to look at the bed that shared his hospital room. He had been drifting in and out of consciousness for two days, but he had yet to see Zane awaken.

Zane still lay quietly, eyes closed, drugged into sleep. He was going to be pissed when he woke up, but he would have to deal. Ty wasn't sure he could tolerate the pain without some chemical help.

He could see the right side of Zane's face, and it was awful: a mass of dark bruises, a swollen eye, and a long line of stitches along his cheekbone that made him look like a patchwork doll. Ty had watched a PA change the bandages, and he'd managed to talk the woman into telling him what had happened to Zane as she'd worked on him. She either hadn't known about the rest of them, or she hadn't been willing to tell Ty their fates, which had damn near sent Ty into a panicked spiral after she'd left. They'd had to sedate him.

Ty watched Zane for a few more minutes, then cleared his throat. "Hey, Lone Star," he said, his voice hoarse. "Wake the fuck up. You're scaring me."

Nothing happened. It wasn't the first time Ty had tried to wake Zane and gotten nothing in response. He was ready to start panicking all over again—Nick had bled out in an intersection, Preston was dead, Zane was practically in a coma, and for all he knew, the rest of Sidewinder was gone too—but then Zane's head turned in his direction, one eye barely open.

Ty smiled, sighing in relief. "Hey there, darlin'," he said, sounding a little more desperate than he'd meant to.

"Hey," Zane croaked.

"God it's good to see you awake. How you feeling?"

Zane drew in a deep breath and blinked a couple times before he muttered, "Like I went through a blender."

"You look it. You haven't been awake. I was getting worried."

"I could say the same to you," Zane said with a ghost of a smile. He turned his head further, grimacing as his stitches pressed into the pillow. "Did we win?"

Ty's stomach tumbled, and his tenuous façade faltered. How was he supposed to answer that question when winning might mean they had lost everything? "Yeah, baby. Yeah, I think we did."

"How?"

"You used the head of the cartel as a parachute."

Zane weakly waved his free hand at Ty; the other was trussed up in IVs. "He flew like a dodo."

Ty's laugh surprised him, and he tried hard to contain it. It would hurt too much to laugh.

Zane wasn't laughing, though. "Who made it?"

Ty nearly gasped. "I don't know," he whispered, fighting a pain in his heart he wasn't sure would ever ease. He smiled, though, taking a deep breath. "You did. I did. You and me, baby."

Zane's eyes opened a little wider and he focused on Ty, looking him up and down. "No one else?"

Ty's heart was going so fast his monitors were beeping at him. "I don't know. Everyone who comes in plays dumb."

They were both silent for a long while. There was really nothing they could do to get more answers until someone came in to speak with them. It was almost worse not knowing, but for right now, Ty could imagine everyone had made it out alive, even Nick, that he and

Zane were the worst of the injuries, that no one had come to see them because they were all out celebrating.

Zane finally wrinkled his nose and winced, reaching up to touch his cheek. "What did they do to me?"

"Things you would not have liked."

"Didn't break my nose again," Zane muttered as he patted his face. Then he raised his arms and stared at the bandages for a long moment. He picked at one to look underneath, and then to Ty's surprise he let it be, resting his arms back at his sides. He checked Ty over again. "You okay?"

"I'm fine."

Zane drew a breath like he was going to say something else, but then stopped for several heartbeats before actually speaking. "How long have you been awake? You've just been over there stewing, haven't you?"

"No," Ty said with a straight face. "I've been flirting with the cute nurse every time she comes in to change your cath bag."

Zane snorted. "Won't take much to be cuter than me right now."

Ty shook his head, adjusting his shoulders to a more comfortable position. "I don't know. You're kind of cute when you're all stitched up like Frankenstein."

"Frankenstein's monster," Zane grumbled.

Ty smiled fondly. He was used to Zane correcting his literary references by now. He'd even started making incorrect ones just so Zane could do it. They both knew it, too.

Zane's chuckling continued for a few more seconds before he fell quiet. Then he asked, "How long have we been here?"

"Nurses told me a day before I woke up. Feels like a week since then," Ty told him as he tried to adjust and get comfortable. He couldn't manage it, though. "Maybe two days?"

Zane huffed. "You're too far away."

"I was here first. Means you're too far away."

"Well." Zane looked down at himself. He pushed the thin blanket and sheet down and sat, bracing himself on both hands.

"What are you doing! Lay back down, you dumbass, you're going to tear your stitches."

"I don't even know where all the damn stitches are." Zane surveyed his bandaged chest and then moved the sheet to reveal the gauze wrapped around his thighs. "Okay, I'm not Frankenstein's monster. I'm the Mummy."

"Zane, lay back down," Ty said again, the beeps of his monitoring machines picking up speed.

"Nothing's beeping on my side," Zane argued as he lifted the edges of some of the bandages again, trying to see under them.

"Don't you make me fall out of this bed trying to stop you, Garrett," Ty growled.

Zane glanced at him, and then carefully lay back down without pulling at any more of the bandages. "I feel pretty okay. Tired, but not too bad."

"Good for you, Rocky," Ty griped.

"How long are we going to be stuck in here?"

"Give me a break, would you, Zane? I deserve to stay here with my IV for a while."

"If I give you more breaks, you'll be nothing but cast."

Ty rolled his eyes. "I broke it when I hit the bottom of the pool."

"You're lucky only bones broke," Zane said, pointing at him. "I'd say what the hell were you thinking, but . . . hell, I would have gone after you, too. And if it hadn't been for you teaching me how to fall fourteen thousand stories to save myself, I probably wouldn't be in one piece right now at all."

"You'd be in a lot of pieces," Ty assured him. He held Zane's gaze, eyebrow arched. Zane stared right back at him stubbornly.

"I'm digging the tough guy routine," Ty finally told him with a smirk.

Zane leered. "Getting the blood pumping?"

"No, that's what the squeezy blanket on my foot is for."

Zane's quirked lips pulled into a full grin. "I'm much more fun than a blanket."

"My blanket isn't attached to a catheter," Ty shot back.

"I was going to fix that, but you told me not to."

Ty rolled his eyes and turned his head away. "You realize we're looking at our future, right? Two of us in a retirement home, bitching about our catheters and heated blankets."

Zane chuckled, the sound somehow both warm and tired. "I'm okay with that."

They both lay silent for a long time. Ty was exhausted and hurting, trying to parse through what he remembered, trying to feel relief over the fact that he had Zane right here beside him and didn't have to worry or wonder about his fate. Zane was probably doing the same thing, trying to adjust to the knowledge that it was all over, that they'd lived through it. They had each other.

Ty glanced over to find Zane still awake, watching him. Ty smiled tiredly. "Hey, do me a favor and press your call button."

Zane did so without a remark or question, and it didn't take long for a nurse to arrive.

"He wakes up mean," Ty told her with a smile and a wink at his husband. "I've dropped my bed thingy."

"Easy enough fix," she said as she walked over to Ty's bed and retrieved the remote. Then she moved to the monitors at Zane's bedside.

"Do you have any word on our friends?" Ty asked, too impatient to let her get through the pleasantries.

"There was a man here during visiting hours, he said he was your brother."

Ty's stomach flipped, and he and Zane shared a worried glance. What the hell would Deuce be doing here? Was the news that bad that he'd had to sail in from his Caribbean vacation to give it to them?

"Would you like me to see if he's still here?" the nurse asked.

"Please," Ty managed.

She left, and Ty and Zane lay in uncomfortable silence. Ty fought not to think about all the scenarios that could come out of this, fought to keep his mind clear and peaceful. There was no use in borrowing trouble, no use in thinking of everything he might have lost until he knew for sure. He rolled his head until he could see Zane again, and they stared into each other's eyes, taking strength and calm from each other.

Zane tried to smile. "It'll be okay. We'll handle whatever happens. Together. I love you, Ty."

Ty swallowed hard and nodded, closing his eyes. He didn't open them again until he heard light footsteps in the hallway, one foot dragging as the other hit hard with every other step. Oh God, it really was Deuce. Ty stared at the doorway, his heart in his throat. Did that mean no one else had made it? None of them had made it out of that maze of corridors alive?

The man who peaked around the doorframe, though, wasn't the brother he'd been expecting.

"Johns?" Ty whispered.

Owen gave him a gentle smile and closed the door behind him as he limped into the room. He had some sort of walking boot on his foot, but otherwise he looked pretty good. A little less fully pressed than usual, but at least he was upright. "I told them I was family," he explained. "It was the only way they'd let me in to see anyone past visiting hours."

Ty could barely catch his breath. He stared at the man, his head swirling, questions flying through too fast for him to grab one.

"Who's left?" Zane asked Owen.

Owen glanced between the two of them. "We lost a few."

"Who?" Ty asked desperately.

"Your FBI man. The tall guy with the dog name."

"Lassiter?" Zane asked, voice breaking.

Owen nodded. He swallowed hard before continuing. "The CIA guy, Preston. We all know what happened to him. His friend, Cross? He disappeared. No one knows where he went. Liam Bell . . . he *said* you wanted us to claim he didn't make it out of the complex." Owen sighed. Ty could see his lips trembling. "Sending a dying message with that jackass, it's . . . it's mean, Six."

Ty nodded. "I'll apologize later. Right now I'm just glad it wasn't a dying message after all."

Owen cleared his throat.

"Our boys?" Ty asked him shakily. If Owen had more bad news, Ty wasn't sure he could take it.

Owen straightened his shoulders and raised his head. "Nick . . ." He trailed off and stared at Ty for a few heartbeats, then shook his head as he looked down at his hands. "They got him off the street."

Ty's world sank into him with a suffocating weight. He fought the tears that choked him, thinking of the way they'd just left Nick in the middle of the road. Those tears would come no matter what he did. At least someone had gotten to him, pulled him out of that mess so he didn't die there, alone.

He opened his eyes to find the world around him watery, and he fought to focus on Owen again, who was still standing with his head bowed.

When he looked up, Ty was stunned to see him smirking. "They say that stupid motherfucker should wake up any day now."

Ty stared at him, not even blinking. "What?"

"Someone got him in an ambulance. He's in bad shape, but he's alive."

"Holy shit," Ty breathed, turning to Zane as a smile began to spread across his face. He couldn't even be pissed at Owen for the way he'd delivered the news. "The others?"

"Doc and Digger came out a little scuffed, a little worse than me. But they're both being released right now. I was on my way to see them when the nurse told me you were awake."

Zane cleared his throat, speaking gently. "What about my other two? Clancy and Perrimore?"

"They're okay." Owen winced. "That redhead is not happy with you, though. She says you shot her."

Zane smiled and relaxed, breathing easier. "I hope she makes me pay," he said with a chuckle.

"By the way. You shot me too, dickface," Owen grunted. Zane just laughed. Owen glanced between the two of them, still looking too smug for Ty's liking. "When you can walk, I'll take you to the others."

"Let's go right now," Ty croaked. He started pawing at his sheets, trying to get himself free as relief filtered through him.

"Six," Owen tried.

"I'm not your Six anymore, bud," Ty said, tears in his voice. He waved a hand as he tried to get out of bed. "I'm just your brother. Now, help me out of this bed."

Owen gingerly got Ty to his feet, trying to keep all the wires and lines from tangling. He fixed them on a rolling stand and hustled to catch up as Ty shuffled across the room and bent over Zane, smiling gently.

"There's nowhere to kiss you," Ty murmured.

Zane gave him a warm smile, his brown eyes dancing with light even though Ty could see pain in them. "It'll keep. Go on. Tell him I said we have a new season of *The Walking Dead* to watch."

Ty gave him a kiss on the very tip of his nose, and then, after a moment to consider, he pressed his lips to Zane's with the utmost care. After making sure he'd had his fill of the way Zane's breaths felt against his lips, he took the arm Owen offered, and they made their way out of the room and down the hall.

Ty was almost at the end of his strength when they finally reached Nick's room. The lights were dimmed, only the one above the bed on. Machines beeped accusingly. Ty and Owen found Digger sitting in a chair in the corner, his chin resting on the handle of a cane. Kelly was in a chair by the bed, both hands clutching Nick's.

They both turned when they heard Ty and Owen.

"Hey, Six," Digger whispered.

Ty shook his head.

"He says he's not our Six anymore," Owen provided, a smile playing at his lips.

Digger scoffed and stood, limping over to pull Ty into a careful hug. They hung on for a few seconds, Digger's fingers clutching at Ty's hospital gown. Then they turned to the bed again.

Nick was still, his eyes closed, his breathing shallow.

Kelly gave them a weak smile. "They say he hasn't woken at all."

Ty wasn't sure what to say or do. He moved closer, shivering as the cool air found its way past his blue socks with the paws on the bottom, up his hospital gown. It was hard to breathe, and he wasn't sure if that was because of his injuries, the drugs, or just seeing Nick in a hospital bed, fighting for his life.

Kelly pulled Nick's hand to his chest, clutching it as he laid his head on the mattress beside him. Ty sat in a chair on the other side of the bed, sliding his own abused fingers into Nick's just to make sure Nick knew not to fucking let go. Digger and Owen drew closer, setting up around the bed. They had a lot of time. They could wait for him to wake.

Zane stepped into the row house, prepared to enjoy the feeling of coming home after being gone for nearly two months between the hospital stay and the ensuing investigation in Florida. He had expected it to feel deserted and a little weird. What he hadn't expected was the utter devastation they found.

The banister was ruined, with pieces of the spindles all over the floor as if someone had chopped them up to use as kindling. A big upholstered chair was upended with boot prints all over it, and the coffee table in the living room was in shards. Zane wasn't sure how the iron base had been taken apart like it was. A kitchen stool was teetering off the edge of the steps, its legs stuck in the treads and the few remaining banister spindles like it had been hurled toward the staircase. Photos were off the walls, glass everywhere, shreds of material and droplets of blood all over.

"What the . . ."

Ty winced. "Did I forget to tell you about this?"

"Jesus." Zane moved deeper into the house. They were going to have to replace half the furniture and the entire staircase. He and Ty stood in the kitchen for a long time, just taking it all in. Their life was in shambles. All they had left was each other and a few friends who'd proven they would literally walk through fire with them.

And it was enough.

Ty set their bags down and turned to Zane. Neither of them said a word as they stared at each other. Then Ty stepped forward and wrapped his good arm around Zane's neck. They stood in the wreckage and held on to each other for long minutes.

Eventually Ty drifted upstairs, and it wasn't long before he was cleaning. Zane sighed as he listened to Ty sweeping up glass. He could probably manage the climb up there with his leg, but he didn't fancy trying it just to watch Ty pluck shards of glass off the hardwood. Instead, he headed for the couch, the only piece of furniture in the living room that had remained untouched in the brawl. He stretched out, wondering where the hell they'd go from here, aside from maybe a hotel with no stairs, as he drifted off to sleep.

A knock came at the door some time later, and Zane managed to heft himself off the couch and hobble over to answer it. He checked the peephole, but no one was there. Fortunately, he didn't have much to worry about now. While they'd been recovering at the hospital in Florida, not only had Ty and Zane been cleared of any wrongdoing, but the NIA had also been summarily stripped of every military and covert resource the government had loaned it. The organization was on its way to being just as weak and toothless as it had once been. Even Liam Bell had been cleared and was out of their hair, wherever the bastard was. Zane still didn't know whether to believe him when he claimed he hadn't tried to kill Ty in New Orleans. Had it been Anna who'd switched that bullet in an attempt to rob Liam of any possible allies when he got burned? Zane didn't know, but Liam had been there for Ty when he was needed, so Zane was willing to call it a draw.

The Vega cartel had retreated back to its roots. It would take years for them to recover from what had happened in Miami, and by the time they did, Ty and Zane would be but a legend among the ranks.

And the CIA, well . . . they had a few hundred million reasons to keep up their end of the bargain.

Really, Zane thought the greatest threat to their lives right now was Michelle Clancy, who was still pissed that Zane had shot her and ruined her perfect track record of not bleeding on the job.

When he swung the door open, there was a manila envelope on the welcome mat at his feet.

Zane glanced up and down the street, scowling. It was a struggle to bend and fetch it—he didn't bounce back from injuries like he used to—and he gave the empty street one last hard stare, but he saw nothing out of the ordinary. He took his new folding knife from his back pocket and sliced through the envelope, peeking into it like he expected trouble to swirl up out of it in a mist.

"What the hell are you doing?" Ty asked from the stairway. He had a gun in his hand.

Zane winced and shut the door, limping toward the dining table. He supposed they'd both go a while on edge after what they'd been through. "Someone left this on the stoop," he said, waving the envelope. "I was checking it for . . . danger."

Ty huffed a tired laugh and came down the steps, standing by Zane's side as he spilled the contents onto the table.

Two innocuous badges slid out, along with two clear silicone earpieces and two standard-issue CIA mobile phones. There was also a stack of crisp bills that drew a whistle from Ty as he examined it.

"Probably from the money Burns stole," Zane grunted. "You can smell the blood on it."

"Sorry, all I see is a sixty-inch flat screen and new furniture," Ty huffed as he opened one of the badges.

"What are we supposed to do with this?" Zane asked. "They don't actually expect us to work in the field, do they? Aren't we a little past our expiration date for the CIA?"

"My understanding was that we're supposed to be field support when called upon. Sort of . . . part-time, I guess." Ty showed the badge to Zane with one eyebrow raised pointedly. "Welcome to the Company, Mr. Bond," he said with a smirk, and handed Zane his badge.

Zane pursed his lips, considering it. "Not too bad, right?" He held the badge up to his face to mimic the photo the CIA had pulled off the FBI servers in order to create the ID.

Ty looked him up and down appreciatively, then picked up the last item in the welcome packet. It was a silver key with a tag attached to it. Ty's brow furrowed as he plucked the tag between two long fingers and read it. "These are . . . the coordinates of the bookstore."

Zane only needed a glance to know they were the same numbers as the ones on the ring he still wore on his right hand. "What's that mean?"

Ty turned the tag over, and on the other side was what looked like a logo. A phoenix made of fire sat atop the words. "Brick & Mortar Books?" Ty read, obviously confused. "How . . . ?"

Zane shrugged.

Ty shrugged back at him and stuffed the key into his pocket. "You feel up to a walk to go find out?"

Zane turned wordlessly, and they both struggled into their jackets, locking up the row house before they headed off on the several block walk toward Fell's Point and the remains of their building.

When they reached the end of Ann Street, though, the brick building on the corner wasn't a ruin like Zane'd expected it to be. Men were crawling over scaffolding, doing masonry work. Saws buzzed as they cut lengths of two-by-fours and measured for new windows and doors. Salvaged molding and antique parts had been collected and stacked inside.

Ty and Zane both gaped, confounded by it all.

"I get it," Zane said with a slow grin. Ty still looked a little confused. "A brick and mortar bookstore. It's our cover. We sell books from the front, and we deal with baby CIA agents from the back."

Ty eyed him, still frowning when he turned his attention back to the partially rebuilt building. "Are you telling me you get to run a fucking bookstore *and* kill things for a living? How is *that* fair? Where's *my* carrot? I don't want to organize books all day!"

Zane chuckled and slid his arm around Ty's shoulders, steering him away to head back home. "Your carrot is also getting to kill things for a living, baby."

"Do you have any idea how hard it is to organize books by subject when they should be alphabetical?" Ty shouted. "This is going to drive me crazy!"

"Too late," Zane said under his breath.

"What was that?"

"Nothing." Zane slid his hand down Ty's arm and worked his fingers in between Ty's, fighting a smile.

They walked on in silence, hand in hand, the warmth inside Zane growing until he thought it just might burn him up.

"Can I get a cat?" Ty asked after exactly one block.

"What?"

"A cat. I want a cat. You get a bookstore, I should get a cat."

Zane suffered through a brief moment of terror as he recalled his many encounters with Smith and Wesson. Then he remembered the smile on Ty's face whenever one of those monstrous, fuzzy, evil felines had bumped its head against Ty's, and Zane instantly caved.

"Okay. You can get a cat."

Ty yanked him to a stop, wrapping his good arm around Zane's neck to kiss him. Zane pressed his forehead to Ty's, his fingers sliding along Ty's shoulder to fix the twisted strap of his sling. He stole another kiss as Ty grinned.

"I love you," Zane whispered.

Ty kissed him again. "I love you." He waited a beat, eyes narrowing, sparkling dangerously. "Two cats?"

"Don't push me, Grady."

AUTHOR'S NOTE

I'm not sure what to say about this book and this series and this piece of my soul. I've spent almost every day of the last eight years with Ty and Zane, and saying good-bye to them as this series comes to a close is bittersweet. My world will be an emptier place without them.

Ty and Zane started their lives as a message between myself and my former cowriter. A message asking, "What should we do now?"

"How about murder?" was my reply, and that was that.

We wrote Cut & Run, and we finished it with enough content to fill two books, and in the end Ty and Zane walked off into the sunset, happy and in love. It didn't feel right. After a day to let the ending settle, it was painfully obvious that this was not the proper end of the story. There was more to tell, and the rewrite began. A story arc formed—a tortuous, cruel story that would force Ty and Zane to work for their happy ending.

It's no secret that I was responsible for Ty. He hopped onto the page fully formed with his entire background and circle of family and friends sitting there, waiting. He was easy. When Zane became mine after the fourth book, I suffered through a few months of doubts. Zane wasn't mine. I didn't know him. How could I do this series justice on my own? How could I do these characters justice?

It didn't take long to get to know Zane, though, and what I began to see among the shadows was a flickering spark. I called him a phoenix hoping to lure him out, and it worked. He's mine now, just as precious to me as any other.

And I suppose that sums up Ty and Zane. They're precious to me. And I hope, along the way, they've become precious to you as well.

Thank you all for letting Ty and Zane, and me, into your lives.

Explore more of the *Cut & Run* universe
with the *Sidewinder* series at:
riptidepublishing.com/titles/series/sidewinder

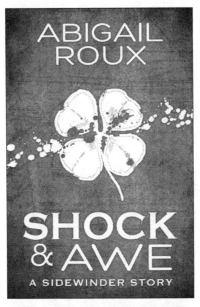

Dear Reader,

Thank you for reading Abigail Roux's *Crash & Burn*!

We know your time is precious and you have many, many entertainment options, so it means a lot that you've chosen to spend your time reading. We really hope you enjoyed it.

We'd be honored if you'd consider posting a review—good or bad—on sites like **Amazon, Barnes & Noble, Kobo, Goodreads, Twitter, Facebook, Tumblr,** and your blog or website. We'd also be honored if you told your friends and family about this book. Word of mouth is a book's lifeblood!

For more information on upcoming releases, author interviews, blog tours, contests, giveaways, and more, please sign up for our weekly, spam-free newsletter and visit us around the web:

Newsletter: tinyurl.com/RiptideSignup
Twitter: twitter.com/RiptideBooks
Facebook: facebook.com/RiptidePublishing
Goodreads: tinyurl.com/RiptideOnGoodreads
Tumblr: riptidepublishing.tumblr.com

Thank you so much for Reading the Rainbow!

RiptidePublishing.com

ACKNOWLEDGMENTS

The culmination of this series has been over seven years in the making. If I tried to thank every person who made this ninth and final book possible, I'd run out of pages before I could do the job well. From the people in my life who gave me inspiration for everything from plot to characters, to the readers who picked up this book and flipped past the title page, everyone who's had a hand in this journey deserves a word of thanks.

Thank you to the readers who've stuck with me, and Ty and Zane, from beginning to end. Thank you for trusting me, and thank you for letting me tell you a story.

Thank you to Rachel and Riptide, who gave me a home when I felt like I was at sea. You're not just my publisher or my editor, you're my friend. And I can't stress how important that's been to me.

Thank you to the handful of people who have the patience to love me day in and day out. You've seen me through the highs and lows and I don't believe I'd be here if it weren't for your voices in my ears, your faces in my memory, and you in my heart.

To my great-grandmother, who fought 'til her last breath, and spent her days in the shade of her porch with a shotgun across her lap. Her spirit lives on in the Grady family.

To my daddy, whose love of history permeated my brain from a young age and who encouraged me to study what I loved. Without him, and without that horribly boring senior-level social studies class I had to take for my degree, I don't believe I ever would have picked up a pencil and started telling stories on paper as I pretended to take notes.

To my granny, my mama, and my baby girl. You've each inspired me in ways I cannot tally. Mara Grady is the mother everyone wishes they had, but I'm so lucky because she came from the two most important women in my life. I hope one day my Little Roux will think the same of me.

And finally, I have to acknowledge a man whose name cannot be given. To Squad Leader, who demonstrated to me that men like Ty Grady do exist. They do exist, and the world needs them.

ALSO BY ABIGAIL ROUX

Cut & Run series
Cut & Run (with Madeleine Urban)
Sticks & Stones (with Madeleine Urban)
Fish & Chips (with Madeleine Urban)
Divide & Conquer (with Madeleine Urban)
Armed & Dangerous
Stars & Stripes
Touch & Geaux
Ball & Chain

Sidewinder series
Shock & Awe
Cross & Crown
Part & Parcel (coming soon)

Novels
The Gravedigger's Brawl
The Archer

Novellas
The Bone Orchard
A Tale from de Rode
My Brother's Keeper
Seeing Is Believing
Unrequited

With Madeleine Urban
Caught Running
Love Ahead
Warrior's Cross

ABOUT THE AUTHOR

Abigail Roux was born and raised in North Carolina. A past volleyball star who specializes in sarcasm and painful historical accuracy, she currently spends her time coaching high school volleyball and investigating the mysteries of single motherhood. Any spare time is spent living and dying with every Atlanta Braves and Carolina Panthers game of the year. Abigail has a daughter, Little Roux, who is the light of her life, a boxer, four rescued cats who play an ongoing live-action variation of Call of Duty throughout the house, one evil Ragdoll, a certifiable extended family down the road, and a cast of thousands in her head.

To learn more about Abigail, please visit abigailroux.com.

Enjoy more stories like *Crash & Burn* at RiptidePublishing.com!

Catch a Ghost	*Peripheral People*
ISBN: 978-1-62649-039-0	ISBN: 978-1-62649-269-1

Earn Bonus Bucks!

Earn 1 Bonus Buck for each dollar you spend. Find out how at RiptidePublishing.com/news/bonus-bucks.

Win Free Ebooks for a Year!

Pre-order coming soon titles directly through our site and you'll receive one entry into a drawing to win free books for a year! Get the details at RiptidePublishing.com/contests.

BRICK & MORTAR
books

Zane sat on a stool behind the salvaged countertop that graced one side of the first floor of Brick & Mortar Books. He rested his head in one palm, using the other hand to flip the electronic pages on his tablet.

The grand opening had been a few months ago, and they'd had a steady stream of business since then. People were drawn in by the unique façade, by the rich and quirky details of the interior, by the comfortable seating Zane had sprinkled throughout the three stories of new and used books. By the free Wi-Fi.

People were also drawn in by the spectacle Ty had set up in the window: Two tiny long-haired kittens who liked to sleep in a lined crate with "TNT" stenciled on the side. One was orange with a fluffy white crest, the other gray with nebulous white stripes. Both had blue eyes that were slowly but surely turning a mystery color between yellow and green.

Zane turned the page of his book, and Cricket the gray kitty patted at the screen as the page swished by. His app exited and left him with the menu screen.

"Ty!" he called, his voice echoing through the rabbit warren of heavy wooden shelving and thick tomes. He glared at the kitten, who was no more than six weeks old if she was a day. The kittens had been so malnourished when Ty had coaxed them out from between two busted-down levels of a dock on the water, the vet couldn't accurately guess their age yet.

Zane leaned closer to Cricket. "Can you go away?"

Cricket blinked innocently and tapped him on the nose. With her claws.

"Tyler!"

Ty poked his head out from an aisle, a load of books in his arms. Zane didn't know if he was stocking them, stealing them, or hiding them so he could read them later without them being bought out from under him like the mystery he never got to finish last week.

Zane had also discovered that Ty was seeding the store, especially the adventure and mystery sections, with spy gadgets. Surprise finds within the pages of books and among the shelves had delighted a few customers already. Zane was terrified to know what Ty was doing in the horror section.

Jiminy the orange kitten was sitting on Ty's shoulder. Jiminy the orange kitten *always* sat on Ty's shoulder, which was how he'd gotten his name.

"What's up?"

"Will you come get your fluffy thing please?"

Ty's expression immediately softened as he came closer. That look right there was why Zane had acquiesced. Ty had been on his way to the rescue facility when he'd seen Jiminy and Cricket at the dock. Convincing Zane to assist him in the operation to extract them hadn't been hard after convincing Zane to let him have a cat—two cats—in the first place. Zane could watch Ty with these kittens all day long. As long as he was an observer and not a participant after the three hours it had taken them to lure the little assholes out.

"Hey there, sweet girl," Ty murmured as he approached Zane's counter.

Cricket meowed and began a little tap dance as she tried to work up the courage to take the leap toward Ty. They loved him like nothing Zane had ever seen. Ty plucked her off the counter, depositing her on his other shoulder. He gave Zane a jaunty grin as Jiminy and Cricket mewed happily and settled onto his broad shoulders.

"What are you reading?" Zane asked, leaning both elbows on the table.

Ty looked down at the stack of books in his hands, then slid them onto the counter. "Nothing," he claimed, grinning in a way that made Zane's heart flutter.

"Uh huh?"

Ty flipped open the cover of a leather copy of the *Complete Works of Edgar Allan Poe*, revealing a cutout with a .38 Special nestled inside.

"Ty!"

"What? It's a display copy, goes behind glass. Customers no touchy."

Zane put his face in his hands, massaging his temples. "Ty."

Ty chuckled evilly, retreating into the rows of books as he began to hum the tune to "When Johnny Comes Marching Home Again."

Zane shrugged, going back to his book with a grin. Whatever kept Ty happy between the occasional buzz from the back door that signaled a delivery from the Company.

Whatever kept them both happy.